G

Amy Sumida

ISBN-10: 148407047X
ISBN-13: 978-1484070475

DEDICATION

For Nick and Kai, may you live forever within these pages.

More Books by Amy Sumida
Available on Amazon.com
http://astore.amazon.com/amysum-20

The Godhunter Series(in order)

(Godhunter)

Of Gods and Wolves

Oathbreaker

Marked by Death

Green Tea and Black Death

A Taste for Blood

The Tainted Web

Series Split:
These books can be read together or separately

Harvest of the Gods & A Fey Harvest

Into the Void & Out of the Darkness

Perchance to Die

Tracing Thunder

Light as a Feather

Blood Bound

Eye of Re

The Twilight Court Series

Fairy-Struck

Pixie-Led

Other Books

The Magic of Fabric

Feeding the Lwas: A Vodou Cookbook

There's a Goddess Too

The Vampire-Werewolf Complex

Enchantress

Pronunciation Guide

Aphrodite: Afro-die-tee

Bilskinir: Bill-ska-neer

Brahma: Bra-ma

Estsanatlehi(Mrs E): Es-tan-AHT-lu-hee

Froekn: Fro-kin

Huitzilopochtli: Weet-seal-oh-POACHED-lee

Járngreipr: Yarn- gri-per

Kuan-Ti: Kwan-tee

Lwa: loa

Megingjord: Mey-gen-yord

Mjollnir: Myul-neer

Persephone: Per-sef-fa-knee

Tawiskaron: Tah-wiss-Kah-ron

Teharon: Teh-ha-ron

Teotihuacán: Tee-oh-tee-wah-kan

Tenochtitlán: Tay-noch-teet-lahn

Tsohanoai(Mr. T): So-ha-noe-ayee

Ull: oul

UnnúlfR: Un- nul-fur

Valaskjálf: Vah-lask-chalv

VèulfR: Vey-ul-fur

Vervain: Vur-vane (not Viviann)

Chapter One

"There were of old certain men versed in sorcery, Thor, namely, and Odin, and many others, who were cunning in contriving marvelous sleights; and they, winning the minds of the simple, began to claim the rank of gods."

Saxo Grammaticus, *Gesta Danorum,* 13th century

When someone asks if you're a god, you say yes!

Those were the words going through my mind the first time I met Thor. In my line of work they should have been words to live by… literally. At least they would have been had I remembered them in time. Unfortunately, Bill Murray's voice taunted me inside my head mere seconds too late. Thanks a lot, Bill.

My forgetfulness left me facing the distinct possibility of an early and creatively painful demise. If only I'd remembered the movie wisdom sooner. Yes, movie wisdom. Scoff all you want but it may surprise you how much useful information is hidden in movie dialog. At least that's what I tell myself so I can feel better about thinking in movie quotes half the time.

"So, Thor," I smirked up at the giant, gladiator-muscled, Viking while he glowered down at me through a fall of his shimmering copper hair. "What's it gonna be? Hammer? Lightning? Fists of fury? Lightning might singe the rug a bit. Odin might not appreciate that, it looks kinda old."

Maybe it wasn't a good idea to taunt a god but hey, what did I have to lose? He'd caught me red handed, bent over the new *Make War, Not Love* campaign plans I'd found in the Human

Relations room of Valhalla. I hadn't even heard the loud-mouthed God of Thunder coming in, if you can believe that. Loud-mouthed didn't automatically equate to loud-footed, evidently. Then to make matters worse, he asked me if I was a god. Like maybe I was a newbie or something, and what did I, the ever quick-witted one say? I said no. Yeah, I wanted to smack myself silly for that one.

Then again, maybe I should cut myself some slack. It's a little shocking to be face to face, well face to chest, with what had to be close to seven feet of gorgeous, vibrant, leather-clad Viking godliness. Did I mention gorgeous? And the leather? I don't mean that yuppie silky lambskin either. I mean hard core, I'm gonna bust your ass if you look at me wrong, well worn but still strong enough to wipe the floor with your face, leather. Just seeing the way it teased me by gripping all that muscle, made me want to rip it to shreds and teach it a lesson. Bad leather, Viking gods should be naked.

"You wanna see my hammer?" Thor's eyes took on a wicked gleam as he looked slowly up and down my body, which took longer than it should have for all five-foot-three (and a half) of me.

"Whoa there, Viking," I leaned back further on the table he'd previously planted me on like I was a misbehaving child. "Raping and pillaging days are in the past. You gotta catch up on the times." I snapped my fingers in his face. "Nowadays there are laws on the treatment of prisoners."

"Not for gods," his lips twitched. It was just a slight movement but I caught it and it gave me the smallest glint of hope that I might actually make it out of this mess alive. Get 'em laughing, then run while they're distracted. It's not the best plan but it's worked for me before.

"Hey, like I always say, gods are people too," I smiled my best P.R. smile. *Gods are great, they're not at all out to manipulate mankind, really, and I'm definitely not here to foil their evil plans.* I smiled bigger.

"No we're not," the frown was back and he set an intimidating fist on the table next to my hip for good measure. A fist that was nearly the size of my face.

The leather around his forearm creaked at me gleefully.

Okay, that was more like it. I could handle an angry god better than a horny one. I congratulated myself on the sharpness of my tongue until I felt his thumb scrape lightly over my jeans. I went still, listening to more creaky leather commentary as Thor leaned in closer and I found myself wondering how much strain the stuff could take. Maybe he'd bust his seams before he had a chance to bust my face. I can't say the prospect didn't have its own appeal, even without saving me an ass kickin'.

The glimpse of chest I had through the V of his leather tunic was something straight out of a male calender. Made for women to drool over, the kind of sculpted, smooth, perfect chest that looked airbrushed. It was mere inches from my face, rising and falling with his deep breaths, and I had an overwhelming urge to lean forward and rub my cheek against it. Then there was that smell. This close to him, I was practically enveloped in it. It was like standing in the middle of a storm while lightning struck nearby; a wild, exciting aroma of rain and electricity. Of freshly washed man.

"Now, now," I chided him like a school teacher as I tried to focus on his face. "You mustn't forget your own history. Shall I refresh your memory?"

"Try me," he made a sound halfway between a sniff and a snort, "let's hear what you think you know of gods."

"Well for one thing," I poked my finger into his massive chest, "I know you aren't gods at all, so you can just stop with the holier than thou attitude, buster."

A thick eyebrow arched up and Thor's lips went into mini spasms.

"For another thing," yes, I was still poking him, "I know where you're from, Atlantean. I know your god abilities are nothing more than technological and magical advances your kind kept from humanity in an attempt to rule the world. Advances that ended up destroying Atlantis but still you all didn't think that was any reason to stop practicing them."

"Practice does make perfect," his eyes started to spark with the very magic I'd referenced and I knew I had only one shot to get out of there alive and un-hammered as it were.

"I know something else too," I whispered and cast my eyes side to side conspiratorially.

He couldn't help it; his smile finally broke free as he leaned in closer, "What's that?"

"I know if I do this," I kicked my leg out as hard as I could and caught him where no man likes to be kicked, "god or not, you're going down."

I jumped off the table the minute Thor landed, groaning and cupping himself on the thick carpet. Then I bolted past him and out the door, already chanting the spell that would get me through the wards of Valhalla and out into the Aether. I felt the magic rush over me like a hot, tickling breath as I ran down a long hallway to the tracing room. It sparked eagerly across my skin, urging me back to where I'd come from. Everything in its place and all that.

As I crossed the threshold, I was pulled through the tracing point and into the Aether. The tracing point sealed behind me with a low murmur of magic and a pressurized pop in my ears. But that physical sensation lasted only a moment before my body became a mere memory with a tingling, freeing ecstasy. I flowed through streams of pure magic, my spell propelling me along to my destination so I didn't have to navigate the waters myself. With another pressure-pop that announced the reformation of my ears, I exited the Aether and felt my body reluctantly become physical again. Gravity was the worst; a jarring, sucking sensation that took a few moments to readjust to.

My momentum sent me straight into a wall. A dirty, alley wall. I pushed off it immediately and swung around to automatically crouch into a fighting stance, just in case Thor had managed to follow me through. Tracing was a rush, add the adrenaline of the chase to it and it left me panting for breath and shaking. My pulse beat heavily in my ears, the thudding drowning out the traffic I could see in my peripheral vision. I was holding my kodachi before me and I hadn't even realized I'd drawn the Japanese shortsword.

Remnants of magic sparked blue and drifted to the ground in a roughly circular outline but the wall across from me remained the same; no ripples, no blurring, no sign of Thor at all. I stood slowly, leaned back, and felt my heart rate start to decelerate as I slid the sword into its scabbard.

"God damn Buffy! Freakin' vampire slayer gets all the props," I muttered. "Vampires, please! Bunch of melodramatic parasites. And werewolves? I'd fight one of those puppies any day rather than a god. At least they can't pull magic out of their furry butts. Now faeries, I might not be thrilled to meet one of them in a dark alley… a dark alley kinda like this one." I shoved myself quickly away from the wall and power-walked towards the street, still bitching about a fictional vampire hunter under my breath.

"Vampire Slayer," I grumbled, "Try killing a god sometime and then get back to me. Blondie wouldn't last a day. She'd be whining to her mommy about the unfairness of it all within minutes. Oh, and falling for your prey... total amateur. You don't poop where you eat and you don't kill where you sleep. Or sleep with who you kill. No wait, that's necrophilia," I frowned and then shook my head. "Oh whatever, it's just dumb to let your prey seduce you." Thor's striking face flashed through my mind, his ocean eyes sparkling with magic, and I decided to just shut the hell up. That guy Spike was sweet to Buffy, in a psycho kind of way.

Ugh. I threw my hands up and shook my head at myself. Staring death in the face can have an odd affect on people. Especially when death's face was that of a Viking god. I had to let it go and stop acting like a crazy person, muttering to myself about vampires and werewolves in an alley. This was just another day hunting gods, nothing special about it.

You might be wondering how someone gets into the god hunting business and all I can tell you is: hell if I know. I pretty much stumbled face first into it. Like hitting a rock when you're riding a bike at full speed; I went flying and landed in a thorn bush. A burning one. A talking, burning one that proclaimed it was god in a booming voice.

I never really was the religious type. I'm more of a hands-on kinda girl. I've practiced witchcraft my entire life, which I kinda look on as a religion of the self. I do mean witchcraft by the way, not Wicca. I know that's a religion but I don't practice it, I just do the spells. Wicca's a little too peaceful for me, though I do like the clothes.

Well, I guess I haven't practiced witchcraft my *entire* life but pretty damn close since Mom was teaching me spells in the cradle. Most babies got *The cow jumped over the moon*; I got sung to about drawing it down. Not that I'm complaining since it's really helping me out these days but I've just never seen the gods as a big part of my life.

Boy has that changed.

I walked out of the alley, into the bright Hawaiian sunshine, and held a hand up to shield my eyes. Well where did you expect the gods to live? Okay, so they don't all technically live in Hawaii but quite a few do and those that don't, seem drawn here. The land is still filled with old magic, practically spilling with it since there isn't much land to begin with. So it's a nice place for a god to go on vacation. Whatever, it's my home and I have to say I'm getting a little tired of sharing it with them. They have their own realm to live in, they need to go there. Or they can go to Hell for all I care... which also happens to be in the God Realm. In fact, from what I understand, there's a few of them. They can take their pick.

About five years ago, I truly started developing a relationship with the gods and I'm not talking in the *Do you have a relationship with God?* Jimmy Swaggart sense. I'm talking about a deep understanding of how truly evil they are. Read your history books, kiddies; most gods were revered mainly because they were so damn scary.

For me it all started with sex. At least it would have if my chosen partner for the evening hadn't been planning on killing me as a sacrifice to the Hawaiian God of War, Ku. You think you've got some bad date stories.

My young, Hawaiian escort for the evening was everything every female tourist (and some males too, I'm sure) fantasized about on the plane ride over. He was tall, dark, handsome, and built like a brick… well you get the picture. He also had green eyes, courtesy of some white ancestor who got lucky with a wicked wahine. Green eyes have always been a weakness of mine.

He took me out on a romantic date, ending with us drinking an entire bottle of champagne at a Heiau (a Hawaiian temple). This particular Heiau was dedicated to none other than, Ku. Now I know that doesn't sound too romantic but take into account that the Heiau was situated on a mountaintop overlooking Waimea Bay and the sun was setting. A deep pumpkin sky painting the cerulean sea pink as it crept into a verdant valley spotted with the flight of tropical birds. Can you see the sexy factor yet?

I may have been tipsy when we started. I'd just turned twenty-one so give me a break on the alcohol consumption, but when I looked up and spotted a large local man watching us from the tree line, I sobered up quick. I shot him a nasty look but he was focused on my date so he didn't see it. Something in his gaze set off warning sirens (definitely sirens, not bells) and I turned back sharply to find a large *Crocodile Dundee* knife plunging towards me.

I had seconds to roll to the side before the blade ended up embedded in the ground, merely nicking my upper arm instead of going through my chest. I rolled back towards the knife, effectively removing it from my date's possession and my bleeding arm, as I kicked upwards. I don't know if I hit him *there* or not but he howled like he was in serious pain.

"Ku," he managed to choke out, "Na waimaka o ka lani." He launched himself at me and in those few moments I saw more than you'd think was possible.

I saw the local voyeur come striding to us, hand extended, face rapturous. I saw my hand gripping the blade and turning it. I saw the look of shock on my date's face as the knife slipped into his neck. Internally I shouted "That's not a knife, *this* is a knife," Australian accent and all, and I almost started to giggle hysterically. It's amazing what the mind will do to protect itself and, like I warned you, I think in movie quotes a lot.

My mind had definitely needed some protection. I used to think those horror movies with blood spraying from neck wounds were ridiculous and inaccurate. I don't think that anymore. You hit a guy in the neck with a big blade and he bleeds. A lot. All over you if you just so happen to be beneath him at the time. It was extremely messy, to say the least, and potentially mind breaking.

I think the only reason I didn't start screaming was that someone else beat me to it. The scream I heard was a terrifying mix of rage, frustration, and pain. It yanked my attention to the left, where I found the local man on his knees. He was right next to me. Way too close for my comfort. He reached for me and I didn't think. I just reacted. I didn't aim either. I just shot the knife out straight and followed through with my body.

I was suddenly grateful for all the self-defense classes Mom had insisted I take. The biggest advantage training can give you is faster action… automatic reaction. Your body moves before your mind has a chance to process things and it saves you precious, life granting seconds.

The man was suddenly gasping beneath me, the blade buried in his chest. He started to murmur some words in a language unfamiliar to me. Surprisingly, it wasn't Hawaiian. I panicked and stabbed him again. I knew a spell when I heard one and I also knew that any spell this guy managed to cast would not be beneficial to my health. He kept going and I kept stabbing, shutting my eyes to block out the carnage. I felt like I had a starring role in *Psycho*, the original not that stupid Vince Vaughn remake. All that was missing was the shower curtain and that ridiculously horrifying music. Although, the sound he made was even more horrific. I didn't open my eyes until he went silent.

The Heiau was gone, replaced by an elegant room in what must have been a multimillion dollar home. That's when I realized Ku had been chanting a spell to open a tracing point, a doorway to the Aether. The Aether, or the Astral as some call it, is a place of pure consciousness. It's also the link between our world and the realm of the gods. Think of reality as a spiritual sandwich. The Aether would be all the tasty filling packed between the bread of our worlds. If you wanted to go from one slice to the other, you had to get through the tuna salad first.

Okay, now I'm hungry.

Anyway, the Aether is also where magic happens. As a witch, I use it for crafting spells. I can tap into it with my mind and create new realities there. It's called spellcraft. Of course it's not as simple as it sounds. There's a lot of work and usually a few ingredients necessary for magic but once something is made in the

Aether, it manifests on the physical plane.

When I was little, my mom told me stories of people who could travel the Aether, a practice called tracing, but the ability was lost to history. The spells had become scarce and unreliable, the destinations vague, the potential risks high. To take your physical body, make it pure consciousness, and send it shooting through the Aether to another location was a mind boggling concept to me. Yet there, beneath me, was proof it could be done. This man could trace, had in fact taken me along for the ride... and I just killed him. Great.

The body was a bloody mess. I'd nearly decapitated Ku in my blind attack. I didn't know it at the time but it's one of the few ways you can kill a god. Don't laugh, there are monsters out there who can put their head back on and keep going without missing a beat. Or just sprout two more. Can you say Hydra? Beheading doesn't always work. I repeat; *beheading doesn't always work.* Remember to take the heart too. Oh and burning is usually quite effective as well but with gods, the head is the most important part to take. But I digress.

After I stopped screaming, (I was actually thankful I'd been able to delay the screaming portion of the evening for that long) I tried to wipe away the blood in a very Lady Macbeth fashion. Out damn spot, out. It was useless. I found the bathroom, not even caring that there could be someone else in the house, and went into the shower fully clothed. I can't even remember what the bathroom looked like. All I recall is the way the water ran bright red and how I stared at it, mesmerized as it swirled down the drain. It was the first time I'd ever killed, as in anything. Well, except bugs but I think we can all agree that they don't count.

I stood under the spray and my body began to shake so I kept adding more hot water. It never occurred to me to take my clothes off. I just sluiced the water off them when I was done and patted myself dry with towels. I remember leaving the towels on the floor like I was an obnoxious hotel guest. What did it matter? I think any attempt at manners had been lost when I'd left a corpse in the living room.

I came out of the bathroom to complete silence. I don't know what I'd been expecting. Shouting. Screams. Policemen waiting to gun me down. There was no one. I was totally alone… in the home of a god. It all sank in. The man praying to Ku. The Hawaiian in the trees. The Aetheric Plane. I had killed Ku. One of the main gods of the Hawaiian pantheon was lying on a white tile floor with his head barely attached because of me. What the hell kind of karma had I just racked up? Would it matter that it was clearly self defense? I decided it did. Then I decided to snoop around.

I mean I didn't even know where I was. Like I said, I knew about tracing but had been warned at a very early age to never attempt it. So I had no idea if I was still in Hawaii or even on the same plane of existence. I had just traced! I could've been anywhere. Tartarus. Niflheim. Minnesota. Oh please, don't let me be in Minnesota. Well, then again, there is that big mall there.

I crept through the god's house and hoped he was a bachelor. The last thing I needed was the Mrs. walking in. What's the proper thing to say in that position? "Hello Mrs. Ku, lovely home you have, sorry about the corpse of your husband. Oh and for making your husband into that corpse." That was one conversation I didn't want to have.

The place was deserted though. I walked past room after room filled only with modern Hawaiian furniture (go figure). The golden gleam of Koa wood merged with Hawaiian textiles everywhere. High ceilings were crossed with wood beams. Creamy white walls were a stark contrast to dark, hand carved tikis placed artfully around the place. The Hawaiian statues looked like they were museum quality and they were all of the same god. Guess who… yep, him.

A set of sliding glass doors opened to a wide expanse of

yard. That in itself screams money when you live in Hawaii, which I was relieved to find myself still inhabiting. Coconut trees crowded the edges of the well manicured lawn like gossiping socialites at a cocktail party, snubbing the shorter kukui nut trees around them. A retaining wall penned them all in, preventing any suicidal snubbed kukuis from leaping over the cliff beyond. The house overlooked Waimea valley. I couldn't see it but I knew the Heiau was below and to the right.

You'd think a god would have an ocean view.

Relieved that I wasn't stranded somewhere impossible to return from, I headed back inside. My brain had started to function again and it was reeling from the reality of my situation. I began to search in earnest, not with thoughts of thievery but simply out of plain curiosity. It wasn't long before I found the one room that seemed special. The big *KAPU* (Hawaiian for sacred – don't touch) written across the door might have given me a bit of a clue.

For lack of a better word, I'll call the room a study. It was full of books and gadgets I'd never seen before. There were weapons everywhere, not just hanging decoratively on the walls but scattered on the floor, as if they'd been tossed there after a long day at the office, if you catch my drift.

As if that wasn't disturbing enough, a wave of magic washed over me, prickling up my arms. When I turned in its direction, all I saw was a massive book. It sat enthroned on a lectern, watching me with the curiosity of a bored tyrant. Covered in dark brown leather instead of luxurious silk, this book wasn't a bejeweled Emperor but a barbarian King. Completely unadorned by gilt or lettering, he needed no crown to proclaim his dominance. Power was decoration enough and this literary monarch wore it like a battle-honed sword, sheathed but still obviously dangerous. I approached it cautiously and it chose to be benevolent, granting me access to spells I never knew existed and information on a race of people who had come from Atlantis. No, not the resort, the actual lost continent.

With new knowledge came renewed fear. It would be wiser to appease my curiosity somewhere else. Somewhere safer than the home of a god I'd just decapitated. So I ran through the house, grabbing up a large bag (a piece of Ferragamo luggage to be exact, Ku had excellent taste) and hurried back to the study. The book went into the bag and then a couple of the more interesting gadgets on top. I told myself I was not a thief, I took them in the interest of knowledge and besides, Ku did try to kill me. To the winner go the spoils right?

By the front door I found a set of keys sitting in a koa bowl. I grabbed them up and continued my panicked flight right out the door, hoping the spoils included a getaway vehicle. I paused to get my bearings for a moment in a huge, circular, covered drive and located the garage set back to the left. A sleek, black Jaguar with an *Eddie Would Go* bumper sticker peered out at me indolently.

Eddie being Eddie Aikau, surfer and local hero who was last seen paddling away from the stranded Hokule'a canoe in an effort to fetch help. I shouldn’t have been surprised to see that little bit of homage to local culture but I was. I mean damn, I’d just found out the gods were real; picturing them purchasing motivating bumper stickers was just a little too much for me. Then I noticed the vanity plate. *KuKuK'chu* stood out against the rainbow background of the Hawaii license plate. Hmph, Ku was a Beatles fan and, evidently, he was also the walrus.

I spared one second to giggle, nearly on the verge of hysterics, and then jumped in behind the wheel. In no time, I was zipping down a private drive and breaking with a squeal when I came to an imposing iron gate. I looked around frantically and finally found the remote clipped to the passenger side visor. With shaking hands, I hit the button and hit the road.

I haven’t dated a local boy since.

Chapter Two

So that was how this whole thing began. That's how I scored this thankless fate that I can't even tell my best friends about for fear of them getting me committed. Or even worse, freaking them out so badly that they'd never be able to live a normal life. Kinda like me.

“I wouldn't wish that on anyone,” I sighed and trudged into the welcoming artificial cool of one of the millions, no make that billions, of ABC stores in Waikiki.

I grabbed myself a coke, thoughts still on the book I'd acquired that horrible day. Not only did I learn how to trace from the Good Book (hey, it’s done me a lot of good) but I also learned about the origins of the gods, the power gods got from sacrifices, and what constituted a sacrifice. It turned out that not only did they receive strength from direct offerings but also indirectly, from any death resulting from battles fought in the name of gods. Most wars have some kind of tie to the divine, even if it’s just plain rage (yes, there’s a god of rage). Also, any god in on the deal could share in the power surge.

So basically it paid off for deities to encourage their followers to fight instead of keeping them safe at home. Why settle for an occasional human sacrifice when you could get it on a mass scale constantly? Most of the gods didn't even have followers anymore, so this was their only energy source. With the downfall of the older religions, war became more necessary and the gods had to come up with bigger and better plans to create bloodshed. The book didn’t tell me that part. The flier I found tucked into the book did:

We will survive!

Come learn how to create panic and discord among the humans!

April 20 at 8pm, Valhalla

Special speakers: Odin and Huitzilopochtli

Potluck to follow. Gods whose names begin with:

A-G bring appetizers or salads

H-L bring main dishes

M-Q bring desserts

R-Z bring drinks

After I stopped laughing hysterically, I decided to begin my career as a god killer, or human liberator as I prefer to be called.

I paid the cashier for my drink and left the artificial air behind in exchange for the natural ocean breeze drifting sluggishly across Waikiki Beach. It wasn't a fair trade in my opinion but the salt air did help clear out those old memories. I plopped down on an only slightly crumbling stone wall and stared out at the Pacific as it battered the golden sand under its frothy fists.

Generally I hated the beach but breaking out of Valhalla can be exhausting and I needed a breather before I headed home over the Ko'olau mountains. The sound of the ocean can be comforting and the waves are pretty to look at, even amusing when you catch a tourist trying to learn how to windsurf. However, at that moment all it did was remind me of how blue Thor's eyes were: deep sapphire with a touch of green, like Caribbean quartz.

I loved light eyes. My own were dark brown and boring as far as I was concerned. They'd been green when I was born but had changed at nine months. My mom told me that she'd bet a friend they wouldn't change and she'd lost. Let that be a lesson to all of you ladies; don't tempt fate when it concerns your child. I shook my head and took another swig of coke. Must be the heat melting my brain. At least I wasn't bitching about Buffy anymore.

I rubbed at the ache in my neck as I pondered a new dilemma along with the old one of how to keep sand from getting all over me when I'm at the beach. Was it just me or had Thor let me go? I mean he didn't even try to chase me. Yes, I'd laid him low but it shouldn't have taken him that long to recover. He was a big, strong, creaking-leather clad god. He should have been up almost instantly. I shook my head. Thinking about Thor was only making the ache in my neck intensify so I gave up and turned my full attention to the sand.

I hate sand. It's probably one of my biggest problems with beaches. Don't laugh, I'm also not overly fond of sun or surf either. Sand, sun, and surf, the SSS, it ranked right up there with the KKK for me as far as evil acronyms went. For those of you who have never seen a beach, much less a Hawaiian one, let me explain.

Sand sticks to you like an alien fungus that believes you're its only hope of survival. Wet or dry it will attach itself to any part of your anatomy it can reach and those cool ocean breezes everyone loves so much? They are in cahoots with the vicious, alien-fungus sand and will happily fling a fine mist of the powdery annoyance all over you while simultaneously lulling you to sleep with its salt-laced caresses. Result? You wake up hours later to find not only has your sun-block died defending you but you're now coated with a thin layer of sand, saltwater, and suntan lotion that has dried to a sticky crust. After you painfully scrape away the crust, you'll find the red glow of your newly crisped skin beneath. The beach is evil, I tell you, evil.

So how could I love my home so much and not adore the pristine glory of the white sand beaches which make Hawaii such a tourist attraction? Well first of all, I enjoy the beach just fine…

through the window of an air-conditioned room with a Li Hing Mui Margarita in hand. Secondly, there is more to these islands than beaches. There's the incredible weather where even the rain is warm and I never ever have to worry about digging my car out of the snow. There's the rich melting pot of cultures and of course, there's the food. Nothing compares to the flavors of Hawaii.

I was just about to get up and sample some of those flavors from a nearby Shave Ice truck when a dark shadow passed over me, sending a shiver down my spine. No, the shiver wasn't because of the sudden relief from the sun. It was magic, strong and confident magic, almost cocky actually. I knew that magic, had in fact kicked it in its balls quite recently. I turned my head slowly, muttering a protection spell under my breath while reaching for my stash of powdered mullein.

"That's not necessary, witch," Thor's previously resonant voice was severely toned down for his foray among the humans.

"I'm nothing if not cautious," I smiled at Thor like he was an old friend as I jumped to my feet.

My legs itched to run but it wouldn't do any good. The crowds around me were thick with vacationing families and honeymooners. If at all possible, I wouldn't involve innocent bystanders and I was hoping he wouldn't either.

"I'm not here to harm you," he grimaced.

He'd taken the time to change his clothes before following me. Maybe he was afraid the leather lace-up pants of his previous ensemble would have made him stand out on a Hawaiian beach. Instead, he wore a pair of khaki pants and a tan silk Aloha shirt. He looked like a local business man on his lunch break. A local business man with golden-red hair streaming past his shoulders, bone structure that would make a Roman statue weep, and a body that looked like it spent more time in a gym than a boardroom.

I kind of missed the leather.

“No, you’re here to wow me with your literally classic good looks and your modern Hawaiian fashion sense,” I looked him over pointedly, just to let him know that I found his outfit amusing. That’s it. Really.

“Would you join me at the closest drinking establishment for a cocktail?” His lips didn’t so much as twitch, even though his eyes sparkled a bit.

“I’m sorry, I think I have sand in my ears,” I shook a finger vigorously in my left ear. I wouldn’t have put it past the alien-fungus. “I thought for a second there that you asked if you could buy me a drink.”

“I did,” his smile spread over his face like a cat stretches in the sun; slowly and sensuously, as if it had all the time in the world and was fully expecting a good scratch beneath the chin later.

I stood gaping for a moment before trying to recover. “Uh… why?” Yep, that’s me, Lucy Loquacious.

I thought seriously about extending the knives from my gloves. The gloves I wore were part of the loot I’d made off with that day at Ku’s. They had 3” long daggers resting inside them, flat against the backs of my hands until a sharp, downward movement would trigger their release. Then they extended over my fingers like lethal claws. I felt like Wolverine when I wore them but more importantly, they were deadly, turning every punch into a four way stab.

They were also a little showy for Waikiki Beach.

So was my kodachi which, for the moment, was camouflaged with a slight blurring of magic that made it blend into my leather pants. Maybe I could go for the dagger I kept down my top. The kodachi and dagger were just of human make but I'd embedded them with magic for increased damage potential. The sword was perfect for taking a god's head. The curvature of the blade gave me the extra oomph I needed to make it a clean cut but

I wasn't about to behead Thor in the middle of Waikiki. The dagger would probably be the best choice for the situation. Maybe I could throw it at him and run away screaming.

"I'd like to talk to you," his eyes strayed to my cleavage and I told myself it had nothing to do with the hidden knife and everything to do with my 36 double Ds. Call me vain but I'd rather have him checking me out than knowing where my weapons were hidden. Mae West said it was better to be looked over than overlooked. Well I needed him to do a little of both, look me over and overlook my knife. It was a survival issue and had nothing to do with him being hot.

I know, I sound full of it even to myself.

"Do I need to bow my head and clasp my hands first?" I backed up slightly and took a quick look around, trying to find a possible escape route.

He laughed, wild and rich, like drumbeats after midnight. It caused a visceral reaction in me, calling to something primitive in my blood and making me sway towards him. People stopped and turned to look at him. Hell, even I stopped scanning the area and just stared at him in shock. The tourists however, looked at Thor eagerly, as if he were some kind of celebrity they might recognize if they stared long enough. In a way I guess he was.

"For you I'll make an exception," he reached out and I tried to back up but the rock wall brought me up short. His hand dropped but his smile stayed put, "Just one drink."

"Fine, follow me," I turned and walked down the sidewalk casually, like it was just another beautiful day in paradise and I wasn't still a little shaky from that sexy laugh. The sun was shining, children were splashing in the waves, and a Norse god was about to buy me a drink. Yep, everything normal here. I dropped my empty coke bottle into a trash can marked *Mahalo* (it means *thank you* not *trash*) and kept walking.

He didn't say a word while we walked, which would normally creep me out, but I was a little too busy freaking out about everything else for it to matter. Was I really going to do this? Sit down and have a drink with an Atlantean? This *so* wasn't part of my job description. What the hell was going on? The only interaction I had with gods was done at the end of a blade. Plus, in my experience guys didn't offer to buy you a drink after you kneed them in the groin. Maybe it was that whole divine forgiveness thing? I glanced back at Thor and he grinned devilishly.

Nope, wrong god.

I led him up the shaded drive of the first building at the end of the beach. We headed up the wide white stone stairs and through an airy lobby to the bar of The Hau Tree Lanai. Very posh. I don't get a god offering to buy me a drink every day, might as well make it a good one.

I found a little table near the rear of the bar and sat down with my back against the wall so no other hot er... *dangerous* gods could sneak up on me. Thor slid in across from me, almost completely blocking the view. I peered around him for a second and then gave up. I figured I could make do with the view I was left with. Mainly him. Hey, I can be accommodating.

"Nice choice," he glanced over his shoulder at the open-air restaurant which ended abruptly in a short wall and then gleaming beach. It was too early for dinner so the patio was empty, wrought iron dining sets waiting patiently for the night's excitements. A mynah bird cawed and took flight from the tree in their midst.

"Robert Louis Stevenson's house was right there," I pointed to the Hau tree, floor tiles imprisoning its small circle of earth. "There's a picture of him lying beneath that tree."

"Interesting. Do you come here often?"

"Really?" I shook my head and pushed a frizzy strand of hair behind my ear. Damn humidity. I had my waist-length dark hair in a tight bun at my nape. Usually, I wore it up when I went out hunting but it was baby fine and was always trying to escape my evil clutches. "That's all you got? I expected better lines from you Thor, you being so… experienced and all."

"Unbelievable," he laughed again as he leaned back. "It's been a long time since I've met someone so entertaining when they're so scared, Ms… ?"

"Miss is good," I smiled again. I wasn't about to repeat my stupidity so soon, "and I'm not scared."

"Then you have the advantage of me, Miss," his eyes gleamed as he leaned forward, completely disregarding my lie. "Concerning my name I mean."

"I'll take every advantage I can get," I looked up at the sudden appearance of a waitress.

"What can I get for you two?" She stared only at Thor.

I couldn't blame her, though it made my lip curl in distaste. Guys as good looking as Thor always came with an attitude to match. Add to that, his "godhood" and you have a grade A egotistical bastard. Give me a nice average human male over Mr. Gorgeous any day. The only problem was, Mr. Average wouldn't understand my hobby.

"I'll let the lady order for us," he smiled at her, nodded graciously, as if he were accepting his just due, and then looked at me expectantly. I shook my head, suspicions confirmed.

"A bottle of Patron Silver and two shot glasses please," I smiled sweetly at the poor woman, who obviously hadn't learned to be more wary around the hotties.

The waitress raised her eyebrows but just asked if we needed limes and salt along with. Very professional. Very used to rich alcoholics. After she sauntered off, I looked back at the god incognito seated across from me.

“I thought you only wanted one drink,” he was smiling again. Did he never stop or was it just a clever way of lulling me into a false sense of security?

“I didn’t say one, you did,” I leaned back and crossed my legs, not to be ladylike but just to have an excuse to be a little further away from him. I had no idea what he was up to and I wanted as much room as possible to reach my weapons if necessary.

“Alright,” he did that head incline thing royalty does but he did it better. “Good choice, I wouldn’t have pegged you for a tequila drinker though.”

“You’ve known me all of thirty minutes,” I smirked, “part of which you spent on the floor groaning. You shouldn’t have pegged me for anything other than a woman to guard your goodies around.”

“I don’t know,” his eyes went suddenly still. “I think I could hazard a few guesses.”

Maybe it wasn’t wise to remind him of the specifics of our introduction but hey, I just couldn’t help wanting to bring him down a notch. Cocky guys put my teeth on edge.

“Try me.” I narrowed my gaze on his twitching lips but then noticed how his eyes remained solemn.

“I’d say first of all that you’re some kind of an artist,” he leaned in even closer as he spoke, “you paint and your favorite subject is people.”

I went quiet and as still as his eyes were. The statement was accurate, too accurate. I started to wonder how much the gods knew about me until I noticed the spot of oil paint on my pinky. Phew, I smiled.

"Very observant," I shook my traitorous finger at him.

"How would I know about your subject preference?" He smiled and leaned back for the waitress to deposit our order on the table between. She poured us each a shot before leaving and I was grateful for the Twix moment.

"Lucky guess," I reached for my glass and eyed him suspiciously over the rim as I sipped. I only shoot tequila when I either; A. Want to get drunk, B. Want to act tough, C. Want to get someone else drunk, or D. Any combination of the above.

He shot his and poured another.

"Tell yourself whatever you want, Miss," he saluted me with his glass and downed it.

Show off. I was *so* not going to rise to the challenge. He was a god. He could probably process alcohol in a heartbeat. Of course I'm part Japanese and could do a fair amount of alcohol processing myself. I'm told it's an allergic reaction a lot of Japanese have but basically it results in me being able to drink with the big boys but look as if I'm embarrassed the whole time (my face turns pink). I didn't want to let him play on my insecurities but then again, I'd been the one who ordered the damn bottle in the first place.

I threw back my shot and pushed it toward him. Oh well, I'm only human, put me down for B. Want to act tough.

"What do you want, Thor?" I pulled my glass closer after he refilled it and lifted it to my lips.

"You," he smiled serenely.

I sputtered and almost wasted good tequila. I said *almost.*

"Excuse me?" My hand hovered mid-air, unsure whether to continue with the drinking program or just give up in favor of open-mouthed confusion.

“I think we’re after the same things,” he reached over and gently nudged my glass upwards. I drank the rest of the shot without thinking and without taking my eyes off him.

“I barely know you,” I turned the glass over this time. “How could you possibly know what I’m after?”

“You were trying to steal the same information I was,” he shot a quick glance around the bar.

“Trying?” Questions flew around my head like annoying gnats. Was he sent to get the plans back? Oh, did I mention I had the forbearance to grab said plans while I was kneeing him? Well I did and now the Norse God of Thunder sat across from me drinking tequila and talking about wanting me due to our similar goals. Why hadn’t he just killed me and taken the plans if he wanted them? Why all the games? What the hell was going on?

“You *do* have them,” he smiled like a cat that had just found a fallen bird-feeder… still full of birds.

“Why would *you* be trying to steal them?” I ignored how sexy his smile was. I am a professional after all.

“Not all gods are as horrible as you think,” he downed another shot, his eyes narrowing briefly under his furrowed brow.

“Yeah, that’s what the Christians keep telling me,” I smirked. “Can’t say for sure though, never met Jesus, just a few Mexicans with delusions of grandeur.”

One perfectly formed eyebrow winged upward over the swirling blues and greens of his eyes. Was it the tequila affecting me or were the colors really flowing together like mist? I pushed the shot glass away from me and sighed. It wouldn’t do to get all sloppy drunk with a god. Who knows where I’d wake up. Or *if* I'd wake up.

"Some of us don't agree with the majority," he pretended to misinterpret my signal to stop drinking and refilled my glass before placing it back in front of me. I stared hard at it for a second so it knew who was boss, then picked it up and took a resigned sip.

"What do you mean you don't agree?" I looked around and faintly realized the sun was setting. Oh great, time for the rest of the monsters to come out and play.

"I don't think we need people to die for us to give us power," he frowned at my distraction and I settled my attention back firmly onto what he was saying. "Most of us believe it's the only way to raise as much power as the freely given blood used to bring but I don't agree."

"The blood?" I smirked at him and shook my head. "You mean sacrifice, specifically human, don't you?"

"I believe that's what I just said," he sighed. "There's no way around the fact that blood holds life and life is magic. When people sacrificed to us, we gained their magic and there's nothing like it. The sacrifice of animals was good too but it was only due to the magic imbued into the blood by human intention and it never came close to the power of a human life. It's that rush of magic that my fellow deities are striving for. They plot to bring war among your kind so you'll kill each other in their name again, this time on a mass scale, and they'll all share in the waves of energy it brings."

"Yes, yes," I waved a hand imperiously. "I know all that. What I don't know is why you, the God of Thunder, God of War, God of the Vikings who were known for their viciousness, would suddenly grow a soft spot and decide you don't want us to fight anymore."

"Trust me, I have no soft spots," his lips twitched a little. "I just don't think mass destruction is a good idea. You know about us, you know we need followers to grow in strength. The more people remember us and respect us, the more we thrive. Some of us have grown immense in ability. What you might not know is that we don't need any more power to survive. Our talents are old and our magic will sustain us until the earth crumbles away and is nothing but so much debris. Even then, we may still survive to find another suitable planet. And by the way, I'm not just a god of war; I also rule the sky, all storms, sea-journeys, and justice."

I could feel my eyes grow round at his candor. I had no idea they were strong enough to survive eternity without our sacrifice. I'd always assumed that without humanity the Atlanteans would have died out long ago. I knew their magic was great but I had no idea it was comic book, super villain great. My own magic seemed a poor shadow to it, although Ku's book held enough of their spells to bring me a little closer to their level. Without that book, I'd already be dead.

"Impressive résumé," I found myself shooting tequila again. Damn it, I had to stop that. "It still doesn't explain why you'd choose to miss out on all the extra power."

"Like I said, I don't think the current course of action is wise. The way things are heading, your kind could blow the whole world apart and I like it here."

"Cause it's where you keep your stuff?" I smirked.

"Some of it," he smirked back.

"So what do you propose?" I could feel the stolen documents crinkling against my waist. The black silk of my top was already limp from the heat so it was a good guess he knew where said documents were. I reached to pull them out but his hand flew across the table and grabbed mine.

"Not here," he caressed my hand along the line of the glove, where the leather was cut to leave my fingers bare. I assumed he was trying to make it appear, to anyone who might be watching, that affection had been his true intention. "You wisely chose a public place to speak with me but if we go any further, we need privacy."

Privacy. Go any further. The words seemed to curl in my gut and try to snake their way lower. I wasn't sure I wanted to be alone with the Nordic giant. It had been awhile since I was alone with any man in a non-killing sense, and the last time hadn't turned out so well.

"What do you have in mind?" I slid my hand out from beneath his and he turned his head to the side, a little wrinkle appearing between his brows.

"I have a boat up at the Yacht Club," he pulled his hand back and used it to refill my glass. The wrinkle disappeared.

"Like I'm going to follow you onto your boat," I huffed.

"Do you have a problem with boats?" His eyes crinkled at the corners and just for a second I wondered exactly how much he knew about me.

"You think you know me?" I narrowed my eyes at him and tried to look as fierce as possible, which is difficult when you're built like I am. Oh, I worked out but I wasn't what you'd call ripped. My love of food prevented that and normally I preferred it that way. A woman should look like a woman. Unfortunately, my lack of height on top of my lack of obvious muscles didn't exactly make me Amazon warrior material. What it did do was make it hard for me to look terrifying. I was about as scary as an angry Poodle.

"I do know you, Vervain," Thor smiled when my jaw dropped. "Did you think I wouldn't know the Godhunter when I saw her?"

"Godhunter?" My whisper was almost a whimper.

"Were you unaware that you'd made a name for yourself?"

His eyes showed a little surprise too. Well yippee-kai-yay, I wasn't the only one in shock.

"I didn't realize I was known to the gods at all," I had hoped my kills had gone unnoticed or at least unaccounted for by the rest of the gods.

"Oh, you're known," his smile returned. "Did you really think you could kill gods and no one would notice?"

"Well it's not like I left my business card." Grisly scenes passed through my head. Images I tried hard not to dwell on and which I sometimes needed large amounts of alcohol to banish. I hunted gods, it wasn't like I was going to give them a fair fight if I could help it. Most of the time I felt like an assassin, sneaking up on my unsuspecting victims and leaving bloody crime scenes in my wake. I never worried about getting caught since most of their homes were in the God Realm. It's not like the police would be investigating. So I never thought to cover my tracks. Maybe next time I'd torch the place when I was done.

"A few of the gods you killed had surveillance systems," he smiled as the blood drained from my face. Gods with security cameras. No, I hadn't counted on that. "You also left your scent everywhere. As soon as I smelled you, I knew who you were."

"What, are you part Bloodhound or something?" I didn't like being in the dark but then I was still fairly new to this game. Maybe I should cut myself some slack just this once. I'd have to be way more careful in the future though. Fire, definitely fire. It would take care of any trace evidence I left behind and be a double guarantee on death. If only I could burn the memories as well.

"We have very acute senses," he licked his full lips and I couldn't tear my gaze away. "Taste, hearing, touch, sight, and smell, they're all heightened on us."

"Well woopdee-diddley-doo," I couldn't help it, I was getting turned on and I needed to cover it up with something.

Sarcasm won out as usual.

Thor did that godly laughing thing again, which did nothing for my efforts to tamp down my libido. Maybe I needed to start dating. Going five years without getting some lovin' was not good for god-resisting. I made a mental note to go out that weekend.

"I forget how amusing humans can be," he was laughing so hard he actually had tears in his eyes.

"Okay fine," I sighed, "I'm funny and I stink. No matter how much you flatter me, I'm still not getting on your damn boat."

"I didn't say you smell bad," he was getting that confused look again but at least the laughter had stopped. "Why don't you accept compliments like a normal woman?"

"There is no normal here, *Thor*," I said his name as if it explained it all. "Lots of interesting things going on but none of them are normal."

"Point taken," he licked his lips again, the bastard. "I'm intrigued."

"No you're not," I put my pointer finger in his face, "you're amused, remember? And the answer is still no."

"I offer you my blood as safeguard," he pulled a tiny blade from his pocket and cut his thumb with it. If the situation hadn't been so serious, I would have laughed to see such a big man with such a tiny knife. But then if you're that big, you don't really need a large weapon do you? He made Mr. Dundee seem like he was overcompensating.

I stared at the blood welling up on his thumb and didn't have a clue on how to proceed. I had the weirdest feeling he was offering me an extreme compliment and I probably shouldn't insult him by refusing, but what was I supposed to do? I couldn't remember coming across this in Ku's book. Did he want me to cut my thumb and press it to his or what? Was I going to be blood brothers, er... blood siblings, with a god? The confusion must have showed on my face because he smiled and suddenly went all deity. He looked at me as if he was bestowing a blessing on me and I had to shake off the sudden urge to kneel.

"Will you accept my protection?" He lifted his hand and his thumb hovered over my lips. The bead of blood seemed to shimmer as it welled up.

Oh damn. Was he going to put his blood on my mouth? Gross. I couldn't even bring myself to say yes, I just nodded and he instantly lowered his bloody thumb. I blinked as the shock-waves coursed through me. Tingling, biting power ran inside me like needle-legged spiders as I felt his blood melt into my skin. I absorbed it and knew immediately that his offer of protection was eternal. I was under Thor's protection. A god protecting the Godhunter. What irony.

"Why did you do that?" I rubbed at my lips and stared at the vanishing cut on his thumb, his body just kinda sucked the blood back in.

"We need you with us," he slammed back another shot and his hand shook for just a second as he put the glass down. "We can't fight both you and them. Now, do you accompany me to my boat or not?"

Chapter Three

I don't mind boats. As long as they stayed afloat and kept me out of the water. It was the ocean I had a problem with and I blame my paranoia on my mother. She'd been a young woman when she had me and instead of staying home, wasting her youth, she took me out with her. I loved my childhood and will physically assault anyone who dares to say my mother was a bad parent but sometimes it's not the best idea to cart a kid along.

One of those outings had been to a yacht party. I don't remember much about the festivities but I remember the boat. When, as an adult, I'd mentioned the memory to her, she had nervously asked what else I remembered. I pressed her to elaborate. She said there was a small space of time when I'd gone missing and they had finally found me overboard. I was three. She sees no connection to my fear of the ocean.

To be completely honest, I must admit that Jaws played a small part in my terror of the deep blue as well, and an even bigger role in me not taking up surfing (I don't like feeling like bait, thank you very much) but I had no thoughts of killer sharks when I boarded Thor's floating behemoth. I didn't think about the water at all actually since the boat... ship... whatever, was so big, I forgot the ocean was even there. No small feat when dealing with me and my paranoia.

Thor took my hand to help me across the gangplank and didn't release it. He pulled me casually through the interior of the thing, passing room after room of shining mahogany paneling and gleaming steel. I caught glimpses of plush carpeting in dark blue and matching curtains fluttering in the warm salty breeze. The boat must have been specially made for him because even with his bulk, he didn't look cramped at all. In fact, we were walking down the corridor side by side and his head didn't even come close to brushing the ceiling.

We stopped at a stairway and went down into the belly of the beast. Maybe not the best description under the circumstances but it fit. At the bottom of the stairs was a large open room. The carpeting down there was crimson, the massive center table was black lacquer, and all the décor had an Asian feel. Not what I expected from a Norse god. Shouldn't there be coarse wooden tables and battle axes? Maybe a buxom wench with blonde braids named Brunhilde?

Instead of axes there were swords. Katanas and the shorter wakizashis were protected in shiny ebony sheaths and displayed proudly on the walls. There was also a brilliant white wedding kimono dominating the wall opposite us, with hand embroidered gold cranes all over it. The walls themselves were covered in soft gold wallpaper with more cranes flying across the expanse, so subtly done that you had to concentrate to see them. On my right was a suit of Samurai armor, complete with a bright red, demon face mask. I swear it was smiling at me and not in a good way, more of a *It''ll be fun to eviscerate you* sort of way. I ignored it on principal.

In the center of the table, a delicate white orchid bloomed in a shiny black pot, colored subtly by light shining through the red and gold lacquered paper parasols above it. The parasol lights gave a pink tint to the room, like the boat was blushing in the face of unexpected company. It shouldn't have worried though, the place was immaculate. Any conquering warlord would have happily dripped blood onto the conveniently colored carpet before shucking off his armor and calling for a geisha. I know, that was terribly white of me but I'm only a quarter Japanese and I've never even been to Japan, so you're gonna have to forgive me my clichés. Plus, I think it's an apt description. The room was fiercely beautiful but even with the kimono and orchid, it was supremely masculine.

To the right of the kimono, a door opened into the galley. I was very pleased with myself for remembering the correct name of a ship's kitchen. I was not so pleased to find a stunning woman standing in the doorway. My pleasure went down even more when she smiled and poured a warm, welcoming wave of magic out towards me. She wasn't blonde and I highly doubted her name was anything even close to Brunhilde but I had no doubt as to why she was on Thor's boat. My sudden jealousy was as embarrassing as it was ridiculous.

Did I really think I was special because he held my hand? Sheesh, what was I, sixteen? I'll tell you what I was, I was an idiot. I dropped Thor's hand like it was on fire.

"I'm Persephone," the newcomer said as she reached a hand toward me.

Her hand enveloped mine and I suddenly felt like the world was a fresh, wondrous place full of new things to discover. I was a little girl again, peering under rocks and crawling through the grass in search of tiny treasures. I shook my head a little and Persephone smiled brighter, her small mouth looking almost too childish for such a sultry face. She had long dark hair the color of rich soil and green bedroom eyes like morning leaves still shaking off the night. A porcelain doll but one that was made for men. She laughed as I continued to gape at her and I felt her power tickle me.

"I'm Vervain," I finally managed to choke out my name and pull my hand from hers. "Persephone, as in the cause of winter, that Persephone?"

"Well I hardly think it's my fault Mommy had a fit because Hades abducted me," she actually pouted a little and I heard Thor sigh heavily behind me.

"Hey, I've never been one to blame the victim," I held up my hands placatingly. It's never a good idea to aggravate the crazies. "I was just repeating what I remember of the myth. Frankly I always thought Hades must be a bastard if he had to kidnap a woman to get a date."

Persephone's smile returned to its former glory immediately "Well it's a little more complicated than that but thank you. I just knew we'd be the best of friends! You're named for a plant after all and I'm a goddess of growing things."

"It's a herb actually," I hated always having to explain my name. It's the same questions every time and always the same replies. It's Vervain not Vivian. Yes I know it's unusual. No it's not a flower. Sigh.

Mom had thought it fabulously witty to name a baby witch after a herb with great magical benefits. Vervain was used for love, money, protection, peace, purification, and even youth. You couldn't ask for a better mix of powers. However, most people were not witches or even versed in our folklore. So I spent a lot of time explaining what vervain was and why my mother would name me after it. If you think that's bad, my middle name is Alexandrite, not Alexandra but Alexandr*ite*, like the gem. People at the DMV are constantly trying to correct the "typos" in my name. There is no creativity allowed in the DMV.

"Yes, I know," she wrapped an arm around me and led me to the table as I cast a *help me* look over my shoulder at Thor.

He smiled broadly and spread his hands as he shrugged. Great, so much for his protection. Meanwhile, Ms. Happy Face pulled me down into a seat beside her. I wondered if she was also familiar with our local herb. Maybe she had smoked some back in the galley. It would explain the permagrin.

"Interesting that you pronounce the H in herb. Were you raised in England?" She went on.

"No," I smirked, pleased to get to use my favorite Eddie Izzard line. "I say herb because there's a fucking H in it."

"Oh, well, um," she obviously wasn't an Izzard fan. "I've

heard so much about you. You're awfully brave for a human girl."

My eyes narrowed as I looked at her and I heard Thor's strangled laugh. Was this innocent child routine all an act? Boy, she was good if it was. No problem, I can throw down with the best of them.

"And you're awfully naive for someone who sleeps with the Devil," I smiled, waiting for the barb to slide home but she only giggled and lightly pushed my shoulder.

"You're funny too. Hades isn't the Devil, he's the Lord of the Underworld," she flicked her thick hair back. Hair-flickers really annoy me. She was probably one of those people with motivational quotes written on Post-its all over her bedroom.

"So I've heard," I looked pointedly at Thor. "What the hell is this Thor, a meet and greet?"

"Pretty much," he slid into the chair on my right and I couldn't help the little jolt of pleasure I felt because he'd chosen to sit beside me instead of Little Miss Sunshine. And I'm back to being sixteen again.

"Is this it?" I looked from him to her and back again. "Just you, me, and your girlfriend here?"

Persephone hooted with laughter but Thor just raised an eyebrow, turned his head to the side, and casually slung an arm over the back of my chair.

"He's not my boyfriend," Persephone giggled again. "I thought you understood; I'm with Hades."

"You only see him three months out of the year if the stories are true," I leaned towards Thor so I could get a better look at her, and yes, it was the only reason I leaned closer to him. It had nothing to do with that refreshing scent of his.

“Uh-huh, Mom’s a little controlling,” she was really starting to get on my nerves with the baby voice.

“So one thing I’ve learned is that the stories of gods are partially based on fact but are mostly fiction. By accepting the power humanity’s worship gives you, you accept their beliefs and allow that power to change you into all they hold true. You are in effect transformed by the thoughts of humans.” I waited for her to nod politely. “However, you still possess free will and can basically do as you please. You are transformed by us but not completely restricted by us.”

“Yes, that’s true,” she murmured and looked away.

“What am I missing?” I looked to Thor for an answer.

“Hades is pretty powerful,” Thor’s lips pressed together. “He’s also pretty jealous. I doubt he'd put up with any competition.”

“So you let this guy rule your life even when you’re away from him?” I couldn’t believe she was that submissive. Well then again.

“Not completely,” her bottom lip pushed out. “I just don’t want to consort with anyone else. Besides, no one wants to get Hades mad either. I’m not worth it.”

Holy crap, it was a goddess with an inferiority complex. The surprises just kept on coming. I looked over at Thor and he shrugged again before running his thumb down the back of my neck. I sat up straight and realized I was effectively trapped between the two of them.

“Back off, Boy Thunder,” I growled between clenched teeth.

Maybe Persephone wasn't his girl but she'd given me a much needed wake-up call. I was out of my league there, playing with the big gods and that was probably all Thor was doing with me... playing.

Thor laughed and leaned in to say something else but before he could speak, the air in front of us shimmered and a figure coalesced. When it was fully formed, there was a striking Indian man standing before us (Indian with a dot not feather). He was under six feet tall but well muscled and his dark skin shone softly against the vivid red silk of his dress shirt. He had on black pants, a thin leather Gucci belt, and matching shoes. His ebony hair curled around his collar and eased some of the harshness from his features but the close cropped beard added a hint of menace. Great, now what?

"Brahma," Thor nodded slightly, "thanks for coming."

Hmph. I knew a little about Brahma. Hindu God of Knowledge; four heads, four arms, red skin, thought himself into existence. He gave new meaning to the term *I think therefore I am*. I counted his head again. Yep, still only one and a measly two arms. I was a little disappointed.

"Of course," Brahma nodded back but then dismissed the Viking entirely and focused on me. "You have a human with you?" He pulled out a chair across from us and slid into it as he inspected me. "She has power too," he closed his eyes and breathed deeply, then shivered, "delicious power."

Okay, that was creepy. I stiffened and looked around me, trying to find the quickest escape route. I had no intention of being this guy's next combo meal. I was keeping all of my energy, thank you. Before I could bolt, Thor's hand came off of the chair and settled on my shoulder. He rubbed gently, then clamped down firmly. I was really starting to worry about his so called protection.

"Remember, I gave you a blood oath," he whispered, "you've nothing to fear when I'm with you."

"You gave her blood?" Brahma sat back as his dark eyes

rounded. "Who *is* this woman?"

"She's the Godhunter," Persephone piped up merrily.

"You?" Brahma leaned in again, turning his head from side to side as if he could catch some previously missed detail if he just got a better angle.

"I'm rather unremarkable no matter how you look at me," I sighed.

I knew I was no great beauty. I'd call myself passing pretty if I had to label it, pretty enough to pass by without gagging. Sitting next to a goddess didn't help. Then there was that whole lack of muscles thing, so I didn't even have the warrior babe look going for me. I told you; angry Poodle. Especially with my humidity frizzed hair.

"I wouldn't say that," Thor's whisper was so close to my ear, it tickled and made me jump at the same time.

Brahma laughed and leaned his face into one palm. "I wouldn't either. You don't have the perfection of a goddess but perfection can be tiring. Your looks are unique, even for a human. I see a charming mix of ethnicity in your face."

"Yep, I'm a mutt."

"I'd wondered about your people," Thor looked down at me intently.

"I'm *human*," I smiled sweetly, "they're all my people."

Brahma chuckled. "Oh, I like her."

"You've already got your hands full, Brahma," Thor narrowed his eyes at the Hindu god. "Are you still cheating on Sarasvati?"

"I'm a god," he drew himself up; "I must attend to my

followers."

"I'm sure your wife finds that comforting," Thor snorted.

"We've gotten off subject," Brahma spread his hands in a *let's not fight* gesture. "I'd still like to know which people you're descended from, Godhunter."

"Call me Vervain, or V if you prefer," I squirmed. Why were we talking about me? "I'm Irish, English, Dutch, French, German, Japanese, Cherokee, and Blackfoot."

Thor's eyes widened. "All of those?"

"I like to think of myself as a preview of what the world will be like someday," I shrugged. "In the future, we'll all be so mixed up, there will be only one race; Human."

"Very noble," Brahma grunted, "but it will never happen. You people take too much pride in what separates you. Look at me for example," he waved a hand over himself. "Do you think I was born this way? No. Humans are so egotistical, they want their gods to look like them. Man was made in God's image, my ass! Man made gods in their own image. It's why Christ looks like a white man, even though history says he was Jewish. He's neither actually, he's Atlantean but when he first became a god, he looked Jewish because those were the people he chose to align himself with. But the Jews didn't want him and when Christianity spread, the white people wanted him to look more like them. With the change in belief, Christ's appearance changed. Actually, it was pretty funny. We used to tease him all the time about how he looked whiter each time we saw him. *My but you're looking awful white this morning*, we'd say." Brahma chuckled as I gaped at him. "Kind of like Michael Jackson but that's a different story entirely. What I'm trying to say is that your pride in your differences is your people's greatest weakness. It's what the other gods use to their advantage. There will always be one race who thinks they're better than another."

"There's still hope for us," I didn't like the bizarre but truthful ring to his words. "I'm living proof."

"That you are," Thor played with the baby hairs around the nape of my neck and it sent tingles over my scalp. "You're also the best mix of all of your ancestors. I like the blending of you."

"Ah, that's precisely what I was trying to say," Brahma smiled widely, showing off even white teeth.

"Well aw shucks, boys," I smirked.

I wasn't entirely sure if they were just messing with me or not, so I felt safer to just go with the old standby sarcasm. Both of the "boys" seemed equally baffled and amused by my attitude but we were once more interrupted by an arrival. This time they just used the stairs.

A Native American couple strode in, hand in hand. I guess Thor wanted to represent both types of Indians. Maybe it was because of my heritage but I preferred them to Brahma instantly. The Hindu god was just a little too slick for my taste.

The man had on a crisp, white, dress shirt tucked into dark blue jeans which were in turn tucked into cowboy boots. His long, black hair was pulled back tightly in a ponytail that caught the light with blue shimmers. He had golden brown skin that practically glowed, high cheekbones, and a generous mouth. Almond shaped eyes, rimmed thickly in long lashes, glittered like chipped obsidian as they settled on us and the man smiled.

"You found the Godhunter," he bowed slightly at the waist and I was shocked to realize that he was bowing to me. "It's a great pleasure to meet you, little warrior. I'm Tsohanoai of the Navajos. This is my consort Estsanatlehi."

The woman moved forward and with her came a warm breeze smelling of rain. She smiled and her long black hair flowed around her hips in a sudden breeze. She was slightly darker than her husband or maybe it was just that his skin was so bright, it made her look darker. Her cheekbones were just as high as his but her lips were fuller and were a deep red, like she'd just gorged herself on blackberries. She was dressed as simply as Tsohanoai, in a cotton dress of light blue.

"I'm sorry our son will not be joining us," her voice was as sweet as her face but there was an underlying strength to it. "Nayenezgani receives the prayers of the warriors before battle and he believes his power is only in war."

Tsohanoai came up behind her and pulled out a chair. She sank into it gracefully, slipping her long hair over the back so she wouldn't sit on it. I was mesmerized and silently hoped she would be the end of the beauty parade for the evening. I didn't think my ego could handle much more.

"Nice to meet you both," I stammered. What was the correct greeting for a god anyway? Where was Miss Manners when you needed her?

They smiled at me warmly and Tsohanoai put his arm over the back of his consort's chair, mimicking Thor and I. The reminder of how intimate I must look with Thor made me wince and sit straighter. I could practically feel him frowning at my movement. I turned and looked over my shoulder... yep, big Viking frown. I think I preferred it to all the smiling he'd been doing anyway.

"Is this everyone?" I was still a little ticked off at being so out of the loop and having to blunder my way through all the surprises. These were beings I hunted for the good of humanity, I didn't expect to be having tea with them and I still wasn't convinced they weren't all evil. The only thing that kept me from bolting was the power of Thor's blood. I could still feel it zipping through my body. I knew deep down that he'd made a true oath and he wouldn't harm me. That didn't prevent others from attempting it though.

"We're waiting on two more," Thor had a little crease between his eyes and I was thoroughly enjoying his discomfort. "Ah, here they are."

There was a loud screeching followed by a muttered oath and the sound of crashing. Thor didn't seem the least bit concerned, in fact he had a little of his smile back. An average sized man walked in waving his arms about his head furiously. A large falcon swept past him and landed on the armor in the corner.

"Curse you, Horus," the man griped. "Watch where you're flying." He noticed the group of us staring at him finally and smiled brightly. "He can be such a birdbrain."

A loud screech filled the room as the falcon launched himself at the man, who then dove for cover. The falcon stopped short and hovered with great flaps of his wings. Bird-form blurred and elongated until it was no longer a bird but a man dressed in a black, short sleeved shirt and slacks.

"The falcon is one of the wisest winged creatures there is," the ex-bird-now-man looked down his long nose at the other, who was climbing to his feet.

"Then why do they even have the term *birdbrain*?" Mr. Average stretched his neck up so he could poke his face impudently into the taller man's. He was dressed more casually, in torn jeans and a yellow shirt which read *Everyone panic, I'm here.* They looked like two opposite sides of the social spectrum.

"It's a ridiculous term made by humans who know nothing of the amazing avian mind." The ex-bird was as regal looking as he sounded and I was back to staring again. His skin was the light gold of a falcon's feathers and his nose was just a step away from the beak it previously was. There was more intelligence in his brown eyes than warmth and his bearing was so grand, my knees buckled with the urge to curtsy. Good thing I was still seated.

"No one knows the avian mind because they have no mind.

Their brains are about the size of a pea." The smaller man batted at his curly brown hair which kept falling into his eyes. It seemed to want to play as much as he did. It was kind of charming. In fact, the more you looked at him, the more charming he became. His lips seemed to be constantly on the verge of smiling, even when he was fighting with the bird. His hazel eyes held even more merriment than his lips and his face ended in a pointed chin like an elf. To top it all off, I caught a glimpse of little horns hiding in all those curls.

"Pan," Thor's voice rumbled out, making the name into a warning.

"Pan?" I couldn't keep the disbelief from my voice. Both men turned to me, Horus with a frown and Pan with a radiant smile. "Pan, as in reed pipes and wood nymphs?"

"The one and only," he bowed gallantly and left Horus sputtering behind him. "And you are Lady…?"

"Vervain," I said as I smiled. Why was I smiling?

"Ah," Pan's smile turned sensual, "I love flowers, they have such sweet nectar in their depths."

"It's actually a herb," I said but Thor spoke over me.

"Pan," Thor's voice was a low growl and the potted orchid on the table actually shook.

"My mistake," Pan backed away still grinning. "I didn't know this bloom was already plucked."

"There's been no plucking," I shot a nasty look at Thor, hoping he caught the message that I didn't appreciate this type of protection. What; did he think it would make it easier if everyone thought we were an item? Not like he could be seriously into me or anything and not like I cared… much.

“Hmmm,” Pan moved forward again, this time he claimed a chair next to the Navajo goddess. “Which is it then, Thor, plucked or un-plucked?”

Tsohanoai moved his wife closer to him as he eyed Pan.

“She’s spoken for,” Thor leaned forward to glare at Pan.

“Hey now,” I shrugged Thor’s arm off. “There’s been no plucking or speaking of plucking and there will *be* no plucking period. Can we find another word for plucking, one that doesn’t rhyme with plucking?”

“Enough,” Horus walked stiffly to the table and sat in one of the end chairs like he was about to bring the meeting to order. Big surprise there. “We’re not here for you to play your silly games with a human, Pan. I would like to know what she’s doing here though.” He looked pointedly at Thor.

“I caught her stealing the same information I went to Valhalla to collect,” Thor leaned back and let that tidbit sink in before continuing. “When I realized who she was, I decided to ask her to join us. I think she’ll be valuable and besides, it’s the humans’ fight too.”

“And *who* is she? What makes her so valuable?” Horus crossed his muscular forearms and the short sleeves of his linen shirt rode up to expose a detailed tattoo of a falcon in flight. Too detailed in fact. I’d never seen ink like it. It was like a real bird had been miniaturized and pressed into his skin. Kinda creepy actually.

“She’s the only human who has ever managed to kill our kind,” Thor spoke very quietly but the words seemed to ring out.

Horus and Pan sat forward with a gasp. Evidently I was known by sight to only some of the gods. I felt like I had just had my superstar status revoked. Oh well, there goes my fifteen minutes. Fame can be so fickle.

"The Hunter?" Horus lifted his head and scanned me dubiously. "*This* is the Godhunter?"

"There's no need to get nasty now," I didn't know what was worse, having a nickname among the gods or not living up to it.

Horus narrowed his eyes. "You don't look strong enough to kill gods."

"Well you don't look like an asshole but there you go," I almost clamped my hand to my mouth.

I had no filter; the words went straight from my brain and out my mouth. It made me a horrible liar and got me into heaps of trouble. I think the only thing that saved me was the immediate laughter of all the other gods.

"Come on, Horus," Thor clamped a large hand down on Horus's shoulder and I saw him wince. "Admit it, that was funny… and you deserved it."

Horus did no admitting and no laughing but the tension did seem to ease from his shoulders. He sat back, nodded, and that was that.

"Okay," Thor said, "let's get started then. Vervain, the documents please."

I leaned back into the chair so I could reach down into my jeans, which also put me further into Thor's side. His breath was in my hair, his scent suddenly stronger, and I quickly yanked the papers from my pants. He took them from me and smoothed them gently on the table. I watched his touch linger over the paper and had a brief moment of imagining those fingers somewhere else. What was it I said about amateurs falling for their prey? I was starting to feel like a supreme moron. Thor turned abruptly and stared at me, slowly raising an eyebrow.

“What?” It came out a little harsher than I intended. Nerves have a habit of turning me into a bitch.

“Did you want to look this over with me?” Thor’s eyebrows shot downward and I felt even worse for being paranoid. So of course I got snappier.

“Why, do you only read Old Norse?” As soon as the words came out, I felt like an ass. “Sorry, I don’t know what’s wrong with me.”

“I could hazard a guess,” Pan piped up from across the table but was shushed gently by Estsanatlehi.

“It's forgotten,” Thor hadn’t even glanced at Pan. He started to skim over the document. “The next strike will be in Washington DC; they’re going to instigate an attack on a peace rally through some al-Qaeda terrorists.”

“Well that’ll put a damper on the party,” I leaned in closer to see it for myself.

“Even the protesters will back the war after being shot at,” Horus twisted his lips into a mockery of a smile. “Nothing like murder and mayhem to beget more murder and mayhem.”

“So what do we do about it?” I looked around the table and the whole thing took on a surreal quality for me. These weren’t just people I was talking shop with, they were gods.

They all looked at me, the lone human in their midst, and I’m sure more than a few of them wondered how I could possibly help. Hell, I wondered it. I was more of a surprise ambush kinda girl and even then, I had to psych myself up every time I got ready to hunt. I guess all warriors have a battle cry to help bolster their spirits. Mine went something like: I don’t wanna diiiiiie! Well it was more of an internal battle cry.

“So we go and we stop them,” Brahma looked bored, in

fact he was paying more attention to the minuscule pieces of dirt beneath his fingernails than he was to us. When he finally looked up and saw our expressions, he huffed. “What? How hard could it possibly be?”

Chapter Four

Five hours later, we arrived in DC. Five hours after Brahma's blasé question. You would think a god would know better than to tempt fate. Did Murphy's Law work with gods? Did words have more power when spoken by the divine? I'd say yes.

We traveled to Washington via the normal way for gods, tracing. I highly recommend it. No lines, no cramped airline seat, no bad food, no fat business man sitting behind you kicking your seat, and oh, it's absolutely free. Yep, it's good to be a god, or at least a witch with travel benefits.

It made me wish I had enough magic to navigate the Aether on my own. Alas, I was a lowly human witch and could only manage to use a spell to link trace points. To get from one place to another, I had to have the exact chant to link the two locations. I couldn't just jump in and jump out willy-nilly. It was the difference between letting the current take you and actually steering a boat. Basically, I surfed the Aether. I could paddle out and ride back in but I couldn't navigate the channels. No helm and no rudder.

Navigating the early morning throng in front of the White House was more my speed, though I hated crowds. I managed to get to the edge of the iron fence, where I stood and stared, Thor keeping most of the jostling people from bumping into me. I couldn't help it, it was America's headquarters and I was one of those very proud Americans. It was also my first visit to DC and I was excited to get a look at the White House. I have to say I was a little disappointed though. Valhalla's way more impressive.

Thor finally grabbed my arm and pulled me along. People flew out of his way, barely even touching him. I don't think they even realized they were doing it. They just sort of were not where he was walking. Fascinating but not as fascinating as my first sight of the President's house. I continued to stare back over my shoulder as he led me off like a deranged puppy who really wanted to pee on one tree in particular; the president's tree.

"Can't I have a minute here?" I tugged on his harsh grip, pulling at individual fingers since his hand was so big I found it necessary to divide and conquer. "I've never seen the White House."

"It's a big house and it's white," Thor kept walking. "Besides we're not here for sightseeing. I'll bring you back when we're done."

I raised an eyebrow at that. It almost felt like I was on a date. A very strange and possibly violent date. Well, probably violent, possibly fatal. Thor held my hand, even after I stopped resisting and started moving purposefully with him. Then there was the mention of a second outing. That's date talk, right? I looked down at our clasped hands and then around at the rest of our group. No one else was holding hands, not even the Navajo couple. Was this just Thor's way of protecting me? He had made a blood oath after all. Maybe he just forgot he was still dragging me along.

We reached the park across the street and stopped abruptly. Thor looked around expectantly and since the only place I was looking was at him, I knew the exact moment he found what he was after. Yes, I was staring at him, I had nothing else to do and he was still holding my hand. I was not completely infatuated. I was not an amateur. I was merely keeping occupied and aware.

I glanced over in the direction he was looking, then looked immediately back for a more thorough inspection. It wasn't everyday that I got to meet two gorgeous Viking gods and I was pretty sure the guy walking up to us was going to be the second. He wasn't as tall as Thor but wasn't by any means short, over six feet definitely, and his long hair was blonde not red. His features weren't as artistically angled as Thor's but they'd give Brad Pitt a run for his money. Hell, I think Angelina would have swapped good ol' Brad for either of these two in a heartbeat. If this kept up, I'd need a bib.

"Ull," Thor finally let me go to embrace the newcomer in a fast manly hug. You know the quick grab, pat hard, and let go kind of hug that says *I must care a lot about this guy because I'm touching him but let's get this clear...I'm sooo not gay.*

"Hey Dad," Ull smiled up at the bigger man before looking me over.

"Dad?" I shook my head to clear it of the lust induced fog and tried to concentrate. "Did he just call you Dad?"

"I'm his stepson," Ull slipped around his *Dad* and closed in on me. "And you are?"

"This is Vervain," Thor stepped between us again. "She's going to be working with us."

"Great," Ull pushed past Thor as his smile grew. "I'm looking forward to it, Vervain." He held his hand out to me but Thor grabbed it before I could and pushed it away like it was a potential threat.

"I made her a blood oath," Thor sounded a little more serious than I thought was necessary over a minor protection.

"What?" Ull wasn't the only one shocked, some of the other gods made sounds of surprise as well. Brahma just looked kinda smug to have known a choice bit of info that the others didn't.

"She's human," Thor let go of Ull and reclaimed my hand. "She didn't trust me and I believe we need her."

"But, Dad," Ull's eyes were getting pretty round, "a blood oath... where? Heart or lips?"

"Lips," Thor locked his gaze on his stepson as if daring him to say more.

"Well," Ull shook his head, "at least there's that."

"So she really is spoken for," Pan looked supremely disappointed. I didn't know whether to be really flattered or really creeped out by all this attention.

"Okay," I used Thor's distraction to yank my hand free and then stood back from the group. "This is starting to sound like something I need to know more about, like right now." I crossed my arms for good measure.

"She doesn't know?" Ull stared at Thor, then transferred his intense attention to me. "You don't know?"

"So tell me already," I was not uncrossing my arms till I had an answer... period.

"It's not your place to tell her," Thor glared at Ull.

"No, it's not," Ull was giving Thor's nasty look right back to him and upping the nasty. "It's yours, as in it should've been done already."

"Thor, you honored a human with *Blood to Mouth* and then didn't even bother to explain it to her?" Horus walked up behind Ull, looking just as baffled as I felt.

"Great," I sighed, "I'm honored. Can someone tell me what I'm so honored about?"

"We don't have time for this," Thor simply pushed his hand between my folded arms, grabbed my wrist, and started dragging me away.

"Whoa, caveman," I tried my best to dig my heels in but let's face it; it was like a parakeet trying to hold back a tornado; just a whole lot of useless squawking. "I don't appreciate this,

Thor. I'm going to ask nice just once. The next time my sword will do the asking. Now please tell me what's going on."

"You have my protection," he didn't even glance behind us to see if everyone was following. "That's all you need to know. You'll not be harmed if I can help it."

"Uh-huh," I looked behind me. The gang was all there and completely fascinated by our exchange. "What's the difference between lips and heart?"

"I don't have time to give you an anatomy lesson," he kept walking.

"Witty, very witty," I looked behind me again, this time for help, but they were all wearing matching *I don't know whether to be pissed off or amused* stares. "What's the difference in the oath?"

"Well obviously a blood oath to the heart is a pledge of love," he sounded like he was schooling a three-year-old. I don't like being patronized. Come to think of it, I don't know anyone who actually enjoys being patronized, including three-year-olds.

"Well *obviously*," I rolled my eyes, "and *obviously* I'm an idiot because I thought I knew enough about blood oaths to be able to assume that you're giving me one meant I could trust you."

"Odin's beard, woman!" Thor finally stopped and turned so suddenly, I ended up smack dab in the middle of his chest. I don't think he even felt it. For me it was like accidentally walking into a telephone pole... which I've done before. Don't laugh, I'm a klutz and it happens to hurt. Don't even get me started on the splinters. "That was the whole purpose of the oath, to let you know you can trust me."

I couldn't stop the laughter, even with my suddenly aching chin. It kind of just spurted out in a surprised guffaw. He looked down at me, then grabbed my upper arms to bring me off my feet so he could glare harder. It served only to burst the giggle dam and

I started laughing even more.

"What's so damn funny?" He actually shook me a little.

"It's just," I had reached the point where exhaustion and anxiety had made me sensitive. If he had said something mean, I might have cried but as it stood, everything had become funny. He could have said *doorknob* and I would have laughed harder. "It's just…"

"The suspense is killing me," Horus's dry voice came from behind me, starting another round of laughter. People walking by were giving us funny looks. The children with those people were smiling though. They knew a busted giggle dam when they saw one.

"Okay, okay," I took a deep calming breath. "It's just that you're a god so it's kinda funny to hear you swear using another god's name. Like, you just took another god's name in vain. Isn't that breaking a god rule or something?" I giggled. "The only thing that would've been more amusing is if you'd said *My beard, woman*, much funnier and probably not a rule breaker."

The assemblage of gods stared at me with different degrees of disgust and amusement. Thor just looked confused.

"I don't have a beard," he said simply. That's when the others finally saw the humor. Their laughter, unfortunately, did nothing to improve Thor's mood. He just snorted, put me down, and resumed walking.

"I've been meaning to ask you about that," I panted after him. I was really glad I'd worn my flat soled boots. "I thought you were supposed to have a great big, bushy, red beard."

"I shaved," his pace quickened and I practically had to run to keep up. "I've been spending a lot of time in Hawaii and it gets itchy with the heat. Beards are for cold weather."

"Okay, great," I felt like that little dog in the old cartoons that jumps around the big dog panting, *What d'ya wanna do today, Spike? Huh, Spike? Huh?* Except this little dog was being dragged. "So you shaved it, looks good. I like the stubble but there's one other thing I've been meaning to ask."

"*What*?!" He stopped again and threw down my hand like holding it was too much encouragement for my mouth.

"Where are we going?" My voice was just a tad too timid sounding for me so I couldn't stop there. "More importantly, are we there yet?" I added a bit of adolescent whine just for good measure.

"Yeah, Dad," Ull jumped up next to us. "Are we there yet?"

I liked Ull immediately. All we had time for was a grin and a wink to acknowledge our new camaraderie before Thor started pulling on my hand again. I was pretty sure I was going to have bruises.

He didn't let up until we'd reached our destination. A secret underground hideout? A chic high-rise loft? No, it was Starbucks. He pulled me with him all the way to the counter.

"I'd like a grande caramel machiatto with whip," Thor announced to the barista as she stared back at him, dumbstruck. He yanked me forward and put an arm around my shoulders. "You want anything, babe?"

The woman transferred her attention to me long enough to determine that I wasn't anywhere near as interesting as he was and then went back to gawking at Thor. I wasn't sure what shocked me more, his ordering what I considered a girly drink (one of my favorites by the way) or his calling me babe.

"Uh, the same please," I gaped at him.

"Make it two," Thor smiled at the girl and for a second I thought she was going to faint.

"You want that hot?" She blinked wide eyes at him.

"Oh, *definitely*," he grinned wickedly and I thought for sure she was going down.

She did sway a little but then she bucked up and rang us up as I silently cheered her on. *You can do it! He's not all that special, just, you know, a god.* Hey, I'm on the side of anyone making me coffee. Thor paid and then steered me to an overstuffed couch to wait as the rest of the gods placed their orders.

When we were all seated with our beverages, I held and sipped my coffee like it was a lifeline. I was sooo not sitting in Starbucks with a bunch of gods who looked like Benetton and Armani got together to make a magazine spread. I looked up, licking whipped cream off my lips and blinking hard. Yep, there they were; sipping from paper cups with the sound of pressurized steam and folk music in the background.

"How long have we got before the rally?" I looked around, wondering if gods wore watches because I sure as hell didn't. I'm not a watch wearing kind of girl. I could go into this whole long diatribe about how I don't like to be restricted by time or some other such granola crap but the truth of the matter is; I'm just too lazy to remember to put one on everyday.

Sure enough, Brahma pushed up his silk sleeve and revealed a Rolex. The diamonds in the face sparkled at me in an attempt to change my mind about the whole watch wearing thing. I have to admit they made a good argument. If someone bought me a Rolex, I might make an effort to wear it everyday. Or at least on non-god-hunting days.

"The rally is at one o'clock. It's now seven forty-six AM, Eastern Standard Time, so that gives us roughly another six hours."

I groaned and took another sip of coffee. It had been a long day… yesterday, and I still hadn't got any shut eye since then. "Don't you guys ever sleep?"

"We sleep," Thor's hand slid up my back and onto my neck, where he began to knead my muscles expertly. "We just don't need it as much as you."

"Figures," I sighed and let him work out the knots. "I know we don't have time for a nap so let's just get on with it."

"Okay," Thor set his cup down. "We need a locator spell, Vervain."

"No prob," I sipped my coffee and thought about it. "Wait, what am I supposed to locate?"

"Can you focus on a magical disturbance?" Horus asked from his big, purple, overstuffed chair. So surreal.

"You want me to find a disturbance in the force, Luke?" I giggled, on the verge of exhausted hysterics.

"Who did she just call me?" Horus puffed up and put his coffee down. "I am not-"

"Relax, Egyptian," Ull chucked Horus on the shoulder. "It's just a movie reference."

"Hmph," Horus picked his mug up but divided his glare between Ull and I, as if we were in cahoots.

"Sure, I can do a locator spell," I got back on topic. "But it'd have to be done while this disturbance is happening and they aren't going to be using magic constantly. Can't you guys just do some god juju?"

"Even we have our limitations," Horus looked like he'd swallowed a bug.

“You know, I've always wondered that,” I just realized I had the perfect opportunity to up my god-hunting game. “I know about beheading as a good way to be sure of the kill but just in case I have to do some hand-to-hand combat, what route should I take? I mean, do you guys just regenerate or what?”

“You want us to tell you how to kill us?” Horus squawked.

“It's a valid question,” Thor frowned. “We'll be taking her into battle. She needs to know our weaknesses.”

“And if she uses the information against us?” Horus narrowed his eyes on Thor.

“Then you'll get to see firsthand if she really is strong enough to kill gods,” Thor glared back.

“Well, as I'm sure you've realized, some of us are a little harder to kill than others,” Ull ignored the banter and focused on me, “How susceptible you are depends on your magic. And that goes for healing too. Only gods whose power includes regeneration can fully regenerate otherwise fatal wounds and even then, they're limited to as much energy as they have stored up. The rest of us can take care of tiny cuts but other than that; if you cut us, we will bleed... and keep bleeding. We have to heal normally or go to one of our healers. If it's really bad, we have to restock our immortality.”

“Ull,” Thor's voice held a warning note, “that's going too far. You know the law.”

“The law?” I felt my forehead wrinkling. “You have laws?”

“Of course,” Ull continued as if Thor hadn't spoken. “We-”

“Could you cast a spell on an item?” Estsanatlehi, who I was already referring to as Mrs. E in my head (along with her husband Mr. T, hehe), pulled a smooth white river stone out of her purse. She cast a weighted look at Ull and he clamped his mouth shut. "A spell that would alert you to excessive magic in the area?"

"I think so," I considered how much effort I would need to put into it to get coverage over as large an area as we'd need to monitor as I took the stone from her. My gaze swept by Ull and I had a sudden thought. "You're his stepson," I blurted like an epiphany. Told you; no filter.

"Yes," Ull frowned.

"That means you're married," I turned and looked accusingly at Thor.

"Why do you care if I'm married?" Thor tilted his head to the side. His eyes seemed to flash bright for a second and his lips twitched.

"I don't," I said immediately. "*Are* you?"

"Let's just say we had a messy break up," his smile came out in full force as his arm crept across my back.

"And you got custody?" I sat up straighter, leaning away from him.

"Custody?" He shook his head a little, like he was trying to clear it of my human insanity.

"Of the kid," I jerked my head toward Ull and Thor's laughter literally boomed out.

Now I don't like overusing the word *literally* because it's so often misused but let me just say that I am definitely using the appropriate word here. His laughter shook the light fixtures, it rattled the windows, and I could swear I heard someone's car alarm go off down the street.

"The *kid*," Thor let his laughter die down to a light rumble, "chose for himself."

"Yeah," Ull leaned forward and winked at me, "Mama's not happy."

"And when Mama's not happy," I looked expectantly at Ull and he didn't fail me.

"No one's happy," Ull finished gleefully. "You can say that again. She's been a holy terror."

"Define *terror*," I narrowed my eyes on Ull. Was I going to have to fight his Mommy?

"You don't see her here do you?" Ull spread his hands wide.

"Well, I don't exactly know what she looks like," I didn't like the cold feeling I was getting in my gut. "I don't even know her name."

"Her name is Sif," Thor answered grimly, "and she looks like him." He pointed an accusing finger at Ull, like it was somehow his fault.

"Hey, don't blame me because you married a bitch," Ull mercifully lowered his voice to issue the insult.

"That's your mother you're talking about," Thor leaned in and matched his stepson's tone.

"She's *your* wife. I didn't have a choice about her being my mother."

"She's my *ex*-wife," Thor grumbled but backed off.

"Wow, she sounds like a charmer," I looked back and forth between their sulking faces. "I can't wait to meet her."

"No!" Both of them shouted at the same time and earned us the attention of the whole shop… again.

"Okay relax, Thunder Twins, deactivate your powers," I held up my hands. "They feel very strongly about decaf," I called over to the onlookers. People laughed and shook their heads but slowly went back about their business.

"You meeting Sif is not a good idea," Thor lowered his voice again, and then his forehead wrinkled. "And *I'm* the God of Thunder, Ull is the God of Justice."

"Whatever," I shrugged. Justice? I don't know why I was surprised; Ull did have a sense of fairness about him but…"I just can't picture you blindfolded and holding scales."

"You can't?" Ull waggled his brows at me and smirked. "Do you want to?"

"Well maybe blindfolded," I waggled mine right back. Thor rumbled angrily, like a brewing storm.

"As amusing as all this has been," Horus's voice had gone so dry, I feared for his safety near any open flames. "Can we return to the reason for all of us being here… in DC… in *October*?"

"Sorry," I stuck my face down into my coffee cup for a minute to regroup. "I'll need a quiet place to work on this." The little white stone felt good in my hands, almost happy to be there. I wondered where it had come from. A river rock definitely but which river? "I'll need some supplies too."

"Ull's got a place here," Thor nodded. "It's why I called him in."

"I didn't notice you making any phone calls before we left," I winced under the look everyone gave me. "Oh yeah, right. God to god direct huh? So much better than AT&T."

"He's my son," Thor raised an amused brow, "I have the right with him. I can't manage it with everyone."

"Did the documents say who was coming in on the job?" It was the first time Tsohanoai, AKA Mr. T, had spoken in awhile, so I was a little startled. He'd been playing the strong silent type well but his voice was pleasant, comforting. I wanted to tell him he should use it more often.

"Yes," Thor didn't look too happy. I felt the cold creeping back with that look. "Huitzilopochtli himself will be coming in."

"Is that a single, a plural, or a sneeze?" I raised a corner of my mouth to try and tease Thor's smile back. Yeah, I know I've been complaining about his smiling but when I wasn't the one making him frown, it wasn't nearly as much fun.

"It's a single," his lips didn't even twitch, damn it.

"So that's good right?" I looked around and suddenly realized everyone had the same sick expression, like someone had just told them all the coffee was Kopi Luwak. You know, the stuff they make from coffee beans pooped out of a civet cat. What a horrible job those coffee makers had, sifting through civet poo all day to harvest coffee beans. I guess I rather do the sifting than the drinking though. "We can totally take out one god," I continued merrily. "There are nine of us, he won't stand a chance. Hell, I'll tell you what; I'll get this one. You all go home and you can take out the next bad guy." I smiled brightly.

No one laughed. No one smiled. No one even breathed. Tough crowd.

"This is not just any god, Vervain," it was Mrs. E who finally answered me. "This is Huitzilopochtli. He's very dangerous."

"What is he, Mayan?" I really needed to brush up on my gods. You'd think I'd know them all by now but trust me when I say; there are a lot of gods.

"He's an Aztec god of war," Mr. T reached over and took

his wife's hand as he spoke and I was shocked to see that it shook. "He killed all of his brothers when they took part in his mother's murder."

"Okay," I frowned. Avenging your mother didn't sound so bad to me. "So he's a mama's boy and he killed his siblings. They couldn't have been very nice if they killed their own Mommy. It sounds to me like he was justified."

"Justified, maybe, but it was *his* mother, not theirs," Ull took over. I guess he felt it was his area of expertise. "The reason he killed them is not the point, Vervain. The fact he *managed* to kill them is."

"Oh? His brothers were pretty bad ass, huh?"

"They were all gods like him, just new at the time, but he was the youngest." Horus must have felt left out because he flung in his two cents, sounding like a professor lecturing first years. "The question you haven't asked yet is; how many brothers he had."

"Fine, I'll bite," all these head games were getting to me. I generally preferred a direct approach to my conversations. "How many brothers did Sneezie have?"

They all looked at each other and then away from me, all but Horus, who seemed to find pleasure in my anxiety.

"Huitzilopochtli had four-hundred brothers," he smiled grimly and just for a second his pupils turned to tiny bird dots, "and one sister, his only ally. She was not so lucky. Coyolxauhqui was killed and in his grief for her, Huitzilopochtli cut her head off and flung it into the sky to become the moon. He sent their brothers up to be the stars and pay attendance on her for eternity."

The cold feeling spread to my whole body.

"That's just a story though, right?" Was that high, squeaky

sound my voice? Crap. I cleared my throat and tried again. "I mean that's one of those human influence things, right? Where we made up a story to explain the universe and you guys are strengthened and influenced by it but it didn't actually happen that way. I mean if all the stories were really true, completely true, then we'd have all kinds of deities up in the sky doing everything from pulling the moon with a chariot to living on it."

"Yes," a flash of some kind of emotion passed over Horus' face. "But most of those stories have a kernel of truth. It's how your people came up with them in the first place."

"So he really did kill all four-hundred of his brothers?" I needed to lie down, or put some Baileys in my coffee, or lie down with some Baileys in my coffee and a straw.

"Yes," Thor's hand crept around mine.

"Four-*hundred*?"

"Yes."

"Wow," I blinked.

"Yes," Thor's hand squeezed mine.

"His father really got around," I snorted. Oh come on, someone had to say it.

Chapter Five

Ull had a beautiful four-story home near the National Zoo. I gaped at the tasteful and modern furnishings as we made our way up to the top floor.

"Are you all rich?" I asked as I looked over a very pricey piece of art. "Stupid question," I snorted, "how could you not be?"

"Well, magic helps," Ull grinned broadly, "but most of us work among the humans. It's just easier that way. I own a law firm."

"A law firm," I stopped climbing the stairs and turned to face him. I looked him up and down, taking in the long hair and carefree attitude.

"God of Justice, remember?" He winked at me. "I'm actually a god of hunting and winter too but I thought a law firm would bring the most financial gain. Orvandil Law is now one of the top law firms in the country."

"Yes, I can see that," I looked at the rest of the group. "What about all of you?"

"I own a line of cruise ships," Thor said.

"A landscaping company," Persephone smiled, "Little Western Flower has the reputation as the number one landscaper in America."

"Oh, sweet," I really wanted to say: well duh, you are the Vegetation Goddess and all.

"We own tanning salons," Mrs. E said for her and her husband.

“I deal in antiques,” Horus sniffed and looked at me like I couldn't possibly understand what that meant.

“I have a bunch of car dealerships,” Brahma smirked.

“Cars?” Well that explained why he looked like a car salesman.

“It's good money,” he handed me a card which read: *Golden Swan Exotics, featuring Lotus, Maserati, Ferrari, Bentley, and Lamborghini; Brahma Kanja: owner.*

“I make porn,” Pan stated proudly, handing over his own card.

“Naughty Nymphs,” I read aloud. “We can satiate any satyr.”

“Catchy, isn't it?” Pan beamed.

“Yeah, like Herpes,” Horus grimaced.

“My girls are all clean,” Pan glared at Horus.

“I'm sure they are,” I tucked both cards into my jeans pocket as I climbed the last step.

We'd finally made it to the top floor, which consisted of a large open space with a small kitchen off to the side. It was obviously made for entertaining and was perfect for our current needs. The walls were painted light green, the overstuffed couches were chocolate velvet, and there were enough potted plants strewn about to change the atmospheric conditions. The paintings on the walls were all modern, which I’m not a big fan of but they matched the décor well. The biggest draw though, was the wide balcony with an amazing view of the Zoo. We were just far enough away to avoid prying eyes but still close enough to hear the calls of some of the more restless beasts.

Speaking of restless beasts, the kitchen was sectioned off

by a counter that doubled as a buffet table. Ull immediately went to work filling it with an assortment of chips and sandwiches that were disappearing down hungry god throats almost as soon as they were put out. It was nice to have a rest after all the craziness but even while they were eating, the gods continued to press me about the spell, so I barely had time to digest before I was at work again. Damn demanding deities. Try saying that three times fast.

I ended up sitting cross-legged in the center of the floor with all of my tools and ingredients placed carefully around me. My circle was drawn, not literally, I wouldn't want to mess up Ull's thick green carpet, but my wards shimmered around me in the air. I was ready to go. If I could just get some privacy, life would be perfect. Life isn't perfect though, is it?

"Do you guys mind giving me some alone time here?" I looked up at the gods encircling my circle and they all frowned down at me. I felt like Prometheus, facing the gods in Olympus and asking them to give me a break over the fire thing. Hmm, maybe Persephone could get me into Olympus. I hadn't found the spell to break into that particular god territory yet.

"Why do you need us to leave?" Thor crossed his arms over his massive chest. Somehow it made him look even more massive, all those muscles squished up like taped supermodel cleavage. It had potential bad-ass explosion written all over it.

"I don't *need* you to, I'd just prefer it," I glared back. "Call me shy."

"Sorry," Ull's grin was just plain cocky. "My house, I get to stay."

"Why do you even care?" I glared at them as they stood around me, staring down at the human as she knelt before her makeshift altar. I felt like a side show freak. Or one of their followers (a god follower not a freak follower). I think I'd rather be the freak.

“We’ve never seen a human twist god magic,” Horus had the look of a scientist peering at a developing petri dish. “I for one, have no intentions of leaving.” There was a murmur of agreement and the ring of them drew closer till they pressed against the wards of my circle like a class of kindergartners around a fish bowl.

“Fine,” I closed my eyes and tried to pretend they weren’t there but even through the circle I could feel their power fluttering against my wards like a flock of multicolored birds. All of it was magic but the breeds were different. They each had their own feel, their own tempo, their own look. It was fascinating and very distracting. I sighed and grounded myself, trying to get the image of feathered gods flocking and squawking around my circle out of my mind, when an evil little idea reared its ugly head.

Gods had been sucking humans dry for centuries. It was about time for a little payback… if my theory worked. I reached out with my magic to connect with the Aether and then sent my focus down into the earth. The bright energy of Nature tickled my toes but I held off on accepting it, choosing instead to push further. I sent my searching tendrils of awareness back up through the ground and into the bodies around me. Soft gasps came from the gods, and a few grunts. Of pleasure, pain, or just plain shock, I didn’t know but no one protested.

I had thought that I could connect with the gods and just siphon a bit of energy from them like I do with the earth or the moon. But their power didn’t just flow into me, giving of itself gently like Mother Nature. It rushed into me like it was coming home after being gone for years. All those birds flapped together inside my body till they swirled into one fiery phoenix, which seemed intent on making sure every cell I had was touched by its flame. It filled me to the brink and kept going like there was more to me than my physical body could contain. My hair lifted up like a breeze was coming from beneath me but the air was absolutely still. Every muscle I had jerked and tightened. I felt as if I were glowing, empowered, recharged, and most of all, I felt incredible.

I inhaled sharply and refocused. I couldn't let their power distract me or I might drain them dry. Wouldn't Horus be pissed then? If he lived. The thought was sobering. For once, I was in the presence of gods I didn't want to kill. How ironic would it be if I ended up killing them anyway? Ironic and tragic. With a head shake, I shut off the flow and they sank to their knees around me. Puppets cut from their strings, staring at me in rapt attention, they seemed unable to move.

I picked up the little white stone and washed it with a bowl of salt water, avoiding their eyes.

"I cleanse you of all negativity, that you may hold only my will, and by the power of water, I consecrate and charge you to be a sensor of god magic." The water dripped from my fingers in glowing drops, flowing over the stone with the viscosity and sheen of oil.

I placed the bowl down and ran the stone through the smoke of some rosemary incense. "By the power of air, I consecrate and charge you to be a sensor of god magic." Smoke curled around the stone, clinging to it sensuously. Particles within the heavy smoke sparked and sizzled.

The few remaining water droplets on the stone evaporated as I waved it through the flames of a red candle. "By the power of fire I consecrate and charge you to be a sensor of god magic." The flames turned blue, splitting around my fingers to lick only at the stone. The stone itself warmed but it was a mellow, comfortable heat.

The scent of rich soil wafted up to me as I scooped some out of a small bowl and sprinkled it over the stone. "By the power of earth I consecrate and charge you to be a sensor of god magic." The soil fell slowly, shimmering as it went, and clung to the stone as if it was magnetized, before falling aside to become regular earth once more.

I traded the bowl for the small silver knife I was using in place of my athame. It had come from Ull's kitchen and was hardly the perfect tool for magic but I'd cleaned it with some alcohol and it would work fine. When it comes down to it, tools are just tools, the talent lies within the individual. I made a small cut in my left pointer finger and rubbed the drop of blood across the stone.

"By the power of my spirit, I consecrate and charge you to be a sensor of god magic," the air thickened around me and thrummed with the energy I poured into the stone. I could feel it push in my ears like I was suddenly submerged in water. "By my blood, I bind power to this stone, that it shall recognize god magic and alert me not only to its use but to the location of the user." I sent energy into the little stone till it glowed brightly. In my mind, I pictured it in the Aether, a bright star of power, and felt the responding weightlessness that signaled the spell's success. Then I added the god magic. The bit they'd all been waiting for was just a few words I remembered from Ku's book. "Ilantre, frangis, antul." I closed my hand over the stone and the light winked out.

Huh. I expected a little more dazzle from god magic. My paltry human magic was more showy than that. Oh well, I knew my little part of it had worked. Maybe it was a god spell beyond my capabilities. I have to admit I was a little disappointed but the stone glowed at me reassuringly and I decided to let it go.

I didn't look at any of the gods while I cleaned up and opened the circle. It was cowardice, yes but I had to finish everything before I confronted their anger. I didn't think I'd be lucky enough to have shocked them beyond rage and into awe but their continued silence did give me some hope. I had psyched myself up pretty good by the time I raised my eyes and lowered my wards.

The first face I saw was Ull's and his eyes weren't filled with anger, they were filled with terror. I was so shocked, my gaze swung about me to the rest of the gods. Only one pair of eyes held anger and they belonged to Horus but even his fury was tempered by another emotion. I just wasn't sure if it was fear or respect. Maybe they were the same to Horus. Everyone else met my gaze with varying degrees of wariness, even Thor looked concerned.

"Well that taught you guys to hang around where you're not wanted," I gave them my half grin but it faded quickly when the mood failed to lighten. Uh-oh, this could be bad. "What?"

"How did you do that, Godhunter?" Persephone's voice sounded even more child-like. She had just regressed from teenager to toddler.

I shrugged and stepped forward, everyone else took a step back. "Would you guys relax?" I held up my hands in the universal symbol of *whoa*. "All I did was pull some energy from you. Normally I just call it up from the earth or down from the moon but I figured I'd try something new. You guys have lived off of our energy for centuries. Are you seriously going to give me attitude for taking some of yours? I wasn't sure I had enough juice to power a spell for such a large area and your magic helped."

They looked at each other, gazes shifting but never losing their intensity. I was getting a little nervous. Anger would almost have been better. Almost.

"You don't understand, Vervain. You shouldn't have been able to do that," Thor finally broke the silence.

"Why not?" I stepped back so I was closer to the knife. I'd removed my gloves so I could work with the magic easier but I was starting to regret my decision. I shouldn't have let my guard down among gods. Stupid, stupid mistake. I really was acting like an amateur.

"The earth gives her power freely," Estsanatlehi stepped toward me with her hands out, palms up, which I appreciated. "As gods, we don't share our power. We've learned only to hoard it and gather more whenever possible. There are none among us who could take from another. Such a talent could be deadly. It's astounding that it has manifested in a human. No offense."

"None taken," I smiled a little, "and I think you may have just answered your own question."

"How so?" Horus had been edging around me but I'd been following him with my peripheral vision. So when he reached out to touch me, I automatically moved into a fighting stance. I may have been a little twitchy, okay? It's one of the reasons I don't carry a gun. I didn't intend to attack Horus but the mere movement sent a wave of energy shooting out of my hand. He was suddenly on his back, half-shifted and surrounded by a cloud of feathers, the likes of which I hadn't seen since the time my cat decided to surprise me by bringing one of his kitty gifts into the house.

"Holy crap!" I jumped and started over to Horus but he held a wing up to ward me off. Yes, a wing. I said he was half-shifted.

Downy feathers drifted down around the largest falcon head I've ever seen, sparkling here and there in the currents of magic that still rode the air. Black bird eyes darted frantically, blinking out of that oversized head. The silky golden feathers at his neck smoothed down into perfectly tanned skin. Perfect until it reached his shoulders, where the feathers began once again. His arms were now an impressive pair of wings, the span of which matched his height.

The linen shirt he'd been wearing was ripped beyond repair at arms and neck but his pants were intact since his legs had remained the same. He didn't seem capable of standing though and continued to flap about furiously, sending me looks that were both terrified and terrifying. He opened his beak and I half expected his snooty voice to spill out but all that emerged was an enraged squawk. I guess his vocal chords had been included in the change. Small miracle but I was grateful for it.

I looked down at my hands and actually saw the magic

rolling along my skin. Like heat on asphalt, it blurred over my body in a haze. For the first time in my life, I was horrified by my power. Not because it was too much but because it was alien, an unknown entity I had no idea how to control. I curled my arms around myself and backed away from everyone, my eyes fixed on the monster I'd created. What had I done? What would I do next?

Thor reached out to me.

"Don't," I shook my head. "I don't want to hurt you."

"Then you won't," behind Thor I could see Horus shifting back into man form. I felt a small amount of the tension in my shoulders release as I realized the damage wasn't permanent. Thor went on gently, "You only changed Horus because you were startled and reacted to protect yourself. You're still filled with our power. Don't fear it Vervain, use it. It's in you now, which means you're its master. Control it."

I took a deep breath and nodded. My hands drifted down to my sides as I thought over the implications. I had their power? Did that mean I could do what they did? How long would it last? I looked at a little potted palm in the corner as an idea struck.

They all watched me steadily as I held my hands out to the plant. I thought of Persephone, the way she felt like springtime, and my hands began to glow. First my palms began to tingle, then warm waves coasted down my arms and out through my fingers. The plant rustled and started to grow. You shouldn't be able to hear things grow. Trust me when I say, you don't want to. Natural growth takes time. Roots drink in nutrients, plant cells multiply, and it all happens way too slowly for the naked eye to catch... or the human ear to hear.

I forced growth into those vulnerable cells, demanded that they separate and multiply at dizzying speeds, and the sounds that resulted from that blasphemy became a raw, primitive music. The beginning of life must have sounded something like that; a creeping, tearing rustle. A sound of struggle, of a creature crawling out of the primordial ooze and taking its first gasp of air with its raw, new lungs. It was a nightmarish noise and it hammered home the truth that although destruction can be explosively loud, creation has its own voice.

In seconds, the palm had burst from its pot and was brushing the ceiling with questing fronds. The roots shook free of dirt like a dog shakes off water and wriggled out to push at my feet. I stumbled back and fell heavily to the floor. The roots kept coming, tendrils waving up before me like snakes, sensing the magic that had freed them, until finally they shivered to a halt and fell limply to the floor. I looked up at the monstrosity I'd made and felt my heart pumping furiously in my chest, my breath sawing through my lungs like it was trying to escape.

Out of the corner of my eye I saw Thor crouch down and start to crawl towards me. "I'm going to touch you, Vervain. I just want to see how much power you've still got stored up."

I looked up at him numbly and suddenly felt very lost. I wanted to be home in my bed where I could pull the blankets over my head and have some time to think. I wanted someone to tell me what the hell was going on, what it all meant. Failing that, I just wanted someone to hold me and make the crazy whirlwind stop for a second. Thor looked like exactly what I needed. I reached carefully to him and nodded.

He didn't just touch me or hold me, he wrapped his entire body around mine. A flesh and blood shield between me and reality. I let my head fall to his shoulder, feeling safe for the first time in years. Damn but safety is such a hard thing to resist. I gave in to the feel of his skin warm against mine, his muscles flexing gently under my cheek. When I took a trembling breath, the clean scent of rain filled my nose and tingles ran over my body. I snuggled closer and felt the air condensing around us, the temperature falling slightly. The sound of thunder rolled through the air. It was soft though, as if heard through a down pillow.

Just let it be a sudden rainstorm. Let this be a normal man holding me. Please give me a normal life for one blessed minute. I squeezed my eyes tighter and buried my face into his thick neck. I could stay there forever just pretending, imagining a world where gods stayed in their heavens and plants took more than mere seconds to grow. A different reality where I didn't behead Atlanteans so that I could feel safer at night. Where I slept untroubled by nightmares, never having to pay a price for that sleep.

In that brief moment, I realized why I did what I did. There, in the arms of a god, I was finally able to admit why I killed his kind. I'd always told myself it was a noble sacrifice. That I fought them so the human race could be safe. I had this image in my head of me being some kind of a comic book hero. Destroying evil in the shadows while mankind walked by, oblivious but safe from harm. What a joke. I was no hero.

The need to save others did, of course, play a part in my choices but it wasn't the only reason. It wasn't the driving force behind my obsession. I hunted them so they wouldn't hunt me. It was a preemptive strike. Hours of training with sword, metal claws, and knives, so I could stand a chance against beings that outclassed me in every way. Even more time spent in spellwork, meditations, and charging my weapons, not to do what was right but simply to be able to walk down the street at night knowing I was prepared for whatever may be around the next corner. It was survival instinct, pure and simple. Nothing noble about it. At the heart of every fighter lies a scared child who just wants to feel safe.

How odd that I'd found that safety with a god.

"Open your eyes, little hunter," Thor's whisper pulled me out of my self scrutiny. "Look at the storm you've conjured."

The funny thing was, storms comforted me. They made me feel peaceful, always had. It was as if when nature raged, I could finally be calm. You can't fight the weather, all you can do is ride it out. So I could relax because all the nasties out there were most likely running for cover too. Storms were like a vacation for me. A way for the Universe to say *Take a breather*. The sound of thunder, the feel of moisture beading on my skin, Thor's lips tingling against my cheek, it all served to calm me. I let go of my anxiety and opened my eyes.

I could barely see the others through the heavy mist cocooning me and Thor. Little sparks lit the clouds sporadically and I realized it was lightning. We were sitting in the middle of a miniature storm; lightning, thunder, and all. I rolled my head back to look up at Thor.

His eyes had gone indigo and within them I saw lightning strike as if it were dancing across waves. He smiled and I lost that wonderful feeling of safety. I didn't mourn the loss though. A part of me seemed to wake up and realize that I didn't want a man to make me feel safe. Going down that road could only lead to disappointment or even worse; if I depended on a man to keep me safe, I could end up dead.

This wasn't even a man, no matter how much I'd like to pretend he was. This was an ancient god. A god that already had some kind of claim on me I didn't even fully comprehend. The last thing I needed to do was get involved with him any deeper than I already was.

Deeper was all I could think about though as he lowered his face and brushed his lips against mine. Deeper into those stormy eyes, deeper into his muscled embrace, and deeper was suddenly where I wanted him. I sighed against his lips and he used the opportunity to invade. His mouth was hot, a vivid contrast to the cold around us, and he tasted wildly metallic with a tinge of salt. Like ozone on the ocean.

My arms pulled him sharply to me, even though I was screaming internally at myself to stop. Electricity mingled with our kiss and vibrations flowed down my skin with the bursting condensation, heading places it shouldn't go in public. I wrapped my legs around his waist and he pulled me up onto his lap with a growl rumbling from his chest into mine. The storm around us grew stronger, more wild. The wind picked up and my hair tangled into his as if it too needed contact.

Thunder rumbled through the floor and rain suddenly beat down upon us. We were soaked in seconds and still he kissed me, his tongue licking at mine, his lips slashing harshly against my mouth. My hands were tangled up in the hair at the nape of his neck, sliding up his face, desperate to connect with him. When his hands pushed up under my shirt, the sound of a throat clearing finally stopped us.

"I appreciate that this is an unusual situation," Ull's voice dripped sarcasm. "But could you tone your lust down a bit? My carpet is not only soaked but it's getting singed."

I pulled back and looked at Thor in horror. Heat flowed over my skin from the neck up. I sprung backwards off his lap, ending up in a sprawl over the tangled roots with my arms propping me up from behind. My silk shirt now clung to me, showing clearly not only my hidden dagger but the pattern of lace in my bra. I was thoroughly mortified.

Thor sat where I'd left him, a little smile on his face. He rubbed his lips with a finger and his smile grew lascivious. The lightning in his eyes sparked and dimmed but the electric look remained. I watched in horrified fascination as his hand slid down from his mouth, over his chest, and between his legs to adjust himself. I gaped and blushed hotter as he laughed loud enough to shake the walls before starting towards me on hands and knees, licking his lips.

"Thor this is neither the time nor the place," Brahma's tone was crisp and his eyes were narrowed on the thunder god.

"Don't rain on my parade," Thor shot over his shoulder as

he crept closer, chuckling at his own joke.

I jumped to my feet and backed away. "Enough! Brahma's right. That was a crazy fluke and it's not going to happen again. I was freaked out and forgot myself for a second. So get up off the floor and go take a cold shower or whatever gods do to calm down. We need to get back to business."

"Gods generally don't have to calm down," Thor got to his feet and kept coming, so I kept backing up till I hit the glass door that led to the balcony. The knowledge of my restricted position jacked up the brilliance of his smile.

"We're not here for this," I held up a hand and it was soon pressed to his wet chest, "and I'm not an exhibitionist."

"Fine," he leaned down and buried his face in my wet hair. His chest pressed into mine as he breathed deep and then exhaled hot across my neck. I did my best to ignore the shivers it ignited. "We'll finish this later," he whispered into my ear.

"No we won't," I slid out from under his arms, cleared my throat, and started another backwards journey across the room. I would not be some god's plaything. Oh hell no, not this witch. Thankfully, Mrs. E saved me.

"Vervain," she grabbed my arm and pulled me over to her. "You were about to explain why you thought you were capable of taking our magic… before you were distracted."

"Right," I blinked and tried frantically to remember anything besides the feel of Thor's hands on me. "Right, I was going to say it makes sense that a human could pull power from gods since it was from humans that the power was taken from originally."

Thor actually stopped halfway over to me and his lust-filled look was replaced with a ponderous one. I squeezed Mrs. E's hand in gratitude before moving away but stopped short when I saw

Horus staring hard at me.

"It makes sense that you'd be able to call the power," he was still standing as far away from me as he could, tearing off the remnants of his shirt. "But not that you could use it like you did. No one has ever been able to make another god shift into his animal form, much less do it halfway."

I understood his fear better then. It wasn't that I'd bested him. It was that I'd forced him into a form he'd never been in before. If the myths were true, he'd be able to shift his head and keep the rest of his human form but he shouldn't be able to shift his arms into wings as well. To have his body betray him like that must have been scary.

"I think she merely forced some of your power back into you, Horus," Ull looked from me to the Egyptian. "She wasn't trying to control it, so it took whatever path it normally takes but went a little further since it was unrestrained."

"Yes, that makes sense," I jumped when Thor's voice came from right beside me. He'd snuck up on me while I was pitying Horus. I didn't like that. It meant I'd let myself get distracted again. Which is fine if you're a god but for us mere mortals it can be bad, fatal even.

I needed to nip this attraction in the bud. Gods were hot. They're gods, it comes with the territory, and if I was going to be working with them, I couldn't go around throwing myself at every one that shot me a lusty glance. Hell, it was probably in their nature to try to score with every human female they came across. They probably couldn't help themselves, what with their need for collecting worshipers and all. I'd have to be the grown up and have some control. No problem, I can be mature, I can be restrained.

I was so totally doomed.

"Aaahhh!" I jumped as the stone in my pocket sent a jolt through my leg. Everyone looked over at me like I was a magician about to do a new trick. I pulled the stone out and was immediately hit with a vision of a hotel room.

It was a large room with two beds, two Middle-Eastern men, and one large Mexican occupying it. Excuse me, I mean one large Aztec. The Aztec had one of the men in what looked like an embrace, arms tight around his chest from behind and face buried in his neck. The third man sat limply on a bed, eyes focused on the floor. I frowned at that but continued to look around, trying to get some idea of where they were. On the nightstand I saw hotel stationary with *J.W. Marriott* printed on top. Great, so I knew what hotel they were in, now I just needed the room number. The phone! I honed in on the phone and sure enough, it listed the hotel phone number and the room number. I took one more look at the men to memorize their faces and then let the vision go.

"They're at the Marriott," I said as my eyes cleared.

"There's a Marriott near the White House," Ull nodded, "makes sense."

"Let's go," Thor was already out the door.

Twenty minutes later, we had passed through the enormous, marble-floored, crystal chandelier hung lobby of the Marriott and gone up to room 512.

Thor took point and kicked the door in. I thought for sure we'd have a hallway full of concerned guests peering out of their rooms but not a peep was made. They must have been calling management to do the dirty work. Not that I blamed them; I probably wouldn't go out either if I saw us on the other side of my peephole.

We surged into the room, hands up and magic ready to confront the baddies. I was last in line so it was hard for me to see what was going on when they all stopped suddenly. I tried to peer around shoulders but I'm kind of short and I finally ended up just pushing past everyone. Gods filled the room but there was no sight of the Aztec or his humans.

"Okay, now what?" I looked around the Aztec-less room and then over to the gods. My body still tingled with the power I'd taken but I was fresh out of ideas.

"It's twelve-twenty," Brahma said, peering at his Rolex, like he'd been doing off and on all day. I guess I knew who Mr. Punctual was. "We need to get to the rally. It's too late for preventative measures now."

The stone seemed to pulse in my jeans pocket, reminding me of the complete waste of time and magic it had been.

Chapter Six

The press of bodies crowding the park across from the White House was overwhelming. Perfume, sweat, and the scent of freshly painted signs mingled with a steady murmur of excited voices in the air. I started breathing more shallow, sweat beading at my temple. Did I mention I was a tad bit claustrophobic? I avoided Waikiki for the same reason; I hate crowds.

We had all split up to try and search the area for the terrorists. Brahma and Horus had gone to search the surrounding buildings for snipers, Horus in falcon form so he could peer into windows as he flew by, but I had a feeling these guys were going to get up close and personal. I searched the crowds anxiously.

My hands kept clenching, like a gunman anticipating the draw. I had a protection spell ready, all I had to do was release it with a throw of the powdered mullein already in my hand. It could cover a space about nine feet square normally but I was hoping with my borrowed power it might spread a little further. If it came down to hand-to-hand, a quick downward shake of my arms would release the knives from my gloves. Then there was my kodachi and the dagger in my cleavage. I really should give in and get a gun but I'd always had this feeling that trying to shoot a god was a bad idea. As a witch, I generally try to go with my instincts.

So I walked through the danger zone with only a handful of herb and some magically enhanced blades to defend myself with. I followed Thor, pressed close to his back, and he guided me through the masses efficiently. He maneuvered us to the front, where a podium had been set up and a man was already addressing the crowd.

"What are we still doing in Afghanistan?" The man was saying. "Obama promised to bring our troops home back in 2009.

This is now the longest war in US history. It's time to put an end to this and bring our people home!" His voice was deep, rich, and carried a slight Irish accent. I was intrigued enough to check out the packaging.

The voice was definitely not false advertising. The man towered above us on the podium but he was probably only a little over six feet tall. His black hair was cut short in sharp layers around a classic Gaelic face with perfect winged eyebrows. Beneath those brows, his green eyes glowed with passion for his cause, outlined in thick lashes a supermodel would envy. Why did guys always end up with lashes like that and we girls had to glue them on?

I sighed unintentionally and Thor looked over and frowned.

"Who's he?" I jerked my chin in the direction of Mr. Green Eyes.

"No one you need to know." His tone grated and I looked up at him with a raised eyebrow.

Did gods get jealous? Duh, of course they did. There were plenty of myths about the jealousy of gods. I wasn't about to let it go to my head though, it was probably just a case of Thor staking some barbarian claim on me and feeling like I should be honored or some crap. Or maybe he just didn't want to lose a potential follower. Either way, I was certain it had nothing to do with the softer emotions and everything to do with an old fashioned power trip. So I ignored him and went back to staring at the new eye-candy.

The stone started buzzing again inside my pocket but when I touched it, my vision remained clear. It didn't need to show me where the magic was, I was already there. I looked around guiltily. I really needed to stop being so easily distracted. Didn't I just give myself a lecture on this? Why don't I ever listen to myself?

Sure enough, there were the two Middle-Eastern men from

my vision. They were sliding through the crowd with ease. Behind them was an empty space which stayed conspicuously empty even in the thick press of people.

"Those are the guys from the hotel," I murmured to Thor.

"Huitzilopochtli," he whispered behind me.

"Let me guess, he's that empty space?" I kept my eyes on the spot behind the men.

"Yes."

"Groovy power," I said with admiration and Thor looked over at me with a lifted brow. "Uh, I mean, what do we do?"

"Wait," Thor's hand slid down my arm and even there, filled with terror, I shivered. So not good.

I looked back at the dark-skinned men. Their eyes were focused on the speaker and I realized they were going after him first. They cleared the edge of the crowd and I saw them both reach into their jackets.

"Gun!" I screamed as I ran forward and flung my hand towards the podium, releasing the protection spell with a cloud of powdered mullein. The herb sparkled as it spread out, drifting down in an impenetrable but invisible protective shell. The spell was good for one attack only so I hoped my target was smart enough to take cover afterward.

The crowd panicked and turned to flee, screaming and shouting as they went. The two terrorists didn't even spare a glance for me, just fired at the speaker like a couple of Stepford wives. The speaker just stood there, staring at them in shock. His eyes grew even rounder when the bullets hit my barrier and dropped harmlessly to the ground. Mr. Green-Eyes turned unerringly to me and our gazes met for a second while I ran across the space that separated me from the gunmen.

"Get down!" I shouted at him as I flung my arms down and felt the comforting click of the knives sliding into place. I didn't have to look to know there were now four, three-inch long blades protruding over my knuckles.

The terrorists finally turned startled eyes to me but they moved their weapons a second too late. I hit both of their gun arms at the same time, flinging my arms wide and then down like some macabre eagle as I ran between them. I felt the blades slice through flesh and skid over bone as the men screamed but my momentum carried me past them and straight into the *empty* space.

"Vervain!" Thor's voice thundered and I glanced back to see him pushing Green-Eyes behind him.

My relief at seeing the speaker unharmed disappeared as I hit a solid wall in the empty air. It felt like I ran into a tank and as I looked up, the air shimmered and the illusion of open space vanished. No tank, just armor covering a very large, very angry, Aztec warrior.

"Huitzilopochtli?" I tried to keep the *oh shit* tone out of my voice as he smiled maliciously at me and metal clad arms threatened to squeeze the air from my lungs.

"And you are?" His voice was thick and soft like silk velvet. It slid over me, brushing against places it shouldn't have been able to touch. I looked up and found myself staring into a pair of exotic eyes the color of freshly spilled blood. I flinched but then a creeping lethargy overtook me, sliding through my veins like an opiate, and all I could concentrate on were how beautiful those horrifying eyes were. Deep and soft, like the heart of a rose. I couldn't look away. Wait, he'd asked me something. What was it?

"Vervain," I offered my name to him like a prayer and felt my heartbeat quicken when his gaze warmed and his smile softened.

He was murmuring something and I had a nagging

suspicion that I should stop him but I couldn't seem to remember how. My arms hung limply at my sides, blades scrapping against my jeans. In the distance, I heard a resonating voice calling to me, a voice filled with thunder and rain, but it grew more and more faint, like a receding storm.

"Vervain," Huitzilopochtli slid a hand through my hair. I felt it snag, my hair caught by the metal plates of his gauntlet, but I didn't care. Pain, pleasure, I wanted all he could give me.

He pressed my face into the gold of his breastplate and the light shining off it was suddenly too bright. I closed my eyes and rested against him. There was an odd feeling of movement, an ecstatic sense of weightlessness, and then my body became heavy again, my newly formed lungs taking a gasp of air.

The glare of the sun was gone and the pressure from his hand released. I looked up and found him smiling viciously at me. I frowned a little as I began to notice how warm I was. Sweat was beading on my brow and I realized the heat was coming from him. His armor was singing my clothes. My vision cleared, the pain jerking me free of his magic, and I screamed.

He laughed and let go of me so that I fell back onto the black marble floor. The cold stone was a relief after the scorching pain and I had to stop myself from rolling over to press into it. It wasn't the time to lick my wounds. It was time to figure out what the hell was going on and the best direction to run in.

Frantically, I searched around me and found the park had been replaced by a large room of stone and glass. White marble walls penned me in, shot through with thick veins of gold. Floor-to-ceiling windows ran the length of the room to my left, devoid of curtains so that the menacing jungle outside could peer in. The furnishings were all stone, not marble, just some white stone that looked as if a forklift would be needed to move it. There was a long table and four chairs, two on each side. How were you supposed to move those chairs? Maybe you just slid in and made due. And why was I thinking about furniture when I needed to be thinking of a way out of this?

I scampered to my feet, accompanied by the sound of my blades scratching the marble floor. Good, they were still extended. I settled into a fighting stance and eyed the man before me steadily, even though my throat was constricting in fear. The memory of wanting him hit me and I had to struggle not to vomit. He'd taken my mind as easily as the sun takes the sky from the night, like it was already partially his to begin with. I'd never met a god who could turn me against myself. How do you win against something like that?

The others were right; I was out of my league and I was about to die.

His head rolled smoothly to the side as he smiled again. He held my eyes with the steadiness of a snake watching its prey as he began to unfasten his armor. First the gauntlets came off, thrown casually onto the table. Then he undid his bracers, they landed with a loud rattle near the gauntlets. By the time he unbuckled his breastplate, a thin trickle of sweat was making its way down my stomach. I was running hot and cold with fear and adrenaline. Should I rush him while his hands were busy or should I just run blindly from the room and hope to find a way out? Neither seemed like a good option but if I was going to die, I'd rather it be as I stood my ground.

"I apologize for the heat," he pulled the breastplate over his head and then started on his legs. "It's a part of me, I'm God of the Sun but also of War and battle excites me. The sun pours through me and its heat can only be cooled by blood. It's why I must return to this room first after a battle. It's fireproof."

"Smart thinking there, flamer," I couldn't help it. It's like as soon as I settle in to fight, my mouth starts the smack talk. It's as ingrained as the stance, just a reflex. Even fear couldn't choke it back. I almost closed my eyes and groaned. This was not a guy to back-talk to. Why couldn't I just be the strong and silent type?

He finished with his armor, completely ignoring my insult, and was left in a thin, black, cotton tunic and loose pants. He picked up a gold pitcher I'd failed to notice. With nonchalance, he turned it over his head and a thick, red liquid poured out to cover him. I gasped, when I realized what he was bathing in. Steam rose off his body and the air was scented with the tang of fresh blood. Fresh blood over a fire. The thick liquid sank into his skin, tinting his dark complexion with a reddish glow for a moment. A deep sigh seeped out of him, like a man sinking into a hot bath after great marathon sex.

“There,” his wicked smile returned and with it I caught the glint of fangs. “Now we can be civilized.”

I shook my head and gaped at him, more horrified that the monster resided in such an elegant package than in the monstrosity itself. He lifted the pitcher to his mouth and drank the rest of the contents like a frat boy downing a beer. My stomach lurched as my body began to tremble and I knew it wasn’t from holding my fighting stance too long. Cold realization had hit and I suddenly knew how he’d stolen my will with his eyes. I was finally meeting the Vampire God, the source of all those little Buffy-plaguing bastards. This man wasn’t just a monster, he was their king.

“I’ve always wondered who made the vampires,” I said it casually but my voice shook a little.

“Ah, yes,” he slid into one of the chairs and brushed his thick, shoulder length, black hair back with the easy movement of an aristocrat. “Please join me and I’ll be happy to tell you about them.”

I eyed the graceful hand he swept toward the chair on his left and thought about it. Evidently he wasn’t going to come out and kill me right that second so it would probably be best to save my strength. I’d leave the claws out just in case. If nothing else, it would buy me a little time. I mean really, I didn't exactly have a lot of options.

"I guess it's a story worth hearing," I shrugged. Then I straightened and walked around the table as I shook out my tight shoulders. I slid into a seat across from his instead of the one he'd indicated. He laughed velvet softness all over me again and I rubbed my arms to try to stop the shivers.

"I could have you on this table, naked and writhing in a second," his eyes glowed a moment as they passed over me. "I could make you beg for me to fill you and then beg for me to empty every last drop of you until you died in ecstasy."

The shaking started again but I tamped it down along with the nausea. I was the Godhunter. I ate gods like him for breakfast. Okay, maybe that wasn't the best choice of words. I tried to give him my menacing glare but I had a feeling it was falling a little short.

"You forgot to add *Resistance is futile,*" I met his eyes… briefly. I had no idea if he needed eye contact to control my mind or not but I wasn't gonna take any chances.

"You're fascinating," he frowned but it was quickly replaced with a greedy smile. "I'm not easily fascinated. Maybe I'll let you live awhile longer. You may prove entertaining."

"Thanks," I smirked, "I'm so relieved. Do I get a collar and a Princess Leia costume?"

His eyes widened for a second before he let out a sharp bark of laughter. There were no velvet tones to it and I had a feeling it was genuine, maybe the first genuine thing I'd seen him do so far.

"You're refreshing as well," he leaned an elbow on the table, placing his chin in it with a precise movement. "What were you doing there today in the company of gods, little witch?"

"You first," I stalled, "you said you'd tell me about vampires."

He made a small grunt of approval. "Indeed. Very well. Vampires, I don't know who came up with the name, many believe it was the Slavs, but I created them. Originally it was an accident. I didn't know I could make humans like me. I was with a lover and I got… carried away," I made a very unladylike snort but he ignored me and continued. "I took too much blood and feared for her life, so I quickly worked a spell for her to accept my blood as a replacement for hers. I thought I could do what you humans now call a transfusion and I believed that the spell would make her blood compatible to mine."

"Worked a little too well, did it?" I leaned back against the cool stone and crossed my arms carefully to avoid the blades.

"Yes, it worked very well," he shook his head. "Isn't that how most great scientific advances are discovered, through accident? I gave her the transfusion and she immediately glowed with health and improved vitality. I was more than pleased until she began displaying the signs of need."

"Need for blood?"

"Yes," he actually looked a little sad. "She grew warm. I thought at first that she was having an adverse reaction and perhaps had even developed a fever but she kept getting hotter till it was obvious what she needed."

"You gave her blood?" He nodded solemnly and I pictured it in my head. Having a god for a lover, believing you were safe and special. Then having your lover almost kill you, turn you into a monster to save you, feeling as if you were about to spontaneously combust, and then discovering the only thing that could cool you down was a blood cocktail. "She must have been terrified."

"She was," there was definitely a note of sorrow in his tone. Wonders never cease. "My priests asked to be changed afterward, preferring to take blood to survive instead of living only off of my life energy as they had been before. They embraced the change but she never forgave me. In fact, she left cursing my name when she was finally able to survive on her own. She in turn created more like her and over the centuries the curse altered, evolved, and became what it is today. It astounds me still, how fast it spread worldwide. I believe she did it on purpose, betraying me as I betrayed her, but I still miss her."

"I'm sorry," holy hell, was I feeling sorry for Big Poppa Vampire? Yeah, I guess I was. Love is love no matter who feels it and the loss of it hurt like a bitch. The mere fact that he *had* felt it made me think better of him. A little.

He smiled gently at me and his eyes softened. "In trying to save her, I lost her. Is it not the way of love?"

"Yeah," I twisted my lips into a smile. "Love sucks, especially for you guys."

He threw himself back into his chair in a surprised fit of laughter. When he finally calmed, he had tears in his eyes. "Oh yes, little witch, I think I'll keep you for awhile."

"Hold on there, Dracula. I already got my hands full. I don't need any more men in my life but thank you for the offer."

"You speak as though you have a choice," his lips were still deceptively soft at the corners but I glimpsed the tip of a fang when he smiled.

"Well, you see what I figure is this," I swung my feet up onto the slab of the table. "You must like your women willing or, like you've already said, we'd have gotten over the preliminaries by now." He raised an eyebrow but kept silent. "So if I'm not willing and you won't try anything unless I am, then I do have a choice."

"I guess you'll just have to stay with me until you are

willing," he shrugged his shoulders like I was his already, it was just a matter of time. I hate men who are too sure of themselves. I don't care how good looking you are, that kind of confidence makes you distasteful in my book. Then he continued and made it worse. "Or until I get bored and decide to kill you."

"Ah, a true romantic," I grimaced.

"A realist," he purred. "When you've lived as long as I, it becomes harder for things to hold your interest and once my interest is gone, so is your purpose here."

"You could always just, oh I dunno," I shrugged, "let me go."

"After you've seen my home, my secrets?" He raised a brow. "That wouldn't be prudent."

A shiver shot through me. If he had his way, the only way out of there for me would be death. I swallowed hard and tried to act nonchalant.

"Paranoid much?"

"Just plain survival instinct," he spread his hands like there was nothing he could do about it.

"So basically, you could attack me at any second." I wanted everything spelled out. "It's not like I got a thousand and one stories to entertain you with and who knows when you're gonna decide my lack of tact isn't funny any more. I'll have to sleep with these on," I raised my gloved hands. "That's not really comfortable."

"No harm will come to you," he let his gaze wander over the blades on my gloves, "as long as you offer none to me or mine."

"Until?"

"Until I decide otherwise."

"I rest my case," I shook my head. If the situation wasn't so serious, I'd be laughing at the guy's childish debate tactics.

"I give you my word to notify you in advance," his lips twitched a little and I strongly suspected he was enjoying himself.

"You're gonna give me a heads up before you try to kill me?" I snorted, "Goodnight, Wesley, good work, most likely kill you in the morning," I quoted *The Princess Bride*, half-hoping for a laugh, but he only frowned at me so I shook my head. "Great, thanks so much, Dread Pirate Roberts."

"It's more than I offer most of my enemies," a little line appeared between his startling eyes. "At least you can sleep without your gloves... and who is Wesley?"

"Fair enough," I conceded, ignoring his ridiculous question. Who doesn't know *The Princess Bride*? Besides, it was more than I'd offer him too. Given the chance, I'd kill him with any means available to me. In his sleep if possible. I know, not very honorable but I'd adjusted my sense of honor when I started hunting gods. I'm only human. Even with my magic, the odds are stacked against me. I do what I have to do to even things out.

We shared a long intense look, sizing each other up. I felt my stomach turn as I watched cold calculation fill his eyes. He looked at me like he could see my entire future, not because he was psychic but because he was going to create it. In those eyes I saw enslavement, torture, and finally death but more importantly, I saw the pleasure he'd find in each. This was one sick bastard.

Before I could give in to the nausea and vomit all over his beautiful table, a group of people walked in and ended our staring contest. Led by a sharp dressed Chinese man, they stopped short when they saw us and I quickly pulled my legs off the table in case I needed them to do some running.

My unease must have been obvious because Huitzilopochtli held his hand up, “Vervain, calm yourself, I've already told you no harm will come to you. You have the word of a god, what else do you need?”

“Less bad asses coming toward me would be a good start,” I muttered but made an effort to at least look like I was relaxed.

“Did you just say you granted this human protection?” The woman speaking was gorgeous and runway model tall. She had long golden hair trailing to her feet in shimmering waves. It caught the sunlight and sparkled, making her look like she was walking in a halo. Her voice was high but soft and curious. I looked down at my sweat-stained self and grimaced. Yay, I'd get to add a feeling of inadequacy to my gut-churning terror.

“I've granted her a reprieve,” Huitzilopochtli’s eyes glittered. “Come in everyone and meet my new guest.” He waved a hand imperiously towards me.

“Is this your new concubine?” A smaller woman stepped around the bright Amazon. She was as dark as the other was light, as petite as the other was tall. They were a perfect foil for one another. And did she just call me a concubine?

“You always did have a thing for humans,” a Native American man with a black mohawk eyed me. His hairdo looked odd paired with his Brooks Brothers suit but who was I, the fashion police? “I have no idea why,” he added scathingly.

“Me either,” I mumbled.

“She's a prospect,” Huitzilopochtli stretched his arms along the back of his chair and looked me over yet again. I gave him a grimacing head shake, like I couldn't believe his audacity.

Frankly, I was beginning to feel like a whore for horny gods. Maybe that was it, maybe the gods just thought all human women were easy. Maybe goddesses were high maintenance and took a lot of effort to get into bed. I looked over the blonde and had a feeling that I'd nailed it.

"You've brought a mere potential lover here? *Now*?" The Chinese man finally spoke and his voice had the clipped tones of a military commander. He held himself like a soldier as well, back straight, arms loose at his sides, one near the hilt of a long sword hung on his hip. He had a thick onyx braid hanging down his back. It swung a little even though he held himself rigidly still.

"She interrupted my work," Huitzilopochtli slowly tore his eyes away from me to regard his friends. "She was at the rally with Thor and a few others probably, though I didn't see them. She saved that son of yours, Lir."

A stocky, dark-haired man looked over at me and his gaze was a mixture of respect, rage, and relief. It was one of the strangest looks I'd ever seen, next to the Vampire God's blood stare of doom, of course. Lir thankfully transferred the look to Huitzilopochtli.

"So you failed, Hummingbird." Lir made it a statement, not a question.

"*Hummingbird*?" I shifted my gaze to the Aztec with a look that clearly said he wouldn't live that one down but he seemed completely unfazed by it.

"Yes, Fiachra lives," Huitzilopochtli shrugged, ignoring my interruption.

"Who's Fiachra?" I looked from one man to the other until it clicked. "Oh, the guy giving the speech was your son? Wow, he must take after his mom, huh?" I tried to compare this guy's craggy countenance to the perfection of his son's and just couldn't see the resemblance. One face belonged on a romance novel and the other on a wanted poster.

Lir went back to glaring at me. "Who are you?"

"Me?" Ooops, now what? "I'm nobody. Just happened to be in the wrong place at the wrong time. You know how it is."

"With Thor?" Mr. Hummingbird raised his perfect brow again.

"Was that who that was? Thor? As in the Norse god?" I was trying real hard to look innocent but I'd never been good at it. "He said his name was Mark."

Huitzilopochtli shook his head. "If you continue to lie to me, Vervain, I'll be forced to take the truth from you. I know you're important to him. He made it abundantly clear when he charged me, shouting your name."

I swallowed past the dry lump which had suddenly formed in my throat. Thor charged him? I vaguely remembered hearing someone shouting for me. It must have been Thor but as far as me being important to him? Doubtful. He was probably just upset that his enemy made off with someone from his group. Then again, he did say they needed me. Maybe I was important, just not in the way my perverted mind had initially assumed. I couldn't help it. You try being surrounded by gorgeous men and not think about sex. Not possible. Plus, there was that kiss.

"Why don't you introduce me to your friends first, Hummingbird?" Stalling was always a good option in my opinion.

"My name means *Blue Hummingbird on the left*, little witch. I'm the Sun God and the sun rises from the South, the left-hand, and is brought by the hummingbird," he made a soft sound of mirth. "You're teasing I'll take as a sign of affection but you'll tell me the truth of your involvement with the Viking or my tolerance will end."

Go figure. I'd been telling my boyfriends for years that my endless barbs were a form of affection. *That's love, baby,* I'd say. None of them had accepted my explanation and now here was this god taking my true insults for affection. How typical.

"Yeah, I'm so into guys who threaten to kill me when they get bored," I rolled my eyes. "Look, you'll get your truth when I get mine. Who are these people and what are you guys up to?" I narrowed my eyes on him.

"She makes demands now?" The Asian was at it again.

"Let her be, Kuan Ti," the blonde actually spoke up for me. It's so annoying when they're beautiful *and* nice. "She's obviously frightened."

The woman had the face of an angel. No, scratch that. She had a face that would make an angel weep to realize that compared to her, he was hideous. Her body was long and slim but curved at hip and chest. Her skin was creamy gold and was so perfect it practically glowed. She was amazing and Hummingbird didn't look twice. What was with these gods? How exactly do you become immune to heart-wrenching beauty?

"Kuan Ti, she's my problem not yours." Huitzilopochtli turned to me and then gestured to the angel. "Vervain meet Aphrodite, Goddess of Love, Sex, War, and Victory."

"Pleasure," I nodded to her. The Goddess of Love, yeah, big surprise there.

"Yes, that too," she winked and crossed her delicate, pale arms over her pristine, white, linen suit. She was all white, gold, pink, and perfect. Her scent wafted to me and I couldn't stop myself from inhaling deep. She smelled plasticky sweet, like a Strawberry Shortcake doll I had as a child. I had a sudden flash of burying my face in the shiny red hair, the fake aroma of strawberries enveloping me. On a very deep level my brain immediately equated her to happiness and I had an overwhelming urge to bury my face in her hair like I used to do with my doll. I quickly blinked away the odd impulse.

Huitzilopochtli got up, came around the table and helped me to my feet. He placed my hand through his arm and escorted me over to the Chinese man like we were at a royal ball. Why he hadn't felt the need to bring me over to meet Aphrodite was beyond me but if he wanted to insult a goddess, it was his business. Or maybe he just thought I wouldn't appreciate being close enough to her to force a comparison.

"This is Kuan Ti," Huitzilopochtli gave the man a nod. "He's a god of war but originally he was a General in the Imperial Army of China and he's also a friend." He said the last bit as if it were the most important achievement of all.

I extended my hand to shake Kuan Ti's but the General took mine firmly in both of his and bent over it to place a quick kiss on my glove, right over the blades.

"What lovely gloves you have," he smiled. "Forgive my abruptness. We are in the midst of battle and it has brought out the soldier in me."

"No prob, General," I pulled away from Huitzilopochtli to pull on the lever that sheathed the blades. "As you can see, I was prepared for a fight as well. But then I was snatched from a crime scene so I guess it's not all that surprising."

"A battle scene," Huitzilopochtli corrected.

"I wouldn't call two men with guns against a crowd of unarmed people, a battle." I put my hands on my hips.

"A small skirmish then," Huitzilopochtli took my arm back, led me away from Kuan Ti, and stopped in front of Lir. "This is Lir, whose son you saved today. Don't expect him to be grateful though, it was his idea to kill Fiachra in the first place."

"What the hell is wrong with you?" I blurted. I hadn't extended my hand to him and I didn't intend to.

"My son was cursed by a jealous mistress. She cursed all of my children in fact. Turned them into swans and turned their hearts against me. Fiachra and his siblings have been plaguing me ever since," Lir huffed.

"I saw a man today, not a swan," I grimaced. A beautiful man who looked nothing like this bad-tempered asshole.

"He changes at will now but it wasn't always so." Lir grabbed my hand and shook it mechanically, then turned away and stalked from the room.

"He's a little temperamental where his children are concerned," Huitzilopochtli turned me with a hand on my back and led me to the man with a mohawk. "This is Tawiskaron."

The Native American man didn't say a word, just held out his hand and shook mine. His eyes narrowed on me and I flinched when I saw them turn completely black. Actually, that's not an apt description. They didn't turn black, they just simply disappeared. In their place were pitch-black holes. As I held his hand, it felt like I was falling into their darkness and it was far from empty. Inside the twin pits of his eyes, things lurked. Horrifying things, whispering and chittering gleefully at the prospect of a new arrival. I tried to pull away, to lurch back, but I was caught firmly by both his hand and his stare.

I felt a scream start to crawl up my throat.

"Vervain!" Huitzilopochtli pulled my hand out of Tawiskaron's and the terror finally abated.

Tawiskaron's eyes were a normal dark brown once more, though they hovered over a sinister smile. My breath was coming hard and fast.

"Tawiskaron!" Huitzilopochtli pushed me a little behind him. "Rein in the darkness. I think I was very clear when I said she was under my protection. I will not have her harmed by your demonic ways."

I blinked and looked Tawiskaron over once more. Demonic? Funny how I'd never considered that demons could exist. I guess the term was as relative as god was. If all the gods were really just Atlanteans, then why couldn't they be demons as well? Some of those bastards sure did act evil enough. Speaking of which... Tawiskaron's face had fallen into a fearful expression and even paled a little. I looked over at Huitzilopochtli and saw why.

The Aztec's eyes were churning pools of blood. Pretty terrifying but I have to say, the pits of darkness scared me more. It must not have been simply the appearance of those eyes that sobered Tawiskaron but the meaning behind their appearance because he obviously disagreed with my assessment. I swallowed hard and began to back away from them both.

Huitzilopochtli's hand snaked back and grabbed me before I could get too far. He shot one more menacing look at the cowed Tawiskaron, then led me to the small dark-skinned woman. Her short hair was a soft brown, so silky it almost looked like fur, and it stuck out from her head, begging for a comb.

"This is Sarama, Messenger Goddess, Mother of all Dogs, and Bitch of Heaven," Huitzilopochtli introduced her.

"Excuse me?" I almost choked.

"Yes?" She looked completely confused.

"Your title is *Bitch of Heaven*?" I was about to lose it. Deep breath; in, out, don't laugh at the little dog goddess.

"Yes."

"Oh, that's just too easy," I couldn't do it. I'd save it for later.

"I don't understand," she frowned at me.

Under my hand I felt Huitzilopochtli twitch but his face

was completely serene. "It's nothing Sarama, you know humans."

She frowned deeper but let it go. "You were with Thor?"

"Sort of."

"Sif will not be pleased," Sarama looked over to Aphrodite and the Goddess of Love frowned. Which meant a slight crease appeared briefly between her brows, giving her a dramatically concerned appearance. Would nothing make this woman look bad?

"His ex-wife?" I blurted, then groaned when everyone stared at me. I really needed to work on that filter between my brain and my mouth.

"You said you didn't know Thor," Huitzilopochtli looked smug, "thought his name was Mark."

"Yeah, yeah, you caught me. Congrats." It was going to come out anyway so what the hell, I just went with it.

"You must know him well if he's told you of Sif," Aphrodite was next to me in three long strides.

"I just met him actually," I felt cold shivers crawl down my spine as I watched them all exchange looks.

"I'll handle this," Huitzilopochtli announced and waved them away. "Let the others know what's happened and we'll join you later."

They left us and I pulled away from Huitzilopochtli without meeting his gaze but still keeping him in sight. I'd been acting like I was truly a guest. How monumentally moronic of me. I was a god damned hostage. I needed to get out of Dodge and I couldn't depend on Tanto, my trusty sidekick, to help me. As usual, I was alone… and what the hell was the Lone Ranger doing with a sidekick anyway, come to think of it? Didn't his name pretty much indicate that he was more the solitary type?

I looked behind me at the glass doors. The jungle seemed more foreboding than accommodating but if I could get out into it, I might have a chance to open a tracing point home. I'd never opened one before but desperation was the mother of success, or something like that.

I wondered briefly if Thor was worried about me and then tossed the idea out as utter nonsense. I couldn't afford to think that way. No one was worried. No one was coming. This wasn't a fairy tale. There wasn't going to be a Prince Charming riding in to give me a happily-ever-after. In real life, Snow White stays dead and Rapunzel grows old, alone in her tower. In real life, you gotta have enough sense to stay away from ugly bitches offering you shiny apples and have enough balls to cut off your own hair and use it as a ladder if needs be. In real life, you gotta save yourself and the only happy endings are the ones paid for in massage parlors.

Huitzilopochtli grabbed my arms, lifted me, and threw me down onto the stone table, all with one slick movement. I landed hard, the breath whooshing out of me, and I was stunned for a moment from the blow to my head. Little spots swam across my vision and bile burned the back of my throat. Was I going to pass out? I frantically held onto consciousness, the possibilities of what could happen otherwise were too grim.

Huitzilopochtli leaned over my chest, trapping my right arm under him while he unbuckled the glove on my left. He yanked it off and then followed up with the right. The slap of leather as he threw them across his shoulder was like a death knell. Then I felt my kodachi removed from my hip and I tried to shake off the shock so I could fight but all too soon my vision twisted again as he threw me over his other shoulder.

"I apologize, my little vicious Vervain," he walked from the room, his heavy boots clomping on the stone floor before the sound was strangled by thick carpeting. "I couldn't let you keep your weapons, you might hurt yourself and I promised you that no harm would befall you here."

He dropped me but this time the landing was soft, my fall completely cushioned by a springy mattress. I was still a little dizzy but I was clear-headed enough to look around and see that I was in a luxurious room. Where the other room had been stark, this one was the exact opposite. It was a lush paradise of silk, velvet, plush carpeting, and polished mahogany. The bed I'd landed on was massive, bigger than a California King. Evidently gods weren't restricted by manufacturer's sizes. The bedding was crimson silk. In fact, the whole room was a bloodbath of color. I guess if you find something that works for you, it's best to stick with it.

I tried to sit up but he pushed me down with a scary show of speed, covering me completely, and let's just say his blood was flowing fine to all areas of his body. His lips, inches from mine, spread in a slow smile as I tried to squirm away. I closed my eyes tight, hoping he couldn't take my mind without catching my gaze. His laugh vibrated from his chest into mine, that velvet sound again, stealing over me, seeping into me. I could feel my legs clenching with pleasure and I groaned in embarrassment.

"This isn't willing," I squeezed my eyes tighter and tried to think of cockroaches crawling on me, anything to disgust instead of excite.

"Are you sure? You body seems to think differently" He rolled, pulling me with him, wrapping his arms around my back and tightening them meaningfully.

"I'm kinda into Thor," I still didn't open my eyes but I felt him go rigid beneath me. Well, more rigid.

"Now you say you belong to the Thunder God?"

"No, I didn't say I *belonged* to him, you pig," his phrasing pissed me off enough to make me open my eyes and glare at him. "I said I was kinda into him, implying that we started something which I was thinking about taking further, maybe."

“That doesn’t sound like he’s claimed you,” his smile returned as his tension vanished.

“No, of course not, I just met him,” oh shit, I just kept telling this guy more and more. Telegraph, telephone, tell-a-Vervain. When would I learn to keep my pie-hole shut?

“Not that it would really matter if he had. I've got you now,” he looked like the matter was completely settled.

“Look, no offense,” I tried to push back but he held me firm. “But I’m not into pushy gods who are trying to get my people to kill each other, or me for that matter. It’s just not a turn on for me, what can I say?”

He let go and I scrambled off the bed, immediately searching for my weapons. They were sitting on an inlaid wood table near the huge fireplace. I started for them but Huitzilopochtli’s voice stopped me.

“Leave them, Vervain,” he sat up and sighed, “I’ve already allowed you to keep your hidden dagger. I cannot allow you to have the gloves, they’re too dangerous. I can feel the god-power in them. And the sword,” he walked over to the table, picked up the sword and admired it. “Beautiful but deadly, just like you.” He put both the sword and the gloves in a long box on the mantle. The lid shut with a click and I knew it had locked with something extra special.

“Magic lock?” I knew I looked defeated but I was past the point of caring.

“Yes,” he closed the distance between us, standing just a breath away, and did nothing but run a hand gently down my hair. “I’ll send for some new clothes for you. The bathroom is through there,” he nodded to a door almost completely hidden by paneling. “Use whatever you desire and then get some sleep. I can feel your exhaustion.”

"And *you'll* be sleeping where exactly?" I couldn't believe he was just going to let me be.

"Here, with you," he smiled again and again I felt that warm, traitorous rush. "But not until later tonight. You've been granted another small reprieve, use it well." He left, closing the door behind him with an ominous click. I felt the rush of power and knew he'd sealed me in with magic, just like my gloves.

Chapter Seven

Two hours later, I was yanked from sleep by a strong hand and a rich voice telling me to dress for dinner. Dinner? What time was it? I normally didn't sleep in the middle of the day and it had messed me up. After going without sleep the night before, I could have done with a lot more of it though.

I struggled up, staring down at my jeans-clad legs with blurred vision. Never a good idea to sleep in jeans but it was either that or my underwear and I wasn't about to get nearly naked in blood boy's bed of lust. The groan poured out of me as I rubbed my eyes. I could feel a bruise beneath the point of my dagger's hilt, where it had dug into my stomach while I slept.

"Come here," Huitzilopochtli held out a hand, something red hung from his other one.

I was too tired to care. I went over and just stood there. He could have struck me down and I wouldn't have lifted a finger. He could have shaved my head or stabbed a knife into my heart and I wouldn't have moved. Instead, he grabbed the hem of my shirt and started to lift it.

"Whoa," I whacked his hands, outraged adrenaline surging through my sleep-heavy limbs.

"I'm going to help you dress," he reached for me again and when I kept a death grip on my shirt, his eyes narrowed, his voice turning to ice. "You'll let me dress you and we'll play nicely or I'll tear the clothes from your body and be everything *but* nice. Your choice."

I felt my fingers go slack as a sliver of fear sliced through me and he immediately reached for me, his eyes shining in triumph. He pulled the shirt over my head. I lifted my arms like a good girl and he sucked in his breath sharply. I wasn't looking at his face but I felt the heat of his gaze. His hands went to my collar, then skimmed down my front, over the black lace of my bra, stroking gently before continuing down to the waistband of my jeans. A cold, trembling horror spread in his wake, closing my throat and burning my eyes. I'd envisioned death at the hands of a god numerous times but never had I considered the possibility of life with one. Maybe because it was so much worse.

I wasn't even sure what the worst part was; the panic, the humiliation, or the fear. Maybe it was the realization that I was in over my head and had been the whole time. That no matter what, there would always be someone stronger, faster, meaner, and out to get me. It was a cold splash of reality that wasn't going to do a thing for his seduction routine, although I wasn't sure seduction was really what he had in mind anymore.

He undid the button and zipper of my jeans and then pushed them over my hips slowly, kneeling to scrape the material down my legs. I stepped from them, barely keeping my knees from buckling, and tried to back away but he grabbed me firmly around the hips and stared up the length of me.

"You're beautiful," he breathed, "why are you trying to hide?"

"Maybe because I don't like being forced to strip." I stared down at him with undisguised hatred. "I don't know what type of woman you normally associate with but I generally don't get naked around a man I've only known for a few hours."

He blinked and got abruptly to his feet. "I only wanted to see you," he jerked the red silk over my head. It caressed my skin and my fear-weakened body shivered in reaction. I pulled my anger further to the surface and used it to push away any trace of weakness.

The silk ended up being a cocktail dress. Versace, I noted

with grim humor. I pulled it down and reached behind me to zip up the back. It was covered in beads and shimmered as I moved. I had no idea how the little spaghetti straps held the weight of it but I had to admit it was amazing. Even with fear filling me, I wanted to check myself out in a mirror. But I wasn't about to give Huitzilopochtli the satisfaction.

He held a pair of red satin stiletto heels out to me and I obediently put them on. He had a hell of an eye because he got both the dress and my shoe size perfect. Like a complete gentleman, he took my arm and led me to a chair, pushing me down into it without a word. His fingers ran across my temples and then undid my hair before pulling the mass of it back. I felt him hold the gathered weight in one hand as he pulled a comb through it with the other. The snarls of my hair swiftly surrendered to his expert ministrations and I closed my eyes to enjoy the sensations. Which only made it worse. I popped my eyes back open, determined to keep them that way through the rest of the torture, bliss, no torture, definitely torture.

Finally, he laid the brush down and offered me his arm. "Our guests await us in the dining room."

What else could I do? He was obviously insane; threatening me one minute and then brushing my god damned hair the next. So I took his arm and let him lead me to the dining room. My head swam from the combination of his insanity and my sleep deprivation. Maybe it was all some weird form of torture. Maybe he just wanted a living Barbie doll he could dress up and parade in front of his friends. Maybe I was still asleep, stuck in one of those nightmares where you keep thinking that you've woken up but you really haven't.

I tried to untangle the mystery on the long walk to the dining room but it was hard enough to remain on my feet. The strange torture habits of Aztec gods would have to wait till later to be pondered. Perhaps the Discovery channel would do a special on it. I choked back an exhausted giggle.

“Are you alright?” Huitzilopochtli stopped me before we crossed the threshold.

“I could use a little more sleep,” I blinked at him and he brushed my hair back gently to study my face.

“Have some food and then I’ll take you back to bed,” he played the concerned lover so well, it made my flesh crawl. I just nodded, not trusting myself to speak.

The room we entered was decorated in cream and gold. The carpet was plush cream, the walls were creamy stone, and the curtains that hung around the two large windows were a color I’d once heard referred to as crème fraiche by a pompous up and coming artist. All the accessories were gold; the curtain rods, the fixtures, even the little chatchkies were all gold… solid if I was judging crazy Aztec boy correctly. I felt like I’d walked into a gilded marshmallow. The gods I’d met earlier were congregated at the far end of the room, around a bar made of golden walnut. There were delicate chairs in the same wood waiting behind them but the gods remained standing.

They turned to us as we walked in and met us at the long table in the middle of the room. The table stood proud under white linen, covered with bone china and more gold flatware than I knew what to do with. The glasses were cut crystal and so were the candelabras placed on each end. A massive floral arrangement of ivy and white roses exploded from a vase in the precise center. Everything was immaculate and it made me immediately search for something with the greatest staining potential.

Huitzilopochtli escorted me to a seat to the left of the head of the table. I fell more than sat into it but he didn’t seem to notice as he took the head chair. Only then did everyone else sit. It made me very nervous and I had to fight to keep from fidgeting. It was all a little too upper class Manson for me (Charles not Marilyn) and I tried to cover up a shudder as the thought of what we might be feasting on struck me. Did they all drink blood? Was I about to be served a banquet of blood or raw meat?

When the servants walked in, I flinched. The gods I'd dispatched before had all lived alone. I didn't think they needed or even wanted servants. Yet here was a whole retinue of help for Huitzilopochtli. It was chilling to think that I could have snuck into a god's home and found not one but several adversaries. I swallowed hard as I looked over the waiters. They all had the look of Huitzilopochtli, restrained ferocity under a guise of elegance, and a horrible revelation hit me when one of them filled my glass with a deep red wine.

"Are they vampires?" I leaned over and whispered to Huitzilopochtli.

"In a way," he shrugged. "They're my priests, the ones I spoke of earlier. They've served me well and will continue to serve me for all eternity."

I shuddered as I thought about being a servant and a bloodsucker forever. Talk about the short end of the immortality stick. One of them placed a dome-covered dish before me. I closed my eyes and took a deep breath. There was a movement of air as he took the lid away but I still didn't look.

"And in the Master's chambers, they gathered for the feast," I whispered as I opened my eyes.

On the plate before me was a beautiful Cornish hen surrounded by a mound of crispy roasted potatoes. I heaved a sigh of relief.

"What were you expecting, little witch?" Huitzilopochtli's laughter tickled my ears.

"You eat normal food?"

"Of course," he frowned slightly. "You've read too much nonsense about vampires. They're as you are. The only difference is, they need blood."

"Then the sun?"

"On me, it has no effect. I'm a sun god after all, it's the source of my power," he sobered a little. "Although something in the transfer did weaken my children. It takes them centuries to be able to stand sunlight. I believe that the heat of the sun must be matched by the heat within. Without balance, one consumes the other."

"Garlic, holy water, crosses, stakes through the heart?" I'd killed a vampire once and it had been easier than killing Ku but if what Huitzilopochtli was saying was true, I'd been careless and lucky… very lucky.

"Garlic is just plain ridiculous," he waved it away. "Holy water is useless; how could something created for blessing be used to kill a god? Crosses are associated with old magic but they've no power over vampires. And as far as stakes go, shove a big pointed stick through anyone's heart and they'll have trouble getting up again but still the only way to kill them is through decapitation, like any god. They're of my line after all."

"But these are all strong human beliefs," I studied him, wondering if he was trying to mislead me. "Gods are shaped by our beliefs. Those things should hurt vampires, if for no other reason than because we believe they will."

"Your belief only shapes gods. Vampires aren't gods, they're the creations of one and as such they're untouchable by human belief. I'm not a vampire but a god, so beliefs concerning vampires don't apply to me." He cut into his hen with relish. "Besides, what human truly believes in vampires? With the creation of artificial light, humanity has gradually forgotten the reasons they should be afraid of the dark."

"That's a bit of a catch twenty-two isn't it?" I still hadn't touched anything.

"It's the truth," he made a prompting motion with his fork at my food. "Vampires are not what you believe them to be and neither am I."

"Enough of this nonsense," Lir's sharp voice carried over to us from his seat, two chairs down from mine. "Do you even know who you've captured, Huitzilopochtli?"

"I've caught a sweet witch in my net," he leaned in and kissed my cheek. I felt tingles dance down my spine. They met halfway with the terror creeping up from my gut and changed into a wave of nausea. I was hoping my identity would escape notice.

"Humph," Lir sneered and looked at me triumphantly. "I thought your face looked familiar, so I did some research and guess what I found?"

Huitzilopochtli raised a brow. "You've ever bored me with your games, Lir. Just say what you must and have done with it."

"She's the Godhunter!" A thick, accusing finger pointed at me and Huitzilopochtli blinked once but none of the others even twitched. I guess I knew what the earlier god huddle had been about.

"Is it true, Vervain?" Huitzilopochtli looked at me as if I'd just morphed from a cute fuzzy caterpillar into a rare butterfly. I wanted caterpillar status back and fast. Where's a hookah when you needed one?

"I have no idea what he's talking about," I wasn't going down without a fight.

"You disgusting little liar," Lir evidently wasn't as impressed with my charms as some of the other gods were.

"Whoa," I held up my hands. "Ease up there, Daddy Dearest, at least I didn't try to off my own offspring."

"My offspring are my affair," he stood up regally but I was satisfied to see that he was shaking. "And I will not be lectured by a human who dares to murder gods."

"I'm rubber and you're glue," I sang out like a three-year-old.

Lir turned a very unbecoming shade of red. For a second the whole table paused and I was sure we were all waiting to see if cartoon steam would start shooting out of his ears. Oh well, I guess it was a no go on braiding each other's hair and gossiping over bonbons. He raised a threatening hand toward me and began to chant something. I automatically went for my dagger but before I could pull it free, Huitzilopochtli stood up and walked over to Lir.

"You're no longer welcome in my home," Huitzilopochtli's dark fingers closed around Lir's neck, showing up starkly against the pale column. Lir's eyes rolled wildly but other than that he did nothing, his whole body going limp as Huitzilopochtli lifted him. Silent but angry footsteps reverberated through the room as Huitzilopochtli carried Lir to one of the large windows. It flew open as they approached. Drawing back a little like a professional pitcher, Huitzilopochtli flung Lir out into the dark. I swallowed hard as I watched his bright shape dwindle until it simply blinked out like a dying star.

The rest of them immediately went back to eating with forced gaiety. I looked around me with wide eyes and felt like I was trapped in an episode of *The Twilight Zone*. Specifically, the one with the boy who could change reality and had terrorized his family until they turned into frightened sycophants. The remaining gods wore the same expressions as that tortured family had. In the episode a woman meets the boy and stands up to him in a maternal sort of way (you know, that whole kind but firm thing) and he goes off to live with her. I do seem to recall that he kills off his entire family first but oh well, the message is the same: power respects courage.

“Pray, do not fall in love with me,” I grabbed my glass and lifted it to Huitzilopochtli in salute. “For I am falser than vows made in wine,” I took a big sip and smiled at him as if I watched gods pitch each other like baseballs everyday. “Besides, I like you not.”

Huitzilopochtli laughed and it was his genuine laugh, loud and boisterous. It startled everyone, including me, but the gods looked truly shocked. They stared from him to me and I saw something I hadn’t expected to see in their eyes… hope. Maybe I should tell them what happened to the boy’s family on *The Twilight Zone*.

“And she quotes Shakespeare,” Huitzilopochtli smiled at me proudly, like I’d just shown my worth. Something I should have probably refrained from doing. “Eat, little witch. I don’t want you to fall ill.” He nudged my plate but I just stared at him. I was suddenly so tired, I wasn’t sure I could even get the food to my mouth.

“Please eat, my lady,” Kuan Ti whispered from my left and I looked over to see his eyes full of genuine concern. Was this the way the bad guys were supposed to act? I don't think Kuan Ti had been given the bad guy book of Standard Operating Procedures.

“Okay, okay,” I forced myself to cut the chicken and take a bite.

“Now tell me why you just lied to me,” Huitzilopochtli’s voice was deceptively neutral.

“What?” I sputtered and nearly choked on my chicken.

“Lir is never mistaken when it comes to his research,” he sliced at his meal, severing meat from bone with surgical precision. “You’re the Godhunter. It makes sense of course. You being in the company of a god known to be a human-rights activist, your magic-filled weapons, your fierce fighting; you’re the God Slayer.”

"I prefer the term Human Liberator, thank you."

He exhaled sharply. "You humans love to justify things by giving them pretty names."

"I don't have to justify anything, especially not to you."

"Don't you?" He took a sip from his goblet and the liquid looked thicker than my wine. It clung to his lips until he licked it away. "I'm a god you'd like to kill. Don't I deserve to know why you want me dead?"

"You know why," I watched the thick liquid drip slowly down the side of his glass.

"I know what you've said. You don't like gods who try to make your people kill each other. This is my crime then? Instigating? It's hardly a crime worthy of the death sentence."

"Millions die because of your *instigating,*" I growled.

"I don't kill them personally," he smiled serenely.

"So humans aren't the only ones who like to justify." I shot him a smug look that wiped the smile clean off his face.

"I think you've had enough to eat," his chair crashed back as he stood and grabbed my arm in one swift movement.

"Well I've had a lovely time, thank you all for such an entertaining meal," I waved the Miss America wave as Huitzilopochtli dragged me from the room. Elbow-elbow, wrist-wrist, elbow-elbow, wrist-wrist.

"My lady," Kuan Ti got to his feet and bowed gallantly.

Huitzilopochtli yanked me down the hall and pushed me into his bedroom. He slammed the door in my face without another word. The coward.

"I just wanted to go back to bed anyway," I stuck my tongue out at the closed door.

Chapter Eight

I was home, on the beach at midnight, and there was lightning dancing on the waves.

I loved storms and the sight of all that power spread out before me was both humbling and intoxicating. I wasn't even cold, thick arms held me to a chest radiating heat. Long hair trailed down from above and hung around me like a comforting cloak. I sighed and snuggled deeper into the embrace.

"Vervain," a voice tickled my ear. "I need you to listen and remember what I say."

I knew that voice but I couldn't place it. I turned my head to look up at the speaker but all I could make out was the flash of lightning in his eyes. The darkness swallowed everything else.

"I'll remember," I said and reached out to touch his face. Maybe if I could feel him, I'd figure out who he was.

He took my hand and pressed it to his lips. "You're trapped Vervain, there's only one place to trace in and out of Huitzilopochtli's home without his help. You must leave where you came in. Do you understand me?"

"Leave where I came in," my fingers moved against the softness of his lips. "Yes, I understand."

"I can't get to you, this was the only way, through our blood link," emotion fought with the lightning in his eyes… fear... sadness? I wasn't sure.

"You don't have to be sad," I stroked the hair back from his face and heard the breath catch in his throat.

"Vervain," my name was a groan on his lips before they

descended. I felt a spark leap between us and heat crept through me on questing tendrils. His tongue tingled in my mouth, stroking against mine and thrusting till I was dizzy with electric wanting. I pulled at his clothes but he stopped me with another groan. "We can't do this here."

"Why not?" I looked across the deserted beach and then back to him.

"We're not really here, darling." My heart fluttered with the endearment but I calmed it, maybe I'd misheard him. "You have to listen and remember."

"Right, I got that, listen and remember," my voice came out a little sharp in my frustration but his sudden laughter chased away my irritation.

"Only you could make me laugh in a dreaming," he shook his head and I strained to see his face but the shadows followed him. "You know the chant to take you home, right?"

"Yes, yes, of course." What did it matter now? Why wouldn't he just kiss me again?

"You need to get out of there, Vervain," his arms tightened around me. "I promised to protect you but he's taken you to a place I can't go and he's dangerous. Don't believe what he tells you." I felt him kiss the top of my head and I sighed. I'd always loved it when a man did that.

"I can protect myself," I smiled up at him and then turned away.

"Please, Vervain," he turned my face back to his again, "Remember. Don't trust the Aztec. Promise me you won't fall for his lies."

"I promise," I met his gaze with my own solemn one and he nodded.

His arms twitched as he looked around us quickly. "He's here, I have to go."

His lips brushed mine and he started to pull away but I deepened the kiss. I slid my hands around his neck and hauled him against me. I felt that electricity ignite again, vibrating through his deep groan, but then it was suddenly gone. His lips changed, becoming more demanding and losing their softness.

I tried to pull back but I wasn't supported in his arms anymore, I was lying in a bed and he was above me, pushing me down. I opened my eyes and the beach was gone, the man above me was dark instead of pale, his eyes glowing red instead of flashing with lightning, and I suddenly knew where I was, where I'd been, and who I'd been with. I pulled away from Huitzilopochtli with a strength I didn't know I had, the name I'd been trying to recall falling from my lips.

"Thor."

Huitzilopochtli hissed and pushed away from me. "You kiss me like that, then dare to speak another god's name? Do not think to play with me, witch!"

I closed my eyes and shook my head. I was so confused, I couldn't even form an answer. He left the bed with a growl and went into the bathroom. I heard water running and sighed, my head spinning a little in relief. Maybe now I could think.

Thor was in my dream. What had he said? It had felt important, something about the Aether. I could only leave in the same place I'd come in. That was the stone room, so I had to make my way back to the stone room… without Huitzilopochtli noticing. I got up and padded over to the door which led out to the hallway. The rush of water from the bathroom was reassuring but I took a quick look over my shoulder anyway before trying the handle. When I pushed against it, I felt the power immediately pushing back. It was still warded. Damn.

Seconds after I let go, a wet, iron grip circled my wrist and spun me around. Huitzilopochtli glowered and dripped all over the carpet while he stood there in breathtaking nudity. To say he had a fine form would not only be an understatement but a crime. He shimmered in the adoring moonlight like a merman given legs. The sheen of water emphasized every hard curve, every dimple and flat plane. There wasn't a single hair to mar the perfection of his chest, and he had a sexy dip on each side of his hips where the bones protruded. Water collected in the small indentations, clinging to him desperately. I was weak and allowed my gaze to wander lower. What a stupid mistake. I almost groaned aloud. He was perfect and growing more so as I watched. I tore my eyes away with supreme effort and looked back at his face.

His initial anger had melted under my hot stare. He looked at me with hard, intense eyes, glittering like rubies in the soft light, and my heart thudded in my throat. His hand loosened slightly to stroke my skin before pulling me forward. I hit his chest, the water on his skin soaking into my clothes and sending a shiver through me.

"What's your game, little witch?" His palm cupped my face as he stared at me intently. "You kiss me and then reject me, you try to escape and then look at me with open lust. These are dangerous tactics and I've ceased being amused by them. Do you want me or the Viking?"

"I don't know what I want," I pushed as far away from him as I could, "but it's not you."

A drop of water fell slowly down the side of his face, rippling over his clenched jaw as his eyes narrowed. My own eyes widened as I realized my mistake. I should have played along. He might have lowered his guard if I'd pretended to want him. Instead, he backhanded me, dropping me to the thick carpet in a second. I ran my tongue along the cut inside my mouth, swallowing blood as I twisted to look up at him.

“You will,” he vowed viciously, towering over me like an angel of vengeance. “You’ll learn to trust me. You’ll learn to love me.”

“Trust my jailer? Love a monster?” I sat up and rubbed my jaw. “Yeah, you're doing a phenomenal job of convincing me. You're a fucking lunatic.”

Huitzilopochtli’s eyes hardened a little but he didn’t say anything. He just bent down and lifted me into his arms like a child. I felt my muscles tighten angrily but I tamped down the feeling. The last thing I needed to do was push him when he was barely containing his rage. He walked over to the bed and laid me back down. I laid perfectly still as he crawled in, still damp, and pulled the covers over us before curling his body around mine. As if we were a normal, happy couple. Yep, he was totally insane. I felt the heavy weight of his leg fall over mine and his breath tickle along my neck. The sound of his even breathing surrounded me as I clenched my teeth and tried to hold back my tears.

Welcome to my world, where the monsters don’t hide under your bed, they sleep in it beside you.

Chapter Nine

When I woke in the morning, it was to the sound of arguing.

"She deserves to die," a woman was screaming. It was not a pleasant way to start the day, especially since I was pretty sure the *she* was me.

"She's mine," the male voice was one I recognized and I tried desperately to subdue the fear it sent spiraling through me. If I wanted to get out of there, I needed to put my big girl panties on and figure it out without letting my fear get the best of me.

"She's bewitched my husband," uh-oh, one guess who that was. It was turning out to be a bad day and I hadn't even opened my eyes yet.

"He's not your husband anymore, Sif," Huitzilopochtli put no emotion into the words, merely stated a fact. Sif still didn't take kindly to it and she wasn't shy about letting him know. She screamed, a sound of pure rage.

"Don't tell me what is or is not between Thor and I!"

"You fought, divorced, and are now on opposing sides of a god war, so you're still fighting," he had a hell of a point there. "That's not what I'd call a happy marriage."

"It's not for you to say," Sif sniffed haughtily.

"It's exactly for me to say," I could feel his power rising, biting along my skin. I snuggled under the covers deeper; to escape it or enjoy it, I wasn't completely sure. "You're my guest here, so you'll have the courtesy of a warning before I bleed you. Leave her be. Don't even contemplate hurting her and then running because even beyond these walls, I'm stronger than you. Don't fight me over Vervain. Don't fight me over anything. You won't win."

"You dare to threaten me?" She tried for scorn but even I could hear the terror in her voice.

Huitzilopochtli laughed and the breath caught in my throat. It was a laugh of cruel confidence. That laugh said *I can kill you anytime, anyplace, and there's nothing you can do about it.* I knew it was true. She was no match for him and neither was I. The thought was a wrench thrown right in the middle of my big girl panties. I barely kept from sucking my thumb and crying for my mommy.

"I don't threaten," his voice still held traces of laughter, "I merely state facts but maybe it's not simple enough for you to understand. I'll make it very clear so there can be no confusion between us. If you harm her, if you upset her, if you abuse her in any way, or try to turn her against me, I will torture you until you beg for death. Then I will let her have you."

A small choking sound was the only response from Sif. I responded by squeezing my eyes shut and wishing desperately that I could believe in gods the way others did. Then at least I could be praying instead of cowering under the covers like a child. Okay, so I'd probably be praying *and* cowering.

"Do you understand me, Sif?" I heard the rustle of hands crushing fabric. "You touch what's mine and not only is our alliance over but so is your immortality. Leave her be or just leave, those are the only choices you have that will keep you breathing."

The sounds of a scuffle sent my heart racing, my whole body tensing for a fight, but the slam of the door shocked me out of my instincts. I had no idea if he'd left with her but I didn't think I'd be that lucky. So when the covers lifted and the bed dipped beside me, I wasn't too surprised. I *was* surprised at the warmth of his body as it slid along mine and by how good it felt when his arm pulled me against him gently. The only thing louder than the steady thumping of his heart was the frenzied pounding of my own.

"I know you're awake, little witch," he breathed into my ear. "Your heart beats like a trapped bird's." His hand slid between my breasts to lay flat against my sternum. "I don't want your fear," the fingers against my flesh started to swirl in lazy circles as the soft heat of his lips trailed down my bruised cheek.

"Would you really torture her for merely upsetting me?" I looked up at him finally; needing to hear him say it, to verify how much of a monster he was.

"Yes," he said it softly, like a lover's vow, and my whole body went cold as I fought to keep my face blank. "You don't approve." He pulled back and looked down at me, tilting his head to the side.

"You sound surprised," I tried to pull away as well but he pressed me down.

"I've just sworn to do great damage to an ally of mine, all for your safety and you not only fear me for it but you think less of me." He sounded as if he couldn't decide whether to be shocked, angry, or impressed.

"I'm sorry, was that your idea of chivalry?" My heartbeat was finally starting to slow down to normal. "Was my line supposed to be *My hero* or something like that? I just hate it when I don't know my lines."

I saw a trace of anger fill his eyes. My breath turned sharp and quick but he quenched the anger as quickly as it came.

"Would you rather I let her in? Do you even know what she would've done?" He pushed off me and leaned back.

"No," I sat up and immediately felt a little better. It's hard to act tough when you're lying beneath someone.

"She was calling for your death, Vervain," he brushed back a stray lock of my hair and frowned when I pulled further away. "She was already armed with her sword and had every intention of cutting off your head while you slept."

I felt the blood drain from my face. As far as ways to die, I could think of more gruesome ones but the idea of someone killing me while I was unaware and unable to defend myself was horrible. The fact that it was my preferred method of killing gods didn't escape my irony meter either but what was even more terrible, was the gratitude I immediately felt towards Huitzilopochtli. Evil or not, it would be better to keep myself in his good graces, so I decided to go with the change of heart.

"You're right," I let my gaze soften on him and my voice drop down to a purr. "I'm sorry, I misjudged the situation."

"You admit you're wrong?" His expression was immediately wary.

"I'm often wrong," I smiled shyly, or at least what I hoped was a shy smile. It probably looked more like a grimace. "I find it easier to just apologize as soon as I realize it. I value integrity more than pride."

"You're a surprising woman, little witch," he lowered his face to mine and my heart went right back to banging on my ribs. I didn't have time to figure out if it was from excitement or fear before he kissed me.

He touched me with his lips alone; softly, carefully. It wasn't the type of kiss I was expecting and he got further with me for catching me so off guard. I slid back against the pillows and lifted my hands to the sides of his face to stroke back the hair that fell around us. He groaned and deepened the kiss. I met him with my own ardor, slipping my tongue further into his mouth. But the instant I did, I felt a sting as one of his fangs nicked me and I tasted my own blood.

Huitzilopochtli went wild like a switch had been flipped, pulling me under his body and grinding his hips against me. I gasped but it was lost in the violence. He was sucking on my tongue, pulling it into his mouth and lapping at it. Fear filled me, unmistakable this time, and I wracked my brain for a way to fight him. The power! The energy I'd borrowed, did I still have it? I reached down inside myself and felt it coiled there, waiting. I tried to channel Thor, to bring the lightning, but his power wasn't there. I must have only borrowed enough for one use apiece. I panicked as Huitzilopochtli's hands roamed over me like they couldn't decide where they wanted to be first. They tore at my top and I finally freed my lips enough to cry out.

"Get off me, you son of a bitch!"

I thought he hadn't heard me but then he stilled and just lay above me, filled with coiled tension. I could feel the magic surging through his body, tingling and teasing my skin. His chest expanded into mine as he took a deep breath and then he relcased it, shuddering.

"Now it's I who must ask for your forgiveness." He raised his head to look at me and I stared at the crimson of his eyes as they swirled frantically. "The blood combined with lust drives me to madness if I'm not prepared for it. Did I hurt you?"

"No," I looked away, unsure what to say or do, "I'm fine."

"Do you forgive me, Vervain?" The pleading in his voice yanked my eyes back to him. His eyes were normal again, as normal as they could get.

"I guess it's only fair," I tried to concentrate on what Thor had said but it was so hard not to be drawn in by the earnest expression Huitzilopochtli wore. Was this the same man who'd struck me last night? Then I realized that his behavior was perfectly in line with that of an abuser. If you asked a battered woman why she stayed with her man, she'd probably tell you something along the lines of, *He's actually a very good man, he just gets angry sometimes.* Abusers know how to keep their victims in line. Insert moments of kindness in between the torture and you'll create a victim who will actually defend you. Child abusers use the same technique.

He laughed and it brought me out of my morbid musings. It was the velvet laugh I both enjoyed and hated. In one graceful movement he rolled off me and helped me from bed. He didn't let go until we were near the hidden door to the bathroom.

"There's a change of clothes for you inside. When you're done, come out to the garden," he motioned to the open doors.

I nodded numbly and entered the bathroom. After the weird wake-up call I'd just had, I welcomed the sanctuary and looked around carefully. I'd nearly been struck dumb by the bathroom the night before so I hadn't been truly able to enjoy it. Yes, dumbstruck by a bathroom, it was that fantastic. The dress he'd left me was hung on a golden hanger across the room from me and it was stunning but it paled next to the beauty of its surroundings.

It was like he'd brought the jungle inside. The bedroom's sumptuous red carpet ended abruptly at the doorway in a green carpet of grass. Not green like grass, I mean there was real grass covering the floor. Along my right was a wall of windows with a door in the center, open to the encroaching jungle. To my left was a slab of stone with a basin carved out of it. A handle placed nearby controlled the release of a miniature waterfall which would pour into the basin from beneath a long mirror. The mirror was set into a rock wall whose every nook and cranny sprouted ferns and bright, monstrous orchids with sword-shaped leaves curling over the slab counter. Antique crystal jars of toiletries hid among the leaves, adding a little sparkle.

There were trees growing inside the bathroom as well; one by the bedroom door and one at the end of the room by the tub.

The dress hung on the later. The bathtub was the most amazing feature of all. Made of the same stone as the counter, it was sunk into the floor to resemble a natural pool. I had bathed in it the night before and it took me forever to find the hidden levers for the water. At the very top of another plant-filled rock wall behind the tub, a platform jutted out. With the turn of one of those hidden levers, water flowed over this and into the middle of the pool, allowing for your choice of shower or bath.

The grass grew right up to the pool and plants grew out of the floor randomly. Near the tub, there were boulders of differing heights with flat tops for toiletries or sitting. One of the boulders actually had a lid which lifted to reveal a toilet. Very ingenious but also very frustrating if you happened to be a person unaccustomed to searching for a toilet inside rocks. I had actually wondered for a few confused moments if maybe gods didn't share our bodily functions.

The room was amazing and so was the dress but it seemed so out of place in it. I walked over and touched the soft material. It was red of course (the man just didn't likc change), made of yards of velvet and lace but not just any velvet and lace. Silk velvet so soft you wondered if they made blankets out of the stuff so you could wrap yourself in heaven while you slept, and Venetian lace, the real stuff some old Italian lady makes by hand with dozens of little spindles. The sleeves were little puffs that ended in a froth of the lace and the bodice was a deep square saved from being immodest by the lace that trimmed it. It curved in at the waist, then out at the hips, and was gathered at different points to show layers of even more lace beneath. It was a dress that belonged in another century or a museum. Definitely not on me.

I stripped, leaving my underwear on the counter with my dagger. Yes I slept with it again, even after the bruising. I washed my face and then frowned at myself in the mirror. I was being seduced by a dress and a handsome face. I glared at the dress over my shoulder, wishing for a pair of ruby slippers to match. *There's no place like home. There's no place like home.* I was being primped, polished, and pampered. It was vastly preferable to some cold dungeon and the seduction of it all was almost too tempting but when it came down to it, the wizard was a bipolar, womanizing Aztec with a thirst for blood and I, like Dorothy, desperately wanted out of Oz.

I saw to the rest of my morning needs and then slipped the dress (I wasn't sure if it was even considered a dress, maybe the correct word would be gown or tent) over my head. It was amazing and I felt like I belonged in some Gothic novel but I soon discovered the reason women used to have maids. I needed help with the laces. I squirmed and stretched but I just couldn't reach. Oh well, so much for making a stunning entrance.

I stuck my head out of the sliding glass doors. "Hey, Hummingbird Man."

"I presume you're calling me," he came through the lush growth holding a magnificent rose.

"I need some assistance," I turned and showed him my back while I held the bodice up with both hands. He laughed softly and I felt his breath tickle my shoulders.

"My pleasure, little witch," he spoke against my skin a second before brushing his lips along my shoulder. I shivered and jerked a little. Then he handed me the flower and went to work on the laces. "There, now turn around and let me see you."

I did as he asked, feeling awkward and wishing I knew why. He stepped back and his eyes feasted on me. There was no other word for it, he looked at me so slowly from head to toe, eyes widening slightly and finishing with a flick of his tongue across his lips. I felt completely consumed by the time it was over.

He took the rose from me, broke most of its stem off, and tucked it behind my left ear. The symbolism wasn't lost on me. Back home in Hawaii, a woman wore a flower behind her left ear only if she was in a serious relationship. If you were single, the flower went on the right. I reached up to correct it but his hand stopped me.

"I may not have taken your body," he pulled a long curl of my hair forward and stroked it tenderly, like he was stroking something much more intimate. "But you're mine, make no mistake about that, Vervain."

"Whatever you have to tell yourself," I glared at him and suppressed the urge to crush the innocent flower in my fist.

He smiled indulgently, like I was a misbehaving child, and it set my teeth on edge but I allowed him to lead me into the jungle. There was actually a little path through the trees and we followed it to a clearing where a stone table was laid with linen and bone china. He seated me in a carved mahogany chair with a red velvet cushion. I peered under the tablecloth at the stone it lay on. Was I about to eat breakfast on an altar? I let the cloth drop. I'd rather not consider the possibility. I focused instead on watching him lift the domed silver lid off my plate.

"Eggs Benedict?" I stared at the perfect hollandaise sauce and the crisp homefries. "How did you know this was my favorite?"

"I shared your mind when I tasted your blood," he grinned unabashedly. "You were hungry and thinking of breakfast."

I looked at him sharply. Breakfast hadn't been in the forefront of my thoughts. Had he heard me turn to the borrowed magic? Did he know what I could do? More importantly, could I still use one of the borrowed powers to escape?

"Coffee?" He poured the steaming liquid into a delicate teacup in front of me.

I added sugar and cream, stirred, then sipped. It was pure Kona. What the hell? Did he just happen to have all of my favorites on hand?

"Thank you," Mama didn't raise me to be rude. "Huitzil… oh I can't keep calling you that. I know it's your name but we're going to have to go with a nickname from here on out and I can't stomach Hummingbird."

"You want to give me a pet name?" He beamed in delight.

"Not a pet name," I glared at him. "A nickname, a shorter word for you. What was your name in English again?"

"Blue Humming-"

"Blue," I interrupted. "I like it. Short, to the point. Blue it is."

"You want to name me after a color?" He wasn't so pleased by that.

"It's just a shortened version of your name," I was very pleased with him being displeased. Then a thought occurred to me and I chuckled. "It'll be an accurate description of certain parts of your anatomy if you keep pursuing me."

He frowned a good five minutes till comprehension flared to life. "You're referring to a state of male frustration, I believe?" I giggled in delight and sipped my coffee as he continued. "Hmmm, I must admit it's never presented itself as a problem to me before. I guess I'll have to pleasure myself if you drive me to such a state and I'll make you watch as your penance."

I choked and nearly spewed coffee everywhere. "You'll *what*?"

"If you're so unaffected by me, then whatever I choose to do to relieve myself will not matter to you, correct?" His eyes sparkled over the rim of his teacup as he took a sip.

"You're disgusting," I felt a shiver run through me as I

pictured him stroking himself next to me in bed. Oh crap, I wouldn't last a week. I had to get out of there immediately.

"We'll see how disgusting you think it is," he cut into his meal. "Maybe I'll try it out tonight if you refuse me again. I knew this would be fun but I didn't anticipate how deliciously naughty it would be. I do so love the chase."

What a typical man and in typical male fashion, he'd probably stop wanting me as soon as I gave in. Except in this case, his waning interest wouldn't mean a break-up, it would mean my death. I swallowed hard and fought back my rising panic.

"Do you still have house guests?"

He looked up and raised both brows at my obvious subject change. "I do, we'll dine with them tonight. I wanted to spend the day alone with you."

"Aren't they here for nasty god business?" The eggs were so delicious, I was having mouth orgasms but it was getting harder and harder for me to enjoy them. "Won't they be mad if you blow them off?"

"Yes and yes," he laughed like their irritation only added to his joy. "Have you not learned yet, Vervain? I'm the master here, none of them can match my power. They'll wait if I tell them to."

"But their goals are your goals, right? I mean wouldn't you rather be working on new ways to destroy my race than be sitting here with me?" It was a bitter comment but I'd had enough with the seduction routine, I wanted the anger back.

"My intentions have never been to destroy your race, little witch," he went in the complete opposite direction of what I expected. "Your race has multiplied to the point of becoming a threat to the ecosystem. Our nasty business, as you call it, is necessary for your survival as well as ours."

“Are you trying to say you’re doing the human race a favor?” I was aghast and horrified because some of his reasoning actually had a twisted kind of logic.

“That’s exactly what I’m saying and if you weren’t such a child of your generation, you’d see it’s truly what’s best for the world. If humans aren’t controlled, they’ll overpopulate the planet and bring ruin upon themselves.”

“A pretty speech,” I rubbed at my temple, it had started to ache. “But it still spells murder.”

“Not murder,” his face looked so serene, “sacrifice. Sacrifice not just to the gods but to themselves and the planet. Your medical advances have made you weak. People who would’ve died had nature had its way, are now allowed to live. This not only causes overpopulation but it passes down those weak genes, making the next generation weaker than the previous. On top of that, the one medical advance which would actually help, often goes unused. Birth control. People keep having child after child. Even those who are so poverty stricken they can't feed the children they birth. Instead of managing your population, you put pictures of these starving children on your televisions and ask other people to feed them. I’ve watched your people for centuries and I speak only the truth, as harsh as it may sound to your ears. The weak need to be culled, the population *controlled*.”

“Who do you think they send to war?” I barely contained my anger. “They don’t send the weak into battle, they send the strong. So you’re little theory doesn’t work. You’re only weakening us further. You’re stealing our brave young men and women and you’re leaving only widows and broken families. Children who will never know their parents, parents who will never see their children again, all because you need your fix.”

“Yes,” he nodded gravely, “they send their soldiers but does war not make them stronger? Does it not make them more attractive to the opposite sex? Does it not in its own way serve to weed out while it replenishes the population? Your military doesn't pick the strongest, they take what they can get but battle sorts out the wheat from the chaff. The most capable survive as nature intended."

"Nature doesn't care whether we fight or not," I growled, "only the gods do."

"Does it not?" He lifted an aristocratic brow. "Have you ever heard of Cordyceps?"

"What?" I frowned at the odd change of topic. "No. What the hell is a Cordycep?"

"It's a fungus," he calmly took a sip of coffee. "When there is overpopulation of a type of insect or arthropod, Cordyceps takes over. They infect, kill the host by sprouting out of the body, and then release their spores into the air to contaminate others until the species is weeded down."

"This fungus," I gaped at him, "you're telling me it knows when there's too much of something?"

"Nature may not have a mind as you would define one but she is aware of what is happening with her children. The planet is aware. Balance must be kept." He held his hands out as if he were the scale.

"Wait... Cordyceps," I frowned again as I tried to remember where I'd heard the word. "Wasn't that the name of the mushroom the trainer gave those three Chinese athletes who broke like five world records?"

"Yes, another of Nature's specialties," he smiled smugly. "To bring life from death. The point though, is that balance is found. Humans aren't outside of her power either. Just look at all the earthquakes which in turn cause tidal waves. Look at the hurricanes she sends. The Earth is literally trying to shake your people off like a dog with fleas. Humanity is just a pest to her and if its growth is not decelerated, Nature will find a way to cull the herd, a way which will not discriminate. Young or old, brilliant or stupid, rich or poor, she doesn't care. She feels no mercy."

"You're using a fungus and earthquakes to rationalize violence and manipulation?" I shook my head.

"You act as if every war on the planet were my fault," he placed his elbow on the table and rested his chin firmly on his fist. "Do you think the violence would simply disappear if I left all alone? Do you think you humans could live in peace with each other?"

"I think it would be more peaceful than having a crazy Aztec pulling the strings."

"Ah, so now I'm crazy," he pursed his lips in thought. "Your reaction proves my point."

"I know I'm going to regret asking this," I sighed, "but what do you mean by that?"

"Humans will never be able to live peacefully," he matched my sigh but added a dramatic flare. "A more belligerent creature has never been birthed. You people actually search for reasons to go to war. I merely direct the current, I do not make the waves."

"Bullshit," I scoffed.

"Cuss all you want," he smiled. "Deep inside, you know it's true. Humans fight over everything. Property, sex, and especially religion."

"Because you so-called gods provoke us."

"You think we *made* you fight over us?" He raised a brow. "Do you really believe that I found a band of humans, got them together, led them toward a homeland, and then told them to go find other people to kill? Do you think I *asked* to be the God of

War? Do you truly think I *wanted* to be drenched in blood?"

"Maybe not at first," I frowned in confusion. My cause was black and white. I fought gods because they made my people fight each other. I didn't appreciate Blue adding some gray to the picture. "But when you stopped receiving so much worship, you had to find a way to get more energy out of us and so you started this manipulation."

"Yes," his face tightened into serious lines, "I do what I have to do to survive. I at least have a reason for warmongering. Your people however, would fight for no reason at all."

"There's always a reason."

"Always a reason?" He laughed scathingly. "There are times when we would cease our manipulations as you call them. We don't need to constantly feed off your energy, you know. Do you know what happened when we did? Boxing was invented."

"Boxing?"

"Yes, you know," he waved his hands impatiently. "With the ring and the gloves and such."

"Yes, I know what boxing is," I growled. "So what?"

"So because your people didn't have anything to fight over, they started fighting as a sport. They'd beat on each other just to see who was the stronger. Two men hit each other until one falls down and doesn't get up, and not only do your people call this a sport but they flock to watch it in droves. They bet on the outcome and then fight with others over winning or losing those bets. Of course it started much earlier than that. The Romans had their gladiators, I just thought you might relate to the boxing thing better. Your people hate far better than they love. They wallow in it while love is tossed aside so easily. I simply make use of it, of your own natures."

“You manipulate everything don't you?” I was shaking, I was so angry. “You think you can manipulate me by twisting the facts to suit your purpose. Yes, we can be violent, we can hate with such passion that it crumbles cities to dust. We study the ways to kill and we teach them to our children. Then we take pride in the learning. We can be horrible and truly evil but that is only one side of humanity.”

I took a deep breath and clenched my shaking hands till they stilled. Blue eyed me with the strangest expression, a slight furrowing of his forehead and a snake-like intensity in his eyes. He nodded for me to go on but didn't say a word, and I was a little shocked to see his own fists clenched on the table.

“We *are* good at hating,” I started again, “but we are so much *better* at loving. You say we fight over property and religion. I say we love enough to give those things up. Prince Edward gave up the throne of England to marry an American woman. Lady Godiva humiliated herself for her husband. The Shah Jahan ordered his kingdom into a two year mourning period when his wife died and then he built the Taj Mahal in tribute to her. We'd sacrifice anything for those we love. You say we toss love aside but even in war, in the midst of hate, men have jumped onto grenades to save their comrades. You've accepted sacrifice from humans for too long, you've forgotten that you're not the only ones we sacrifice for. We also sacrifice ourselves for each other.”

“Yes, very moving,” he frowned as he searched my face, “but you forget that most of your great love stories end in hatred. Guinevere betrays her husband for Lancelot and the King tries to burn her at the stake. Cleopatra is just as untrue to Julius Caesar and kills herself over the mess she made. Even the renowned Napoleon and Josephine split up due in part to adultery. Troy was demolished for the love of one woman and King Henry VIII killed his wives so he could trade them in for new ones. Then his daughter Mary tried to bring the Spanish Inquisition to England to please her husband. You love fiercely because you cannot, even in this, separate yourselves from your hate."

"Those are extreme examples," I gritted out. "Stories are told about things that are unusual or shocking. You don't hear the millions of simple tales about how everyday people struggle through life, standing beside each other faithfully until the day death finally parts them. How sometimes their love is so strong that even death cannot stop it. Their souls find each other again in the next life, searching the world until they are once more with their beloved. The reason I fight you gods isn't hatred, it's love."

"Look at you," he huffed. "You don't fight for love! You sit there so indignant, judging me, *hating* me. This is what I meant by you proving my point. You blame me for all this bloodshed so that you may have a reason to hate me, to kill me. You heard one side of the story, discovered one little piece of the puzzle, and you lifted it up and shouted *Aha! I've found the problem!* You decided you'd fix it without ever stepping back and taking in the whole picture. You can't admit that I may be right because then you would lose your reason to hate. It has nothing to do with love! If there is anything else, it's fear that motivates you."

"No," I stood up and he followed suit. "I'm not going to sit here and listen to you rationalize your actions to me and I'm certainly not going to listen to you tear apart mine!" I pushed my chair back and started towards the house. When I heard him following, I sped up. I'd almost reached the glass doors when he grabbed me and swung me around.

"Don't run from me, little witch," his hands squeezed my upper arms tight. I was going to have more bruises. "It's useless, the sooner you learn that the better."

"Maybe you'll catch me in the end, Blue," I used his new name deliberately and felt a small twinge of satisfaction as his jaw clenched, "but it's not useless. As long as you're chasing me, you won't have me and I intend for you to *not* have me for as long as possible."

His hands tightened for a second and then he smiled. It was an icy smile, smug and devoid of any other emotion. He let go and stepped back to bow to me. "Then by all means; run, little witch, run. I think I'll enjoy the chase."

I looked up and the heat in his eyes terrified me. When they began to glow, I turned to run, lifting my skirts up as I went. Through the open doors of the bathroom I went and his laughter followed me mockingly. He was so sure of himself that he was giving me a head start. I glanced at the closed door to the hallway and realized why he was so confident. I still couldn't leave the room. I screamed at the door in frustration and the door clicked open, swinging wide on silent hinges.

I gaped for the space of two heartbeats before I gathered enough wits to grab the box that held my weapons and bolt out the door. In the hallway, I almost ran straight into Aphrodite. She steadied me and then pointed down the hall towards the stone room. Had she opened the door?

Blue's startled shout carried to us and she gave me a push. I mouthed *thank you* to her and she nodded with big exasperated eyes, pointing again before making a shooing motion. I smiled and ran in the direction she indicated. Hooray for sisterhood, I guess even goddesses could feel it. The stone room was just a little further. If I could make it there, I could trace out and escape.

I entered the room and threw a quick glance back over my shoulder. Aphrodite was nowhere to be found but Blue had just entered the hallway. Our gazes met for a second and in his eyes I saw shocked defeat. He knew where I was headed, he knew he'd miscalculated, and he knew he'd never reach me in time. I was already chanting the spell to take me home when I hit the spot where we traced in. Instantly, I was sucked through, dissolving into the Aether with the sounds of Blue's anger nipping at my heels.

I blinked at the blinding Hawaiian sun, back in the same

alley I started in days ago, and I began to laugh. I laughed like a raving lunatic. A couple passing by glanced at me and then quickened their pace. Not such a bad idea for me as well. I needed to get out of there.

I ran from the alley, garnering a few startled gasps and stares. I heard one little girl ask her daddy if I was a princess, which almost started me on the hysterics again. Instead, I held it together long enough to reach the parking lot, where I'd left my car.

Oh crap, it was going to cost a pretty penny to get my car out. At least I'd parked valet. I always do when I go hunting, so I don't have to worry about my keys. The guys knew me there, so losing my ticket wouldn't be a huge problem either. When you drive a Jag (yes, I kept Ku's car; surprise, surprise, no one reported it stolen) and you're a woman, you tend to get noticed. I also had enough sense to leave my purse in a hidden compartment in the trunk.

I hurried to the valet booth and Jimmy smiled up at me. Jimmy was an old surfer who'd spent his life on the waves and finally woke up one morning to realize he was forty years old with no marketable job skills. So he was a parking lot attendant and he was surprisingly happy about that.

"Hey, sista," he jumped up and grabbed my keys. "Wassup wit' da kine?" He motioned to my dress. "What *is* dat?"

Jimmy spoke the local dialect known as Pidgin. It made me smile every time I heard it come out of his very white face. The surfers had adopted it but originally it was a way for all the different immigrants to understand each other. It was a mix of English, Hawaiian, Japanese, Chinese, and Portuguese. Tourists thought it was funny, some even thought it made people sound ignorant, but I loved it. My ancestors had come here to work in horrible conditions, with people from many different cultures, and they had triumphed together by creating a new language and a new culture all of their own. The language was a part of their legacy and it was also the sweet sound of home to me. I'd take it over Blue's cultured accent any day. I smiled brightly at Jimmy.

"I was at an early Halloween party," good thing it was October. "What do you think?"

"Looks sic!" He ran off to get my car as I laughed.

Jimmy pulled up quickly because he always parked my car near the front. "K sista, here ya go," he jumped out and I popped the trunk to retrieve my purse.

"How much?" I fished out my wallet and hoped I'd brought enough cash.

"Five bucks," he grinned, "I went lose your ticket cause you so pretty in dat dress."

"You're so full of it but thank you," I laughed and slipped him twenty-five dollars. That was another reason they all remembered me, I tipped big. I threw the box with my gloves and sword in it, on the passenger seat and jumped in.

"No worries," he waved as I drove off.

No worries indeed. Turns out that I didn't need the ruby slippers after all, I had my very own Glinda. Out of respect for her saving me, I sent up the first prayer I'd ever made.

"Thank you, Aphrodite," I whispered as I stepped on the gas. "There's no place like home."

Chapter Ten

I drove home carefully. I always drove carefully now that I had Ku's Jaguar. Although if I ever did get pulled over, I wasn't above using magic to get me out of trouble. I went over the Likelike (pronounced lee-kay-lee-kay not like-like), the trees crowding the road on the way to the tunnel. Long branches stretched out, reaching, grasping at me like an angry Aztec as I passed, then shaking angrily in the rear view mirror. I tried to blink my eyes free of the crazy hallucinations as the dark mouth of the tunnel gulped me down.

I sped through the poorly lit passage and almost slammed on the brakes when a pair of red eyes appeared in the gloom. I swallowed a scream as I realized it was just the brake lights of the car in front of me. I took a shaky breath, slowing down around the last sharp turn before bursting out into full sunlight again. A wave of relief hit me as I wove down the mountain. Sheer lush peaks soared on my left and a steep drop fell on my right, allowing for a great view of Kaneohe, where I've lived for most of my life.

The sun was out in full force on this side of the island, gilding the verdant slopes and framing the rapidly growing city at the foot of the mountains. So much light was more unusual than you'd think. Kaneohe rarely went a day without at least a sprinkling of rain. The mountains caught passing clouds expertly and liked to wring them dry before letting them go on their merry way. Having grown up in the wet conditions, I loved the rain and would normally have hissed in the face of so much sunlight but after shedding the dark feeling of pursuit, the sun shining my way home seemed like a good and welcome omen.

When I finally pulled to a stop in my driveway, my head thumped back against the seat heavily. Half of me didn't quite believe I could escape Huitzilopochtli so easily. My heart finally got the message that it could relax and my mind used the opportunity to process the last seventy-two hours.

It had been a wild ride, even for me. I'd actually allied myself with gods and even kissed a couple. I shivered through the memory of Thor's wild kiss and groaned through Blue's. I still didn't know what to make of the Aztec. He'd been so sincere in his beliefs, so uninhibited in his passion, but then had been offhandedly cruel and terrifyingly cold in his scientific reasoning.

It didn't help that his assessment of my motivations for fighting gods had struck a chord of truth. Hadn't I just admitted to myself that fear was a huge part of it? I wondered if he'd wrung that from my mind when he'd made himself at home there earlier. And let's not forget about the way the bastard had hit me.

The memory of Thor took over and I grasped it greedily. I much rather think about the way it felt to be held by him, how the heat of his skin contrasted with the cold rain. I trembled, I actually trembled like some nympho perv. What kind of a god-chasing slut was I turning into? I covered my face with my hands, trying to block out the sexy images. I hadn't made love to a man since before the episode with Ku. It was just too difficult to get close to someone without explaining my strange lifestyle. I mean what was I supposed to say? *Hi, I'm Vervain. I'm an artist and a Virgo. I like Moroccan food, Roger Moore best as 007, and hunting gods.*

My friend Jackson always said, *If a woman isn't having sex, it's because she doesn't want to*. Well sure, I could go out and pick up a guy for the night but I just didn't like casual sex. I botched it up without fail. The two times I'd tried had both resulted in long-term relationships. One guy I'd even told up front that it wasn't going to be more than one night. He called me the next day and asked how many times he could call before it was considered stalking. I almost married him.

Wrapped up in sex and ex thoughts, I didn't see Thor until he rapped on my window. Then I screamed like a little girl.

“I’m sorry,” he held up his hands and tried hard to look apologetic while suppressing a huge grin. “I was just wondering when you were going to get out of the car.”

I opened the door and flowed out in a loud rustling of fabric. Before I could say anything, I was wrapped up in two thick arms and pulled off my feet. His clean, electric scent filled my nose and I inhaled it greedily, instantly winding down to a state of perfect calm. Muscled chest filling my arms, a steady heartbeat pounding through him and into me, and fiery hair caressing my face as his cheek pressed into the top of my head. It all sang a song of solace and seduction. Standing there with him, I felt like I’d truly come home. I had to remind myself that I’d just met Thor. I didn’t know him well enough to feel this comfortable with him.

“Let’s get inside.” He put me gently on my feet and then leaned over me to shut the car door.

“What are you doing here, Thor?” I asked as we walked to the front porch.

“Let’s get inside first,” he kept a firm hand on me, scanning the neighborhood as we went.

I found my keys and fumbled with the lock. The keys jingled and I stared down accusingly at my shaking hand. Warm fingers closed over mine and Thor gently took the keys from me, opened the door, and ushered me inside.

The interior was dark, cool, and smelled faintly of nag champa incense. I let its welcome sink into my bones. The house was small by mainland standards, only three bedrooms, but in Hawaii it was a fair size. More importantly, it was all mine and I loved it.

Gauzy white fabric draped down the living room walls and hung across the ceiling to peak at the center around a Moroccan lantern I'd outfitted with an electric bulb. Directly beneath the lantern was a low, inlaid wood table, and gathered around the table were sofas, in the original sense of the word; low Middle Eastern couches with bright pillows in a rainbow of colors. The dark carpet was overlaid with Persian rugs up to where it met my kitchen and the Middle Eastern theme faded into plain Eastern.

My kitchen table was heavy wood, hand-carved with oriental dragons. The walls were bright crimson, adorned only with an antique wedding kimono. Red drapes in the exact same shade as the walls hid the window that looked out onto my back yard and kept the sunlight out completely. A graceful vanilla orchid stretched elegantly out of a china pot in the center of the table, its fragrance adding its own welcome. I frowned a little when it occurred to me just how similar my dining room was to the one on Thor's boat.

"Ummm, Vervain?" Thor was still standing in the doorway.

"Enter Thor and be welcome," I recited the ritual words that granted him limitless access to my house. I could always renew the wards and revoke his welcome in the future if I had to. That made me feel better. I just didn't trust any hot gods yet, at least not completely.

"Thank you and may I bring no harm with me," he replied just as formally and slipped inside, shutting and locking the door behind him with a loud click. He looked like he was about to say something else when a gray blur streaked through the room, screeching like a banshee.

"Nicholas," I threw my keys and box on the sofa before bending to pick up the tabby. I'd bottle-raised the cat after finding him abandoned as a kitten. In his head, I was Mommy. Hell, in my head as well. I scratched beneath his chin, receiving deep purrs for my efforts, in between sassy meows.

"You have a cat?" Thor reached out and stroked Nick. The cat eyed the god critically with bright green eyes before approving the attention with renewed purring.

"Why does that surprise you?"

"It doesn't surprise me," he looked around. "I was just wondering who cared for him while you're away."

"I have an automatic feeder, a pet fountain for water, and a cat door so he can get outside on his own." I plopped down onto one of the sofas, still cuddling Nick. "I also have a friend who checks in on him if I don't check in for awhile."

"He must get lonely," Thor eased his big frame down next to mine and resumed petting Nick. I realized with some surprise that he must genuinely like cats, a trait I loved in men. Most men liked dogs, it was manlier. Only a special type of guy appreciated felines, the kind of guy who was secure in his masculinity and didn't need a pet to constantly fawn on him.

"I don't go hunting very often," I handed Nicholas to Thor, who took him with a big grin. "He can fend for himself for up to a week but I'm rarely gone more than a couple days, which is why I just got scolded."

"Ah," Thor nodded. Nick had stretched up Thor's chest, leaning his head back for his neck to be scratched.

"Now tell me how you know where I live."

"Simple," he let Nick crawl down before turning to face me. "I've given you my blood. Once you've shared blood with a god, they can always find you." He pulled me onto his lap casually, settling my voluminous skirts around us. "I like," he stroked my puffy sleeve and sniffed at the rose behind my ear.

"You can track me? Like a LoJack?" I felt a shiver of dread slide down my spine and it had nothing to do with Thor. "Anywhere?"

"Unless you guard against me specifically, yes," his soft smile was slowly replaced by an intense stare. "I knew exactly where Huitzilopochtli had taken you but without the proper chant, a god can't enter another god's territory. I'm sorry I couldn't free you."

"It's alright," I leaned around him to flick the light-switch on and the filtered light from the lantern filled the room. "I managed on my own. I always do."

"You're not alone anymore," he leaned closer but before he could kiss me, I scooted off his lap.

"I dreamed of you."

"Yes," he reached for me but I scooted further down the couch. I couldn't think with him touching me and I really needed to think. "It's another side effect of the blood sharing. There's some of me in you now, so I can seek you out. I can enter your mind if you allow it or if you're sleeping and your defenses are down. Are you upset with me for invading your dream? It was the only option left to me."

"No, that's not it," I held up my hands when he moved closer. "Does it work both ways? If I had given you some of my blood, could you still do all those things?"

Thor's face stilled, then tightened. "You gave him blood?"

"It was an accident," my voice ghosted into the space between us.

"How do you accidentally share blood, Vervain?" Thor looked at me like I'd cheated on him.

"Look, one second I was kissing you in a dream, the next I was awake and kissing him," okay so maybe that wasn't exactly how it happened but why the hell was I defending myself? It's not like I was in a committed relationship with Thor. "He didn't get very far but he managed to nick my tongue."

Thor shot to his feet with a roar. "I'll kill him! He'll wish for death a thousand times before I'm done!"

I grabbed his hand and pulled him back down beside me. "That's very sweet but it was just some heavy petting, we didn't go that far."

Thor's eyes swirled and lightning flashed in their depths. "You make it sound consensual."

"Why didn't you tell me he was the father of all vampires?"

Thor's eyes widened as I effectively derailed his jealousy train. "I didn't know he was. There have been rumors but most vampires don't know their origins."

"Then you didn't know he could hypnotize with his eyes?" I really didn't want to believe Thor had let me go up against Blue unprepared.

"No, I didn't know," his shoulders sagged and his face fell with them. "So that's how he was able to take you without a fight. What else did he do?"

"At first, he did nothing really," I shivered thinking of how weak I'd felt. Damn but that was an awful feeling. I pushed aside the memory and went on. "Though he made it pretty clear he could've made me happily consent to anything, even my own death."

"He can do that?" I heard a tremor in his voice and it scared me even more. If Thor was afraid of him, where did that leave me?

"Yes, I believe he can," I rubbed the chill from my arms and this time when Thor pulled me against him, I didn't resist. "He said it would be more entertaining to get me the old fashioned way, through seduction. How quaint, don't you think? Oh and then when I stopped being so amusing, he would kill me."

"Did it work?" Thor had tucked my head into his shoulder, so I couldn't see his face but his voice had lost all its normal vigor.

"Did what work?"

"The old fashioned way," his hand twitched against my back.

"A little," my voice wasn't too strong either. "He was very sincere and very suave, despite all his casual threats. I might have fallen for it if he hadn't slapped me around a bit. I've never been into abusive relationships."

"He hit you?" Thor growled and started to sit up.

"It's done," I pushed him back down.

"But you didn't fall for it?"

I sat back and looked into Thor's face, a soft smile tugging at my lips. "You sound very worried, Thunder Cat," I placed a hand to his chest and felt his heart pounding rapidly beneath my palm. "Why does the idea of me wanting Huitzilopochtli upset you so much?"

"You know why," his eyes were intense, his voice the barest trace of sound.

"We hardly know each other," I don't know which of us I was trying to convince. "We've only had one kiss. Well, at least in real life."

"It was a hell of a kiss," those intense eyes started to sparkle. The lightning flashing in them took on a new meaning when combined with his sultry smile.

"That it was," my lips curved up into a half grin. "I'm not into the Aztec. I'm here aren't I? I escaped as soon as I could."

"You won't escape me so easily," his lips were suddenly on

mine and I was drowning in his storm.

I felt the fire of his hands sweep up my back, over my throat and up my face to hold me against him. His heat pulsed through me, searing me from the mouth down. Little tremors of excitement trailed along my skin and I automatically started to push myself against him.

"Wait," I gasped and pulled back, remembering suddenly what I needed to ask him.

"I'm tired of waiting," his voice had deepened to a rumble.

"You've barely waited two days," I swatted him. "If you think I'm going to jump into bed with you that easily, the gods really are crazy."

"I didn't think we'd make it to the bed at all," he looked down at the wide sofa with its soft cushions and then back at me.

"Enough, Thor, this is important. I need to finish our conversation."

"Talk is overrated," he pulled me back.

"Thor, can Huitzilopochtli find me now too?"

Well that worked. He went still beneath me.

"Shit," he cursed and then his arms tightened.

"I'll take that as a yes," I grimaced.

"How good are your wards?" He reached over the couch and pulled back both the gauze and the black-out curtain that hung over my picture window, so he could scan the front yard. I looked under his arm and didn't see anything out of the ordinary but that didn't mean Blue wasn't out there. I'd already seen how well he could hide.

“The wards will hold,” I settled into Thor. “Even against him they’ll hold but I can’t stay inside here forever.”

He looked down at me sharply. “You can block him from your mind, it’s not easy but I can teach you.”

I felt some of the tension slide away. “We need to do that now, before he finds me.”

“You're right,” he took my face in his hands. “I can do a quick, temporary block right away to tide us over, if you let me in.”

“Let you in?”

“To your mind,” he nodded seriously. “Completely.”

I sighed and squeezed my eyes shut as I dropped my mental defenses. Immediately, I felt his presence but he wasn't alone. There was a shadow there with him. Thor's presence brightened, growing stronger and stronger till the shadow screeched angrily and fled. I felt impervious shields slide into place, practically hearing the clang of metal as they fell.

“Whoa,” I blinked up at Thor.

“A few minutes more and he might have found you,” Thor had a tiny trickle of sweat dripping down his cheek.

“And you can teach me to do that?”

“I believe I can,” he smiled. “You're already familiar with warding, I felt your mental wards when I passed into your mind, so this shouldn't be too difficult for you.”

“It felt like steel walls falling around me,” I thought about how I usually meditated each morning to put a psychic shield into place. “Normally I visualize a glowing web of light surrounding me and everything that hits it, makes it glow brighter.”

“Good technique,” he nodded, “but not good enough to keep out the Aztec. You need something stronger than a web. He's had your blood, it allows him to slip in past your normal defenses. He's the one carrying the link, so it's going to be harder to shut him out than if it were reversed.”

“Like with you?” I watched him very carefully. How much would he try to hold back in order to keep the upper hand?

“Exactly,” he frowned as his eyes flew over my wary expression. “I didn't give you a blood oath to bind you, Vervain. I gave it to you to free you. If you want rid of me, the same techniques you'll learn to block out Huitzilopochtli will work on me.”

“No, it's fine,” I smiled apologetically. “Trust issues, sorry. I just want to know that there's an escape clause. I don't like feeling trapped.”

“I offered you protection, not prison,” he smiled back. “The very oath that binds us, prevents me from doing anything to harm you and in fact, requires me to do everything I can to prevent you from being harmed. It's a very old ritual, very powerful, and I've given you an advantage over me by using it with you.”

“That's what's so hard for me to understand,” I looked over this amazing man and just couldn't believe he'd want anything to do with me, much less want to watch over me for the rest of my life. “Why would you do that? You barely even know me. Am I that important to your cause?”

He looked away, the tips of his perfect teeth showing as he bit his lip.

“What?” I angled my face to peer up into his. “Why are you suddenly reeking of guilt?”

“I didn't have to use our bond to find your home,” he lifted his head but there was a thick furrow in his brow now. “I've been waiting here for you since I ran up against Huitzilopochtli's wards."

"What?" I slid a little away from him. "How?"

"When you first started killing my kind, there was an uproar," he slid back too, giving me more space. "The gods were furious that some human could kill one of us, could steal our immortality. But I wasn't furious."

"You weren't?" Nicholas crept into my lap and stretched out a paw so he was touching Thor's knee. I looked down at the feline bridging the gap between us and wondered if he was trying to tell me something.

"No," Thor smiled briefly at the the tiny paw. "I was intrigued. I've been fighting other gods on behalf of humans for so long without barely causing a stir but you came stumbling into the middle of it all and they took notice. You were what we were lacking: the human element. There we were, trying to fight for humanity without any humans even knowing there was a war going on to begin with. The other gods wouldn't take us seriously because our main allies didn't even believe we existed."

"So when I joined the party, they got worried that the rest of the humans might catch on?"

"That and..." he frowned harder, his jaw clenching enough to cause his cheeks to flutter.

"And?"

"Like you deduced earlier, most of our power comes from humans," he stared at me hard, his eyes gone very serious. "It makes it difficult for one god to kill another. Your human magic fuels us all and though we each use the power differently, at the heart of it we're all the same. We can harm each other easily enough but to bring a true death is complicated. It's almost like trying to kill yourself, it can be done but not without a lot of mental anguish. The only time I've seen it managed was under the influence of mindless rage."

"So if you killed a god, you'd suffer for it?"

"A little but that's not really the issue," he ran an unsteady hand through his hair. "Think of the power like a virus. Once someone is infected, that's it. The virus isn't going to attack another infected host, the damage has been done already. We're all infected and it's a symbiotic relationship now. The magic needs us as much as we need it. When the host is destroyed, the magic is released and will immediately search for a new host. But when all it finds is uninhabitable, it's forced to disburse. The disbursement can be unsettling for us but it's minor. The problem isn't the after effects, it's the magic itself. It will try to stop us from killing another host either by misfiring or twisting our thoughts. You have to be very strong willed or very determined to control the magic in such a situation, which is why strong emotions help."

"So what am I; Typhoid Mary or something?" I laughed but quickly sobered when he didn't see the humor.

"No, you're not a carrier," he shook his head. "You're the disease. Sorry, that sounds horrible but it's about as close as I can get. You're the source, we're merely vessels. In taking your power, we've ceased to be our own source and only the source can kill indiscriminately."

"Wait a minute," I felt my body grow still as the ramifications hit me. "You're saying that as a human, it's easier for me to kill gods?"

"As a human and a witch," he added. "You have more magic than the average human and you know how to use it, how to manipulate it and direct it. You're a lighthouse shining through the darkness, calling it home."

"Calling it home," I frowned, "like when I pulled it from you."

"Now you see why you scare them," he nodded. "Now you see why you draw us to you. The magic wants to return to its source."

"So it's the source of your magic you're attracted to," I grimaced. Go figure. I knew all these hotties couldn't really be into me.

"Partly," his head tilted questioningly. "How is that any different from being attracted to someone because of the color of their hair or the curve of their breast?" His hand snaked out and swept up my side, just brushing the underside of said breast.

"Hey," I slapped at him and he pulled away laughing.

"I'm sorry," his eyes were beautiful when he laughed. "It's just funny that the infamous Godhunter would focus on the attraction part instead of the killing part."

"It wasn't easy for me to kill any of them," I frowned at his amusement.

"I didn't say it was easy, just easier," his eyes flicked down a moment. "With that show you put on in Ull's apartment, you pretty much confirmed it: humans are our weakness."

"I guess God isn't the only one who can giveth and taketh away," I tapped the end of his long nose.

"I guess not," he stroked Nick a bit before he looked back up at me. "You realize what I just told you would cause many of my kind to label me a traitor?"

"Do you think they'd be right?" I took his hand from Nick and held it.

"No, I think I've finally behaved like a god."

"And why should a god care what another god thinks?" Oh crap, his hand felt really good in mine.

"I don't," he smiled as he leaned closer, "it's just going to make family reunions awkward."

"Wait a minute," I stopped his mouth's descent with my pointer finger. "You never told me how you knew where I lived."

"You made them nervous," he kissed my fingertip, "but you made me curious. I watched for you, followed every trace of you. I researched you; what you did for a living, your history, where you lived, and the more I learned, the more I wanted to know. I started watching over you, following you when you hunted, making sure you were safe. I know your habits. I know your motivations. I even know where you buy your groceries. So forgive me if I act too familiar with you, because I am. I know you, Vervain Lavine but I want to know you even better and I want you to know me too."

"You stalked me?" I made a little huffing sound of disbelief. "I have a god stalker?"

"Yeah," his lips twisted into a quick smile before descending toward mine again, "I guess so."

"I'm oddly okay with that," I murmured before I lifted my face to his.

Chapter Eleven

I was standing on top of a huge Aztec pyramid. It must have been twenty stories high and its base was massive. A wide row of steps cut through the tiers like an arrow shooting straight at me. Looking down that long stairway left me feeling a little dizzy. Like one wrong step would leave me tumbling forever. I blinked and the feeling was gone.

The doorway of a dark temple arched above me while the temple itself stretched out behind me to cover the pyramid's tip. From my vantage point I could see a broad avenue at the foot of the pyramid, it spanned to the right and led to a smaller pyramid. To the left, it reached out to an enclosure with yet another little pyramid, guarded by a circle of buildings. In the flickering light of torches, bright colors were revealed, painted over the stones and statues. Angular designs seemed to pulse and carved faces shift in the dancing glow, making me feel like I was in the center of a crowd even though I was utterly alone. The rich smell of fecund marshes was sweetened by the perfume of night blooming flowers. The scent was so thick, it felt like I could run my fingers through it.

More pyramids gathered in a courtyard around the main three like anxious children, reined in by a massive wall crowned with snake heads. The snakes stared viciously out at the city beyond, sending a silent yet effective warning to all who would approach. I knew suddenly that I stood on sacred ground and it was guarded by more than stone serpents. A shiver skated over my spine.

Just out of reach of the staring snakes were palaces, huge buildings with sparkling courtyards, and beyond those were smaller homes, all circling around the pyramids in great vibrant wheels. The buildings glowed white in the moonlight and there were flowers everywhere; in the courtyards of the palaces, in the gardens of the smaller homes, and in every nook and cranny they could find. Cutting through the whole city were waterways, crisscrossed by bridges, which led to an outer ring of floating gardens; patches of crop land surrounded by canals. The canals in turn led out to a huge lake which surrounded it all.

I was standing in the exact center of an ancient island city.

"Welcome to Teotihuacán, Place of the Gods," Blue's velvet voice draped over me from behind. "We stand at the center of Tenochtitlán, the home I led my people to, the city near the cactus."

His hands slid over my shoulders, the skin to skin contact startling me. I looked down and saw that my body was wrapped with gauzy white material, held in place by a thick, gold belt. I closed my eyes and tried to remember who I was. I didn't want to be here with this man, this god, but I couldn't remember why.

"You're mine," he whispered against my bare shoulder before he kissed my chilled skin. His kiss promised warmth and I turned to him, welcoming his heat.

Lean arms closed around me and a heavy veil of hair slid down to enclose us as he bent to kiss me. When his lips touched mine, he was all I wanted, nothing else mattered. I forgot about the incredible city, the chill in the air, and most importantly, I forgot to remember who I was.

I felt him lift me and carry me further into the temple. He laid me down carefully and I felt smooth stone at my back. The rock beneath me was warm, pulsing with energy and excitement. Around us, the walls were covered with paintings of priests, gods, and animals in bright colors. The paintings were violently beautiful, war and sacrifice featuring predominantly. A quick flash of terror spilled through me as I spotted a picture of blood and altars but the emotion was quickly replaced by the feel of his hands.

He undid the belt and then untied the cloth around me slowly, carefully, before laying it all at his feet. A breeze brushed against my naked skin and I reached for him, wanting desperately to be covered by his warmth. He laughed softly and I heard victory in it, victory and something deeper, something darker. I frowned, vaguely disturbed by that laugh but then he undid his own belt and let the cloth at his waist fall with it.

Standing naked before me, he truly looked like a god and I couldn't help but worship him with my eyes. I drank in his magnificent form, the sleek expanse of chest, his curving biceps, the flat plane of his stomach, the thickness of his thighs, and all that lay between them. His eyes glowed red but I wasn't afraid, I was anxious. It felt right and wondrous and I wanted it so badly that I heard myself whimper. A part of me cringed at the submissive sound but I couldn't focus on my little misgivings, couldn't grasp them, they just slid away like silk pulled through a grasping hand.

"No, my sweet darkness," he took my hand and kissed the tips of my fingers. "Don't worry, no one will take this moment from us. I shouldn't have allowed you to run from me. I should have claimed you at the start."

Tears rolled down my face but I didn't know why. Something was wrong, what was it? He began to lick my palm, then kiss his way up my arm, and I lost the feeling of unease. His teeth scraped along my collarbone, sharper than I'd expected, and I gasped. Then his hands flowed over my body like molten rock, liquid hot but with the promise of something solid to come. They rubbed away my tension, relaxing and exciting at the same time.

I felt his lips close over the crest of my breast just as his fingers went below to call forth my own liquid heat. I moaned and pulled his head closer, raking my fingers through the heavy silk of his hair. The flick of his tongue drove me over the edge. I was reeling already when his mouth sent me plummeting faster into ecstasy, his hands working their magic in tandem with his lips.

Warm flesh slid over me, then down my body. My legs fell apart to accept him and all I could think about was the feeling of his skin on mine, the strength of his muscles flexing beneath it, and the scent of him, like spicy chocolate, teasing me. I lifted my head a little to gaze down at him poised between my thighs, his eyes glowing ferociously at me.

"Tell me you're mine and let me claim you," he drew his tongue up the middle of me slowly and I writhed. "Tell me," he covered me with his mouth, licking and then plunging his tongue deep.

My throat went dry and I shook my head. Why was I denying him? He was my god, my lover, and I did belong to him, but some part of me screamed, *No!* The paintings around me seemed to come to life, the people shouting out a warning. My heart sped up, my breath coming in short gasps as I tried to pull away from him.

He looked up at me sharply, his arms holding me still. Suddenly, all I could see were his eyes, burning into my soul, filling my world with churning crimson as he continued to lap at me. He wrapped his arms under my thighs and pulled me tighter, closer.

"Tell me you belong to me," he growled, "tell me now!" His voice cracked through my mind like a whip and I broke beneath the sharp spikes.

"Yes," I fell back, finally free of his gaze, "yours."

His eyes widened and his breath puffed hot against me, sending quivers of pleasure through my limbs. I thought he'd get up and slide into me then but he didn't. He growled low in his throat and rubbed his face against me, savoring his triumph.

“So much magic,” he whispered and licked me again, “mine.”

He looked up at me and lowered his head as his lips pulled back to reveal sharp fangs. I screamed as he sank those teeth into me, all the while continuing to flick his tongue, taking blood as he gave pleasure. My orgasm rushed out of me as my blood rushed into him, washing away my terror. The sound of him drinking, sucking at me, should have repulsed me. Instead it excited me further, as if it was a normal expression of desire, something to be expected and cherished.

I lay convulsing with after-shocks as he licked my wounds carefully. Warmth spread as he blew a healing fire over me. I felt the cuts close quickly, my skin itching for a moment as they healed. One last lick and he raised himself above me, coming up my body to kiss me again. I tasted my blood on his tongue before he pulled back and looked at me with eyes gone tender despite their savage color. He stroked my face, the pads of his fingertips barely touching me, and then covered my face with soft kisses.

“Sweet sacrifice,” his voice whispered through me, “I will treasure your gift. You'll see that I can love you like no mortal man can, with the strength of centuries, and I will never give you up. Together, we will bring them to their knees.”

He slid inside me then and the feel of it was so perfect, we both cried out, our voices mingling like our bodies. When he started to move, I thought I’d shatter from the pleasure. My body was so filled with it already, I couldn’t possibly hold more. The slide of his hot flesh branded me and made me feel complete while the stone beneath me seemed to push me up, offering me to him.

“I will come for you, my Queen,” he gasped. “Drop your shields and I will come for you.”

“I don’t understand,” I wrapped my legs around him and clawed his back, pulling him deeper. I didn’t want to talk. I just wanted more of him; more and more. “I don't have any shields, just come.”

“You *will* understand,” he kissed my neck gently, the warm wetness of his tongue briefly flicking out before his fangs pierced me lightly. The pleasure crested with his bite and we came together, him pouring into me as I poured into him, a complete circle, a divine sacrament. “Now you’re mine, Vervain!”

My name on his lips sent me shooting out of the dream and I bolted upright, shaking in terror. Nick was crouching in the corner against the carved walls of my Chinese wedding bed. He was hissing at me, something he’d never done before, and I began to cry. He stopped abruptly and crept closer, as if to see if it was really me.

“I’m sorry, baby,” I stroked his fur and he snuggled back against me, purring. “I wasn’t myself for a while there.”

I let the smells and sounds of home ease into me and relax some of the tension in my muscles. I was home, it was just a dream. There, the whir of the a/c. There, the spice of the sandalwood oil I used to polish the bed. There, the heartbeat of the animal in my lap. Then the sound that should have been frightening but only comforted me more: the soft shuffling of a man asleep in the next room.

My heartbeat calmed completely when I remembered that Thor had spent the night. He didn't want to leave me alone, even after he was satisfied with my ability to shield. I'd thought it was just a ploy to get me into bed but he'd gallantly offered to sleep on the sofa. I pulled out a futon instead and fixed it up for him in my art studio. My third bedroom was used exclusively for magic so it wasn't an acceptable guest room. He'd insisted that he'd enjoy sleeping surrounded by my paintings if he couldn't sleep beside me. I'd laughed and thought he was being excessively paranoid. Now I was glad he'd stayed.

Part of me wanted to creep into the other room and crawl into bed with him but instead, I'd satisfy myself with the knowledge that he was nearby and take the comfort of my cat beside me. I laid back down and focused on adding more power to my shields. I didn't think Blue would be able to sneak into my dreams with all the shielding I'd put up but evidently my mind slipped a bit when I slept. I should probably have woken Thor but I didn't want to go running to him like a child afraid of the dark. I could talk to him about it in the morning. Hell, maybe it was just a bad dream. Maybe he hadn't made it past my shielding at all.

I smiled as the thought comforted me and turned my head into the softness of my pillow. A sharp twinge went through my neck and I sucked in my breath as my hand flew to the spot. My finger came away with a drop of blood and I jumped up, displacing Nick, who yowled at me as I scrambled out of the opening at the foot of the bed. I ran to the bathroom, flicked on the light, and stared aghast at my reflection in the mirror.

There was Blue's bite, gleaming like twin jewels against my throat.

"Thor!"

Chapter Twelve

Asgard was the home of the Norse gods. A part of the God Realm which could only be reached through the Aether. Near Earth but not of it, it lay on a parallel plane to our world with the Aether holding us together like glue. When Thor saw the bite on my neck, he immediately carted both me and Nick to Asgard. More specifically, to his home; Bilskinir Hall.

It was as massive as the man himself and not even remotely resembling anything I thought a Viking Hall should look like. It was more of a palace, an edifice of soaring ceilings, wide windows, and not a single room smaller than my entire house... including the bathrooms. It perched atop a sheer cliff that I was told guarded the entrance to Asgard. Far below it ran a channel where the lake of Asgard met the sea.

Across the sea lay other god domains, probably hundreds of them, but I really didn't want to think about it. I focused instead on the crashing of the waves against the rocks below. The sound flew up the cliffs and permeated the whole place like constant background music but the briny smell didn't reach us. All I could smell was Thor, fresh and electric.

Nicholas had settled in nicely. Cats are naturally drawn to magic (I lamented this fact every time he got loose in my altar room) so a realm built by magic probably felt like home to him. He walked prouder and stalked the Hall as if he were its true master. Okay, so not much of a change in behavior for him.

I wish I could say I was just as comfortable as Nick was but it was the first time I'd been in the God Realm by invitation and it took awhile for my body to realize it wouldn't have to fight its way out. I was tense while Thor led me to his library and chilled enough that he started a fire in the large hearth there. I settled into a leather wingback chair beside the fireplace.

"I'm going to contact Teharon," he said as he laid a quick peck on my forehead.

"Okay," I murmured, not knowing who this Teharon was or why he needed to be called but feeling way to shell-shocked to be able to muster any interest.

I stared into the flames, the fire sparking and waving wildly at me. It was so close, I could feel the heat radiating off it, and yet I couldn't get warm. The cold felt bone deep, freezing me from within. I started to shake, a fine tremor which soon turned into full blown palsy. I tried to focus on calming my twitching limbs but flashes of my dream kept replaying in my head. Red eyes staring at me tenderly, dark skin glistening in the firelight, sin-black hair swinging in a shining arc, and those teeth.

I fell off the chair and landed on my knees, covering my face with shaking hands as I cried out in denial. The shame hit first, crawling up my throat to choke me. I told myself that I'd done nothing wrong, that the shame was his for taking advantage of my dream-bewildered self and that nothing had physically happened but still it consumed me. He'd made me want him, want what he'd done to me, and that was the greatest damage of all.

I didn't fight him. I hadn't even known that I should have. He'd stolen my ability to defend myself, my right to say no. He'd made me complicit in my own rape, turned me against myself. He had defiled more than my body, it was my mind, and in doing so, he'd planted a seed of doubt. I could feel it taking root, spreading out through my veins and arteries. Pulsing through my blood like a pathogen was the idea that I wasn't strong enough. I wasn't going to win this war. I was a human trying to fight gods and my abilities just wouldn't make the cut.

I remembered the sharpness of his teeth in my neck and then lower, the vivid memory of him lying between my thighs made my face heat. I squeezed my eyes shut, rubbing at my forehead as if I could simply smooth away the horror. My cheeks were wet and I wiped at them distractedly, then pulled my hands away to stare at the evidence of my tears. Weakness.

"Oh, hell no," I felt my upper lip curl into a snarl as I picked myself up off the floor. "I may not be a goddess but I am a witch and I'm not without power." I'd be damned if I'd let that son of a bitch destroy me with one little dream. "Next time I'll know better. Next time you'll be the one wiping away tears, you bloodsucking bastard!"

I felt the vow settle inside me, forcing out the poison he'd left. I may not win the war but I wasn't going to sit it out, crying in a corner, just because Blue had got the better of me in dreamland. I pushed away the lingering visuals with determination and decided I was done brooding on it. I needed to distract myself with something else. I lifted my chin and looked around the room with more interest.

I was in a very English looking library, two stories high. There was a little ladder attached to the wall on casters which could travel about the room along a brass rail. In one corner of the library was a tiny painting displayed in a very large and ornate gold frame, which perched on an easel. A small light attached to the top of the frame illuminated it gently. Was that a Renoir? I sniffed away the last of my tears as curiosity caught hold of my artist's heart and thawed the chill away.

Nearby was a long mahogany table scattered with books, some were spread open as if in the midst of being read. A few chairs clustered around the table but the main seating was more centrally located, in the form of a couple sofas and wingbacks like the one I'd originally been deposited into. The room was all shiny wood and maroon leather with plush hunter green carpeting. For me, it was love at first sight.

I got up and walked around the library in a daze. My

fingers trailed over the leather spines, the embossed gold titles. Mark Twain, Jane Austen, Shakespeare, it went on and on. Most of the books were costly, some were probably priceless. I peered into a glass case installed directly into the floor-to-ceiling shelving. A book was propped open, revealing delicate drawings interspersed with loopy script in sepia ink filling every inch possible on its aged linen pages. A brass plate beneath it read: Leonardo da Vinci *Codex Leicester* 1506-1510.

"Holy Shit," I breathed as I reverently touched the glass.

"You like Leo?" I hadn't even heard Thor return.

"Leo?" I spun around to gape at him. "What, were you like friends or something?" I laughed, then started to choke when he merely raised a brow. "Mother-of-pearl! You really did know him, didn't you?"

"I've been around for awhile, Vervain," he chuckled and the man beside him joined in. "Leave it to you to be more impressed with an artist than a god."

"Leonardo da Vinci wasn't just an artist," I sputtered, "he did much more than paint. That book right there is proof of it. He was a genius."

"Hmph," Thor smirked. "He was a step away from insanity, taking all the stories I used to tell him about Atlantis and trying to turn them into reality."

"Stories?" I lifted a brow. "Are you trying to tell me that you were Leonardo's muse?"

"Yes, well," Thor frowned and the man beside him laughed harder, hitting him on the shoulder.

"She's more charming than I expected," Thor's friend said.

The newcomer was bare-chested and I wasn't complaining.

That chest was as much a masterpiece as any da Vinci; wide, smooth, and sculpted. It should have been on display in its very own glass case. His hair was long, down to his waist, and it was loose except for a thin braid that ran down the side of his face. The braid was wrapped with leather and adorned with a white feather tipped with red.

His large, long-fingered hand reached out to take my own and I forced my gaze up to his. There I saw one of the most serene faces I've even seen on a man. High forehead and cheekbones with a widow's peak, a square chin, and strong lips. His nose was long and proud. His eyebrows, like raven's wings, curved delicately over almond-shaped eyes and had an upward flip at the ends. It was a beautiful face but it was the bright turquoise of his eyes which really made it striking. Against the rich brown of his skin, those eyes seemed to glow, demanding attention till everything else simply became background.

"Vervain Lavine," the rich smoothness of his voice flowed over me. "I'm Teharon of the Mohawks."

I cocked my head and stared at all that pretty hair again. "Did you miss the memo on the hairdo?"

His eyes crinkled when he laughed. "I'm not a warrior, I'm a healer. They call me *He who holds Heaven in his hands*."

I had to clear my throat twice before I could speak again and even then, it came out a little hoarse, "I bet they do."

"I brought Teharon here to teach you to spirit-walk," Thor growled, "not flirt with you."

"I'm not flirting," I felt my face heat. "Okay maybe a little but I can't help it, you're all gorgeous. What's a girl supposed to do?"

"*Choose*," Thor rumbled and Teharon laughed louder.

“Be at ease, Thunder God,” Teharon patted Thor's shoulder, reaching up since Thor was a good foot taller than the Indian. “I came to teach, not steal, there's no war-party at my back.”

“Oh great, an Indian joke,” Thor sighed and took the chair I'd vacated by the fire.

“What's spirit-walking,” I was finally regaining my brain power, “and why do I need to learn it?”

“Thor has told me about your situation,” Teharon gracefully sank to the floor and sat, well, Indian style. He gestured to the floor before him and I sat as well. “I know of Huitzilopochtli's powers. His ability to control minds is great but like all great magics, it has its limitations. It only works with him in the vicinity. The greater the distance between him and his intended victim, the less control he has. When he took your blood, he was able to form a link with you that has let him surmount this restriction. With his bite, he has strengthened the link even more. That he was able to do so in a dream is troublesome to say the least.”

“You're telling me,” I sniffed.

“I can show you how to use that link,” Teharon continued, “turn it around on him. With proper training you could not only protect yourself from his invasion but invade his mind in return.”

“This could be the chance we've been waiting for,” Thor leaned his forearms on his knees to get closer to the conversation. “They know we have their plans now, so they'll most likely alter them but if you can peer into the very mind of one of their most aggressive leaders, we'll have the upper hand once more.”

“I'm game,” I smiled at Thor's relieved expression. “What do I need to do?”

Chapter Thirteen

Two hours later, I had the basics mastered. I knew how to find my link with Blue and project my consciousness down it. I knew how to slip quietly through his mind and filter through his thoughts so he wouldn't even know I was there. I knew how to protect myself from him by not only building shields around my mind but by shielding off his link *inside* my mind. I'd learned, processed, and practiced as much as could be practiced without actually doing the deed.

Thor had long since left the library. The process was tedious and involved a lot of silent communication through meditation between Teharon and I. He shared parts of his mind with me so I'd be able to get the feel of sifting through someone else's thoughts. I was shocked and so grateful that he'd allowed me the intimacy. Teharon's thoughts were peaceful. He was a man who pondered, who took the time to consider things like consequences. It was a calm night to the violent glare of my own mind.

"I think you've trained enough for now," Teharon nodded and let go of my hands.

"You think I'm ready then?" My heartbeat sped up. I wanted to get in that bastard's head and get some retribution.

"No, I just think you need a break," he smiled gently.

"I don't need a break," I huffed in disappointment. "I need to get into his head. We continue."

"After lunch," Thor announced from the door.

I turned to find him leaning there with his arms crossed, looking at me with a small smile and a large possessiveness which was both thrilling and extremely annoying. He also looked amazing in a lime-green, silk, dress shirt and black slacks that clung to his muscular thighs in just the right amount. The green showed off the strawberry highlights in his hair, turning it into a richer copper color. I was so caught up in admiring him that it took me a second to realized that the man from the peace rally was standing behind him, watching our exchange avidly.

"What are *you* doing here?" I blurted in surprise.

"I live here, woman," Thor frowned, "this is my home. I'll go where I please."

"Not you, you ass," I got to my feet and walked around Thor to gesture at the man who had recently been ousted to me as a swan-shifter, "Fiachra."

Swan boy's brows rose and his deep, ivy eyes widened. "How do you know that name?"

"Did you just call me an ass?" Thor interrupted.

"I met your father," I glanced at Thor, "and yes, I called you an ass."

"I go by Finn now," Fiachra-now-Finn reached out a hand and I shook it.

"Vervain Lavine," I offered my name.

"I've been anxious to meet you, Vervain," he released my hand slowly, sliding his fingers along mine. "I owe you my life."

"All in a good day's work, sir," I put my hands on my hips, puffed out my chest, and did my best cop impersonation.

His eyes lingered a little too long on my chest, even though the jeans and sweater I had on were pretty modest. I raised a brow when he finally raised his gaze and he had the grace to look embarrassed.

"I'm sorry, I caught a glimpse of you before and thought you were pretty. Now I find that I've severely underestimated your appeal."

"Yeah, a lot of men underestimate me," I tried for flippant but the blush still crept up my neck. It must be that feast or famine curse and boy was it feasting time. I almost felt the need to do a little happy dance. Almost.

"We've yet to finish discussing your insult, Vervain," Thor took my arm and escorted me to a loveseat.

"Thor, you might as well learn this now," I sat down and he took the seat right beside me. "I will probably insult you a lot. It just shows how comfortable I am with you."

"So you only insult people you like?" He chewed at his lips and frowned, then the tip of his tongue rolled his bottom lip beneath it.

"No, I insult people I don't like, worse," I forced my eyes away from his lips, wondering if he was doing it on purpose.

"You're a strange woman," Thor looked up briefly as the other two men joined us.

"That I am," I laughed. "Welcome to Vervain World, party on, excellent."

Thor looked at Teharon. "Did you understand any of that?"

"It's a movie reference," Ull smirked at us from the door. "You're getting old, Dad."

"Of course I am," Thor glared at Ull, "older and more powerful every day. Remember that, infant."

"I'm sorry to interrupt this witty repartee," Finn focused on me, "but did you say you met my father? Does that mean he was with Huitzilopochtli?"

Oh poop, I hadn't thought about having to tell the son that good ol' Dad wanted him dead. Surely Finn knew his father's intentions but what if he didn't? I should probably tread carefully.

"Yes and yes," I nodded. How was that for careful?

Finn took a deep breath and let it out slowly. "He tried to kill me, didn't he?"

"Sort of," I tried to keep the pity from my voice but some must have leaked through because Finn laughed bitterly.

"My father does not do *sort of*, Vervain," Finn grimaced.

"No, I don't expect he does." A vision of the cold-hearted man popped into my head, his face closed down, cut off from emotion. "Let's just say he didn't try to prevent it."

"What did Lir say to you?" Thor put his arm behind me on the couch, attempting that sly move normally reserved for movie theaters.

"Not a lot," I let his hand slip onto my shoulder without comment and shook my head at the triumph in Thor's eyes. "He said his children had been plaguing him, whatever that means."

"Did he tell you about my curse?" Finn looked grim, sidestepping my implied question.

"Yeah," I stared at all that male beauty and wondered how it looked in swan form.

"I'm a black swan," he smiled at my raised brows. "You looked curious."

"I'm sorry," I smiled ruefully. "You must get tired of it."

"Not from beautiful women," he made a slight bow. "I'll shift for you if you'd like to see."

I felt my body twitch at his words, intrigued despite myself. I don't know for sure why the thought of him transforming into a swan did it for me but it did. Maybe it was the idea of seeing someone so masculine change into something so sublimely graceful. Zeus bagged a Queen with his swan form so I wasn't the only woman who found the idea interesting. Or maybe it was simply the way Finn had said it; with an Irish purr which seemed to imply that everything he did was sexy.

I swallowed hard and cleared my throat when I noticed all of them watching me with different types of interest. Finn's eyes were wide and bright, Ull's were twinkling with mischief, Teharon's were calm but knowing, and Thor's were narrowed and twitchy around the edges.

"Maybe some other time," all I could manage was a whisper.

"Anytime, anyplace," Finn claimed my hand and kissed my knuckles.

Thor moved so fast, I barely felt it. One second he was sitting beside me, the next he was holding Finn off the ground by his shirtfront. I had a passing thought that the shirt was going to be horribly wrinkled and possibly ruined.

"You accept my hospitality and then insult me by trying to seduce my woman?" He shook the smaller man but Finn only laughed.

Finn patted Thor's forearms like an old friend. "All's fair in love and war, especially with a woman as rare as our Vervain."

"She is not *our* Vervain," Thor's voice was taking on the deep rumble of thunder that seemed to precede his storms.

"Okay," I stepped up and slapped Thor's ass hard, the downward swipe-slap that really stings. "I've had just about enough of this."

Thor almost dropped Finn but managed to reassert his grip at the last second as looked over his shoulder at me. "You spanked me?"

I almost laughed at him but I valiantly controlled myself. "You're behaving like a child so you'll be treated like one and for your information, you've called me *woman* twice within the last thirty minutes. I happen to already know my own sex and have no need of your reminders."

"What?" Thor lowered Finn to stare at me in confusion.

"Stop calling me *woman*," I snapped as I took both of his hands, gently liberating Finn's shirt. "It makes you sound like a caveman."

"It's an endearment," Thor let me lead him back to the loveseat as Finn tried to smooth out his shirt... totally called that one.

"No, honey," I patted Thor's leg after he sat down. "See, that was an endearment, *woman* is not. Would you like me to call you *man*?"

"It would be better than *ass,*" he said with a grimace.

The room was quiet for about two seconds before all four of us started laughing at Thor. It was just such a perfect, dry delivery and his expression was priceless. By the time we were done, tears were streaming down my face.

"Okay," I held my hand out to him, "I won't call you *ass* if you don't call me *woman*, deal?"

"Deal," he nodded and we shook on it. See, I can compromise. "Now how about lunch?" Thor got up and helped me to my feet. "We can talk over pizza."

"Pizza?" I followed him out into the hallway. "Is it delivery or DiGiorno?"

"Neither," Ull laughed while Thor looked confused again. "I picked it up on my way. Hope you like Chicago style."

"I love it," I smiled as the scent of garlic, tomatoes, and buttery crust filled my nose. "Where'd you get it?"

"Uh, Chicago," Ull gave me a *duh* tone.

"You went to Chicago for pizza?" I blinked in surprise.

"It's just as far as anywhere else from here," he laughed at me.

"Oh," I felt like an idiot, "right."

I walked into the dining room and just stood and stared for a second before recovering and following Thor to a seat. Imagine a Viking dining hall; long trestle tables, stone walls with torches poking out of them, piles of fur, poles for practicing your ax throw, those kind of things. Okay, got it? Bilskinir's dining room was nothing like that.

The table was made of wood but that's where the similarities ended. It was mahogany, polished to a mirror-shine, the kind that would make your glass do the condensation-slide eerily across the table without anyone touching it. The dining set looked modern American but everything else in the room looked Indian, as in India, forehead dot not feather. There were saris instead of curtains and carved fretwork adorning everything. A mirror edged in brass was hung at the far end of the room. It loomed over a statue of an elephant holding a bowl of marigolds balanced precariously on its tusks.

The walls were gleaming white marble and the floor was covered in a enormous Persian carpet. A double-domed ceiling was adorned with brass lanterns hanging on long chains from their apexes, and the windows were actually arched doorways. Their wide curves were separated by sinuous columns and they opened to a balcony filled to overflowing with plants. The sound of surf and the cry of birds trickled in on the breeze.

Gods sure did know how to decorate. Maybe there was a god who was good at interior decorating. The God of Décor. He was probably gay with a really thick French accent.

"Damn," I whispered in awe as I looked down at my gilded china plate with its huge piece of cheese-oozing pizza.

"Something wrong?" Thor sat in an elaborately carved chairs on my right, once again ignoring the seat at the head of his own table but somehow commanding the room nonetheless.

"Nope," I smiled and took a bite. The pizza was unbelievable. "Everything's just perfect."

"Good," he poured me some red wine and the food was suddenly lead in my belly.

"Uh, do you have white?" Flashes of my dinner with Blue and his glass of *wine,* snapped into focus.

"Sure," he frowned, taking my glass for himself and replacing mine with his fresh one. He poured me some white wine, staring more at me than my glass. "What is it?"

"Nothing I want to talk about right now," I took a swig and felt some of my strength return.

"Alright," Thor gave me a quick nod and let it go, bless his little Viking heart.

"Ah, we have perfect timing I see," Pan sauntered in, followed by Horus, Persephone, Brahma, Mr. T, and Mrs. E.

"Help yourself," Thor waved at the open pizza boxes at the end of the table. "I called you all here because we've had a new development."

"Oh?" Brahma took the seat on my left and reached immediately for the red wine. I looked away. It was going to be a long time before I could enjoy a glass of red again.

"I think it's safe to assume they won't be following the *Make War* list now that they suspect we have it," Thor's arm crept around the back of my chair as he leaned back and addressed his friends. "So it's fortuitous that Vervain now has a link to Huitzilopochtli."

"A link?" Mr. T stopped with his fork lifted halfway to his face (Chicago style needs a fork).

"Huitzilopochtli bit Vervain but Teharon is training her to use the mark as a way into the Aztec's mind," Thor spoke into the shocked silence. "With a little luck and a lot of skill, we should have some information very soon."

"Yeah, like right after lunch," I started shoveling pizza faster into my mouth. The sooner I could become competent at spirit-walking, the sooner I could find out what Blue was up to, and the sooner I could kick his mind-raping ass. The thought brought back my appetite fully.

"Slow down, Vervain," Teharon shook his head at me. "You won't be ready until we've completed at least one more session. You definitely won't be trying it tonight."

"But..." I gaped at him, a small piece of pizza falling forlornly off my fork.

"No," he shook his head again, more firmly.

"Thor?" I looked at Thor for help.

"I think you should listen to the expert," he shrugged. "What's a couple more days in light of your safety?"

"Fine," I grumbled, "but we're doing it first thing when I

come back tomorrow."

"Come back?" Thor dropped his arm from my chair and turned to face me. "I thought you'd stay the night."

"Oh really?" I raised a brow at him.

"I brought your cat and everything." The entire table was watching our exchange like a tennis match. Back and forth, back and forth.

"I know. I'm taking him home with me," I took another bite of pizza, took my time chewing it, then looked up at him. "I like sleeping in my own bed and I'm perfectly safe now. I may not be up to spirit-walking but I'm solid as far as shielding goes. Isn't that right, Teharon?"

Teharon frowned a little at me, clearly not pleased that I involved him in our argument, but finally nodded. "She's more than competent enough with her shielding now. She should be safe in her own home."

"See?" I smiled smugly at the sullen Thor and sent Teharon a grateful look.

Chapter Fourteen

A loud knocking on my front door startled me and when I lost my concentration, my magic surged. It proved to be just the thing I needed though, blowing open the box I'd been working on for hours.

“Yes!” I held up my gloves and kodachi triumphantly while I kicked the box that had previously held them hostage. Then I did a little victory dance, waving my weapons in the air with glee before laying them down. “Who is it?” I called as I continued my dance down the hallway and to the front door.

“Ull,” came the reply. “You okay in there?”

“Yeah, I'm fantastic,” I opened the door to Ull's smiling face. “What are you doing here?”

“Dad was getting impatient,” he smirked. “He was about to come down here and get you himself but I talked him into being more subtle and sending me. You gonna ask me in or what?”

“Enter and be welcome, Ull,” I stood aside, Nick peering around my feet and adding his meow to the welcome.

“Thanks,” Ull reached down to scratch the cat's head before coming in. “Nice place,” he looked around curiously. “So what are you doing in here that's got you so excited?”

“Huitzilopochtli sealed my gloves and sword in a box and I’ve been trying to find a spell to get them out. I finally succeeded.” I headed back to my altar room, waving for him to follow.

“Your Wolverine gloves?” Ull was a fan of the X-men too.

“No, my opera gloves, I’m just dying to see La Bohéme,” I

crossed my eyes and stuck my tongue out at him as I sat back down in the white outline of a circle which was painted on the floorboards in front of my altar.

Ull whistled sharply as he looked around at the shelves of books, bottles, and assorted witchcraft paraphernalia. He picked up a piece of mammoth ivory carved into an offering bowl with intricate knotwork along the sides. His fingers traced the delicate carvings before putting it down and moving to my altar. I was about to tell him not to touch anything, when I noticed that his hands only hovered. I watched him a bit more, observing how his fingers wavered over my tools like they were dancing in a breeze, before I pulled my discarded book back into my lap.

As soon as I reached to close the book I'd been using, Ull turned sharply to point at the book. “Where did you get *that*?”

“It belonged to Ku.”

“Oh,” he sat down next to me and ran a finger along the edge of the cover. “You killed him right?”

“Yeah, I was trying to prevent myself from becoming his next sacrifice at the time.”

“Hey,” he held up his hands in surrender, “I don’t have a problem with you taking out the competition.”

“Hmmm,” I closed the book. “Speaking of competition, I met your mother.”

“You think of my mother as competition?” His mouth twisted in mirth.

“More importantly,” I pushed at him, “she thinks of *me* as competition. She would’ve decapitated me while I slept if Blue hadn’t told her to back off.”

“Blue?”

"Sorry," my face burned red. "I mean Huitzilopochtli."

"You have a pet name for the big bad vampire god who kidnapped you? What is this, Stockholm syndrome?" He had totally sidestepped the part where his mother had tried to kill me.

"It's not a pet name," I rolled my eyes. "He thought the same thing. Do they give all you guys the same script or what? I was getting tired of his long-ass name so I shortened it, that's all."

"How is Blue short for Huitzilopochtli?" Ull narrowed his eyes.

"It's not, it's short for *Blue Hummingbird on the left*, the English translation of Huitzilopochtli."

"I bet he liked that," Ull chuckled, sharing my delight in Blue's irritation.

"He was thrilled," sarcasm dripped from my words. "Especially when I told him how apt a description it was going to be of certain parts of his body if he continued to chase me."

"You said you'd give him blue balls?" Ull roared, smacking the floor beneath him. "Holy shit, woman, talk about balls, you've got brass ones."

"Why, Ull," I batted my lashes at him and slid into my southern belle accent, "you say the sweetest things."

He picked up the remnants of Blue's wood box, still laughing a little as he looked it over. "What did you use, a sledgehammer?"

"Ha ha," I smirked. "I needed to use god magic."

"Oh hey," he dropped the box and moved backward in the conversation. "So you met Mom?"

"Uh, well, noooo, not exactly," I extended the no to convey

my annoyance. “I got to listen to the dulcet tones of her voice but I never had the pleasure of actually meeting her. She woke me up by screaming at Blue to let her in so she could chop my head off for bewitching her husband.”

Ull snorted. “She said she was going to kill you for bewitching Dad?”

“Yeppers.”

“Whoa, Mom needs to move on,” Ull shook his head sadly.

“How long has it been since they um, divorced?” I wasn’t sure god unions worked the same as human ones. I mean it wasn’t like they had to file paperwork.

“About five-hundred years, give or take,” Ull shrugged and when I gaped at him, he laughed. “Some of us hold grudges a long time.”

“Grudges sure,” I snorted, “but she’s just plain in denial. How can she possibly think he’s still her husband?”

“She can think whatever she likes,” Ull grimaced, “she’s a goddess.”

“She’s an Atlantean and so are you but I’m not going to argue semantics,” I huffed. “Either way, she would’ve killed me for nothing because I’m not sleeping with Thor.”

“You’re not?” Ull waggled his brows at me. “So you’re available?”

“What she meant to say,” Thor’s booming voice cut in, “was that she’s not sleeping with me *yet* but she will be… soon.”

“Holy shish kebabs,” I flinched and turned to see Thor standing in the doorway. “How'd you get in here?”

“You invited me, remember?” He frowned as if I was daft.

"Once," I glared at him. "That doesn't mean you can just waltz on in whenever you like."

"You want me to knock?" His brow furrowed.

"It would have been polite, yeah." I got to my feet. "I could've been doing something."

"Yeah, like me," Ull just had to pipe up.

"Stay away from her, Ull," Thor growled and Ull just smiled bigger.

"Fine, whatever," I pushed Thor back out the door. "Let me get my purse and we can go."

"Good," Thor calmed a little. "Teharon is waiting. He thought you'd be there already since it was you who was so eager to get into Huitzilopochtli's head."

"Blue," Ull corrected and I shot a glare over my shoulder at him.

"What?" Thor started to look confused again.

"Blue," Ull was all smiles. I guess he figured if he wasn't going to get to screw me, he'd just screw *with* me. "It's what Vervain calls Huitzilopochtli. It's her little pet name for him."

We were losing Thor to his storm eyes again. Great.

"It's not a pet name and I will make you pay for that, Ull." I pointed viciously at him.

"So what is it then?" Thor's voice was tight with irritation and I was getting irritated about defending myself to a man I wasn't even technically dating.

"It's a simple shortening of his English name and I intended it to be insulting." Okay, that was a stretch but I didn't think Thor would like the idea of me teasing the bad guy.

"You were trying to insult him by calling him Blue?" Thor narrowed his eyes. "I can think of several things more insulting, right off the top of my head."

"She told him it would be the color of his balls if he kept trying to boff her," Ull's voice inserted helpfully.

"You what?" I didn't know if Thor was going to laugh or choke.

"Well not in those precise words," I mumbled.

Thor settled on laughing. He laughed and laughed and laughed. The shelves shook, the windows rattled, and Nicholas came zipping through the hallway to hide in my bedroom. I may have cringed a little.

"You are lovely," Thor grabbed my face and planted a kiss on my nose.

"For telling some dude I'd give him blue balls?" I couldn't see the *lovely* in that.

"For defying him with humor when most women would have cried, laid down, and..."

"Closed their eyes and thought of Mother England?" They both raised their brows at me. "What?"

"Nothing, darling," Thor squeezed me against him and I remembered the dream with him on the beach. So he had called me darling. Then he whispered in my ear, "You just have a way with words."

Sweet tingles spread out from the spots his warm breath hit. I pushed him a little and rubbed at my ear as he laughed. I was doomed, so doomed.

Chapter Fifteen

“I'm just not convinced you're ready,” Teharon said for like the fiftieth time. Or maybe the third.

“I'm done waiting,” I growled. “Let's just do this.”

I'd been over and over the same exercises with him for hours. I knew what to do, the only thing left was practical application.

“I guess we can give it a try,” he sighed.

I let out a whoop before kissing his cheek. “Thank you. I know I can do this, Teharon.”

“I don't doubt that you know what to do, Vervain,” he looked really worried. “There's just a big difference between knowing and doing. There's so much that can go wrong.”

“And you'll be here to help me if something does,” it was the same argument I'd been using for half an hour. There really wasn't a need to repeat it except that it seemed to finally be sinking in.

“Alright,” he scooted back on the library's floor to give me some space. “Close your eyes and sink into your subconsciousness like I taught you.”

“Okay,” I smiled, “sinking.”

“Find that part of yourself that seems hollow,” he kept coaching but his voice soon became distant, as if he'd retreated to the far side of the room even though I knew he was still seated right in front of me. “There should be impenetrable walls around this emptiness. Let them down slowly, carefully and gently.”

I found the place where Blue had taken a piece of me, easily enough. I'd erected psychic walls around it that I pictured as thick, seamless steel. I reached for the top of the steel box and began to push it down gently. Something slipped, I pushed too hard, was too eager, and the walls fell apart with the clang of a large bell, reverberating through my head.

"No! Gently!" Teharon cried.

"I know," I mumbled in my half aware state but before I could say anything more, I felt Blue surge through the unguarded hole.

I had no time to block him or fight back. The walls had crashed down and he was there before the echoes faded. I felt his heat seep into my mind and spread. There was a flash of crimson eyes, deadly midnight hair falling over me, and then pure panic. My entire body tensed as if to fight while I vaguely heard shouting around me. I went numb, arms falling limp, eyelids too heavy to lift, before suddenly being revived with fresh imperative, a new focus and direction.

Home, I had to go home. I got up quickly, brushing away something that was trying to hold me down. I headed into the hallway, my vision hazy around the edges. Dark shapes fluttered around me as I walked but I kept batting them away. I just needed to get out of this place and go home. Yes, home where *he* would come for me. My god and lover commanded that I return to him. I had to go.

Then suddenly I wasn't moving anymore, there were strong arms around me and I fought them but I couldn't make them let go.

"Vervain!" I heard my name and frowned. I knew that voice, it was important to me.

"Little witch," my lover whispered inside my head, blocking out the other voice. "I ache for you. I need you, do not fail me."

My chest ached at the sadness in his words. I had to get to him. He was grieving for me. How could I have been so cruel? I knew he loved me, I knew he needed me with him but still, I'd left him. I'd been vicious and spiteful. I'd behaved like a child but I'd gladly spend the rest of my life making it up to him.

Vaguely, I felt the sensation of more hands on me and somewhere in the background, I heard voices shouting but all I could concentrate on was Blue. He kept calling to me, urging me forward and lending me his strength. He loved me so much he was giving me a piece of himself so I could fight the monsters trying to restrain me.

I bucked and writhed. I twisted and kicked but I couldn't break free. I felt the cold bite of steel around my wrists and ankles, sending me into a screaming rage. I had to get to him, why were they trying to keep us apart?

"They're evil," his voice caressed me inside. "They want you for themselves. They will all use you, one by one, and then they'll kill you and toss your body into the sea. I'm the only one who truly loves you, little witch. You must come to me so I can protect you."

I fought viciously, knowing my life depended on it. Hands reached out to calm me and I bit at them, clawed at them. They wouldn't win without a fight. If they thought I'd just lie still while they all took their fill, they'd be sorely surprised. I was the beloved of a god. Nothing could keep me from him.

"Huitzilopochtli!" I cried. "Help me!"

"I'm giving you my strength, little witch. Fight them, you must use it to fight them."

I felt his magic pour through me and I strained at the chains. Something warm coursed down my wrists, which brought on another round of shouting until someone placed a damp cloth over my face. I inhaled a sharp scent and sank into oblivion.

Chapter Sixteen

I was warm. No, make that hot. I was burning hot, my screams boiling up my throat and my blood sizzling in my veins. I would've given anything for a drop of water, sold my body and soul for it in a heartbeat. The thought of the cool relief it would provide made me whimper. I would have begged but I couldn't get words past the desert my throat had become. Then something cold caressed my skin and I sighed. The cloth skimmed over my body but as soon as it left, I burned once more.

Someone held a cup to my lips and told me to drink. Heavenly water poured into me, a temporary balm; it doused the flame for only a moment. Like fighting off a lava flow with a garden hose, it merely crusted the surface until the magma moved on and swept it away. My mind was fuzzy, my brain becoming nothing more than stewed meat. I fancied that I saw flames licking at the inside of my closed eyelids. My muscles were clenching and pulsing, desperately trying to escape the inferno.

"He said only he could save her," a voice echoed through the room, the acoustics sounding strangely hollow. "Would it not be better to let him have her than to let her die?"

"She will not die!" That voice was so familiar, I almost wept. "Teharon will save her."

"No more," I whispered and heard them move closer.

I forced my eyes open and saw that I was in some kind of a cave. The sound of waves crashing echoed around me and the smell of salt filled the air. The men who had been speaking came slowly into focus. Two were light-skinned with fair hair, a third was pale but with dark hair, and the last was dark-skinned with dark hair. It was the darkest one who approached me and when I tried to move, the clinking and weight of chains alerted me to my situation. Why was I chained to a bed in a dank cave?

"Don't try to move yet," the dark one said. "I'm here to help you. Trust in me, focus on my voice, join your eyes with mine."

I looked at him as he leaned over me and realized that I knew him. His name was... "Teharon," I croaked.

A gruff sound erupted from the dark on my right but I couldn't take my eyes from Teharon. I saw the Indian make a calming motion toward the darkness and whoever it was quieted.

"I'm going to do some healing magic on you and I'd like your permission to enter your mind," Teharon's hands glided over me with a cool cloth. "The evil has settled there and taken root, so I must follow it in to weed it out."

I was about to say yes when I felt the heat rise and a voice that wasn't mine pushed its way out of my throat. "No! You will not have her!"

"He's here," Teharon spoke as he moved but I could no longer see him clearly, my eyes were covered by a red haze. "Throw these herbs on the fire and I'll start the journey."

"Teharon the weak," that voice was scathing. I couldn't believe it was coming from my throat. Was I possessed? Did I actually need a priest? Holy cannoli, I always thought all that exorcism stuff was crap. The voice went on, despite my efforts to hold it back. "You cannot fight me, healer. This one is mine and I'm the only one who can save her."

"Yeah, yeah we've heard the same routine from you all night. Try something new."

"Don't speak to him, Ull," I felt Teharon settle his body over mine and I sighed as it began to absorb my heat. "You give him more to reach out to when you acknowledge him."

My body started to convulse and the red over my vision seemed to spread through me. I would've screamed if I could have made my voice work but all I could manage was a whimper. Strong hands took mine and Teharon's heavy body held me down. I heard him chanting above me and the words spread calm through my limbs.

Inside me I felt a rush of cold, like a glacier-fed river had been released. Water met fire in violent fury, sending searing steam against the inside of my skin. The lava had reached the sea yet it continued to rage on underwater. This fire could not be quenched by mere water. It called for blood and I shook my head in denial. I'd let it burn me alive before I gave in to that horrifying urge. The effort cost me and I was panting with exertion when I heard someone inhale sharply.

"Do you see her teeth?" I think it was the one called Ull. "She's growing fangs." I hissed at him. I was so angry, furious, though I didn't know why. "Fuck, her eyes are red."

"Teharon," someone spoke carefully, like he was about to fall apart, starting with his voice. "Please, I can't fight this battle."

The man above me kept chanting, like nothing else was important. But he wasn't really above me, he was inside of me. I felt him stroking me from within, searching through every hidden part and soothing as he went. I felt the fire retreat from him. I felt the fresh water of his soul heal and renew me. It may not have been blood but water's persistence won out over fire's passion in the end. A terrible scream echoed through my head. Then the last ember was extinguished. I took a deep, cleansing breath and opened my eyes.

Everything came into sharp focus and my cooling mind began to make sense of it all. Above me was Teharon, his body still laid along mine, his chest propped up by his arms. On the right side of the bed was Thor and when I met his gaze, his face filled with relief. Beside him, Ull was just lowering his arm from Thor's chest, as if he'd been holding his father back. Finally, there was Finn, standing at the foot of the bed, and his face lit up with a bright smile when I met his eyes.

"Aunty Em," I rasped, "I had the strangest dream. And you were in it … and you …," I looked from face to face.

Finn and Ull laughed, relief amping their voices so that the sound echoed through the cave. Teharon's blue eyes looked into mine with a trace of confusion.

"Haven't you ever seen *The Wizard of Oz*?" I smiled as best as I could with my dry, cracked lips.

"Maybe you'll show it to me?" He gently kissed my forehead and eased off my body before Thor could do more than growl at him.

I felt energized and tried to sit up but the chains still held me down. "Hey, I'm all for a little kink every now and then but the group thing doesn't turn me on. So either all but one of you leaves or someone needs to unchain me."

Thor was the only one who didn't find that funny. He stepped over and unlocked my chains with quick movements and then helped me to my feet. His fingertips stroked my forehead gently and he looked into my eyes like he could see the healed parts of my mind through them. Finally, he nodded and that's when I noticed his forearms. They were cut deeply on both sides. He looked like a wild animal had used him for a scratching post.

"What the hell happened to you?" I waved at his arms.

"You did," his eyes still held a little of the horror he must have gone through and I paled as I stared into them.

"What did I do?" I sat back down on the bed with a heavy thump and stared up at him.

"Let's go back to the Hall and we'll talk there," he reached for me but I shook my head.

"No, just tell me," I held up a warding hand.

"It's nothing. I just haven't had the time to heal myself yet," he shrugged it off.

"I can take care of that," Teharon lightly touched Thor's shoulder.

"Thank you," Thor finally pulled his eyes away from me to look over at Teharon. "I owe you a great debt."

"You owe me nothing," Teharon's eyes strayed to me. "I have this odd feeling that I just saved myself by saving her."

For a second I wondered if the fever was back but then I realized I was only blushing. I was sure doing that a lot lately. I looked over at Thor and saw the relief back in his face. He hugged the Indian roughly and then turned away, giving us all his back. I thought I saw him swipe at his eyes but that's just ridiculous. Why would he be crying?

"Well, that must have been one hell of a fever to get you all so worried," I looked around at the surprised faces. "But I still don't understand why you needed to chain me or why I would attack Thor. I must have been really delirious..." Even as the words left my lips, my eyes started to widen with memory. "Oh no," I whispered. "No. It was Blue wasn't it? That bastard possessed me."

"That's one way to put it," Teharon nodded and crossed his arms.

"Another way would be?" I remembered Blue's voice and the things he'd said to me, and had to swallow back the rising bile.

"Another way to put it," Ull stepped over and sat down

next to me. "Would be to say he mind-raped you, stripped away your will, and forced his soul into your body."

"I think I like possession better," I said in a little voice.

Ull laughed and helped me to my feet. "Come on, Vervain, let's get you cleaned up."

Thor returned to take me from Ull and I saw his cuts again. "Damn it," I crumpled in misery. "I'm so sorry. I should have listened to Teharon. I never wanted to hurt you."

"Vervain, don't," Thor knelt and wrapped me in his arms as I began to cry.

Hot, frustrated tears poured down my cheeks. I couldn't believe I'd been so stupid, so foolish. Never loose your temper when you're fighting. Lose your temper and you lose the fight. I'd lost mine and let it push me into action too soon.

"It's alright, darling, they're only scratches. I've had far worse," Thor comforted me.

"Who else did I hurt?" I pulled back and looked at the others. "Are all of you okay?"

"Thor held you down until I could medicate you," Ull's normally carefree voice was low and serious. "He was the only one injured. We chained you after that."

"Oh… good," I said weakly.

"It's going to be alright now, Vervain," Thor picked me up and carried me out of the cave.

We were on the shore of Asgard's lake, at the base of the cliffs of Bilskinir. The lake was a black mirror, reflecting a gibbous moon on its surface. Gentle waves were flowing in, barely disturbing the wide expanse of water as they made shushing noises against the rocks. The rest of Asgard obeyed the admonishment and remained silent. I looked up, awed by the view of the cliffs looming over us, but it didn't last long. Thor opened the Aether and traced us through in a heartbeat.

We stepped out into a large, sea-blue, marble bathroom. There were grand columns everywhere, like the ceiling was too heavy to be supported by mere walls. Artwork was spaced at intervals on the walls, each with its own spotlight. A counter top with twin sinks stretched down one side a bit before giving up the fight and ending just short of a cream colored chaise. The window behind the chaise was open, devoid of any glass, like all the other windows I'd seen in Bilskinir. Baby blue curtains fluttered in the breeze. At the far end of the room was a white Jacuzzi bathtub with golden fixtures and turquoise tapestry curtains held back to either side of it. As I watched, the water started to pour into the tub.

"You need to bathe and relax so your mind can start to heal. If you're hungry when you're done, come out to the dining room and join us. But if you're too tired, you're welcome to sleep in the guest bedroom out here," he pointed back through a door behind him. "Okay?"

I nodded and he kissed my forehead before turning to leave.

"Thor?"

"Yes?" He turned back with raised eyebrows.

"You just saved my life didn't you?"

"Teharon did," he began to get that wounded look again. "He's in his rights to pursue a relationship with you now, even though he's already renounced the claim. God laws are pretty clear about a life for a life. If you wish it, I won't stand between you two."

"Are you kidding me?" I thought back to what had been said in the cave. "Is that why you seemed so relieved when he said you didn't owe him? Is that secret god code for *Don't worry, I don't want your woman*?"

"He never said he didn't want you and I saw the way you looked at him," Thor didn't even try to hide his hurt.

"He's hot and he'd just basically felt me up from the inside," I made an unladylike snort. "Give a girl a break would ya? I'm surrounded by sexy gods who, for some reason beyond me, seem to think I'm attractive too. I can't help lusting every now and then. I'm not dead."

"Is that Vervain code for *Don't worry, I don't want Teharon*?"

"I guess it is," I shook my head and laughed at myself. "And he doesn't want me either, Thor. You need to relax." I'd just had Teharon inside my head and I knew his feelings for me were platonic.

"Thank you," he smiled. "I'll give relaxing a try sometime when you're not being possessed by a bloodthirsty Aztec."

"Don't thank me yet, you might wish I'd chosen Teharon before we're through," I chuckled.

"Vervain," he filled my name with wonder. "There isn't a god out there who wouldn't trade places with me right now, no matter the cost."

"You know what, Thor?" I was equally bemused. "I really don't get it. I've met a few goddesses now and I know you could have a lot better than me. Is my magic really that appealing or are you all just tired of beautiful women?"

"You're a witch, you know the call of magic." Thor came to stand before me and slid his hands over my face. "Yours is like a siren's voice, singing of strength, all the more shocking for the fragile body it's housed in. Seducing with passion hot enough to burn a god and brand him for eternity. It lures with promises of love to outlast the stars and laughter to light the world. The magic inside you, the magic that *is* you, is more beautiful than any face I've ever seen."

My stunned silence turned into nervous twitching, culminating in me ruining the moment like I always did. "Most of the stars we see have already burned out. It just takes a really long time for their light to reach us."

I wanted to clap a hand over my mouth. He'd just given me the most romantic speech of my entire life and I was arguing over the lifespans of stars. I stared at him, hoping he wasn't about to take it all back. *Sorry, never mind, I thought you were someone else, someone who wouldn't babble like an ass when given romantic flattery.*

Surprisingly, he didn't get mad. He laughed, sweeping me up and around in a circle. "See what I mean, my little witch? I haven't had so much fun in centuries."

I paled as I heard the endearment and he went still, studying me.

"Please don't call me that," my whisper belonged to a lost little girl, not me. I hated it and I hated the man who'd put the fear in my voice. "It's what he calls me."

"Huitzilopochtli?" Thor's jaw clenched.

I just nodded.

"I'll never call you that again," he pressed me into his chest, the rapid pounding of his heart filling my ear. "It's going to be alright now, darling. I promise you."

"Yes, I like that better," I snuggled against him. "Say it again."

"It's going to be alright."

"No, the *darling* part," I smiled against his chest.

"Oh," his laugh jostled my face. "Anything you want, darling."

Chapter Seventeen

“I don't want you doing this.”

“Your opinion has been duly noted, Thor,” I sighed. He'd been throwing a god tantrum for the last hour. “We all know how you feel but if I don't do this, we've got no leads and everything I just went through was for nothing.”

“She's ready,” Teharon said as he placed a hand on Thor's shoulder, “and we'll be right here, just in case.”

“You were right beside her last time,” he grumbled but sat down next to me on the library's carpet.

I met Teharon's eyes and his lips twitched. I didn't bother to say anymore. I was done talking, this needed doing. So I forgot about Thor beside me, the others gathered around us nervously, and just focused. Teharon wasn't even going to prompt me this time, I was on my own.

I focused inward until I found the steel box imprisoning Blue's link. I thought about him tearing through my mind like a surgeon on Crack, cutting up my personality with insane precision and reforming me into the woman he wanted. Now it was my turn. Instead of pushing down the walls, I just imagined them slowly evaporating. The steel became gray mist and then disappeared entirely. I went still, waiting for some kind of reaction, but nothing happened. It was calm and quiet inside my head.

Now for step two. My connection to Blue was a deep pit in the floor of my mind. It seemed bottomless but I knew better. Blue was down there, hopefully unaware of my imminent leap into the abyss.

The blackness within the link seemed thick, the kind of

dark belonging to back alleys and primeval forests after midnight. Things lurked in black like that and if you stared long enough, you might see them staring back at you. I didn't want to stare at all. I didn't need to see the red eyes to know they were there, searching specifically for me. Waiting for me to be dumb enough to wander into their reach.

I crept forward, slid down the rabbit-hole, and carefully peered into a warped Wonderland. The darkness fell away and I blinked my mental eyes in the light of Blue's thoughts. I had interrupted his lunch and I don't mean food. It took all the willpower I had to calm myself and not flee in terror. After a few deep breaths, I was able to take a better look.

But it wasn't just looking.

All of Blue's senses became mine. Solid floor replaced the feel of carpet and I was suddenly standing instead of sitting The sound of the fire beside me morphed into a woman's moans. My nose filled with the scent of expensive perfume with a top note of blood, making my heart race in time with his. Metallic saltiness was sweet ambrosia on my tongue and I felt my body shudder in response, heat filling me with an almost sexual pleasure.

I pulled the woman closer, feeling her hands sink into my hair, her hips press into mine. When Blue's male response threatened to overwhelm me, I was finally able to pull back. I drug myself away from his present to search the vault of his mind for his recent past.

Memories surrounded me as the sensations of his current exploits receded and I lost track of time as I searched, filtering through them by sensing the gist like a glowing marquee above each one. I became more efficient the longer I looked, until I was able to sort through batches of them by subject. Unfortunately, there were a lot of plots concerning humanity and I had to find and trace the one he'd settled on to his final decision.

After I grasped it fully, memorizing all the details, I pulled away gently, flowing back into my own body. I reformed the walls around Blue's link and sank carefully into my physical self. I focused first on my breathing, the way it filled and lifted my chest. In through the nose, out through the mouth. I heard the fire pop, a foot shift across thick carpet, breath easing out of several throats in different rhythms. My face was warmer on the left where it was closest to the fireplace. My right foot was starting to go numb and I wasn't looking forward to the pins and needles I'd soon be experiencing.

"There is no spoon," I whispered as I opened my eyes to a roomful of expectant faces.

"What happened?" Thor's eyes were wide, on the verge of going stormy.

"It worked," I smiled. "He didn't even know I was in the Matrix."

"Good job, Vervain," Teharon praised.

"Yes, yes but what did you learn?" Horus circled me, his head cocked at a sharp angle.

"What do you know about the Russian government?" I countered.

"Enough to understand whatever you've discovered, I'm sure," Horus settled into place to peer at me.

"Okay good," I got up and shook my leg out, grimacing through the sharp pains, "because I know very little."

"Blue's going to attack Russia?" Ull had really taken to the new nickname for Huitzilopochtli.

"He's going to plant a car bomb to kill a woman named Maria Putina," I frowned as I replayed it in my head. "Well he's not going to plant the bomb himself but he's going to put the whammy on some poor schmuck who works for Prime Minister Medvedev and then make sure the guy gets caught on camera planting the bomb. How does he do that exactly? When I was staring into his eyes, he could control me but once I was able to break contact, I was myself again. Yet with the guys at the peace rally, he was barely even paying attention to them and they were practically zombies."

"It's not the eyes, that's a myth," Teharon explained. "Like I said before, it's a facet of his magic but it requires proximity to work. If you broke free from him, it had nothing to do with your eye contact. It was probably an outside influence."

"Oh, right," I thought back to those first few terrifying moments with Blue. "It was the heat rolling off him. He burned me. That must have snapped me out of it."

"That would have done it," Teharon confirmed. "He probably worked a spell in addition to using his magical abilities with those terrorists. He would have needed a boost to control more than one person, unless the people in question were really simple minded or already inclined to behave the way he wanted them to. As far as controlling someone to the point of doing something against their nature, like planting this bomb, he'd have to be in fairly close proximity to his subject. So we can assume that he'll be nearby."

"Wait, Maria Putina," Horus frowned as he interrupted. "The President's eldest child?"

"Is the Russian President's first name Vladimir?" I plopped down on the loveseat, suddenly exhausted.

"Yes," Horus sat down beside me, earning a glare from Thor, who'd been on his way over. "Vladimir Putin."

"Then yeah," I leaned my head back and talked with my eyes shut. "He wants it to look like the Prime Minister was trying to assassinate the President but got his daughter instead."

"Putin is overly protective of his young," Horus mused. "The girl is in her twenties and has only recently been introduced to the public. Her murder would destroy Putin. At the very least, it would hurt his friendship with the Prime Minister."

"Don't Putin and Medvedev both have ties to Gazprom, the Russian oil company?" Brahma asked. "If their bond goes bad, they could bring Gazprom into it, which could ultimately lead to war with the European countries they export to. The relationship is already strained from the increases in price."

"Hmph," I could barely open my eyes. "Bad juju."

"So who's up for a Russian vacation?" Pan piped up.

Chapter Eighteen

"Pulkovo Airport, St. Petersburg, Russian Federation."

"Yes, very good, Vervain," Horus patted me on the head. "That's exactly where we are. Maybe you can learn your Arithmetic next."

"Sorry," I shrugged and gestured to the view before us. "I was having an *X-Files* moment. It felt like the scene could use some groovy subtitles to let the audience know where we are."

Where we were, was standing off to the side of the main terminal of Pulkovo, watching people come and go through the glass doors. Some looked exhausted, some excited, but none of them looked like the guy I'd seen in Blue's head. I frowned as I watched a tall woman dragging an overstuffed brown suitcase behind her. It was so strange to have arrived at the airport without actually stepping off a plane.

"So where's this guy supposed to be?" Brahma sounded bored.

"He should be walking into those doors at any second," I pointed to the entrance of the parking garage. "And there he is," I grabbed Thor's hand and started walking briskly but casually after Medvedev's man.

The man's eyes were glassy, his movements robotic. He banged into the shoulder of a red-faced man bundled in black fur and barely noticed. The fur pile yelled something nasty after him but he just kept walking. He was obviously under Blue's control already, which meant Blue was probably somewhere nearby. So all we had to do was stop him from planting that bomb without alerting Blue and we'd be golden. No problem.

We entered the parking structure right behind Blue's zombie. It was Brahma, Pan, Persephone, Thor, and I. Horus was out flying recon around the airport and Teharon was on standby with Ull, Finn, Mrs. E and Mr. T at Bilskinir. Thor had thought too many of us would draw unwanted attention. As if he didn't draw attention all on his own. Please. His height alone was worth a second look. Though I have to admit, in Russia it wasn't as unusual as it was in Hawaii.

Medvedev's man headed toward priority parking, which was a row of sleek black sedans and limos. One red Porsche stood out like a whore in church but he passed it by, heading for a limo on the end with tinted windows. When I saw how far ahead of us he'd gotten, I started to jog. How had he moved so fast?

"Excuse me," Pan called over to the man. "Do you speak English?"

The man shot an alarmed look over his shoulder and then ran the last few steps to the limo. In a move any Pro-Baseball player would admire, he slid the last bit and disappeared under the car.

"What the hell?" I looked up to where I knew the security camera would be and sure enough, it had been focused right on the guy as he made his home-run slide. "Thor, we gotta get rid of that security tape. There can't be any evidence pointing to the Prime Minister."

"Brahma?" Thor turned to face the Hindu god.

"No problem," Brahma smirked as he faded into invisibility.

"Now what?" I grimaced as the bomber ran off, having completed his mission.

About ten feet away, his steps faltered, then he stopped altogether. He looked around in confusion before starting off again in a much slower shuffle. He was going to be really annoyed when he saw that big oil stain on the back of his coat.

"You don't happen to know how to diffuse a bomb, do you?" Persephone asked, her voice muffled by the huge scarf she had wrapped around her face.

"Not one of my skills," I sighed.

"What did you see happen next?" Thor asked.

"The driver comes in from there," I pointed to a door on our left. "He picks Maria up in front of the airport and they make it down the main road about a mile before the car explodes. At least, that's how Blue envisioned it."

"Okay, hold on while I contact Horus," Thor's forehead creased. "He's on his way."

"Why do we need the birdbrain?" Pan stuck his hands on his hips and pouted. He actually looked pretty cute in his cold weather gear. His hair was desperately trying to escape the confines of his knit cap and his thin frame looked good with the added bulk of the gray down jacket.

"Because I'm the only one who can fly," Horus answered smugly from behind us.

"Big deal," Pan huffed, not the least bit startled by Horus' amazingly fast arrival.

"It's a big deal when we need someone to steal a limo and then fly out the window while it's still moving," Thor clapped a hand on Pan's shoulder. "We don't have time for this. Go, Horus."

Horus nodded and ran for the car. Within minutes, he was driving out of the parking garage. I felt immediately relieved. For the moment, Maria was safe. Stranded at the airport for a bit but safe. Horus would drive the limo into a ditch and fly away unharmed. Everyone would be fine.

I smiled a bit as I watched the driver walk into the parking garage and start searching about for his missing limo. He made a frustrated motion with his arms and stalked away, muttering to himself.

"Trust me, buddy, you're better off," I chuckled.

"Hello, little witch."

We all spun around to find Blue leaning casually against the cement wall, one leg crossed over the other. He'd somehow managed to sneak up behind us. I threw my hands down, grateful that I had my full combat gear on beneath my coat; gloves, sword, knife, black leather, and my heavy boots with the hook blades in the heels. I was all set for any hurt he tried to dish out.

"Calm yourselves," Blue looked amazing in a blue wool and fur coat, his hair gleaming against the bright cerulean. "You won this round. I concede."

What do you want?" I started forward but Thor stopped me with a hand on my arm.

"So you've chosen lightning over lust," Blue's mouth twisted as he stared pointedly at Thor's hand.

"Lightning over *blood*lust, you mean," I growled.

"Did you wear that coat to match your new name?" Persephone asked Blue with a sweet smile. Oh, that girl was dangerous.

"No, to match my mood," Blue smirked at her before looking back at me. "I've been so melancholy lately. Don't you want to cheer me up, little witch?" His voice oozed sarcasm and snark but his eyes were intense. Oh, this guy did not like to lose.

"I want you to drop dead actually," I started forward again

and again Thor held me back. I pulled my arm away but stayed put to add, "And I'd be happy to help you with that."

"I just want another taste," Blue pushed himself abruptly away from the wall and we all tensed. He smiled like a shark circling prey as he looked me over slowly. "Your blood is better than ice cream," he licked his lips, "better than anything I've ever known."

"The line is *love* not blood," I shot back. "Don't fuck up Sarah's song."

"Love or blood, it doesn't matter; I'll have them both," he took another step forward.

Thor stepped between us. He didn't say a word. He didn't have to; the lightning in his eyes said it all.

"Have you tasted her yet, Thunderer?" Blue licked his lips. "She tastes like midnight, dark and sweet."

Thor frowned till he realized it wasn't my blood Blue was referring to. The air went still and crisp, static sparking like fireflies. My hair started to lift in the breeze and thunder boomed somewhere above us. I wanted to throw up all over Blue's shiny black boots.

"Sounds like a no," Blue peered around Thor as if completely undisturbed by Thor's thunder, and focused on me. "So you haven't decided after all."

"Oh, I've decided alright," I edged out to face him. "I've decided to kick your ass before I kill you."

"You don't mean that, little witch," Blue's eyes went soft and for a second I thought I actually saw a glimmer of hurt. "When you gave yourself to me, it was the most beautiful moment of my life. Tell me it meant something to you as well."

Pan, Persephone, and the recently returned Brahma gave gasps of various degrees but Thor just grew more still. A snowstorm began to rage outside, sending icy flurries into the parking garage. I spared a moment of concern for the planes trying to land before I rounded on Blue.

"I didn't give you anything, you malicious son of a bitch. You mind-raped me and now you want to mess with Thor's mind too by throwing it in his face," I felt my body go cold beneath my warm layers and it had nothing to do with the storm.

Some people feel anger as intense heat, some shake with the rush of adrenaline, some even cry as they throw punches. I get cold when I need to fight. Not numb, just a light chill that steadies me. Cold enough to kill. I'd worry about morals later, after I got warm again.

"Oh but you did," Blue's eyes brightened. "You told me you were mine. Now I'm holding you to it."

"It was a dream, a dream which you controlled!" I wanted to cut off his smirking lips and stomp on them. "You manipulating, evil-"

"Enough," Blue held up a hand. "I can wait. A woman always changes her mind."

Then he was gone.

"Not this woman!" I shouted at that empty space but then Horus flew right into it and hovered there to change back to his man form.

Horus smoothed out his ruffled fur coat, took in our tense expressions, and shrugged. "It's done. Relax."

Chapter Nineteen

"Thor, will you say something please?" We were alone in his library but he hadn't said a word to me since we'd returned from Russia. He just sat and stared at me while lightning flashed in his eyes.

"Why didn't you tell me?" His voice was a low rumble.

"It's not something I wanted known," I sighed. "Especially not by you. I'm humiliated that he controlled me so easily."

"It never occurred to you that he might taunt me with it?" Thor glowered down at me. "Do you know how horrible it felt to be blindsided like that?"

"As horrible as someone taking advantage of you in a dream?" I shot back.

"Vervain," Thor groaned. "You've suffered alone when you didn't have to. You should have told me."

"It wasn't real, Thor," I looked away from the hurt in his eyes. "It was a dream, we didn't actually have sex."

"Oh, it wasn't real?" He shoved my hair over my shoulder to expose the bite marks that had yet to heal. "What's this then; a figment of my imagination?"

"No, it's proof that I need to be more careful around gods," I muttered.

"Careful?" His eyes narrowed on me.

"I'm just saying; I'm glad I know how to shield now," I shrugged, trying to look nonchalant when I was anything but. I didn't want to talk about this, especially not with Thor. I still felt ashamed even though I knew I was the victim. “It wasn't sex, Thor. It was a mental attack and thanks to Teharon, I know how to protect myself from it now. That makes me feel safer around you too, I might add.”

Without the new shielding I'd learned to create, I may not have allowed things with Thor to go any further. But now I knew I could block him out if I needed to. Which meant that I could safely proceed with him... at least for a little while.

I know it's a little fatalistic but I had no illusions about a relationship between me and an ancient Viking god working out. Come on, it wasn’t like we’d end up picking out china patterns or anything. I wasn’t even sure I wanted to take things further with him, even with the shielding. Thor's kisses were toe curling madness, I could only imagine what sex with him would be like. Mind-blowing, addictive… life-destroying if I was denied it. If I slept with Thor and he dumped me, I may never be happy with sex again. I didn’t like that kind of attachment, that kind of vulnerability. My life is hard enough as it is.

“Safer?” Thor angled himself so he could glare at me better. “Do you really think I could ever do that to you; push my way into your mind and rape you?”

“Wow,” I shook my head in astonishment. He was sure good at catching the underlying message... and taking it to a whole new crazy level. “That’s a little extreme. I was thinking more along the lines of not wanting a god to have access to my mind after we’ve dated.”

“You just assume our relationship will fail?”

“I didn’t say that,” I sighed. Why did I say that? I knew he’d take it badly.

“You said *after we’ve dated.* That implies an end,” Thor growled.

"Well we can't date forever. We're not even technically dating now. I don't think Starbuck's counts," I huffed. "Either way, there comes a time when dating ends."

"So you're saying that even if I marry you, you won't like me having access to your mind?" He was staring at me so intently, I almost didn't catch the *M* word.

"I really don't think marriage between us is a possibility, Thor." My stomach lurched. I really didn't want to have to face this so soon. I would've liked a few more weeks of blissful denial before I acknowledged the cold hard truth.

"Why not?" His face was flushed and his eyes had gone all twitchy. I thought women were supposed to be the ones who got upset about a man's commitment issues, not the other way around.

"Come on. Did you really think this could be a long-term thing?" I searched his twitchy eyes but there was no understanding there. Was I the first human he'd fooled around with or did he just not care about the future?

"I can think in longer terms than any human can, Vervain."

"Okay, let's think about those terms." Crap, this was going to suck but it couldn't be stopped now. "Let's say we're really great together."

"I already know that," a smug smile settled over his face.

"Oh yeah, and how could you possibly know that?"

"I've been in your head," he looked at me like I'd asked how he knew the sky was blue. "I know we're compatible, very compatible."

The smile turned into a leer. I've never seen someone leer so well, expressing every naughty thing he'd like to do, by simply raising a brow.

"You're getting me off track," I pushed him back a little. "So we're good together, then what? You watch me grow old and die? Or do you dump me when I start to sag too much and trade me in for a younger model?"

"I wouldn't leave you because you got old," he scowled.

"So I'll grow old while you stay as you are and I'll know you're staying with me out of loyalty, even though you'll never touch me. *Then* I'll die." I watched him swallow that down. It was a hard pill for me to take too. My throat was constricting in rebellion.

"It's too soon for these concerns," Thor waved his hand like he could chase the bad thoughts away.

"No, it's perfect timing." Why did I feel like my world was shattering? "If this goes any further, I'll be in too deep, either way it ends, it'll hurt."

"I would never hurt you, Vervain,"he whispered. Damn but he did earnest eyes well. Maybe he'd been a boy scout, a baby god scout, whatever.

"Every man says that at the beginning," I shook my head, reminding myself of other men who'd looked at me the same way before going on to rip my heart out and stomp all over it. "Along with the old *A man would have to be a fool to leave you*. Ironically, that one's usually said right before they leave."

"I'm not a man, I'm a god," Thor grabbed me and yanked me against his chest.

"That's the problem," I should've pushed away from him but I couldn't. Maybe it was selfish but I needed some small bit of contact before it ended. Just one more little memory to take with me. So I soaked in the feel of his body against mine as I went on. "A man could actually mean those words. He could also break my heart but there's at least a chance that he won't. I could marry a man, have children and grow old with him. I could even be buried with him someday."

"That's what you want?" Thor snorted. "To live a normal life and then rot together when it's over?"

"It sounds better when I say it."

"I can give you children," his eyes were vivid with fervor. I had to remind myself that I barely knew him. This was way too soon to be talking about children. Then again, I guess I started it.

"That's not the point and what would they be anyway; Atlantean or human? Would they grow old like me or live forever like you?"

"Whatever they wanted," Thor looked away with a guilty twitch.

"What was that?" I pointed my finger up at him. "What the hell is that supposed to mean?"

"They'd have a choice, Vervain," Thor sighed, hunched over, and hugged me, pushing my head into the nook his neck made. "There are things I can't tell you about yet but what I *will* tell you is there is hope for us. Just because you're one thing today, doesn't mean you'll be the same tomorrow."

"You sound like you're saying I could become a goddess," I huffed. What poppycock.

"It's happened before."

Oh hell, he was serious.

"Kuan Ti?" I recalled the Chinese god.

"Among others," Thor leaned back and looked down at me, the surprise evident in his voice. "How do you know about Kuan Ti?"

"I met him at Blue's place. Blue said he'd been a General in the Imperial Army. He meant that Kuan Ti been human, didn't he?"

"Yes."

"You're not going to tell me anymore?"

"I can't, Vervain, it's forbidden. Just don't give up on us because of what may or may not be."

"Alright, I'll let it go for now," I pushed out of his arms and headed for the door. "But I need some time to think about this."

"Vervain," Thor started after me.

"No, don't follow me," I held up a hand. "This is me doing you a courtesy. I'm leaving before I say anything awful. Or rather, *even more* awful. In times like this, it's best to just let me leave."

He sighed but nodded curtly and let me walk out. I went straight to the tracing room and traced myself home.

Ever since Thor had taught me the spell to trace directly to my house from Bilskinir, things had become a lot easier. Especially when I was trying to leave with my dignity in tact. It would have been embarrassing to have to walk back into that library and ask him to take me home.

Of course that meant I was completely alone when I arrived on my doorstep as well as completely distracted by thoughts of Thor. So I didn't see the large shadow detach itself from the others and launch itself at me until it was too late.

The shadow and I landed together in a tangle of limbs, leather, and what felt like fur. I gasped for air as the weight of my assailant pressed into my chest. Consumed with thoughts of breathing, I kicked up with all of my might and became immediately grateful that I was still wearing my hunting outfit.

The hook on the back of my boot caught something tender on the down swing and I heard a yelp as the weight lifted and I could breathe again.

It was about eight o'clock at night and the moon was hidden, so I wasn't able to see much but a huge black shape for awhile. The shape did look a bit odd and my attacker was making some weird growling noises but even all of that in combination with the sensation of fur I'd felt earlier, didn't prepare me for the sight that met my eyes when the moon finally poked out from the cloud cover.

He stood at least as tall as Thor and was covered in a mottled gray pelt. He had the head and paws of a wolf but the upright form of a man. Yes, he was definitely male. Funny how horror stories never mention that sex is very apparent on a werewolf but let me assure you, it is. Thankfully, it wasn't all that distracting when they were trying to kill you. I barely gave his swinging package a glance before I released the metal claws from my gloves. It was a good thing too, because within the space of time it took me to release my blades, he was already in the air, bound straight for me. I spun aside and landed a blow to his arm. I knew my blades had gone deep but his bright green eyes glared at me without even a hint of pain.

"You smell like witch," his voice grated out of his throat, harsh and inhuman, and my brows rose in surprise. I didn't know werewolves retained the ability to speak in their wolfman form. You learn something new everyday.

"Yeah?" I smirked. "Well you smell like wet dog."

He lunged for me and I ran for the back yard, knocking potted orchids into his path as I went. I wanted him out of the front yard where my neighbors might see him and come to my aid. Yes, people in Hawaii actually helped when they saw others in trouble. Even when that trouble could get them seriously maimed. I thought of Tahnee and Justin next door. They'd send their German

Shepherds out in a second if they knew I was being attacked and the girls would be torn to pieces. I loved Roxy and Vasse, there was no way I'd let them get hurt by this monster.

"I like witches, their blood has a spicy kick," his voice was much closer than I expected and I ducked just in time to miss the blow he'd intended for my throat.

He caught me on the upper arm instead and I rolled away, screaming in pain. I'd never actually been mauled by a bear before but I was pretty sure the experience would be comparable. I ended up half under the mock-orange bushes bordering my back yard, and a small sound caught my attention. Nick was huddled under there as well, pressed up against the wall separating my yard from the yard next door. He was shaking and looking at me with wide scaredy cat eyes.

"It's okay, baby," I whispered. "Mama's just gonna to go kick some werewolf ass. You wait here." I clucked my tongue at him reassuringly before I rolled away and backed up to face the wolfman.

Funny but that little furball gave me the extra determination I needed to face down the monster. As pathetic as it may sound, that cat is like my child and I was as enraged as any mother would be when their baby was in danger. Mess with me and I'll defend myself but mess with my cat and I'll obliterate you. The wolfman was going down.

I ran at him just as he started forward but at the last second, I dove low and punched out at both of his knees. I kept going with my momentum and he toppled over my back. As he thrashed, one of his flailing legs caught me in the head.

My vision shifted sharply as the werewolf crumpled, howling in pain. I went down as well, battling nausea until I was finally able to stand again. I don't know how much time I lost but when my head finally cleared, the wolfman was on his stomach, crawling toward me with as much menace as a crawling thing can muster. Let me just say here that a crawling werewolf can reach deep and come up with a lot of menace.

I dove at him again, ignoring the pounding in my head and the sour taste in my mouth as I kicked him in the muzzle as hard as I could. His head spun and blood sprayed out in an impressive arc but he just shook it off and snarled at me. I know I, like most women, hold most of my strength in my legs, so it had been one hell of a kick yet it had barely fazed him. Tough bastard.

"I'm going to kill you slowly, bitch." His voice was even worse now that his mouth was filling with blood.

"It's witch with a *W* and you're the one on the ground, dog breath." I kicked him again and his arm shot out, claws sinking into my left thigh and toppling me.

He roared in triumph as I screamed. Then he lunged forward to finish me off but I stopped him with my foot in his face. The claws in my thigh shook and cut deeper, grinding my kodachi into my leg and effectively trapping it as well. His other paw batted at me as I continued to kick him. It tore through my leather pants but the wounds were minor compared to what would happen if I let up, so I kept thrusting my foot at him till I heard a snap and he went limp.

"How's *that* for a spicy kick?" Yes, it had to be said.

He was heavy but I dragged myself out from beneath him, digging into the grass with my blades for leverage. The hardest part was trying to pull out his claws. They were sharp but ragged and clung to my flesh with a final determined vengeance. When I finally got free, I crawled away from his body and stretched out on the cool grass.

It felt so good on my face. I breathed in the scent of crushed lawn and night blooming jasmine, reveling in simply being alive. I knew I was bleeding but it was only a trickle, so I was pretty sure he hadn't nicked my femoral artery. I shouldn't bleed out… hopefully. If I was wrong, I had about five minutes to live.

I made a sound that was part sob and part laugh, the small movement sending pain twitching through me. The cuts in my arm had subsided to a dull burn but the pain in my legs more than made up for it. If I lay very still, it hurt a little less. So I took slow shallow breaths while I waited for my body to stop screaming at me. Right before I slipped into a welcome oblivion, I felt a rough tongue begin to lick my face and a warm, purring body nestle into my side.

Chapter Twenty

"Vervain," a rich, warm voice, like spiced cider sipped on a winter night, invaded my dreams. "Vervain? I think she's waking up."

I blinked and looked around in confusion. There was a whole lot of blurry faces surrounding my bed and I couldn't imagine why. I blinked some more as I tried to remember who all these people were. Then it hit me and with the knowledge came the pain.

"Oh, hell," I groaned, my voice all dry and gravelly, reminding me of the werewolf. "Did someone get the license plate of that semi?"

"What, darling?" Thor's face came into view and I realized that he was curled up next to me in the bed. "Is she hallucinating?" He looked up and I followed his gaze to Teharon, who was standing over me on my left.

"I just meant that I feel like I've been run over." I smiled weakly at the Indian. "Did you save my life *again*?"

"No," he chuckled softly. "You'd most likely have lived this time. All I did was speed up your recovery and make sure you weren't concussed. Now that you're awake, I can finish." He ran a hand over my body, a bright glow emanating from his palm, and the pain disappeared.

"Thanks, bu-u-udy," I did my best Pauly Shore impression with the finger flutters and all. It was lost on everyone but Finn and Ull, who made strangled snorts. I looked around again. There was also Mrs. E and Mr. T, Pan, Horus, Brahma and Persephone in attendance. The gang was all there. "Aw shucks guys, you didn't all have to come. Flowers are always acceptable in times like these. Or even a nice fruit basket."

"We never left," Horus sniffed.

"Oh," I grimaced.

"I would've come back to see you if I had left," Persephone sat at the foot of the bed; a large, masculine bed that I was betting belonged to Thor. Looked like I was back in Asgard.

"Thanks, Sephy," I smiled weakly.

"She gave me a nickname," Persephone giggled and shot a happy look back at the others before leaning towards me. "Hey I heard you kicked wolf booty. I'm so-o-o-o jealous."

"Why? You got a bone to pick with the werewolves?" I chuckled over my play on words and then looked over at my shoulder, expecting to see scars, but there was nothing but a red splotch. Teharon had mega talent.

"Oh, I don't mind werewolves at all," Persephone shook her head. "I think they're kind of sexy actually." We all gave her horrified looks but she didn't seem to notice. "It's just that I heard they're pretty strong and you beat one. You're so cool."

"Yeah, Vervain," Pan sashayed up in his usual jeans and T-shirt. The shirt read *By the biting of my thumb, something wicked this way cums*. It had a picture of a naked nymph, looking over her shoulder and biting her thumb seductively. Pan didn't look half as seductive when he struck a pose, elbows out, hands flat under his chin as he batted his lashes. "You're my hero."

"Shut up, Pan," Persephone hit him in the gut but he just laughed.

"How are you feeling?" Thor studied my face carefully.

"Like some werewolf just tried to make me into pâté and spread me on a cracker." I laughed at his grimace and turned my head so I could kiss the hand he had against my cheek. "I'm fine, babe. Hey, speaking of the werewolf who almost made me into his midnight snack, did you guys happen to do something with his body or is there a furry corpse for Mulder and Scully to find?"

"Excuse me?" Thor had an expression of extreme pain... mental pain.

"Oh please tell me that you've heard of *The X-Files*," I begged him.

"Is that something to do with the American government?" Horus came closer, his interest piqued.

Ull, Persephone, Finn, and Pan were laughing their asses off. At least I wasn't completely alone in a room full of communist bastards.

"You're never going to be able to relate to this woman if you don't start watching some TV," Ull gave his father a pat on the shoulder. "Sounds like you may want to start with the Syfy channel."

"At least some of you understand my jokes," I sighed. "It's like I'm talking to my Grandpa sometimes."

"Yeah, except Thor's older," Pan smirked.

"Okay, that's disturbing," I waved a hand, "and a complete tangent. Let's get back to the body in my yard."

"I took care of it," Thor grunted. "Which reminds me of something else. Nick was curled up around you when I found you, so I brought him along too. I'd like you both to stay."

"As in live here?" I felt my eyes go wide.

"Yes, that's what *stay* means," he took my hand. "You're not safe alone right now."

"I like my house," I scowled, "and I don't like the idea of hiding."

"Vervain," Thor took a deep breath. "You wouldn't be hiding, just protecting yourself."

"Sounds like hiding to me."

"You're in danger there," he growled.

"Don't get mad at me, I'm wounded." I blinked up at him dramatically but then something occurred to me. "Hey, I've been bit by a werewolf. Does this mean I'm going to get hairy when the moon gets full?"

"No," Teharon's soft voice reassured me. "Werewolves are born, not created like vampires."

"Well, that's a relief," I sighed.

"Damn it, Vervain," Thor jumped off the bed so he could tower over me. "I don't want you unprotected."

"It's too soon to live together," I glared at him. "We haven't even been on a date yet."

"Again with the dating thing," he threw up his hands in frustration. "That's it, everyone out."

Thor shooed the God Squad (as I was affectionately referring to them inside my head) out the door before turning back to me. I could hear Pan bitching all the way down the hall.

"What are you doing?" I eyed him warily as he approached the bed.

"I'm taking you to dinner," he threw back the sheets and I was shocked to find that all I had on was one of his shirts.

"I think I'm going to need some pants for that," I smirked at him. “I know some restaurants have a policy of *No shirt, no service* but I don't think they'd serve me without pants either.”

“*I'd* love to serve you without pants,” he waggled his brows.

“Hmmm, maybe after dinner,” I laughed at his shocked expression. “What; you thought I was holding out for marriage?”

It could be my near death experience but I was beginning to think that I should start living for the moment, and at the moment I wanted Thor.

“No, I, uh...,” he blinked rapidly. “Are you up for this?”

“Dinner or sex?” I laughed again when his legs gave out and he sat heavily on the bed.

“Both,” he swallowed hard, “either.”

“Why do I get the feeling that discussing sex is difficult for you?”

“Not difficult,” he shook his head. “I'm just not usually so blunt about it. I either flirt or seduce. I don't really know what to say to a woman who talks about sex in the same sentence as dinner and with the same nonchalance.”

“You say yes,” I gave him a devilish smile.

“Yes,” he leaned in to kiss me.

I'd actually been concerned that I might not be recovered enough to make love to Thor but his kiss removed all doubt. Adrenaline filled me with his very first touch, spreading from my lips to my belly and then even lower. His hands on my back kneaded away any remaining tension till there was nothing left but pure, hot desire.

I pulled back, gasping, “Maybe we shouldn't wait for

dinner."

It was his turn to laugh at me. "Absolutely not. I'm taking you on a date. I don't want to hear anymore talk about us not being good together. We'll do this the human way."

"Humans have sex before dating." What the hell was wrong with me? I could wait a few damn hours.

"Yeah, it's called a one night stand," he got up and went to a large wooden trunk set against a wall. He pulled out something green and a belt. "I don't want a one night thing with you," he handed the clothes to me. "I want the real thing."

"Wow," I stood up, clutching the garments to my chest. "I... uh, yeah, that sounds good."

"Then it's decided," he ushered me towards the bathroom. "Go and change, that tunic should be long enough to serve as a dress for you and the belt will give it some shape."

"Okay," I stumbled through the doorway.

The tunic fit great, though the sleeves were a little long and had to be pushed up. It hung to my knees and looked pretty good when I belted it. Of course, the belt was too long and had to be angled into a loose knot but it ended up looking like it had been designed that way. I splashed some cold water on my face, lamenting my lack of make up, then finger-combed my curls. Lastly, I bit some color into my lips and went back out to Thor.

He had changed into tan dress slacks, a matching jacket, and a pale green shirt. With his hair brushed and shining down his back, he looked amazing. I wanted to hide my face and run away in shame. People were going to think that I was his sister or maybe his sugar mama.

"What?" He came rushing over. "Are you okay? Do you need to rest some more? I knew this was too soon. Here, let me help you back to bed."

"No," I pushed my insecurities aside and smiled. "I'm fine, let's go."

"Are you sure?" He lifted a brow.

"Absolutely," I smiled brighter.

"Okay then," he took my hand and started leading me out of the bedroom. "Where would you like to go? London? Venice? No the Venetians hate everyone but themselves. Paris? Hmmm, no, the French are just as bad. How about Brazil? Or there's Germany."

"How about Hawaii?"

"I can take you anywhere in the world and you want to go home?" He cocked his head.

"I want my focus to be on you tonight, not the scenery." I pulled him along toward the tracing room. "If we go someplace I've never been, I wouldn't be able to give you the attention you deserve. No, that's not true," I rolled my eyes at my own weakness. "I wouldn't be able to give the scenery the attention it deserved."

"We'll save Brazil for another time then," he had that grin men wear when it finally dawns on them that a woman wants them. You know they're completely clueless till it reaches the obvious stage.

"I know a great place in Kailua," I grinned back at him.

Chapter Twenty-One

"So tell me about the real Thor," we were at a corner table in Peppino's; an Italian restaurant with great food made by a real Sicilian mama. Sigh.

"You know the real Thor," he got that little wrinkle going between his brows.

"No, I know myths and I have a feeling about the kind of man you are," I paused to smile at him. "But I don't really know about *you*. Like for instance, where were you born?"

"Atlantis," he lowered his voice and glanced around the crowded restaurant. It was a little hole in the wall place and we were pretty close to other diners.

"Oh," I blinked. "So you're one of the originals."

"I was a young man at the time of the diaspora." His stare went distant. "It was frightening. The world I knew had fallen apart and my family was forced to find a new home amid a culture we knew little about. Up until that point, we had nothing to do with the people who lived on the other continents."

"What happened?" I was completely engrossed. Here was my chance to hear about a historical event from someone who'd actually been there. I'd never even considered the gods as sources for factual history. "I read about the fall of Atlantis in Ku's book but it wasn't very descriptive, more of a bland recounting. Tell me what it was like."

"The High Council," his lips twisted as he focused back on me. "Twenty men and women, our brightest minds and most talented magic wielders, ruled Atlantis. They were brilliant but maybe that was their downfall. Ever unsatisfied, they constantly experimented with powers that should have been left alone."

His hand shook a little as he reached for his beer. He took a hefty swallow and when he replaced it on the table, I took his hand. The haunted look in his eyes eased up a bit but it lingered. I was starting to feel bad for asking.

"I don't know what they did exactly," he continued. "Like I said, I was just a young man and not privy to the decisions of the High Twenty. I just remember my father's face when he came for me. I'd never seen him scared before. His fear terrified me the most. More than the earthquakes or the blue flames that engulfed the Council Temple."

"You don't have to tell me anymore," I rubbed his hand. "I didn't mean to bring back such horrible memories."

"It's fine, I want you to hear about this," he sighed. "My mother was already dead and part of me was grateful she didn't live to see Atlantis fall. But I remember Frigg, my father's second wife, holding Balder so tight that he cried out for me to take him. I had to wrench him from her arms."

"Balder is your brother?" I asked gently.

"Yes, he was two," his other hand fisted on the table. "We made it to our boat and took as many on board with us as we could. Teharon was there and Horus with his parents but I don't remember who else. It was so long ago."

"So the three of you have been friends since then?"

"Yeah," he gave me a half grin. "That was before Horus gained the power to shift. He was just a wild teenager then." Thor's smile faded as he went on, "I don't think he ever fully recovered from the horror of it. You know, he really is a good man. I hope you don't hold his haughtiness against him. I think it's his way of protecting himself. He lost three sisters and his first love along with them that day. Now it's especially hard for him to get close to women."

"I can understand that," I said gently. Horus kinda made sense now.

"You've been good for him, I think. You ruffle his feathers like Pan does," Thor squeezed my hand before resuming his story. "Anyway, we made it to the new continent and stood on the shore to watch as Atlantis crumbled into the ocean, lighting the night with blue fire."

"How many of you made it?"

"Not a lot," he looked away. "Less than a thousand out of hundreds of thousands."

"So then you just left?"

"We had managed to salvage a few things," he said. "So we made camp on the beach, took stock of our supplies, and planned our next move."

"Very sensible," I smiled, thinking that was just like Thor.

"Yes," he made a self-mocking sniff. "We were all very sensible back then. We knew the humans inhabiting the other continents were inferior to us in both intelligence and magical talent."

"So you decided to become their gods?" I raised a brow.

"No, that was never the plan," he glanced over as Claudio, the owner/waiter trudged by, yelling back at his mother in the kitchen. He waited a moment and then continued. "We planned on simply ruling them. No one suspected what their magic would do to us, what their adoration would change. Your people made mine gods. We found our divinity, our immortality, in you."

"Well, I happen to know that already but it's nice to hear you acknowledge it," I winked, trying to lighten his mood.

He rewarded me with a grin. “My father took us North, where it was cold but very beautiful. The harsh conditions bred strong men and we inherited their strength. It was a good decision. Eventually, we gained enough power to build the God Realm but it took us all working together to accomplish it.”

“Is Balder your only brother? I thought I'd read that there were more,” I mused.

“Odin's called the Allfather, so people got confused. There are a few gods whom humans say are his sons when they aren't but Dad was married a couple times after Mom died. So I have two more brothers; Vali and Vidar,” Thor smiled.

“Good for him,” I swallowed past a strange lump in my throat. I cleared my throat and continued. “It's nice that your father was able to find love again.” The words seemed to pour cold water all over Thor's improved mood. “What did I say?”

“No, nothing,” he smiled but it was bitter. “It's just that his last wife was human and when she died, it nearly killed him. It was worse than when he lost Mom. He's let it turn him bitter. It's very hard to be around him now. Only Balder visits anymore. Vali's disappeared into his beloved forest and no one's knows where Vidar is. Sabine's death has destroyed my family. The only time I see Father anymore is at Yule.”

“And yet, here you sit, on a date with a human,” I felt that lump in my throat constrict harder. I guess it was my intuition, warning me that Odin had failed in the exact same way I knew I'd fail with his son. “Are you sure you want to make the same mistake your father did?”

“There's more to the story than I can tell you now,” he kissed my hand. “Just know that it could be very different for us.”

“It *will* be different,” I took a deep breath and lifted my glass.

His eyes widened but he lifted his glass to mine and clicked it with a smile. I just didn't mention that I knew it would be different because I wasn't going to stay with him. This may not be a one night stand but it wasn't going to be a lifetime commitment either. I'd just have to deal with that bridge when I reached it.

“You change your tune fast,” Thor said after he swallowed his sip.

“Maybe it was my brush with death,” I offered.

“Whatever it was, I'm glad for it.”

“Me too,” I smiled past the knot of anxiety my thoughts were tying. “Now eat your pasta, I want to go for a walk on the beach.”

“Yes ma'am,” he started eating with enthusiasm.

Chapter Twenty-Two

Kailua Beach was deserted, an odd occurrence even at eleven o'clock at night. Usually there were at least a few lovers or teenagers partying and hiding from the occasional cop who decided to patrol the beach. Yet the sand was empty for miles, it was only us and the endless waves sweeping the shore.

"Did you do some juju or something?" I looked up at Thor.

"I wanted to be alone with you," he admitted as he took my hand.

"Hmph," I shook my head and let him lead me further down the shore. "Must be nice to be a god."

"It has its perks," he stopped abruptly and pulled me against him. "Here's another," he whispered as he brought his mouth to mine.

I tasted the hops on his tongue but I didn't mind, even though I hated beer. On him, it seemed to just enhance his masculinity, just another flavor of male. His hand snaked through my hair as he deepened the kiss, holding me tight. I groaned at the feel of his chest, hard against mine, and the tingles his hand made as he slid it down my back. Everywhere he touched seemed to come alive like he was some kind of Dr. Frankenstein and I, the monster's bride.

Lightning flashed out on the water and thunder rumbled in response. I pulled back, a little dazed, and looked up to find the flashes mirrored in his eyes. No wait, they began in his eyes and mirrored into the world. Didn't Frankenstein use lightning too? My head spun and I would've fallen if he hadn't been holding me so tightly.

“You never told me *your* stories,” his voice had gone low, sultry vibration.

“You said you knew me already,” I teased.

“I also said that I wanted to know you better.”

“Okay,” I drew back and sat in the sand, trying to push away thoughts of mad scientists and monsters. “What do you want to know?”

“Do you have any siblings?” He sat next to me, looking as comfortable on the sand as he did on his loveseat in Bilskinir.

“I have one half-sister and two half-brothers.”

“Why half?” He frowned.

“One brother is from my Dad's marriage to another woman. My remaining sister and brother are from my Mom's marriage to another man.” I cocked my head at his confusion.

“So you don't consider them to be fully your family?” He seemed surprised.

“Of course I do,” I finally understood. “It's just a way of saying that I only share one parent with them, not both.”

“Family is family,” he brushed back a strand of hair that had blown across my face. “It's silly to have labels for the quantity of blood you share.”

“Maybe. I never really thought about it,” I shrugged. “It doesn't make me love them any less. I just wasn't raised with them, so it's a different relationship from siblings who have grown up together.”

“Ah, yes. I have a different relationship with Vidar and Vali than they do with each other because they were so close in age. Even though they had different mothers, they were raised together. I think Vali saw Sabine as more his mother than Frigg. Balder though, has always been his mother's son," Thor grimaced.

"So you understand," I leaned a shoulder against him and he swept his arm around me.

"I do," he agreed.

It was amazingly sweet to sit on the beach beside Thor. All the annoyances of the beach which I usually hated were dimmed in the dark. Moonlight was kinder than sun to my skin and made Thor into a mysterious stranger. The salt breeze was gentle and the sand was soft beneath me. Honestly, the only reason I wanted to bring him there was to see if the reality of Thor on a beach at night was as good as the dream. I was shocked to find it was even more so. Thor made the beach beautiful. For me, that said a hell of a lot.

A pueo, a Hawaiian owl, flew by us, its white feathers shining in the night like a star.

"Oh," I pointed, "did you see it?"

"Yes," he nuzzled closer. "A good omen."

"Maybe if you were in Greece," a deep feminine voice startled us and brought Thor to his feet instantly, "but here you may find that the sight of an owl is quite different."

I was a little slower to rise, spending more time on locating the source of our interruption than on gaining my feet. I found her in the least likely place; walking in with the tide. I stared open-mouthed as a beautiful black woman walked up to us wearing a dress that seemed to be made out of the waves themselves. When she reached the shore, her dress broke free and formed a full hemline of froth. Upon her brow was a silver crown draped with pearls and topped with a gold starfish.

"Yemanja," Thor nodded with respect.

"Hello, Thor," her voice sweetened and I felt a terrible emotion swirl through my gut; jealousy. "Hello, Godhunter."

"Hello," I followed Thor's lead and nodded.

"Did you send the owl?" Thor took my hand and squeezed it reassuringly.

"You've never been one for subtleties, Viking," she sighed. "That used to be something I found charming but now that you no longer share my bed, I don't see the appeal. It's funny how sex changes your perspective."

"If the owl wasn't a blessing, then what was it?" Thor was being unusually patient with her and it was making me increasingly angry.

I was creating a list in my head of all the reasons this woman was better for Thor than I, the top of which was her being a lwa (a voodoo spirit) of the sea. The fact that she was stunningly beautiful didn't hurt either.

"It was a warning," she ventured another step forward but seemed unwilling to go too far from the water. "There's trouble coming for you and most of it is standing right there," she pointed at me.

"Hey now," I started forward but Thor held me back.

"I know she's trouble," he grinned, "but she's worth it."

"Then be warned and be careful, love. You're walking your father's path, treading in his footsteps, and the price may be higher than you suspected," she shook her head before looking at me. "The warning is for you as well, Godhunter. You may not believe this but I've watched over you since you were a child, even though you are not mine to protect. Do you not remember me?"

I blinked and frowned through a sudden flash of memory;

my accident on that yacht back when I was a little girl. I did remember someone in the water with me. A beautiful face on a dark-skinned woman with pearls in her hair. I'd thought she was one of the guests, come in after me, but when I concentrated, I recalled that the woman had come from beneath me. She'd never been on the boat at all... and she'd had a fish tail. How had I forgotten that?

"You," I breathed as shivers raced along my arms.

"You do remember," her voice was sweet as she smiled brightly. "You were so little. You had climbed the railing and slipped. No one saw you fall and your party dress was pulling you under. I lifted you up till they came for you. There's great magic in you, even back then it was enough to catch my notice. I knew you weren't meant to die so young and so I saved you. What I didn't know was that you'd end up seducing my favorite Viking when you got older." Her voice teased and I found myself smiling in response.

"You saved my life," I had no idea if she had ulterior motives but for whatever reason, she'd helped me once. "Thank you. It's way overdue but thank you."

"You're welcome, Hunter," she raised a hand and the owl came to perch lightly on her fingers. "Remember my warning and I just may save it again. You've become the prey. The wolves have your scent and the only way to stop them is to save them. Your gentle touch shall force them more than your force shall make them gentle." She lifted her hand and the bird flew toward us, only to disappear in a shower of stars. "Remember," she whispered and when my vision cleared of starlight, she was gone.

Chapter Twenty-Three

She's right though," we were back at Bilskinir and I was pacing the length of Thor's library. "That wasn't just a random attack, someone's trying to kill me."

"It could be anyone," Horus scoffed. "It's not like you don't have any enemies."

We had to put off the lovemaking in light of Yemanja's warning. Thor called the group together to brainstorm who might be behind the werewolf attack now that we had new information. Everyone was here, including Nick, who was curled up in front of the fire. There had been a few suggestions but only one name held any weight in my opinion.

"I've only been seriously threatened by one person lately," I threw Thor an apologetic glance. "I think it's Sif."

"Sif would come and kill you herself," Thor ran a hand through his hair, the skin around his eyes twitching and tightening. "I really don't think she'd send a werewolf. I doubt she'd even know how to contract one."

"She knows Fenrir," Brahma looked steadily at Thor and something passed between them. "And everyone knows the wolves are assassins for hire, my friend. I'm sure he'd be happy to explain it all to her."

"Werewolves are assassins?" I blinked rapidly as I thought of all the werewolf lore I'd read.

You didn't hear as many myths about the other shapeshifters, it was mainly werewolves. I'd always assumed the wolves were just unlucky or not as adept at secrecy but maybe it was the plain fact that they were hired to kill and so were seen killing.

“Well yeah,” Persephone chewed her lip. “You know it's difficult for a god to kill another god, so we hire the wolves. It's just a job to them though, they're really not all that bad.”

“Say that to Tyr,” Ull grimaced. “Fenrir took his hand off. They’re all thugs and killers, just like their father.”

“I’ve met a few nice ones,” Persephone's eyes shifted down and away as she continued to chew at her lip.

“Oh, please,” Ull threw his hands up into the air.

“Who’s Fenrir?” I was trying hard to catch up... and get rid of the images of ninja werewolves I suddenly had in my head.

“Fenrir is Loki’s son,” Thor looked really serious, not exactly the best sign. “He’s the Wolf God and the father of the werewolves.”

“Great,” I sighed and tried to smile. “So now I know where vampires and werewolves both come from. The secrets of the universe are unfolding,” I said dramatically. “Does anyone happen to know the source of the Fey? Then I could really rest easy.”

A hush fell and Thor looked at me in horror. “Don’t even mention them here, Vervain. They’ve withdrawn and we’ve no wish to summon them back.”

“Okay, okay,” I held up a placating hand. Boy, I knew fairies were nothing like Tinkerbell but I didn’t think they were bad ass enough to make the gods nervous. “So Sif knows the Big Bad Wolf. Are we talking old buddies kind of thing or just acquaintances?”

“Acquaintance is enough,” Brahma looked a little tired. “She’d know where to find him.”

“Yes but how would she know where to find Vervain?”

Thor had started pacing.

"Who knows," Ull chimed in. "*Someone* found her and that's all that matters. I have to admit, it looks like it could be Mom."

"She's never even seen Vervain," Thor walked by me and I grabbed his hand.

"Do you still love her?" The room stilled, little shuffling sounds and nervous coughing dying out to silence as everyone waited for him to answer my question, while trying to appear completely uninterested.

"Why would you ask me that?" He looked so shocked that I almost let it go but I had to know.

"You don't want it to be her," I tried to look as understanding as possible but it felt like a fist was twisting my gut, so I probably looked more pained than sympathetic. All I needed was a god with baggage. Hell, I had enough baggage for the both of us... big Louis Vuitton, steamer trunk baggage.

"Of course I don't," he went down on one knee in front of me, bringing him a little closer to eye level with me and completely consuming my view. "Would you want to believe someone you once shared a life with was a heartless killer? That they were so bitter they'd deny you any happiness, even if it meant murder? I don't want to believe that of her but it doesn't mean I still love her. She destroyed our love a long time ago."

"Sorry," I whispered, feeling like an insensitive ass. I wondered what she'd done to him but I wasn't about to be even more of an ass and ask.

"It's alright," he got to his feet. "You'll be safe here. Either way, we'll get to the bottom of it and if it is Sif, I'll take care of her. For now, I think we've talked this out as far as we can and it's time to call it a night."

I swallowed hard as I realized what that meant. The others got to their feet in agreement and wandered out to their guest rooms with a chorus of goodnights. I felt awkward after all that had happened. I'd had to face a gorgeous ex-girlfriend and details about an ex-wife who wanted to murder me. The mood was kinda gone and I wasn't sure I was up to getting it back.

Then he held his hand out to me.

He was backlit by the fire, his hair glowing red at the edges like it had joined with the flames, while his face was soft gold from the light of scattered lamps. His broad shoulders looked even wider with the dramatic shadows playing them up and when he smiled at me, he looked like every fantasy I'd ever had rolled into one.

"Are you tired, darling?" His voice sent shivers racing down my spine.

"Not at all," I smiled and took his hand, letting him pull me to my feet.

"Good," he led me to the door, "I have every intention of watching the sunrise with you."

Something tightened low in my body and my heart sped up till I couldn't separate the beats. It became one complete and unbroken note, one long vibration waiting for the touch that would quiet it. All I could do was nod. His smile softened as he walked me down the hallway to his bedroom, the artwork lining the walls blurring into obscurity. The details of the bedroom were the same, just a hazy background. All I saw clearly was Thor and the massive four-poster bed we were heading toward.

"I feel like I've been waiting forever for this," he whispered as he pulled me into an embrace.

"It's been barely over a week," I whispered back, completely fascinated by his lips.

“Not for me,” his hands snaked into the hair at my nape to angle my head up. “For me it's been two years. Two years of watching and wondering, fantasizing and waiting. Two years of wanting you here like this.”

“That's a long time to wait,” I gulped, suddenly worried I wouldn't be up to his expectations. Two years is a lot of pressure to put on a girl.

“I'd have waited longer if you needed me to,” he brushed his lips over mine. “I can be a very patient man.”

“Well, I'm not patient at all,” I reached up and held him still for a more thorough kiss. When I pulled back, I pushed his hair away from his face and saw something I hadn't noticed before. It kind of looked like a small piece of stone embedded in his forehead. “What's this?”

“Ah, that is a long story,” he grimaced. “Let's just call it a bar brawl.”

“Is that a piece of rock?” I was fascinated.

“Yes, let it go.” He started kissing my neck.

“Oh, the dilemma,” I murmured appreciatively over his endeavors.

“What's that?” He didn't even lift his face. In fact, it was slowly lowering.

“There's just so many jokes,” I groaned. “Blockhead. Rocks for brains. Sorry, I had to get a couple out or I was gonna explode.”

He finally pulled back and looked down at me like he didn't know whether to strangle me, laugh, or just ignore me altogether.

“Right,” I smiled lasciviously. “It's *your* explosion we need to be working on.”

"*Our* explosion," he chuckled and pulled me back against him.

"Rock my world, baby," I giggled and he threw his head back, making a very frustrated sound.

Then I started rubbing him the right way (yes, that way) and he groaned, his arms crushing me to his chest. My hands shifted to his back, learning all those dips and planes his muscles made, like a blind girl reading braille. He was my new language, a doorway to knowledge and undiscovered worlds, and I intended to become fluent in him. There was a library of learning for me to do but all the books had only one title, one author.

"Vervain," he pulled back, panting a little. "I don't want to rush this. Let me look at you. Let me savor this moment."

"Oh, you're good," I started to unbutton his shirt.

"Good?" He smiled but it was a tad confused.

"Smooth," there went another button, another, and another. Oh sweet sacred Viking, look at that chest. All golden skin and curving muscles. "I guess you've had centuries to practice your pillow talk though."

"Pillow talk?" He threw his unbuttoned shirt aside and grabbed my questing hands. "You think what I'm saying is meaningless romantic coercion?"

"Then again," I frowned, "that just ruined the mood a bit."

"Vervain, what do I have to do to make you believe I want you?"

"I believe, I believe," I reached for his belt and he took my hands again. I sighed and went further, "I could sing a damn *Monkeys'* song, I believe so much."

"Now who's pillow talking?" He rolled his eyes.

“Ugh!” I threw up my hands. “What do *I* have to do to get you to fuck me?” He looked like I slapped him; blinking hard, his mouth hanging open. “Oh, for the love of the blessed Moon, what now?”

“I just realized how little this means to you,” he backed up a step. “I've been waiting years but for you it's been barely any time at all. You think of me as nothing more than a pleasant diversion.”

“*Seriously*?!” I was ready to scream. “All your flirting and seduction and now you're upset because I actually *want* to have sex with you?” I rubbed at my temples with frustrated fingers before flinging them out in exasperation.

“Vervain,” he ran a hand over his face. “I want to make love to you, you want to fuck me. That's why I'm upset.”

“You want me to be in love with you before we have sex?” I couldn't believe it. The Norse God of Thunder was a romantic... and stuck in a Jane Austin novel. Didn't Jane die unwed because the man she loved married another woman? But I digress.

“Yes,” he growled, “no. Shit. I don't know. I can't expect you to love me after only a week but I guess I expected you to feel *something* for me. I didn't think this was as base as fucking for you.”

“It's not,” I groaned. Was I going to have to give him therapy every time we had sex? If he hadn't been half naked and completely hot, I would have left. “I was frustrated and blurted that out. I have no filter. In my head, out my mouth. I do feel something for you. Trust me, this wasn't just going to be a good time.”

“It wasn't?” A little spark of interest lightened his look.

“Thor, I haven't had sex in years. Do you really think I'd just jump into the sack with you because you're hot? That's not how I was raised. If I didn't feel something for you, I wouldn't be here."

I walked over to him and slid my hand around his waist. He started to smile and reached down to undo my belt. It fell to the floor with a thunk. Then his hands were pulling up the tunic and I was suddenly reminded that I had no underwear on. He sucked in his breath and ran a hand lightly over my face. It trailed down my neck, then fluttered between my breasts before snaking around my waist. I was yanked against him suddenly as his lips descended.

I fumbled for his belt and undid his pants without bothering to remove it from the loops. He kicked them off, his boxers quickly following. Then he was pressed against me and I was able to feel all of him, especially the hard length rising between us. I reached for it without breaking the kiss and he growled low in his throat as I stroked slowly. Strong hands lifted me and carried me over to the bed.

Lightning flashed outside and illuminated the room a second before thunder boomed. With the storm came a chill in the air which shocked me a little as he laid me down but soon I was warmed by the heat of his skin. He smiled down at me, easing between my legs, and I gave myself a moment to enjoy the breadth of him. His massive shoulders were too wide for me to wrap my arms around so I slid my hands down the smooth skin of his chest, then slid them around his waist and up to grip his back.

"You look perfect in my bed," he rumbled over the tempest brewing outside his balcony.

"And you look perfect above me," I nipped his chin and he chuckled.

His hair trailed across my face as he lowered his mouth to my neck, nibbling and kissing his way to my collarbone, and I inhaled his invigorating scent. Everywhere he touched seemed to spark to life; dancing tingles spreading over me from top to bottom and back again. I felt like I was the center of an electrical circuit, conducting his energy through me and back to him. My exhaustion vanished; fueled by his spark.

His hands trailed down my arms, captured my wrists, and raised them above my head. With a firm push to convey his desire for me to keep them there, he left my hands to trail his fingertips down the underside of my arms and over my breasts. I shook as the tingles spread, tiny blue sparkles glinting from his fingers to my flesh.

"I wanted to take my time with you," he looked up at me and I was mesmerized for a moment by the lightning flashing against the bright blue of his eyes. "Vervain?"

"We have all night and I don't want to wait anymore," I slid my hands down to the curve of his ass and pulled him closer.

He grinned and gave up resisting, "I don't either."

The storm outside lashed the walls of Bilskinir with a violence perfectly in tune with our passion. Thunder rumbled, growing in strength till the vibrations shook the bed, and lightning struck right beside the balcony. The room was illuminated with bright flashes, like snapping halogens, and everything blurred into a tribal pounding of rain, flesh, and hearts. One last flash of lightning cast the erotic look on Thor's face into stark relief as we cried out together, hands clenching ecstasy. Then the wind whistled into a gentle breeze and the rain lightened into a delicate shower. Our heavy breathing replaced the sound of thunder as his head fell to my shoulder and his body collapsed over mine.

Even in his exhaustion, he was considerate, shifting his weight to the side so he wouldn't crush me. He ended up with a leg and an arm draped across me, his face buried in my neck. I smiled, feeling my heartbeat return to normal and enjoying the little aftershocks coursing through my body along with the random blue sparks that still jumped between us.

"Sweet mercy," I breathed. "What was that?"

"Well it wasn't fucking," Thor smiled against my neck.

"It was fucking phenomenal," I smiled back as his hands started to roam again.

Chapter Twenty-Four

I watched the sun rise in Asgard from the bed of a Viking god. It couldn't get much better than that. Unless you added in the fact that I'd yet to go to sleep because said god had kept me up all night with a marathon bout of the most incredible sex I'd ever had. I smiled and snuggled deeper into the sapphire silk comforter as I sleepily perused Thor's bedroom.

He'd gone to get us coffee and breakfast so I finally had an opportunity to really take a look around. The massive, four-poster bed I was in was draped with deep blue silk, the thick posters carved with runes and Scandinavian scroll-work. Beyond it, the walls were the same dark wood as the bed, divided with pillars carved in the same style, adorned with eclectic artwork, and divided by bookshelves. Persian rugs littered the floor haphazardly and antiques were strewn about just as carelessly. In front of the stone fireplace were two chairs upholstered in deep burgundy leather, one with a thick animal pelt thrown over it. Dominating a corner was an amethyst cathedral crystal which would probably stand about waist high on me. Opposite it was a Native American headdress set on a stand, long feathers trailing to the floor.

It was the room of a scholar, with piles of books and prime pieces of art from extensive travels. It was the room of a warrior, with weapons of every size and shape hanging proudly on the walls. It was the room of a sensuous man, comfort and seduction oozing from every surface. It was the room of a god.

What the hell was I doing there?

The god himself walked in carrying a tray with a silver coffee pot, two ceramic mugs, and two plates of steaming food. I grinned and sat up, the comforter falling to my waist, forgotten. His eyes glowed appreciatively and my hand shot down to replace the cover. I couldn't handle another round yet.

"Food first," I wagged a finger at him.

"Puny human," he teased as he laid the tray on the bedside table and then poured me a cup of coffee. "First I want you to see something." He held a hand out to me and helped me from the bed. "Here," he picked up a discarded robe and helped me into it before handing me my coffee.

I wobbled a bit and he steadied me with a smug look as I added cream and sugar to my coffee. When I had it perfect, he led me out to the balcony with one hand on me and one carrying the tray of food. There was a small cafe set there and he placed the tray on the round wood table before he pulled out a chair for me. Amazingly, the table and its cushioned chairs had survived the thunderstorm, remaining completely dry. I raised a brow at their obviously untouched condition and Thor smiled.

"Bilskinir is mine. Nothing enters without my permission, not even the rain."

"Must be nice," I sipped my coffee as I looked out over Asgard.

Unsurprisingly, his balcony had the best view in Bilskinir. Asgard was laid out before us, the steep cliff we were situated on practically giving us a bird's eye view. Speaking of birds, big white ones darted in and out of sight, their cries carrying gently up to me, along with the sound of the surf pounding endlessly on black boulders below us. The mountain we were on stretched out to the right, continuing around the lake, where it was bisected by a channel of water leading out to the sea. High above this channel, at the edge of each cliff, were twin stones; tall boulders carved with runes.

"The Guardian Stones of Asgard," Thor said from my left.

"I thought *you* were the Guardian of Asgard," I smiled at

him.

"I am but I'll take all the help I can get," he smoothed my tangled hair back from my face. "Especially when I have such treasure to protect."

I blushed and looked down into my cup. I should have been used to his sweet talk, he'd been pouring it on thick all night, but I wasn't. It felt like a movie to me, everything too soft and too shiny. Life wasn't like that, especially not mine, and it was hard for me to believe someone so perfect could want someone so far from it.

"Those mountains separate my immediate family from the rest of the Norse pantheon," he pointed to some white-capped massiveness which I assumed were his mountains. "Although Balder's hall is beyond the peaks as well. And there runs the herd of Asgard, Odin's favorite horse comes from their line," he gestured to a group of magnificent horses running through a valley on our left. They went straight to the lake below us and hung their heads to drink.

"Are they divine horses?" I pulled my plate over and took a bite of french toast. "Do they listen to the prayers of regular horses?"

"Only Nordic ones," he winked at me.

"Is that the forest your brother Vali lives in?" I pointed to the thick woods surrounding the valley.

"Yes, though he tends to favor the region around Valhalla," Thor pointed to the shining hall, roofed with golden shields. It spread out, wider than a football stadium, on a patch of open land across the lake from us. "Even though he doesn't visit Father, he still likes to be close to him."

Then sunlight hit the shields, flashing red and gold, and setting the surrounding trees aflame with light. The rest of Asgard seemed to shiver with that first strike of sun. Everything flashed, everything sparkled, though that might have had something to do with all the raindrops left over from the previous night. The Viking realm stretched and yawned, sparkled one last time, and came awake.

"Wow," I breathed, my fork forgotten on my plate.

"That's what I wanted to share with you," Thor smiled and took my hand to place a quick kiss on it.

"Thank you," I whispered.

"I want you to feel at home here, darling."

"That may take some time," I chuckled but stopped abruptly when he frowned. "I just meant it's a lot to take in, a lot to get comfortable with, but it's wonderful. Asgard is amazing."

"I agree," he relaxed and started to eat.

"So how long has it been since you've visited your father?" I asked casually.

Thor swallowed and looked at me sideways. "Does sneaking in to steal his war plans count?"

"No," I pushed at his shoulder. "Is it really so bad between you?"

"Well, we're on opposite sides of a war right now," he sighed. "I think I'm an embarrassment to him but I also think he secretly agrees with me. He's a leader but after Sabine died, he started letting his people lead him. They want the power and so he goes along with their plans."

"That's sad, baby." I frowned when he smiled at me. "What?"

"I just like hearing you call me *baby*," he grinned wider.

“Well, if that's all it takes to make you smile,” I held up my coffee in salute. “Thanks for breakfast, Baby Thunder.”

“You're welcome, Darling Witch,” he kissed the syrup from my lips.

Chapter Twenty-Five

"Miss V," Jackson exclaimed as I walked up to the table. "Where you been, shug?" He drew out the endearment with a hint of New Orleans, so the shortened *sugar* came out sounding like shuuug.

"Fighting gods," I laughed and hugged him. "Oh and one werewolf."

"You're never satisfied with the normal are you?" Jackson's boyfriend, Tristan, stood up to hug me next. "The rest of us just have demons to slay but you get gods. I wanna live in your world."

"No you don't, trust me." I loved teasing the boys with the truth because even though they assumed it was just fun fiction, there were times when they got a sharp look in their eyes and I knew they suspected something.

"Gods or demons," Jackson sent me a penetrating look, "we've missed you. You should spare some time for us mere mortals."

"Hot stuff, you ain't a mere anything," I settled down into my seat and picked up my menu.

I'd been putting my guys off for as long as I could and honestly, I really needed some Jax and Tryst time. So I'd snuck out of bed to meet them. It was actually evening in Asgard even though it was late morning in Hawaii. Thor and I had gone back to bed after breakfast, completely exhausted from the previous night's activities, and I had woke up just as the sun was setting.

"This is going to be my second breakfast in eight hours," I laughed as I looked over Cinnamon's selection. I don't know why I bothered, I knew the menu by heart.

"Oh noonsies," Tristan clapped his hands, his bright burgundy hair slipping into his eyes.

"No, no, second breakfast, then noonsies," I corrected him.

"I know," he rolled his gorgeous blue eyes, as if the thought of me knowing more about *The Lord of the Rings* than him was ridiculous. Which of course it was. "I meant we could do noonsies after this."

"Ah, pardon me. How could I ever doubt you?" I rolled my eyes.

"So, Miss Vervain," Jackson interjected before the conversation became pure LOTR. "What have you really been up to?"

"Oh, you know; painting, witchcraft, and having wild sex with *my new boyfriend*!" I did a little squeal and Tristan joined in. Jackson just smiled and reached for my hand.

"Oh no," I jerked my hand out of his reach. "None of that. I don't want to know how horribly it's going to end."

Jackson was a clairvoyant and it was a constant battle to keep him from seeing too much. I probably should just give in and tell them already, if anyone would believe me about Atlanteans becoming gods it would be those two.

"Why do you assume it will end badly?" Jax moved his coffee aside to try and get a clearer shot at my hand. "Or that it will end at all? This may be the one. Could you pass me the cream, porfa-please?"

"He isn't the one," my bright mood faded a bit when I thought about the future Thor and I would never have. It didn't matter what he thought, I knew there was no hope for us. Human-god relationships had a notorious reputation for ending badly.

“Hah!” When I passed the cream, Jackson grabbed my hand. “Oh,” his eyes went distant as he focused on a point somewhere beyond my left shoulder. “He's magnificent. What is he; Scandinavian?”

“You could say that,” I grimaced and tried to pull away but the guy had a kung-fu grip.

“Vervain, this man's in love with you already,” he whispered. “He's appointed himself your guardian. He's scared to death of you getting hurt. How very gallant, very old world.”

“*Very* old world,” I nodded as inwardly, I groaned. Please don't see anymore, please don't see anymore.

“Or very paranoid,” Tristan frowned as he watched my face.

“He's got a right to be afraid,” Jackson's hand clenched on mine. “Vervain, what are you into?”

“Nothing!” I tried to jerk my hand back again.

“There's so much blood,” Jackson's voice took on the monotone reserved for his predictions. “The Queen of Love brings only pain. Take her pain, take everything she is, and you change pain to pleasure, pleasure to love, love to heal the blackest hearts and make them yours.”

Jackson blinked and refocused on my face. Tristan and I were staring at him like he'd just announced his preference for Payless shoes over Gucci. I was terrified. Jackson was never wrong and coupled with Yemanja's warning, it was pretty much carved in stone. Pain was coming my way; pain and blood, evidently.

“Well that was really helpful,” Tristan twisted his lips into a grimace. “And by that I mean you were completely useless. More trouble than honey on a pig's ass.”

“What I say?” Jackson's brows lifted. Sometimes he'd instantly forget what he prophesied. I breathed a sigh of relief. My secret was still safe.

“Well you started out great,” Tristan narrowed disapproving eyes on him. “Then you started blabbering about blood and pain, and something about the Queen of Love, whatever that's supposed to mean.”

“It's fine, Tristan,” I started to reassure Jackson as well but the waitress came up to take our orders.

When she finally left, the dark mood had dispersed and I just wanted to let sleeping hellhounds lie. So I left Jackson's strange prediction alone and focused instead on the happy news of the long awaited end of my abstinence. They teased me with merciless intensity and fished for every bit of information on Thor they could get and I offered them every normal tidbit I could think of.

It was a surprisingly relaxing morning after that. I scarfed down my carrot-cake pancakes, drank way too much coffee, and basked in the general wonderfulness of my gorgeous friends. Every female eye in the place was fastened on me with envy. If only they knew.

Why is it that gay men are usually hotter than straight ones? I have one word for you: hygiene. Well that and great genes. Jackson had modeled at one time and had kept himself in top shape. He was not only gorgeous but was one of those gay men you didn't realize was gay until two hours into a conversation when he moved his hand a certain way or sent you a sassy look. But by then it's too late, you're hooked.

Tristan, on the other hand, had just a touch of flamboyance. It was enough for you to realize you weren't getting any play in this lifetime but reserved enough to compliment Jackson instead of embarrass him. He was Versace to Jackson's Armani. They were a great pair and loads of fun. I hadn't realized how much I'd missed them until it was time to leave. We said goodbye amidst hugs and kisses. Tristan pouted when I told him I couldn't stick around for noonsies but brightened back up when I promised to introduce them to Thor at the soonest opportunity.

I crossed the parking lot Cinnamon’s shared with all the other cute restaurants and shops in Kailua, making my way to my car in a happy food haze. Buildings boxed in the lot on all four sides; two high-rise office buildings guarding one entrance and looking grotesquely out of place next to the quaint two-stories around them. In the alleys between the smaller buildings, trees grew amid thick plant life, gaily adding their appeal to the country cottage façade and further alienating the massive cement monstrosities.

The alleys were clean and bright, nothing like you’d expect an alley to be, and short on shadows to hide in. They weren't scary. They were the domain of stroller-wielding yuppies, not monsters. So when I passed by one of those alleys and heard a low growl, I was startled enough to jump. I looked over just as a massive dog emerged from the bushes. It was the size of a pony. What the hell did they feed that thing? Or should I ask; what *in* Hell did they feed that thing? ‘Cause I was pretty sure that’s where the beast was born… hatched… conjured… whatever.

No, wait, it wasn't a dog but a wolf. A shiny black wolf with honey-colored eyes. He padded towards me, claws clicking on the cement. I flung down my arms and released my blades immediately. Bless Yemanja for warning me and making me paranoid enough to wear them to lunch.

The beast kept coming, like my gloves didn't make a lick of difference. If I hadn’t been so damned scared, I might have appreciated the beauty of him but as it was, the animal simply looked formidable. Okay, that’s an understatement. It looked terrifying, monstrous… and very hungry.

It cocked its head at me and bared a set of the sharpest fangs I'd ever seen... and I've seen some pretty sharp ones lately. Exhibit A: Blue AKA Huitzilopochtli. The sun glinted off those perfect white teeth, a little too well cared for, for an animal. His eyes surveyed me with more than animal intelligence, and then there was the fact that Hawaii doesn't have wolves. Much less mutant, giant, killer wolves. My slow-processing, terror-filled brain finally put two and two together and came up with werewolf.

"Damn," I backed up along the chain-link fence which ran down one side of the parking lot. It wasn't the best idea to retreat, everyone knows it's a sign of fear and fear was like candy for werewolves. "Not another one," I groaned as I forced my legs to stop and stand their ground.

I took a quick look around me. The lot was full of cars but thankfully empty of people. How long had the wolf been watching me from the bushes, waiting for the right moment to strike? A chill went down my spine as I realized how pathetic my senses were compared to those of a true predator. I had completely underestimated my enemy again. This was becoming a habit, the kind of habit that could kill me.

It leapt at me and I side-stepped but it had jacked-up, animal reflexes and twisted mid-air. Pain rocketed through me as its teeth sank into my shoulder and we both went down. It landed on my chest, straddling me while it worried at my wound like a piece of meat. Even through the agony, I noticed the sharp claws protruding out of his massive paws on either side of my face. I was becoming more and more certain that this was the painful, bloody end Jackson had just foretold.

Straddling my body was a vulnerable position for the wolf but then it probably wasn't expecting a human to be armed with god weaponry. If my claws had been normal steel, they may not have even penetrated his thick hide. They weren't normal though, so when I punched both hands up into its underbelly and pulled them down, I gutted the beast horribly. Blood gushed over me, along with the slide of thicker things, before the wolf fell back with a sharp howl to kick uselessly at the air.

I rolled onto my unchewed shoulder and stood up on shaky legs, clutching my wound to try and staunch the blood flow. The bite was deep, ragged, and wide due to the head-thrashing technique my attacker had employed. I tore away my already damaged sleeve and with some awkward maneuvering, I was able to bind my wound. Pain burned through me, threatening to steal my consciousness, but I breathed through it and focused instead on my would-be assassin.

The creature was panting furiously as its eyes rolled up to me in terror. Entrails oozed out of the shredded mess of its belly, blood pooling quickly and matting the beautiful coat. It was enough to turn my stomach and my automatic reaction was to look away. But I forced myself to stare at it and acknowledge what I'd done. Death should never be easy, not for either party involved.

So I stared and what I saw was just a wounded animal in horrendous pain. My pain seemed to dull in light of his and when he whimpered, my breath caught on a sob. I was a major animal lover and hurting one was so against the grain for me, it felt like a part of my soul was shriveling. I told myself that this wasn't just any wolf, this was a werewolf sent to murder me. But my heart wasn't listening. He was just so pitiful and monstrously beautiful, I couldn't end his life. I just didn't have it in me.

Rule number one when fighting gods and monsters: No sympathy and no mercy. But what had Jackson said? Something about pain to love and love to heal? And Yemanja had said something about being gentle. It was all fuzzy at the moment but it resonated within me and I knew that going with my heart was the right thing to do. I'd killed so many gods, giving up a part of my humanity to save humanity. Killing this wolf was a sacrifice I wasn't willing to make. Killing him would kill the only goodness I had left.

"If you shift now, will you be able heal?" I asked with as steady a voice as I could manage through the radiating pain of my shoulder. The wolf's eyes narrowed and it nodded in a very human way. "Then go ahead and change. I'll guard you while you do and we'll call this round a draw." I was shaking and I wasn't sure if it was from blood loss or the possibility of having just made a fatal mistake.

The wolf shifted immediately and I glanced around to be sure we were still alone. When I looked back, there was a large, naked man sitting against the chain-link fence, and I mean *large.* No wonder the wolf was so big, the man was almost as big as Thor. Short, black, silky hair poked out from his head in clumps, giving him a wild, unkempt, and very sexy look. His eyes were still the color of honey and still tilted in the same manner; more wolf than human. Those unusual eyes stared at me with both animal intensity and an intelligence superior to most humans. I tried hard to focus on them and ignore the fact that he was naked, hot, and... a shower not a grower. Not that I looked. Much.

"Why?" His voice was raspy and his breathing ragged.

For a second I thought he was asking me why I was trying to avoid looking at his nudity. Then my mind snapped back into focus and I almost slapped myself for being such a perverted werewolf-ogler.

"I guess I'm just a sucker for a wounded wolf," I tried to look casual and yet still be prepared for an attack. He had a distinct advantage over me now. My shoulder wound would make self defense difficult at best while he was completely healed. "I'll probably regret it later but it felt like the right thing to do," I shrugged and then hissed from the pain of the movement.

"You're the one who killed Kenny," he swallowed hard and I suddenly realized that he wasn't a threat to me. He was still weakened from the effort it had taken to heal.

“Is that the werewolf who attacked me the other night?” I pulled up the levers that sheathed my claws and the naked wolf-man nodded.

“You've got to be kidding me. I killed Kenny? Great, my life has just morphed into an episode of South Park,” I huffed. Kenny the Werewolf? Werewolf Ken? Wouldn't you know it; Barbie's Halloween date had tried to assassinate me. “Look, he attacked me first, Fido. I was just defending myself.”

“It’s just a job,” his lips twitched. Was he going to laugh at me? Of all the inappropriate… oh, who the hell am I kidding?

“Time to find a new line of work then,” I looked around again. “You need to go. Someone could see,” I waved vaguely to include his still very naked, very sexy body and my tied off shoulder. Did werewolves have extra pheromones or what?

“You’re really just going to let me walk away?” His voice caressed me with a lilting measure of both wonder and fascination as his eyes continued their intense scrutiny.

“No, I wanted you to heal so I could stab you all over again, it’s more fun that way,” I rolled my eyes and grimaced around the throbbing pain of my shoulder. “You may wanna change back to a wolf. I think you’d garner less attention than if you walked around naked, although it's a tough call.”

“You’re not even going to ask who sent me?” His wolf eyes widened, his brows lifting.

“Would you tell me if I did?” I lifted my brows back at him.

“No,” he grunted with a twisted grin.

“Well, there you go,” I searched the parking lot again and saw an elderly couple coming out of the antique store. I could just imagine the headlines; Double Heart Attack, Elderly Couple

Shocked to Death by Werewolf Flasher. I focused back on the werewolf anxiously, “And you *should* go, like *now*.”

“I’m Trevor,” he crawled over to me and I barely controlled my urge to back away. He sniffed the air around me thoroughly, then grabbed my hand and rubbed his face against it like a cat scent-marking its owner.

“I'm Vervain,” I shook my head and laughed a little hysterically. “How very nice to meet you, Trevor.”

“Vervain,” Trevor stood and it took all of my willpower to focus on his face. “I’ll find you again but I’ll hunt you no more. You’re safe from me now and I’ll do everything I can to keep the others away from you as well. I swear it on the life you gave back to me.”

“Thank you but really, that’s not necessary. Don’t come after me again and we’re all square.” I didn’t want to get him killed by his family for disobedience or something like that after I just saved him. Wouldn't that be ironic?

He blinked as if I’d said something profound and then shifted suddenly. One second he was a hot, naked man, the next, a giant fur ball. I sucked in a shocked breath as he circled me three times, rubbing against me as he went, then lowered his head in a bow before he ran off in great, lopping strides.

“Well what the hell was that about?” I mused as I watched him go. Then I shook my head and stumbled to my car. I had to get home so I could trace over to Bilskinir. Hopefully I could get to Teharon before I passed out.

Chapter Twenty-Six

"Vervain, where have you been?" Thor asked as I lurched through the door. "What the hell happened? Teharon!" He caught me just as I was about to fall.

"I'll be okay," I smiled weakly, "it's just a little bite."

"A little bite?" Thor carried me to the bed before shouting again, "Teharon!"

"I'm here," the Indian walked in with his perfect forehead creased into lines. "What's the problem? Ah," his eyes fell on me. "Trouble again, Godhunter?"

"When is she not in trouble?" Thor grumbled.

"Thanks, babe, really helpful." I grimaced when he untied the torn sleeve from my shoulder.

Teharon gently nudged Thor aside and came up to carefully inspect the damage. He made some pensive sounds as he prodded lightly. I hissed, sharp pain streaking through the numbness that had been taking over. Teharon frowned and held up a hand when Thor started to move forward.

"Give me space," Teharon touched the edges of the nasty wound.

My shoulder had been reduced to a mass of chewed meat but I felt a tingling warmth start to spread it, immediately reducing the pain. I watched as Teharon's fingertips began to glow, the light growing brighter till it flowed from his hands and sank into my flesh. It itched like crazy but I clenched my fists and held them still at my side while he finished. When he finally pulled away, my skin was whole again. A little pink but whole and pain-free.

"Thank you," I took Teharon's hand and squeezed it. "You must be sick of saving me already."

"Not at all," he patted the top of my hand like I was a little girl. "My magic is happiest when it's being used. Your constant need fuels me."

"Well, stick around," I chuckled. "I've just been told I've got a boatload of blood and pain coming my way."

"What?" Thor took a seat near my feet as I scooted up into a sitting position. "What exactly were you doing today?"

"I think I'll leave you two to it," Teharon nodded to me and discretely left.

"I went to breakfast with some friends," I shrugged.

"Vervain," Thor shook his head. "You know better than that. How could you go out alone and unprotected?"

"I wasn't alone, I was meeting friends," I frowned down at the huge bloody mess that used to be Thor's tunic. "Sorry about your tunic. Looks like I need to go home and get some clothes."

"Does that mean you're staying?" Thor lifted a brow.

Aha, the one thing that would distract him.

"For now," I gave him a little smile. "I just need to grab some of my stuff. My paints and some canvases as well as clothes. There's a couple of portraits I need to finish by the end of the month. All of us non-god types have bills to pay."

"I'll go with you to get them," he said decisively.

"I'm staying but I'm not going to barricade myself in Bilskinir, babe," I got up when I saw Nick come striding in. "Hey you," I reached down and scratched his chin.

"You can't go gallivanting around with fragile mortals when the wolves have your scent," Thor looked like he was going to start yelling at any second.

"Look, it's cool, okay?" I left Nick to go curl up in one of the heavy chairs by the fire. "The werewolf that attacked me today is on my side now."

"I figured that was a werewolf bite," Thor gave me an exasperated look. "Wait, what? He's *on your side*? What's that supposed to mean?"

"I demolished him," I gave him a saucy grin. "Then I felt bad so I backed off and let him heal. He said he'd try to stop the others from coming after me."

"One wolf is not going to make a whit of difference against the whole Froekn family," Thor huffed.

"Froekn?"

"It's what the wolves call themselves and it's also besides the point," he got up and pulled the useless tunic off me. Then he inspected my shoulder, making satisfied sounds, before he picked me up and carried me back to bed. "If I have to, I'll make you too exhausted to leave Bilskinir," he declared.

"That may not be such a bad idea," I wrapped my arms around him but then frowned as I recalled Jackson's prophecy in full. "Does Sif call herself the Queen of Love by any chance?"

"Not that I know of," Thor pulled his face back to gaze down at me. "Why do you ask?"

"A good friend of mine is a clairvoyant," I sighed. "He read me today because I mentioned I had a new boyfriend."

"You told your friends about me?" He got the cutest goofy look on his face.

“Yes, and they want to meet you but focus,” I snapped my fingers and he blinked. “Jackson said some nice things about you,” I blushed when I remembered what he said about Thor already being in love with me. Was it true?

“Did he now?” Thor's face was going from goofy to cocky and I preferred the goofy.

“Cut it out,” I slapped his arm. “He went on to say how you were terrified of me getting hurt but you had good reason to be scared. He said there was going to be a lot of blood and then he mentioned something about the Queen of Love only bringing pain. I don't know what it means but it doesn't sound good.”

Thor sighed and got to his feet. “We need to tell the others,” he fetched another tunic, this one in powder blue. “You get dressed and I'll go call them all together.” He took one last long look at my nudity before handing me the tunic, then groaned as he left.

Fifteen minutes later, I was dressed and telling the God Squad about my latest adventure.

“It has to be Sif,” Finn was pacing the library. He seemed to be taking it the worst. “You have to do something, Thor,” he stopped in front of us and glared at my guy, who was seated on the couch beside me. “You swore *Blood to Mouth* to protect her, you have a responsibility.”

“Don’t remind me of my vows, Black Swan,” Thor was about to stand up but I patted his thigh and he relaxed a little, shooting me a little smile before continuing. “I want her safe even more than you do and I’ll stop at nothing to see that she is.”

“I have to say I’m not too impressed with your results so far,” Finn’s eyes narrowed.

Thor stood up and I jumped to my feet to stand between them.

"Enough," I growled at the both of them. "I'm not some child in need of protection. I'll be happy for some help but I'm not going to cower behind any man, even if that man happens to be a god."

Thor looked at me, then back at Finn with a twist of the mouth which clearly said; *You see what I have to deal with?* Finn nodded and snorted as he backed away. Silent male communication could be the most annoying kind.

"Fine," Finn sat down and we followed suit, "but I still think Thor should handle his ex-wife."

"We're not even sure she's behind this," Horus was perched on the end of his chair and I don't mean that he was sitting close to the edge. He crouched on it like a bird, balanced on the balls of his feet with his forearms braced on his knees. How he managed to make it look both elegant and casual was beyond me.

"Who else could it possibly be?" Pan was twisting his hands together. I'd never seen him so worried and I found it deeply unsettling. Pan had two moods; happy and happier, the later usually due to besting Horus.

Everyone looked at me and I shook my head. "I haven't got a clue but I have to tell you, it sucks having someone gunning for me without even knowing what they look like. They could walk by me on the street and I wouldn't know it."

"I'll do it," Thor grumbled.

"You're going to talk to Sif?" I couldn't hide my surprise.

"What else can I do?" He pulled me against his chest. "I can't allow these attacks to continue."

"Thank you," Finn fell back into his seat and threw his hands up in the universal *finally* gesture.

“Thank you,” I whispered and Thor kissed my forehead. “When are we going?”

“What?” The whole room seemed to ask the question.

“Well, I’m going with you of course,” I looked around at the others like it was a given.

“No you're not,” Thor shook his head as if the discussion was over. I thought he knew me better than that.

“I want to meet her,” I stood up so I could glower down at him for once. The room emptied out behind me quickly but Thor barely spared them a glance.

“It’s not a good idea, Vervain.”

“Why not?”

“For one, if she is behind this, she may try to kill you.”

“So?”

He groaned. “Vervain, this is not a contest of who’s the toughest. She’s a goddess. You're a hunter of gods. I understand that it’s in your nature to confront her but I don’t want to deal with the fallout.”

“You mean you don’t want to referee,” I started to smile.

“Exactly,” he stood up and grabbed my waist. His smile spread as he looked down. “You’re so tiny. I can span your waist with my hands.”

I’ve waited forever for a man to call me tiny and give me that hand-spanning, romance novel line. My waist is small in comparison to the rest of me, I definitely have an hourglass figure, but in comparison to women's waists in general, it wasn’t all that little. There was a bit more sand in my hourglass.

“That’s because you have huge hands,” I tried to hide my pleasure but it was difficult. You tiny girls will never know the joy of a comment like that and I pity you for it. I hate you and pity you but at least I’m not bitter.

“The better to touch you with, my dear,” he growled and let his hands wander.

I laughed in delight. “Oh, Grandma what big-”

“Don’t you dare,” he laughed and picked me up.

“What?” I blinked up at him innocently. “You know what they say about big hands.”

“Would you agree with them?” His eyes twinkled.

“Hmmm…” I pretended to ponder it.

“That’s it,” he threw me down on the couch and started unbuckling his belt.

“What are you going to do; give me a spanking?” I looked up, my face filled with a mixture of disbelief and amusement.

“No,” he scoffed. “I’m going to give you another look.”

“Thor!” I laughed and got up to stop him.

“Admit it,” his hands were at the zipper of his jeans.

“Alright, alright,” I put up my hands in surrender. “It’s monstrous, the biggest I’ve ever seen. I fear for my life every time we make love.”

I heard a muffled laugh outside the door and Thor rolled his eyes. “Find somewhere else to be,” he shouted.

“We just wanted to hear who the winner is,” Pan’s voice filtered through the thick door.

“Pan, I always win!” I shouted and Thor raised a brow, so I wiggled mine at him.

“Oh, really,” he grabbed both of my hands suddenly and pulled them behind my back. Then he transferred them both to one of his huge hands and when he pulled down on them a little, I was bent backwards. I gasped as he pushed my blouse up and undid my front-snap bra. “You wanna try that again?”

“I win,” I laughed that deep way women do when they know the effect they have on their man. Oh, it's a good laugh.

His lips covered me with a scalding kiss and I sighed until he bit down just enough to make me cry out. I bucked and lifted my head to glare a warning at him.

“What are you going to do, Godhunter?” He had lifted his face barely an inch to taunt me and his eyes held the lightning I loved. “Who wins?”

“I do,” I breathed out but sucked my breath back in as he sucked more of my breast into his mouth and bit deeper into the meatier flesh. “I do,” I said again defiantly. He tongued the nipple as he bit deeper and I cried out in pleasure and pain. “I do!”

He took one last lick and then released me. “I guess you do,” he got up and started to walk away.

“Damn it, Thor!” I screamed in frustration.

“Yes?” He looked back over his shoulder.

My blouse fell back down a little as I huffed. “You do.”

“Do what?”

“You win,” I mumbled.

“Again,” he turned around fully and smiled in smug satisfaction. “Say it… loud.” It was his turn to wiggle his brows.

“You win!” I screamed.

I heard Brahma say “Pay up,” and Pan cursed.

Thor closed the distance between us in two strides, then proceeded to make me feel like I’d been the winner after all.

Chapter Twenty-Seven

"She swears it wasn't her," Thor slumped on the couch, back where we'd started just a few hours earlier.

"And you believe her?" I tried to make my voice sound as neutral as possible.

"Yes," he looked at the others and they nodded like they all knew some secret god code.

"What?" I looked around at everyone and then back at Thor.

"It wasn't her, Vervain," I saw the lines of strain around his eyes and knew he was half relieved and half worried.

"How can you be so certain?" I pressed him.

"Vervain, they were married," Teharon sat down next to me and took my hand.

"So?" I didn't like the way everyone was looking at me, like they were about to tell me my cat had just died. I started looking around for Nick.

"They have a connection," Teharon answered but Thor waved him to silence.

"I should tell her this," Thor said to Teharon over my head and the Mohawk god let go of my hand.

I looked back at Thor.

"You know how I can slide into your mind?" Thor looked at me like he expected me to get it immediately. I did.

"You've shared blood with her. Oh, of course," I sighed in

relief and everyone stared at me like they were waiting for my real reaction. "What? That's it, right? You have the same kind of connection with her that you do with me and you read her mind to see if she was behind the attacks."

"You're not mad?" He still looked wary.

"Why would I be mad about a relationship you ended centuries ago?" I frowned. Maybe I was missing something.

"I should've known you'd be reasonable," he smiled and shook his head.

"Well, I try," I smirked. "It's just hard sometimes when I have to deal with gods who have their own idea of reason."

"It's good to be a god," Thor laughed but I heard the relief in it.

"So if not Sif, then who?" Finn's voice was back to being impatient.

I caught his gaze and the intensity of it scared me. There was something there that I'd have to deal with someday and I wasn't looking forward to it. I had a feeling he wouldn't take the friend speech well. I partially blamed myself for encouraging him with the swan thing -insert sigh here-. Just as long as he didn't turn into a bush-lurking stalker, I'd be fine. I narrowed my eyes on him in consideration. Maybe I'd better trim the hedges around my yard.

"She didn't know," Thor grimaced. "She was supremely pleased that Vervain's in danger but just as supremely confused on who it could be."

"Then you just don't leave Bilskinir Hall unattended," Finn waved at me angrily when I started to speak and turned to Thor. "Back me up here, Thor, you know I'm right."

"He is," Thor said simply and begged me with his eyes. I

hated it when he did that.

"Fine," I crossed my arms and gave in to a good pout. No fair; a bunch of gods ganging up on poor little ol' me.

Chapter Twenty-Eight

"I'm not so bad, little witch," Blue's voice was a gentle purr.

We were seated at a beautifully decorated table next to a railing, on a balcony two stories above the beach. The moonlight created silver stripes across the water and turned ships into mysterious shadow creatures. Candlelight warmed Blue's skin to caramel and reflected back to me as twin flames in the sunglasses he wore. His hair was slicked neatly into a ponytail and he was dressed in a black tailored suit with a white shirt, open at the neck. He looked sophisticated in the shades but they made me a little uncomfortable. I felt bare, torn open, while he hid behind those black lenses. Then, almost as if in response to my unease, he removed the sunglasses and set them aside. The thing was; I still couldn't clearly see his eyes. The shadows deepened them to an indistinguishable color.

"I have dreams and desires. I pursue them as any man would. Can you fault me for making you a part of my dreams, for desiring you?" He took my hand gently in his.

"You don't pursue as a man," I whispered as a shiver went down my spine. "You pursue as a god and gods don't play fair."

"Neither do men," he lowered his mouth to the back of my hand so slowly, I had every opportunity to pull away. But I didn't. I let him caress me with his lips. I let his teeth graze over my flesh and I shivered again.

I'd gone completely batty. What was wrong with me? What was I even doing there with him? I looked around the restaurant for some clue, something to jar my memory. I couldn't even recall how I'd arrived. People filled the tables around us but their conversations were soft, muted. I couldn't focus on a single word being said. Then I realized that I knew the place. I'd been there before. Frowning, I tried to concentrate.

"You're like a cool rush of wind," Blue's voice went breathless. "You soothe my skin while you stoke the fire within me."

"Have you stolen my memories?" I rounded on him suddenly.

I'd finally figured out where we were. *Bali by the Sea*, one of my favorite posh restaurants. How else could he have known of this place? He must have seen it in my head.

"When I entered your body before, I saw glimpses into your past," his face seemed to soften as he spoke. "I wanted you at first because you fascinated me. You made me feel interest for the first time in centuries. Interest beyond the sweet flesh and blood of a woman."

I felt my face flush and he smiled at me fondly. Somehow it embarrassed me even more.

"You wanted to seduce me and then kill me when you were done," I looked him over like he repulsed me. "Let me give you a tip. The next time you want a woman, don't tell her you intend to kill her when you get bored. It tends to ruin the mood."

"We were enemies," he shrugged like killing women after he had sex with them was a natural, everyday occurrence. "I was being honest and if you were honest with yourself, you'd admit that you're attracted to me as well. You resist me only because of our different opinions. It's this struggle between your lust and your ideals that made me want you even more but I didn't *love* you until I saw into your mind."

He leaned forward and the light finally caught the blood red of his eyes. They shimmered and stared hard into mine, like he could see through me, into every dark place inside me. I swallowed hard and felt my teeth clench. I felt even more violated than I had from the altar dream. Here he was professing his love for me and all I could think was; he's obsessed with me because he took advantage of me in a dream and he knows I would never be with him in real life. He simply wanted what he couldn't have. How could he possibly think this was romantic?

"When I saw your strength tempered by kindness," he continued relentlessly, "your passion for your art, your search for beauty in all things, your determination to fight for your race even though you fear it will turn you into a monster, your effort to train yourself to be strong but retain the femininity you love, all the conflict and glory of you, I was overwhelmed. I didn't stand a chance."

"Oh, my god," our waitress had returned to pour our champagne and she caught the tail end of his declaration. I hadn't even noticed her, I was so enthralled with his twisted speech. "I think I'd kill to hear a man say that to me. If you don't snatch him up, you're insane, sweetie." She smiled brightly but her hands shook a little as she poured my bubbly. I understood how she felt. I was a little shaky myself, though for an entirely different reason.

Blue gave her a gentle smile and she flushed before she returned it and hurried away. I was still dumbstruck. Say something, Vervain, speak! I opened my mouth but all that came out was a rush of air. I closed it and then opened it again. Still nothing. I must've looked like a fish. A dying fish.

"Did, uh," I cleared my throat. "I'm sorry, did you just say that you love me?"

"Yes," he shook his head like he was a little surprised by it as well. "I believe I did. I haven't spoken those words in a long time. I think I like saying them to you. I love you, little witch." He smiled brightly, like a child who'd just learned to tie his shoes.

I sipped my drink and let its warmth slip through me, doing

a little to calm my racing pulse. Breathe; in and out, in and out. I could handle this situation. I am a professional when it comes to gods. I could distance myself and analyze this thoroughly. He was the Aztec Satan, the Father of Vampires, the CEO of Bad Gods Incorporated. I hated him, I had to hate him, it was kind of a job requirement… and he loved me. Well, at least he might not try to kill me now.

Unless it was a trick. He was clearly insane. He actually thought this little speech had a shot at winning me over. Maybe he thought he could steal me away from the God Squad by spouting some romantic bullshit. Then he'd either use me for some nefarious purpose or kill me outright. Those options made much more sense to me but I was pretty sure we had completely different ideas of sense. What if he really did believe himself to be in love with me? What a twisted son of a bitch.

I took another sip of champagne since I couldn't think of anything to say that wouldn't prompt a physical altercation. The silence stretched on and he finally took my hand from my glass and held it, just held it. I looked up at him with both annoyance and trepidation.

"I wanted you to understand why I'm pursuing you," he explained. "I wanted you to know you're safe with me, will always be safe with me. I didn't say those things to make you uncomfortable or make you think I expected you to immediately return my feelings. I've had the honor of sharing your mind. You know nothing of mine, so you can't possibly feel the same. I would share that with you as well but I fear that some of my memories would haunt you."

I sighed, "Okay, I officially feel safe." Not. "I'll try and relax but it's a little hard after a declaration of love from a god." From a psycho god. I had a fleeting thought that there was another god who loved me but I couldn't remember his name. Why was everything so fuzzy? I looked down at my drink suspiciously.

Blue laughed his sweet laugh and that sound was something I did remember. I breathed it in and let it slide over me. He was passionate heat and silk velvet and he was going to make my life hell, I just knew it. Even knowing how evil he was, how he'd probably kill me if given the chance, I couldn't deny his appeal. Must be that bad boy thing. Damn, we women could sure be dumb when it came to men. Blue got up and held a hand out to me.

"Dance with me?" I took his hand and suddenly the restaurant was gone. What the hell?

We were alone on a wide expanse of ruby floor. The room seemed to go on forever, fading into darkness at the edges. I stared around me in confusion but then he pulled me in close and started moving me expertly around the floor. There was music playing but I had no idea where it was coming from, it was simply there. Hidden speakers I guess.

I leaned my cheek on his chest and it struck me how perfectly I fit against him. There was that quick sensation of another man again, that the man who should have been holding me was much bigger than Blue. That my face belonged somewhere around mid-chest instead of right beneath his chin. But then Blue's scent hit me, sweet and dark, like spiced chocolate, and I lost the trace of thought again. Didn't I hate this guy? What was wrong with my head?

"I want you to trust me, little witch," Blue whispered into my hair. "So I'm going to be honest with you now."

"What is it?" I pulled away from him and looked up into his face warily.

"This is a dream," he bit his lip self-consciously and I noticed the point of a fang. "I've come to you in your sleep because it's the only way I know of to reach you, to speak with you, without any interference."

"Interference from who?" It all clicked back into place as soon as I questioned it aloud. It was like my mind had just been waiting for me to say the secret word for it to blow away the cobwebs. "Thor," I breathed as I backed up, pushing out of his embrace. Blue looked stricken but I knew it was all a trick now. He'd been messing with my mind again. "Thor!" I screamed and sat up in bed as the dream fell away.

"What?" Thor sat up beside me, sparks dancing along his skin to broadcast his anxiety. "What is it?" He scanned the room and then came back to my face when he noticed nothing out of the ordinary. "Are you alright, darling?"

"It was Blue," I held my hands out before me and snarled in anger when I saw how they shook. "Damn that bastard! Why won't he just leave me alone?"

His declaration of love felt more like a declaration of war, echoing in my head ominously. Talk about your fatal attractions.

"I thought you were able to keep him out now," Thor's arm went around me and pulled me in close.

"I can but it's harder when I'm sleeping," I let out a shaky breath and let him lay us back down.

"Tomorrow you train with Teharon again," he said decisively as he pulled the covers back over us.

"Okay," I whispered and snuggled into him as I formed steel boxes around Blue's link to me. Box after box after box. No more dream dancing with diabolical Aztecs for me.

Chapter Twenty-Nine

"It's your dream, Vervain," Teharon's gentle voice seemed out of place in Thor's bedroom. The only time I ever heard it in there was when I was injured.

We were seated before each other on the bed because he thought it would be helpful to be in the place I'd be sleeping, while he trained me to keep Blue out of my dreams. But keeping Blue out of my dreams wasn't really what Teharon wanted me to do. He wanted me to take control of my dreams and use it as another opportunity to get into Blue's head.

"But I need my sleep," I whined. "I fight when I'm awake, I don't want to have to do it while I'm sleeping too."

"I'm sorry, Godhunter," his eyes went soft and sad. "We all have our own battles. I would fight this for you but I can't. This one is yours. All I can do is give you the weapons you need."

"What about a weapon to stop him from getting into my dreams?" I asked for about the fifth time.

"We've tried that," he was so patient. I would have strangled me by now. "It appears that Huitzilopochtli is too strong."

"Can't I just practice more, train harder?"

"No," his voice finally took on a firm edge. "We're wasting time, Vervain. You must train, that's true, but you must train to be aware in your dreaming. Once you've mastered that, you can turn the dream on him. He is the invader. It's your world and you can mould it into whatever you want it to be."

"Hmmm," I contemplated that for a second. "That has

possibilities."

"Finally," he leaned his head back in relief. All that shining black hair swished back with him and I couldn't help admiring it. When he looked up, he caught me staring and smiled slowly. "Those are not thoughts you should be having in your lover's bed."

"Then stop being so damn sexy," I crossed my arms petulantly. "I can't control my every thought."

"*Yes*, you can," Teharon leaned forward and took my hand, pulling my arms free. "It's what I've been trying to tell you all along. Now concentrate. See yourself in the dream from last night."

"Alright," I closed my eyes and pictured the restaurant.

"Have you got it?"

"Yes," I mumbled.

"I'm doing this for you, Godhunter," he said sternly.

"I know," I sighed. "I apologize for my churlishness. Go ahead."

"I was thinking it was more *child*ishness but okay," he squeezed my hand when I started to make a comeback. "Recall what he said, the feelings, the smells, everything around you."

"Got it," I remembered so much more now. Odd that I didn't notice the smell of the sea in my dream but I remembered it when I was awake.

"Now change it," he took my other hand and I felt his strength reassure me. "Think about how you'd have preferred the dream to go and change it to be that way. Start by concentrating on the little details, what he was wearing, a table, a lamp, the food. Change the little things and the rest will become easier."

I nodded as I tried. There, on the table, was a crystal bowl full of red roses. Blue's favorite color. I focused and changed them to yellow. It took a bit of trying but once they went, I was able to grasp the feeling of the transformation and it became easier. I got rid of the bowl completely, then the table. I emptied the restaurant till we were just standing in an open space.

“Okay,” I smiled as I continued to focus. “I've changed the scene, now what?”

“Change your interaction,” Teharon instructed. “You won't be able to control his response because he isn't a part of your world, he's an interloper, so don't waste energy on trying. What you *can* do, is use his presence as a door into his head. He has to enter a dreamstate to get into your dreams. He's just as vulnerable as you are, even more so since he's putting out the effort to get into your mind. He's laying siege and has left his own castle unguarded, as it were. You can steal into his thoughts while he's distracted in your head.”

“Anything else?” I smiled maliciously.

“It's your dream,” I heard him chuckle. “You can do whatever you want in it, be whomever you want.”

“Sweet,” I returned to the scene in my head eagerly.

I turned it into an interrogation room. Blue was strapped to a metal chair, a harsh light shining straight into his face. He squinted up at me, shadowed in the dark of the room, and I laughed. Perfect. It was easy once I got the hang of it.

“No problem,” I opened my eyes and let the vision go.

“Very good,” Teharon scooted back against the wall. “Now we try the real thing.”

“The real thing?” I looked over at him in surprise. “I'm not tired.”

"I'm a healer," he spread his hands. "I can put you to sleep and wake you back up again if need be."

"Oh," I frowned, unsure of how I felt about that.

"Lie down," he patted the bed beside him. "I can keep a light contact with your mind if I keep contact with you physically."

"Okay," I eased myself down next to him and closed my eyes. I felt a little better knowing that Teharon would be there.

"Sleep, Godhunter," his voice swept over me like a warm blanket pulled up to my chin. I found myself drifting down into myself; my body heavy and limbs languid.

Then I was in lying in another bed, in another part of the God Realm. I turned my head and Blue rose above me, a soft smile on his lips. I looked past him and took in the details of the rest of the room. It was his bedroom I was in now, his bed I was lying in. Big surprise.

"Back so soon, little witch," his hand played down my cheek. "How about a different type of dancing tonight?"

"What were you doing; just sitting around waiting for me to fall asleep?" I lifted a brow and ignored his question.

"Your shields weaken as soon as you enter REM," he rolled his body over mine and I realized we were both nude. "I can feel it."

"Whoa there," I pushed him off and visualized my fighting gear on me.

"Someone's been teaching you," Blue's eyes narrowed on my leather vest.

"You don't think I'm capable of learning on my own?" I got up from the bed and slowly, I started to alter the room around us.

“What are you doing?” He jumped up, still naked, and stared at the room in horror.

“I just thought you might like to see the actual room I'm sleeping in,” I swept my hand out. “What do you think?”

“This is your bedroom?” He calmed and started to look around with interest. “It's not at all what I expected.” He peered at the huge cathedral crystal in the corner.

“No, not mine,” I smiled as his eyes shot to me. “I'm living with Thor now.” I failed to mention it was temporary. Sue me.

“You're *what*?!” The red of his eyes started to churn like blood in shark-infested water.

“I tried to tell you nicely and you wouldn't listen. So you've forced me to be mean. The reason I'm so exhausted right now is because I just had amazing sex in that bed,” I pointed at the dream version of Thor's bed. “With Thor.”

“You lie,” he stalked forward and grabbed my arm.

The second he touched me, I pushed my consciousness into him and flew down the link into his mind. He screamed and tried to pull away but I grabbed him with my other hand and I was amazingly strong in my dream.

It was easier to filter through his thoughts now that I'd had some practice and I soon found what I was after; another plot to kill Maria. I knew the details within a moment and wasted no time in escaping his thoughts.

“Invading my mind won't stop me from coming here,” he growled.

“And invading my mind won't stop me from cumming with Thor,” I smirked, relieved that he seemed to have no idea what I'd been after in his head.

He shouted in frustration, pulling away from me and raking his hands through his hair. “You're cruel, little witch. All I want is some of your time, some consideration.”

“I might have been more inclined to give it to you, if you hadn't, oh I don't know, *abducted and raped me!*” I screamed the last part at him.

“That again?” He looked truly baffled.

“Yeah, that again,” I threw down my hands and felt my claws make a comforting click as they extended. “I should castrate you. Maybe then you'd realize how evil what you did to me was. It's only a dream right? You won't actually be missing your cock when you wake up.”

“Hmph,” his lips twisted into a little smile. “You still haven't learned how useless your weapons are against me.”

“Not here, they're not,” I smiled viciously and leapt forward, punching him in the face before he could react. Then I spun around into a crouch, preparing for any counter attack.

He was screaming, holding his face as if it might fall apart. Blood gushed from between his fingers and he pulled his hands away to stare at it in shock. The whole left side of his face, from cheekbone to jaw, was in ruins. Flesh was hanging free and I could see the white of bone glinting through all that red.

“Now,” I stood up. “Get the fuck out of my head.”

He started to fade away, still naked and bleeding, but right before he disappeared, he smiled grotesquely and said, “You're the first woman to make *me* bleed.”

“What the hell?” I exclaimed as I sat up in Thor's bed and looked into Teharon's worried eyes. “Is it just me or was he turned on by the way I flayed his face open?”

“It's not just you,” Teharon sighed. “Huitzilopochtli has gone mad, I fear.”

“At least I succeeded in taking control of my dream.”

“Yes, well done. I just worry that it's going to be harder next time, now that he knows what you're capable of,” Teharon grimaced.

I felt a wedge of cold fear slide into me. Next time? I wasn't sure if I wanted to do that again, even if I did have the upper hand. Teharon laid a hand upon my shoulder and I slid into his arms for a sympathetic hug. I just wasn't sure who was comforting who. Then the door opened and Thor walked in to stand at the foot of the bed.

“Do you mind taking your hands off my girlfriend?” Thor glowered at Teharon but when we shot apart, he started laughing. “Sorry, I've just been waiting for an opportunity to call you my girlfriend,” he laughed again. “Girlfriend, it's so quaint.”

“Yes, lovely,” I sighed and sank back against Teharon.

“I didn't mean it was okay to go back to hugging him,” Thor glowered and crawled up into the bed on my other side. “If you need hugging, I'm available.” I rolled my eyes at Teharon and transferred myself into Thor's embrace as he asked, “Why do you need hugging?”

“I've never been in bed with two men before,” I waggled my brows at Thor in an obvious attempt to distract him. “How close are you and Teharon?”

“Vervain,” Thor growled while Teharon chuckled.

“I am *not* getting into the middle of this,” Teharon scooted off the bed and made a hasty retreat.

“So no threesomes?” I pouted at Thor.

"Not unless it's you, me, and my cock," Thor rumbled.

"I can't seem to remember his name," I crawled into his lap and gave him a wicked smile. "You might have to reintroduce us."

Chapter Thirty

I stared up at the red castle walls stretching away from me to either side. They were topped by the occasional turret and manned by Russian guards. The medieval looking exterior was appropriate in my opinion. The Russian government was a collection of barbaric crusaders, torn between their desire to save their people and their greed. Or maybe I'm just a biased American.

"How are we going to get in?" I stood in front of the Kremlin, those imposing rust-red walls towering over us as the river rushed past behind us.

"We're not," Thor looked over to Horus. "He is."

"Me again, eh?" Horus smirked.

"All you have to do is get in and replace the poison with this," I held up a bag of sugar cubes. "Ilya will be under Blue's influence so he won't know the difference."

The poison Blue had given Prime Minister Medvedev's son to use on Maria Putina, had been dripped onto cubes of sugar with the intent of Ilya serving them to Maria Putina with her coffee. She and her father, President Putin, were visiting with the Medvedevs that very second. Ilya would be implicated in Maria's death with assorted planted evidence (which Medvedev would most likely cover-up) but the President would assume the poison had been intended for him and the seed would be planted.

"No problem," Horus changed into falcon form and took the little bag of sugar cubes in his talons.

"Be careful to stay invisible," I called after him as he flew away. "Blue's going to be close by."

"He knows," Thor took my hand and led me down the sidewalk like we were simply two tourists out for a stroll. "We're watching the perimeter just in case Blue shows his face. It'll be fine."

"My face is right here, Viking," Blue was leaning against the railing next to the river, looking as if he'd been standing there the whole time.

"You just don't give up," I huffed as Thor angled in front of me.

"Neither do you," Blue frowned, his eyes losing focus for a second, as if he were watching another scene entirely. "So you've thwarted me again. Enjoy your success, little witch. It won't last for long."

"I'm sorry, could you just say *Bwahaha* and rub your hands together after you say things like *thwarted me again*?" I smirked at him from the safety of Thor's side.

"You'll slip up," Blue scowled at me. "I don't know how you're getting your information but the flow is going to stop. I'll find your spy and plug the leak. Just a warning between friends."

"Oh you should put a plug in it alright," I smirked.

"There will also come a time when you won't have your bodyguard," Blue lifted his shades and looked me up and down with his disturbing eyes. "I count the hours."

"I'll give you something to count," I growled as I dropped my claws. "I don't need a bodyguard."

"Vervain," Thor put his arm out to hold me back, "not here."

"Yes, listen to your thug," Blue dropped his sunglasses back in place. "I'll see you tonight, little witch."

He traced away before I could say anything more.

"Oh, I hate it when he does that," I seethed.

"Threatens to abduct you?" Thor turned to me and stroked his hands up and down my arms gently.

"No; leaves before I can have the last word."

Chapter Thirty-One

"I thought we could go out today," Thor said casually as he handed me a cup of coffee. We were having breakfast on his balcony. "The only time you've left Bilskinir has been to stop Blue from killing Maria and I know how you hate being cooped up here."

"Where did you want to go?" I poured some cream and sugar into my cup as I considered his suggestion.

"I thought we could take my boat out."

Me and him alone in the middle of the ocean. No Aztec invading my dreams and no Russian woman to save. It sounded like heaven. Well, except for the ocean part.

"I'd like that," I said, only actually half sure of my statement.

"Great, take your time here while I go gather some things." He got up from the table, kissed me quickly, and left humming *A Pirate's Life*.

I huffed a little laugh, then relaxed and ate my breakfast. The previous day with Blue seemed like a nightmare, dispelled with the coming of the sun. Horus had been successful and Maria was still alive but part of me knew this could become a never-ending battle. I needed to find a more permanent way to stop Blue's attempts on her life.

"*How do you solve a problem like Maria?*" I sang into my coffee. "*How do you catch a cloud and pin it down?*"

I giggled when I realized I'd reduced my Blue issues to a song from *The Sound of Music.* Truly though, there was nothing to be done about it immediately, so why not let it go? I started to feel better with every mouthful of food, every sip of coffee. Humming Julie Andrews songs seemed to help.

When I was through, I got up and went to the closet to get dressed. I put on a bikini, which I didn't intend on actually swimming in but which showed off my cleavage nicely, and then a batik sarong over it. I tied the sarong at my waist casually. I could always retie it into a dress if I needed to cover up more later. Then I slipped on some sandals and a pair of sunglasses before I pulled my hair back in a ponytail. Done.

I found Thor in the kitchen, which was a huge stainless steel monstrosity, so modern it made me ill. I liked cozy kitchens with baskets, center islands, and pot racks hanging over them, not brushed steel. I tried to hide my distaste as I wandered over to him. He had a large bag stuffed with food and was wearing a pair of green swimming shorts. He looked heavenly.

"You ready, babe?" He slung his free arm over my shoulders and led me to the tracing room.

"Yep," I slid my arm around his waist, loving the feel of his tight stomach. "Let's go."

We traced into his ship's dining room. The place where I'd first met everyone. He put the food in the fridge and then took me up top. I watched while he undid the moorings, fascinated by the play of his muscles, and that's when I the thought struck me that the boat seemed way too big for one man to handle alone. Not that I knew anything about boats.

"Don't you need a crew?" I followed him to the helm, which was up a flight of stairs and in an enclosed, air conditioned room.

He stopped short and gave me a patronizing look. "I'm a god, remember? Not just any god but a god of seafaring. I think I can handle one little ship all by myself."

“Oh,” I watched in fascination as he started the engine of his *little ship* and steered it out into open waters. “Aye, aye Cap’n,” I saluted and he chuckled.

“I hereby hire you on as my First Mate.” His face filled with so much joy as he looked out on the wide expanse of sea. He was completely at home. Too bad the place where I felt completely at home at was fading fast behind us.

“Ooooh, First Mate, eh?” I snuggled up against his back and wrapped my arms around his waist as he steered.

His laugh rumbled through his back and into my chest. “First and only, darling.”

The amount of joy those four words filled me with was ridiculous. I thought back to my previous life and couldn’t believe where I’d ended up. If you'd told me a month ago that I'd wind up happily setting off to sea wrapped around a Norse god in just a few weeks, I'd have called you several names, the least of which would have been *crazy*.

“You seem different,” I drifted off to the side and took a seat in one of the huge chairs which were bolted to the floor.

“Different from what?” He spared me a quick glance.

“From how you are on land,” I shrugged. “More playful I guess.”

“I used to be like this all the time,” his smile wavered a bit. “I don't know if you've ever read any of the stories they tell about me but I was a *live in the moment* kind of man.”

“Does this have anything to do with that rock in your forehead?” I smirked.

“Not my finest moment,” he grimaced, “and not the most light-hearted of stories. You know, I once dressed in drag.”

"Shut up," I laughed and leaned forward in my chair. "Tell me all about it."

"It was a long time ago," his grin widened. "I was more fun then."

"I think you're pretty fun now."

"I think you've brought back the joy to my life," he shot me a quick look that warmed me down to my toes. "Fighting against my father has robbed me of most of my humor but with you, I remember how to laugh."

"You are *so* getting lucky today," I gave him a sexy wink.

An hour or so later, I was wondering if he was ever gonna stop the ship so I could get on with the getting lucky portion of our day. I was once more plastered against him from behind but he didn't seem to be getting the message. What did a girl have to do to get her some hot Viking loving?

"Where are we headed, Baby Thunder?" I peered around Thor's side just as a dolphin broke the surface of the water in front of the boat. "Look, look," I pointed.

He laughed and put an arm around my shoulder, bringing me up beside him. "They're playing in the froth. Do you want me to stop the ship so you can join them?"

"Uh, no, I prefer to play with you," I smiled nervously.

"Are you scared of dolphins?" He looked like he was surprised I'd be scared of anything. It kinda made me fall a little harder for him.

"No, just a little paranoid of deep water." I looked away, worried that he'd take it badly.

"You're afraid of the ocean?" He was astounded.

“I don’t like my legs dangling into someone’s backyard,” I tried really hard for a light tone. “Especially when that someone has sharp teeth. I just feel like bait.”

“Bait?” He laughed and it was his booming, glass-shaking laugh. I glared at him but it only made him laugh harder. “You live on an island.”

“I didn’t say I couldn’t swim,” I crossed my arms and huffed, “I just don’t want to frolic in the deep blue.”

“Oh you’re going to frolic,” he pulled me against him, crossed arms and all. “You’ll frolic with me in the deep blue and you’ll like it.”

“Anyone ever tell you you’re a pompous jerk?” I kept my arms crossed, even though he was pulling me tightly to his chest and it was getting uncomfortable. That’ll show him.

“Vervain, nothing will hurt you when I’m in the water with you,” he shook his head at me like I was being silly. “The predators can feel my presence and will keep their distance.”

I heaved a sigh. “I know you’re right but paranoia doesn’t make sense, that’s the whole point.”

“It’ll be alright, you’ll see,” he kissed my forehead.

Then he let me go so he could stop the boat. Great, this so wasn’t what I wanted him to stop the boat for. He took me by the hand and led me down to the back of the ship. I looked at the ledge hanging off the back of the boat, slapping the water with each wave, and blanched. I could feel my breath coming faster and I was pretty sure I was shaking but everything kind of took a back seat to the sight of all that blue I was about to get into. Blue, huh; I guess there was more than one I didn't like.

There were things in all that water, things that liked to nibble on the toes of stupid humans who dangled their feet into someone else's territory. The ocean was so deep, we couldn't even explore it all. Deep sea was like deep space; who knew what was down there? Who knew what could come up at any moment for a look see? Or a light lunch.

"Ah," I tried to pull away but I was weak from terror. "You just go ahead and I'll watch from here."

Thor frowned and studied me. I don't think he really understood the depths, no pun intended, of my paranoia.

"You really *are* afraid." He blinked at me. Nope, he just didn't get it.

"No, I'm a compulsive liar," I snorted, my hands clenched tightly at my sides.

"Darling, nothing will hurt you, I swear it." He held both of my fists in his hands.

"Sure," I nodded a little too quickly. "I believe you."

"Okay," he let me go and started towards the ledge. "I'm going to go in and I want you to come and just sit here."

"Yeah okay," I walked over slowly.

He jumped in, splashing me, and I even laughed at that, I was so relieved that I wouldn't have to go in. He smiled at me as he tread water, then looked over his shoulder at the pod of dolphins swimming nearby. They immediately swam closer. I watched in amazement as they approached him, nudging him with heads and flippers. He swam almost as well as they did and the dolphins seemed to enjoy his company.

After awhile, he came back over to my ledge and a dolphin trailed after him. I laughed like a little girl when it popped its head up next to me, clicking and chirping in its secret language.

"What's that, Flipper?" I leaned toward the dolphin like I

could understand it. "Someone's in trouble?" Thor's smile looked a little confused, so I explained. "It was an old TV show with a little boy who was friends with a dolphin."

"Well, I think *you've* got a new friend," he stroked the high gray forehead and the dolphin dipped underwater, then came up a little closer. "Come in with us, baby."

Oh crap, I should've known this was where it was headed. I stalled by reaching out to the dolphin. It jerked its head up and tapped my hand with its snout. I laughed and a little of the fear eased away. Two more heads popped up around us and loud chirping sounds filled the air. I didn't know dolphins behaved like this without being trained.

Most people would have loved to have been in my shoes. What was wrong with me? I looked at Thor, smiling brightly, the sunlight rebounding off the water to coat him in gold and all those beautiful mammals swimming beside hi. I was about to relent when the soundtrack to Jaws started playing in my head. Duh nah… duh nah, duh nah.

"Darling, even if I weren't here," he laid back into the middle of the pod and more heads broke the surface, "you'd be safe because of them. Dolphins can kill sharks and their mere presence will discourage attacks."

He was telling me things I already knew. It didn't help. You can't reason with paranoia. Why do people always try to fix you with reason? I frowned and hugged my knees to my chest. I didn't need fixing. I just needed to be left alone. On the boat.

"I'm fine where I am, thanks." I scanned the horizon for more fins. "*Discourage* doesn't mean they won't attack. Sharks have no fear."

"Vervain," Thor swam up to the boat again. "I want to feel your soft skin rubbing against mine. I want your legs wrapped around me while we swim together," he held onto the ledge and caught me in a piercing, lightning-filled stare. "I want to feel the heat of your mouth on mine while the ocean cools us."

As quickly as that, the fear was gone, replaced by hot desire. I held his gaze as I stood and the look on his face was pure sex. Tingles of excitement rushed through me as I undid the sarong and flung it behind me. It fluttered to the deck as Thor swam back a little to give me room.

"Oh, you're good," I dove into the water and came sliding up against his chest. "I give up. I'm no match against centuries of sweet talk experience."

His breath was warm and fast against my neck when he pulled me tighter to him and whispered, "I love your surrender almost as much as your conquest."

"Conquest?" I wrapped my legs around his waist, just like he wanted, and let him tread water for the both of us.

"You know I'm yours," he kissed his way up my neck and met my gaze with such heat, I was grateful for the water's chill.

"Are you?" I was suddenly out of breath, "For how long?"

"As long as you want me," he silenced any more questions by putting my mouth to much better use.

I felt a long, silky body slide along my back and stiffened for a second before I remembered the dolphins. I almost giggled, I was so excited. I leaned back and reached out to them. A head surfaced beneath my hand and big dark eyes regarded me with amazing intelligence. The long mouth opened and an excited clicking came from it.

I let go of Thor and he gently pushed me toward the dolphin. Slick, thick skin flowed under my hands as the dolphin dove. I caught its dorsal fin and it pulled me along with it under the water. I grabbed on tight with my other hand as we broke the surface and shook the water out of my eyes. Thor laughed and I felt so free that I joined in. Where had all my fear gone? A small part of me knew this was Thor's doing in more ways than one but I didn't care. I was having too much fun.

Have you ever rode a horse? Felt the power of a beast beneath you? Known the exhilaration of being carried along by the speed of another creature faster than yourself? Had the kinship of being connected to an animal you'd previously thought of as untouchable, too wild to be touched? Riding a horse is wonderful but it pales in comparison to riding a dolphin.

Never before had I felt so honored, befriended by an animal whose grace and intelligence set it apart from other species, almost to the point where it became otherworldly. Sliding through the water with them, I felt the lure of the ocean for the first time. The beauty and power of a separate world within our own, a world in which these creatures ruled. A world into which I was being welcomed.

The dolphin brought me in a complete circle and I ended up in front of Thor again. I reached for him and he pulled me back in against his chest. He felt so good, all slick and solid. His bright, red hair was plastered to him and glittered darker than when it was dry. He had a perma-grin plastered on as well and I realized how important it was for him to share this with me.

"I knew you could do it," he licked the salt from my lips. "Nothing scares my girl for long."

I kissed him deeper and he groaned as he pressed up against me, hard and ready. The dolphins splashed around us, chattering and sliding against our skin. I leaned back and wrapped my legs around Thor, so I could float on the surface but still be connected to him. His hands slid up my waist and over the mounds of flesh that rose out of my blue bikini top. I sighed and rubbed little circles over his forearms, amazingly content and happy.

Then he reached behind me and undid the tie that held my top on. He quickly pulled it from me, tossing it on board the ship before I could protest. I screeched, covering my chest with my arms and sitting back up against him. The water gushed up between us.

"There's no one here but us and the dolphins," Thor laughed. "I really don't think they're interested in you like that."

"Anyone could sail up," I scanned the horizon for ships.

"By the time they got close enough to see you, we'd already have you covered." He slid a hand between us and twirled a nipple in his fingers. "Let me see you. I've been dreaming about what your body would look like surrounded only by the sea and me."

"You're slick, you know that?" I gave him a Mona Lisa smile and lay back into the water slowly, drawing my hands down his arms as I went. I felt my hair float out around me, swirling like seaweed. His face went still and his chest rose faster.

"You make reality so much better than fantasy." He stared at me, his eyes flashing brighter and brighter.

Then his hands were sliding over me, stroking my breasts before going lower, and I tightened my legs around him to keep myself lifted. One of his hands reached under to support me so I could relax my grip and I briefly wondered how he was staying afloat without kicking.

"Relax, darling," he leaned over and licked first one then the other breast as I sighed in delight. "My magic is holding us, just let go."

So I did. I let go of my fears and inhibitions as he held onto me and changed my mind about the sea.

Chapter Thirty-Two

We spent the whole afternoon playing with the dolphins, making love, eating sandwiches, and drinking champagne. It was heaven and I didn't want to leave. I had never had so much fun in the water. Thor one, Paranoia zero.

When it started to get dark, we showered together in the main cabin, then rested a bit on his huge bed before heading in to shore. Thor steered while I helped. Which basically means that I held the wheel and he stood pressed up behind me as he did the real steering. Lately, life had felt like a car chase and letting go of the wheel was not an option. It was almost a relief to let someone else have control for a little while.

The sun was making its last curtain call as we approached Waikiki. It clung to the tips of the buildings, turning glass and steel into a sparkling masterpiece. From a cheap print to a priceless original, the city had a moment of supreme glory before the sun finally left the stage. Artificial lights were already sprinkling on all over the island but the man-made illumination seemed a cheap imposter. I was never one for worshiping the sun, being more of the moonstruck variety, but right then, as I watched those last rays die out, a chill crawled over me and I had the strangest feeling that I'd appreciate the sun more when next I saw it.

I shook off the unsettling sensation as Thor docked the boat and took me ashore for some dinner. We walked up into Waikiki from the Yacht club and then into The Hawaii Prince Hotel. On the ocean side of the hotel, the lobby had a two-story wall made entirely of glass. It was beautiful but glass walls made me nervous. Nothing to hide behind. So I passed through the cavernous lobby, sneaking glances over my shoulder at the fragile barrier. Night had turned the glass into a mirror, making it even more disturbing. There could be monsters lining up outside and I wouldn't know it till they came crashing through. I shook my head free of my violent musings and focused back on Thor. If I could face the ocean, I could handle a simple glass wall.

Thor led me up an escalator to the hotel's restaurant for a meal that we were both supremely under-dressed for. The staff barely looked twice though. It's Hawaii, casual is the dress code everywhere. You can get dolled up if you like but being under-dressed doesn't earn you the same stares as it would on the mainland. So I stopped worrying about dining in my bikini-sarong combo and just enjoyed my dinner.

It was fabulous. The food, the view, and the company. I forgot about my earlier unease under Thor's admiring stares. How could any woman keep thinking morose thoughts with that kind of attention? It's just not possible. So I let it all go and allowed myself to relax.

It was one of the best days of my life, right up until I headed into the ladies room. Someone grabbed me by the hair and pushed me into the cold marble counter. My forearms took most of the impact and I used the force of it to fling myself around and face my attacker. She was blonde and very pale.

"You think he loves you?" She spat at me. "He doesn't love you. Just look at you; you're disgusting. Fat and ugly with hair the color of dirt."

"What the hell?" It took me a second to figure out. "Oh. Sif, right?"

"Yes, right," she sneered and threw a punch.

I ducked and punched her in the belly. She made a nice satisfying grunt and then I slammed her head into the marble and heard an even more satisfying sound. Crack.

"I don't give a shit what you think about me," I spat into her ear as I kneed her in the stomach. "You're not the one he just had crazy ocean sex with." I pushed her away and she landed sprawled against the far wall. "I am."

I walked out of the bathroom and back to our table with a huge grin. It was terribly petty and part of me was disappointed in myself but I had enjoyed beating up Thor's ex-wife. The only problem was; I still had to pee.

Fortunately, Thor had already paid the bill, so we were able to leave immediately. He raised his eyebrow when I headed into the first public restroom we came across but he was a gentleman and didn't say anything. I wasn't sure if I should tell him about Sif or not. Would it make a difference for him to know that his ex really was hunting me down?

As we headed down the backstreets towards the Yacht Club, a growl came out of the darkness and I automatically threw down my hands to release the blades from the gloves *I wasn't wearing*. You'd think I'd have remembered from my recent fight with Sif that I was completely unarmed, not even a protection spell handy. You would also think that I'd be more on my guard just in case she had followed us. And while you're doing all of this thinking, maybe you could think up a way for me to not be such an idiot.

"Damn it!" I searched the shadows. "Another werewolf."

"Froekn?" Thor glared at the shadows around us.

As I continued to scan the night, I heard a second and then a third growl. They were getting cautious and increasing their numbers. I should've been flattered I guess.

"How many are there?" Thor wondered, just as a wolf launched itself at him.

"Thor!" I screamed but the wolf wasn't actually after Thor.

He kept sailing over Thor's head and landed on me,

knocking me to the ground. I felt the asphalt tear into my back and hissed as the road-rash spread but my main concern was the wolf snapping at me from my chest.

I had raised my arms as I fell, so he didn't get my throat but he was snapping at my arms and clawing up my belly. The sharp tang of my blood was already in the air and the pain from multiple wounds was beginning to consume me. In seconds, I'd either be gutted by those thick claws or lose my throat to his teeth. Thor would never make it in time.

They say before you die, your whole life passes before your eyes. Well, I don't know about everyone else but my past didn't show up at all. What I saw was my future, or maybe it was just what I hoped my future would be. I saw everything I wanted to do, places I wanted see, and people I hoped to meet. I saw the children I'd never have and felt a great despair that they'd never be born. Which was really weird since I wasn't even sure I wanted children. In fact, my lifestyle kind of worked against it. Then I saw Thor and the kind of father he'd be to those potential babies.

All of it flashed by in a second and before it was through, the wolf was off me, dangling in the air above me. I looked up, a little shocked to be relatively whole, and saw a werewolf shaking the wolf like he was a bad puppy. In the shadows around us more wolves crept, snarling and snapping in our direction.

"Enough," the werewolf growled back at them. "Don't make me kill you all to protect a human. She's mine, you smell my scent on her and still you've track her. You've brought this on yourselves. You know I'll fight you all if I have to. Is that what you want?" He threw the wolf at the others, barreling them down like bowling pins, and they rolled quickly away, whining as he continued to shout. "I don't want to but I will. A life for a life; I'm bound."

The wolves receded and the werewolf reached a paw down to help me up. I eyed the dangerous claws sticking out of that monstrous paw but really had no reason to fear them. He'd just saved my life after all. So I took the soft but dangerous paw, his claws closing gently around my hand, and let him help me up. Thor was standing beside us, lightning flashing not only in his eyes but in the sky as well. He reached for me as I regained my feet.

"Vervain, I'm sorry I failed you," Thor pulled me against him and I hissed in pain when his stomach brushed mine. "Shit," he swore and pulled away. Then he bent over to inspect the cuts closely. "They're superficial. Teharon can take care of them when we get home." He looked up at me but I was staring at the wolfman who had saved my life. Thor stood and turned to face him too.

"Trevor?" I peered cautiously into the werewolf's face.

He was even bigger than the last wolfman who had attacked me, taller and broader even than Thor, and he had a thick, beautiful black coat that shone silver in the moonlight. His muscles rippled under all that fur and although he had the head of a wolf, he practically oozed virile masculinity. Man and beast together in one fuzzy package. I knew then why Persephone thought they were sexy.

"Yes, I'm sorry I couldn't prevent the attack entirely," Trevor looked down toward his wolf feet, took a deep breath, and then stared up at me like he'd made an important decision. "I vow it will not come to that next time. I'll defend you with my life."

"You did more than enough," I reached out a hand to him and after a moment, he gave me his paw. "I saved you and you saved me. Thank you for your offer but we're even now, consider the debt paid in full."

He nodded curtly, like I'd said exactly what he'd expected me to. "We Froekn are a stubborn race and we take our obligations very seriously. As long as the contract stands, they'll come after you. You must be more careful, Godhunter."

"We will be," Thor put an arm around my shoulder and I rolled my eyes. He was being a possessive ass in front of someone who had just saved my life.

"Thor," I chided. "This is Trevor, he just saved my life. Trevor this is Thor, my well-meaning but rude boyfriend."

Trevor smiled, at least I think it was a smile, and surprisingly Thor smiled as well before he said to me, "I like it when you call me your boyfriend. I don't think anyone's ever called me that before."

"Okay," I shook my head. "We can talk about your strange Atlantean ways later but for now I'd appreciate it if you showed a little gratitude to the man who just saved your *girlfriend's* life."

Thor grimaced in embarrassment and extended his hand to Trevor immediately.

"My apologies and heartfelt thanks," Thor said as they shook. "Vervain's right; I wasn't able to reach her in time. I owe you a great debt."

"You owe me nothing," Trevor's voice was still that deep rumble. "Vervain spared me and I spared her but watch her well in the future, Thunderer. I can't control every wolf and I won't be able to hold off the entire pack."

"I'll do my best," Thor said stiffly. "Give my respects to Fenrir."

"He'll be pleased that you sent greetings, though probably not in the way he'll receive them." Trevor smiled that wolf grin again, full of teeth and a shockingly long tongue. Then he nodded goodbye to me and disappeared into the night.

Yep, when the sun came up again, I'd be happy to see it.

Chapter Thirty-Three

“We need to call the God Squad together,” I announced as I walked into Thor's bedroom.

“Why, what's happened now?” Thor sat up in his chair by the fire, placing a book on the table beside him.

“I just got through with another spirit-walk and Blue's got a new plan to kill Maria,” I shook my head. “What is it with him and that girl?”

“I think mainly, it's that her death will destroy not only Putin's relationship with Medvedev but Putin's mind as well,” Thor sighed. “However, it could also be that once he locks onto a target, Huitzilopochtli doesn't give up.”

“It would sure explain his obsession with me,” I sniffed in irritation. “Anyway, can you call them all and have them meet us at my place?”

“Sure,” he stood up. “Wait, why your place?”

“I need to pick up some things and there's food in the fridge I should use before it goes bad,” I shrugged. “Having them over will kill two gods with one sword.”

“Maybe lay off on the god killing analogies when you're living with one, darling,” Thor grimaced.

“Point taken,” I nodded and headed out to go find my cat. Nick needed some time to prowl the real world.

“And, darling,” Thor called after me.

“Yes,” I poked my head back into the room.

“What's a God Squad?”

Chapter Thirty-Four

"Thanks for coming, everyone," I placed the platter of meat and cheese down on the low table in my living room. They all dug in instantly. "And thanks for bringing your appetite."

"Anytime you feel the need to feed people," Pan waved a chicken leg at me, "I'm your god."

"Well, I didn't want it to go to waste," I sat on the sofa next to Thor. "It's been awhile since I've been home and I was worried that the meat would go bad."

"No worries with us," Persephone nibbled at a piece of cheese. "You can't give a god food poisoning."

"Oh, I didn't even think of that," I saluted them with my coke can. "Eat up, I have some sausage I wasn't going to serve but you're all welcome to it if you'd like."

Enthusiastic grunting was all the response I got.

"So, I noticed you haven't put up any Christmas lights," Pan said with a mischievous look.

Horus made a disgusted sound in response; half snort/half choke.

"What; you got a problem with Christmas?" I raised a brow at Horus while Pan giggled.

"It's not Christ's birthday," Horus stared morosely at the floor, the chicken forgotten in his hand. "JC's birthday is in March."

"He's just got a burned butt over it because it's actually *his* birthday," Pan elbowed Horus, who pulled himself upright like a bird ruffling its feathers.

"December 25 is your birthday?" I blinked in surprise. I knew the whole Christmas thing was really about taking the Winter Solstice from the Pagans but I had no idea Horus was involved.

"Horus," Thor rubbed a hand over his face in annoyance. "Get over it. It's been hundreds of years, man. A lot of religions got intertwined, it's no big deal."

"No big deal?" Horus puffed up. "*I* was called the *Lamb of God. I* had twelve apostles, and *my* myths spoke of my crucifixion and consequent resurrection in three days. His stories were my stories *first*!"

"They called you a lamb?" I squished up my face in horror.

"Among other titles... also stolen," Horus sniffed.

"You were *not* called a lamb," Thor sighed. "It's been so long, even you don't remember things accurately. And by the way, everyone thought it was my birthday too."

"Wait, it's your birthday too?" Shoot, I had to go get a gift. What does one give their god boyfriend?

"Nah," Thor shrugged, "my people just thought it was. I was born in July."

"Oh," I sighed. Good, I had awhile to prepare then. "Wait, the Vikings celebrated your birthday on Christmas? So, it should really be Thormas?"

"No," Horus ground out while everyone else laughed. "Haven't you been listening? It should be Horusmas."

"Horusmas!" Pan started to cackle. "You've got to be shitting me! That's fucking hilarious. Horusmas. Happy Horusmas!"

"What's wrong with Horusmas?" Horus inhaled sharply.

"It just doesn't roll off the tongue, now does it?" Pan kept laughing. "Merry Horusmas!"

"I think it has a regal ring to it," Horus sniffed.

"It almost sounds like *whore's a miss,"* Pan giggled.

"That doesn't make any sense," Horus glared at Pan.

"Oka-a-ay," I blinked slowly. "So anyway, if anyone's interested, I know Blue's next move."

"Just ignore Horus, Vervain," Brahma shot the Egyptian god a wry look. "We all do. Go ahead, what did you find out?"

"He's planing on murdering Maria when her family goes on vacation," I announced. Honestly, I was getting really tired of saving this woman. "The Putins own a dacha, a little Russian vacation house outside of Moscow. Blue's going to use Medvedev's driver to gun them down on their way to the dacha but he only intends to kill Maria. He needs Putin alive for everything to work."

"So we take out the driver?" Thor asked. He had Nick's forepaws on his shoulder and was stroking the cat's back soothingly. Whether it was more soothing for him or Nick, I wasn't sure.

"I'm not down with killing an innocent," I frowned and started stroking Nick. I needed some kitty comfort too.

"He's a potential assassin," Horus pointed out.

"He's a potential *victim*," I clarified. "And I'm not killing a man for something Blue is compelling him to do."

"So what do we do?" Teharon pondered. "This isn't a bomb or poison we can just remove from the situation. We could protect the family but that would still leave the driver looking like an assassin."

"We don't have to kill him to stop him," Mrs. E said simply. "Set a trap for the driver, head him off and grab him right before he reaches the Putins."

"That's why I love you," Mr. T kissed her cheek. "You're brilliant."

"We'll have to hold him till they leave the dacha," I pointed out. "Otherwise Blue can just have him try again." I dropped my head into my hands and scrubbed my face. "This is going to be endless, isn't it?"

"They won't stay more than a few days I'm sure," Pan stuffed a piece of roast beef into his mouth and continued talking as he chewed. "I'll look after the dude, it'll be fine. I've got a lot of vodka."

"No, I mean this," I looked up and waved my hand out to include everyone. "Sneaking into Blue's head and trying to prevent whatever horror he's got planned next." An endless line of spirit-walks, invaded dreams, and frantic chases stretched out before me. "When's it gonna end?"

"When he's dead," Thor said grimly.

"But none of us are powerful enough to kill him," Ull looked around the room and then back at me. He raised a speculative eyebrow.

"I don't think I can kill him either," I shook my head. "So that means it'll never end. Blue's right; we'll slip up eventually. No one wins all the time. He's going to sneak something by us. Maybe I won't catch it or maybe we won't be able to stop him in time but either way, he's going to win from sheer perseverance."

"So do you stop fighting?" Teharon stared at me

speculatively.

“What?” I stared back in shock.

“When you know you'll lose eventually,” Teharon lifted one perfect brow, “do you still fight?”

“Of course,” I looked at Thor like maybe he knew why his friend had suddenly gone nuts. Thor just made an amused sniff and shrugged.

“Why?” Teharon planted his elbows on his knees, folded his hands beneath his chin, and stared harder.

“Because giving up is not an option,” I huffed. “Because if I'm going down, I'm going down fighting. Because the bad guys don't get to win that easily.”

“But it's not your fight,” Teharon's voice never rose above the level of polite conversation.

“I'm human,” I ground out, “this fight's more mine than yours.”

“That's right, Godhunter,” Teharon smiled like he'd just taught me an important lesson. “It's your fight because you made it so and you're not going to stop fighting, even when the odds are against you. So why waste your time worrying over what will or will not be? We have plans to make.”

“Okay,” I exhaled gruffly. “I'm shutting up now.”

“Holy hand grenades,” Ull exclaimed. “You shut up the Godhunter!”

Before I could yell at Ull, *The Devil went down to Georgia* started playing from the vicinity of Persephone's butt. She jumped guiltily, grimacing when everyone stared at her, and then pulled her cell phone out of her back pocket.

“Hey, baby,” she said into the receiver. “Uh… nothing... no I’m… uh, I’m hanging with some friends,” she swallowed and listened. “This isn’t really a good time… yes but… I don’t think that’s… well, I, uh…”

There was a knock at my front door and Persephone turned to look at it with round eyes before swinging her horrified gaze to me. I frowned as she flipped her phone shut and started to smile the smile people use when they're just about to tell you something you’re gonna want to throttle them for.

The knock came again; louder.

“Persephone,” I took a deep breath and let it out slowly. “That wouldn’t happen to be the Lord of the Underworld at my front door, would it?”

“Maybe,” she looked as if she were in pain and when the knock came again, she hid her face in her hands.

“Who is it?” I called in a sweet sing-song voice.

“Hades,” a low, gravelly response came through the door. “You’ve got my woman in there and she’s supposed to be with me.”

I looked back at Persephone in shock as I realized he was right. It was winter (it’s hard to remember seasons in Hawaii, give me a break). This was his time of the year to be with her. I’d be a little pissed off if I only got three months out of every year with Thor and he kept taking off on me too. I kind of felt bad for the guy, so I got up and opened the door.

In my doorway stood a man of average build and height with dark brown hair and clean-cut looks. His smile was boyish, his hair carelessly tousled, and his clothing was casual but tailored. He seemed very normal until I looked into his eyes. They were plain brown in color but behind those average irises, a fire raged and blazed through, as if his irises were made of colored glass. I had the eerie feeling that if I looked any closer, I'd be staring straight into Hell.

So if eyes were the windows to the soul, what did that say about Hades? I swallowed hard and smiled despite my unease.

“Hey, baby,” Persephone came to the door, giving me a minute to compose myself better. “I was just helping my friends out but I guess I can go now.”

Hades nodded to Persephone but he kept his gaze on me, looking me up and down, then up again. His head tilted to the side sharply.

“There’s something very familiar about you,” his eyes narrowed.

“Yeah, everyone says that about her,” Persephone went to cross the threshold at the same time that Hades tried to come inside. There was a little flash and Hades jerked back, looking stunned.

“Your home is warded,” Hades glanced over to the gathering of gods in my living room and then back at me. “Who *are* you?”

“Look, babe,” Persephone put her hands on her hips and faced off with him. “You said you were too busy to help me with my little projects, so I can’t tell you who she is. This is all top secret stuff that you’d already know if you were a good consort and supported me.”

Hades frowned and lifted a brow all at once. Which is really hard to do. I've tried it since then and failed.

“Is this really that important to you, Bunny Nose?” He asked.

Coughs and sputters erupted from the group behind me but

I managed to keep a straight face. Bunny Nose pouted and crossed her arms.

"You know it is," she let out a harsh puff of breath. "Don't try to *Bunny Nose* your way out of this. Other goddesses have consorts who support them completely," she looked pointedly over her shoulder at Mrs. E. "I'm tired of you ignoring me for nine months and then smothering and controlling me the other three. I get enough of that from my mother."

Holy crap, there was about to be a lover's spat of divine proportions on my doorstep. I had to do something. What to do? What to do?

"Hades, please enter my home and be welcome," I blurted.

Hades blinked at me, then smiled a surprisingly genuine smile. "Thank you," he stepped inside, "and may I bring no harm with me."

"I'm Vervain," I held out a hand to him and Persephone just gaped at us as Hades shook my hand excitedly.

"I'm Hades," he smiled wide and continued to shake my hand for a bit longer than necessary. "It's a pleasure to meet you, Vervain. I don't get introduced to many of Persephone's friends and this is the first time I've been invited into someone's home."

"That's just sad," I pondered Persephone for a moment, then looked back at him. "Okay you two, follow me," I turned and started heading towards my art room but I stopped when I realized they weren't behind me. "Come on, I don't have all night," I snapped.

They shot a look at each other, then followed me. When we got inside the room, I indicated a chair for each of them but I remained standing.

"You two have issues," I looked back and forth between

them. “Now normally that wouldn’t be any of my business but your issues are about to explode all over my living room. So I’m going to help you out just this once.”

“You think we need counseling?” Hades frowned at me.

“That would be a good start,” I sighed. “But I don’t have time for that you right now, so it’s going to be speed counseling.”

“Vervain, don’t you think I’m right?” Persephone had a small whine to her voice. “He should be more supportive.”

“No time for you guys to complain,” I waved a hand imperiously. “I’m going to tell you how it is and then you’re going to do your best to fix it… somewhere else. Do you understand me, Bunny Nose?” I glared at Persephone and she nodded, her face slack with shock, “How about you, Hot Stuff?”

Hades blinked rapidly but said, “I’m willing to try.”

“Okay, great,” I nodded curtly and mused a moment, trying to sort things through. “You’re feeling abused and controlled,” I pointed at Persephone and she nodded. Then I pointed at Hades. “You’re feeling neglected and horny.” Hades looked like he didn’t know whether to laugh or slap me, so he compromised and nodded too. “Alright Miss Sephy, here’s a really important question. Do you love him?”

“What do you mean?” Persephone looked even more shocked, if that was possible.

Hades just stared at her intently.

“Hades,” I hardened my gaze on him. “You’re going to have to step up here. I think our girl’s a little shy. Do you love her?”

“Yes,” no hesitation from Hades. Hooray for the Lord of the Underworld.

Persephone nearly got whiplash looking over at Hades in disbelief, "You do?"

"Bunny Nose," he kissed her cheek sweetly. "How could you ever doubt it?"

"I...," she looked at me and then back at him, "you never said."

"I show my love for you all the time," he frowned. Typical man.

"Okay," I held up a hand. "Common male misconception. Truth is; women need words. We like to be shown how much you love us after you *tell* us how much you love us. So now that we got that clear; Persephone, for the record, do you love Hades?"

"Yes," she whispered.

He smiled so radiantly, I almost needed to shade my eyes.

"Bravo," I held up my hands in the *at last* motion. "Now the really hard part. You," I pointed at her again, "need to grow up and stand up to your mommy."

Hades hooted with laughter as Persephone sputtered, "I'm very mature." Hades howled even louder until she smacked him.

"Don't argue with me," I shook a finger at her, "take a pointer from Nike and just do it."

"What does the Goddess of Victory have to do with this?" Hades' face twisted up in confusion and Persephone elbowed him.

"If you'd let me get a TV, you'd know what she's talking about," she stuck her tongue out at Hades.

"Thank you, Persephone," I said and she nodded, sweetly smug, until I continued, "that was very mature."

“Hey,” she pouted.

“Shu-u-ush,” I pointed to her again. “Tell your mama that you’re a grown woman and then start acting like it; move away from home.”

“What?” She looked like a doe caught in headlights.

“Either get your own place away from mommy dearest or move in with him,” I pointed back at Hades and he grinned at me like I was the best thing since beer. “Don’t get too happy with me yet, Sizzle Butt, you aren’t entirely blameless.”

He sat up straighter and raised both brows in surprise. “I’m the most loving of consorts,” he said defensively.

“Yeah, yeah somehow I don’t think your idea of loving and her idea of loving are the same.” I looked to Persephone and she nodded tightly.

“He wants sex all the time,” she crossed her arms. “Sex, sex, sex. I’m sore by the time I go home.”

“But Bunny Nose-,” he started but I cut him off.

“Shu-u-ush,” I narrowed my eyes on Hades. “Go buy a book on romance and try it out. You’ll be surprised how far a little consideration gets you. If you love her, show some interest in *her,* not just her body, and give her a little space. No one likes to be smothered. Got it?”

They both nodded.

“So what have we learned?” I quizzed them.

“I’m going to tell my mom to shove it and I'll move in with Hades,” Persephone intoned dutifully.

“Really, Bunny Nose?” Hades hugged her tightly and kissed her forehead. “I’ll try to be more supportive of you and I’ll romance you till you get fat on chocolate and the smell of roses makes you sick."

Persephone giggled and kissed him back, "I love you, Sizzle Butt." She giggled more.

I groaned and shook my head free of the knowledge that my joke nickname would be used in their sex talk for years to come.

"Okay, talk amongst yourselves, I'm going back to the others," I said as I stepped out of the room. They hardly even noticed when I left. The sound of smooching followed me down the hallway but I entered the living room to complete silence and steady stares.

Thor stood and took my arm to ask, "Are they both still alive?"

"What do you mean?" I'm not sure what my face looked like but I am sure it was horribly, totally, shocked.

"We didn't hear any screams but we heard Hades laugh and that could be just as bad," Pan grimaced.

"I gave them a bit of counseling, that's all," I shrugged.

"You what?" Thor sat back down. Hard.

"You gave relationship advice to the God of the Underworld and his reluctant bride?" Brahma spoke slowly like every word was difficult to pronounce.

"Well, I wouldn't call it advice so much as instructions," I sat down beside Thor.

"Instructions?" Teharon leaned forward.

"Yeah," I huffed in surprise. "I think it worked too, they seemed pretty happy in there." A high pitched giggle came out of my art room, right on cue. “The plan is for Persephone to move in with Hades and in return, he'll be a better consort.”

“Vervain,” Thor groaned.

“What?” I looked around and they all had matching expressions of dismay.

“Demeter’s going to throw a fit,” Ull seemed to say what everyone was thinking because they all nodded in agreement.

“So what?” I snorted. “She can’t control her daughter forever.”

“You don’t know Demeter,” Thor rubbed a hand over his face.

“Okay,” I shrugged, “she throws a fit, so what? She can have her temper tantrum and then she can get over it.”

“Demeter’s pretty good at the tantrums,” Ull scrunched up his face.

“Look, I know the story,” I spread my hands. “I also know that she’s not actually the cause of the seasons. She can’t keep the world in constant winter.”

“Not the whole world, no,” Teharon’s voice was a calming wind. “But she could probably keep a portion of it pretty cold. She's a single mom with hardly any friends and no family besides her daughter. Demeter is overly controlling when it comes to Persephone and her anger over her daughter leaving home for good could be disastrous.”

“Whatchu talkin’ bout, Willis?” I stared hard at Teharon and he raised his brows at me.

“She’s got weather magic,” he continued. “Demeter can alter the temperature and Persephone can make things grow. They’re a good team.”

“And I’m Yoko,” I groaned. “I just broke up the band.”

Chapter Thirty-Five

"Just set a trap for him," I mocked as I swung my kodachi at another vamp. "Head him off," the vamp's head went flying. "Grab him before he reaches the Putins," I fell back into the packed earth of the country road, to avoid being run down by yet another vampire on a motorcycle.

Everything had gone just as planned, up until we realized that Blue had changed his plans. Well not changed so much as amended. We'd prepared for a sleek black sports car to come plummeting down the dirt road. In light of those expectations, we'd dug a hole across the lane, covered it with tarp and dirt, then waited. The car had indeed arrived and wrecked as we'd hoped it would but a dozen motorcycles had followed closely on its heels. All of them pulled up short when the trap was sprung.

The bikers weren't just an honor guard, they were vampires. Which actually wouldn't have been a huge problem if we'd been prepared for them. But we hadn't expected such a large attack and so we'd thinned out the ranks, sending Ull, Horus, Brahma, and Persephone ahead to watch over the Putins; just in case. Who knew the *just in case* would be a bunch of blood-sucking bikers?

War cries echoed as Mrs. E and Mr. T did their thing, lightning struck nearby as Thor fried one of the vamps, and Pan's gleeful laugh carried over it all as he used his influence to make our enemy panic. The panic was working great but we needed to do some beheading to finish these guys off. It was a good thing I had spell-enhanced weaponry or I wouldn't have made it past the first vamp. I don't know if I've mentioned this before but beheading a man isn't as easy as they make it look in the movies. It takes a lot of strength to separate a head from a body. You have to cut through muscles and tendons, not to mention bone. Why do you think the French invented the guillotine? They were tired.

“Vervain!” Finn put his back to mine as we fought and it struck me that he didn't have a cool god magic either.

All Finn could do was turn into a swan. Not so helpful in times like this. I glanced over and saw his forearms bulge as he lifted his own sword and sliced the head from a vampire. I felt a kind of kinship with him then, the two normal fighters trying to survive amidst those with aggressive god magic. We had to train twice as hard to accomplish even half of what they were capable of naturally.

I threw out a handful of wormwood, activating a stun spell that I had intended to use on the driver, and dropped a vampire who was about to launch himself at Pan. Okay, so maybe I wasn't exactly normal.

“The driver,” Finn nodded to a man getting out of the wrecked car.

He threw a long gun out of the ditch and then climbed up after it. Slipping the rifle's strap over his chest, he headed for an abandoned motorcycle.

“Dang it,” I ran towards him but there wasn't anything I could do, I don't carry projectile weapons and the guy was beyond my reach.

“In the car,” Finn pointed and I saw a stash of guns laid out on the passenger seat.

I ran over and dropped to the ground so I could reach down and pull one out. I was already starting to sweat. Did I mention I don't like guns? I couldn't even tell you what I was holding, just that it was large and black. A machine gun, I think. I stood up and pointed it after the fleeing man. How hard could it be, right? All you do is point and shoot. I pulled the trigger but nothing happened.

“Damn, damn, damn!” I was about to throw the gun at the

man when Finn's hand reached over and pushed a button next to the trigger.

"Safety's on," he smirked. "Try again."

"Don't say it," I growled and lifted the gun once more.

I didn't even try to sight, just aimed in the man's general direction. Turns out, that's all you need to do when you're using a machine gun. The man, bike, and all went down in a shower of dirt. He laid there groaning while me and Finn ran over.

"Wow," I looked at the gun in my hand. "Maybe I'll keep this."

"You didn't kill him," Finn looked the guy over. "In this instance your inexperience was a plus. We can take him back to Teharon and patch him up."

"Great," I looked back over to the battle, where Thor was taking care of the last of the vamps with his blunt but very large hammer. As I watched, he swung his weapon in a wide arc and a vamp's head went spinning off into the dark. "Whoa," was all I could say. I have to admit, it turned me on a little. I gave myself a mental shake and ran over to join my hot, hammer-wielding boyfriend. "We need to get the driver outta here now," I gestured over to where Finn was trussing up the Russian.

"Right," Thor nodded and started heading over. "I'll take him back with Finn. Pan, get Vervain home," he called over his shoulder.

"No prob, Chief," Pan sidled over to me, eyeing the weapons I was holding. "You wanna at least put the sword away."

"Oh, right," I handed him the gun while I slid the kodachi into its sheath.

"Gods don't use guns," Pan looked over the weapon. "We

generally don't have to, but you did well with this. Why don't you carry one?"

"Well, I'm kinda afraid of them," I took the gun back, "and swords are better for severing god heads. But I think I may be warming up to the idea."

"Looks good on you," he nodded appreciatively.

"Yes, it does," we jerked toward the sound of Blue's voice while Mr. T and his Mrs. ran over to back us up.

Automatic reaction, I couldn't help it, I just pulled the trigger and sprayed out bullets in a wide arc. Blue jerked with the impact, looking confused as he inspected his ruined shirt. There was no blood. His chest was whole beneath the holes, the bullets no doubt lying around him in the dirt.

"What the hell?" I looked from the gun to Blue.

"That's why we don't use guns," Pan said dryly.

"Damn it," I threw the weapon at Blue's head.

"So angry," Blue laughed after dodging my throw. "Why do you want to kill me, little witch?"

"Why do you want to kill Maria Putina?" I shot back.

"Because her death will launch a war of epic proportions." He closed his eyes and smiled as if he could see it playing out on the back of his eyelids. "Putin's hatred of Medvedev will grow till he loses control and takes down not only Medvedev but Gazprom as well. The oil crisis that follows will pit the Russian Federation against the Europeans. Then it may even become worldwide."

"You really are an evil bastard," I breathed in horror. How could I have ever found this man attractive?

"Your people make snuff films and movies such as *Faces*

of Death. Violence and gore are entertainment for you but I'm the evil one? At least what I do has meaning for me. This is not about pleasure, this is about survival. I do what I believe is best for not only godkind but humankind as well. I truly believe my cause is honorable but I'd give it all up for you," he focused on me intently.

"What?" I stared back in open-mouthed horror.

"Let's go, Vervain," Pan suddenly had a death grip on my arm.

"No, wait," I held up a hand and turned back to Blue. "What are you saying exactly?"

"Come with me now," he held a dark slim hand out to me. "Be with me willingly and I will cease my efforts to kill Maria Putina."

"And simply launch another plot," I smirked. "I'm not that stupid."

"Vervain," Pan was tugging on my arm now. "Why are you even wasting time listening to him?"

"You're right," I turned to Pan and felt his arms go around me. As we faded away, Blue's voice followed us.

"Not just Maria then. I'll give it all up for you, little witch."

Chapter Thirty-Six

An hour later, I was seated between Thor and Teharon in Bilskinir's dining hall. Medvedev's driver was recovering in a locked guest room and I was still mulling over Blue's proposition.

"Vervain, let it go," Pan whispered to me. "You can't trust him."

"She can't trust who?" Thor looked up sharply.

"Thanks a lot," I grimaced at Pan.

"Sorry," he looked down at his plate morosely.

"Who can't you trust?" Thor took my hand. "Me?"

"No, of course not," I took my hand back and rubbed at my face with it. "It's Blue. Pan's talking about the Aztec."

"And why would you consider trusting him?" Thor's eyes narrowed.

"Because it might mean the lives of hundreds of thousands of people," I sighed.

It was a dilemma leaders had been facing for centuries and a moral debate that never fails to spark tempers. Do you sacrifice one life to save many? A friend of mine had once tried to persuade me by taking the question further. Do you kill ten people to save a thousand? How about a hundred to save ten thousand and so forth. I'd answered yes every time. She couldn't understand my logic, that it was a simple case of numbers.

She argued that taking a life was wrong no matter how many it saved. I asked her if it would make a difference if the lives saved included her parents, her brother, or her husband? What if the life taken was that of a murderer? She had no answer for that. The equation had changed for her, whereas I saw it the same no matter what. I fought gods for humanity, all of humanity, be they criminals or toddlers. As Spock so eloquently said, *Logic clearly dictates that the needs of the many outweigh the needs of the few*. I bet you thought it was some great philosopher who said that. Nope, it was Spock. I don't even like Star Trek but I agree with his logic.

“Explain,” Thor's curt tone pulled me out of my logical musings.

“Blue showed up after you left,” I studied Thor's face. Could I really give him up? “He made me an offer. He says he'll stop his warmongering if I-”

“That's not going to happen,” the finality in Thor’s voice grated on my nerves. This wasn't his decision to make.

“We were just talking about how this was a losing battle,” I sighed. I was so tired of fighting. I just wanted it to end. This wasn't the kind of life I wanted and the thought of changing it was attractive, even if it meant living with a lunatic. “Blue's never going to give up.”

“And neither are we,” Thor declared calmly.

“I started this to save lives,” I tried another tactic. “I could stop it all right here.”

“By becoming a whore!” Thor growled.

“Excuse me?” I leaned back to glare at him.

“Bad move, Dad,” Ull spoke out of the side of his mouth as he focused his attention firmly on his plate.

“What? That's exactly what she'll be if she gives in to him,” Thor looked from Ull to me. “I won't allow it.”

“You know as well as I, that taking Blue out of the

equation would be a huge gain for our side," I barely controlled my tide of fury. "I'm not so proud that the use of my body matters more to me than that."

"And taking you out of the equation would be a huge gain for *their* side," he was breathing carefully, like he was about to explode. "I can't believe you would even consider this."

"Consider what; sacrificing myself for the good of others?" I leaned back in my chair. "It's kinda what I do."

"That was before," he looked away.

"Before what?" I pinched his arm and he sucked his breath in sharply and glared at me. "Before I became Rapunzel and you decided to lock me away in a tower? I'm sorry, babe but if I'm not mistaken, I'm the witch here. I should be locking *you* up."

A strangled, choking sound came from Ull's direction before he murmured, "Thor, Thor, let down your long hair." A lightning bolt zapped the carpet beside Ull and he looked up in complete innocence. "What I say?"

"Stay out of this," Thor gave Ull a menacing stare before focusing on me again. "You know I don't want to lock you up."

"No, you wanna protect me," I glared at him.

"Why is that so wrong?" Thor huffed in exasperation, then took my hand and pulled me from the room. "We're going to discuss this privately."

By the time we entered the library, I was enraged and I didn't even know why. He'd just pushed the right buttons I guess. If you wanted to piss me off, the surest way to do so was to imply that I couldn't take care of myself. I had completely lost sight of the reason we were fighting in the first place. Blue and all of humanity took a back seat to my injured pride.

“So, what did you want to say to me?” I sat down and laced my fingers over my stomach.

“I don’t want you to face Huitzilopochtli again. He's manipulating you,” Thor's voice went soft, and damn if his words weren’t reasonable.

“I can’t hide from him,” I sighed and looked down at my hands, suddenly clenched together in my lap. “I don't want to accept his offer but it may become our best option.”

“I don’t care about options, I care about you.”

“That’s very sweet but I do care about what he can do to my people. I refuse to ignore the opportunity to end this all peacefully,” I shook my head. “It would be selfish to do so.”

“I tell you that I care for you and you speak of battle?” Thor looked at me like I’d stolen the last brownie. And it was a pot brownie.

“Do you want an honorary bitch badge because you sure do sound like an abused housewife?” I snapped at him.

“That’s enough, Vervain!” Thor shot to his feet and towered over me. “You will not be whoring yourself to that perverted Aztec! You’re staying right here where it’s safe and I will fight him without you from now on.”

“Oh? You think you can stop me?” I smirked up at him and it was the last straw on Thor’s camel's back.

“Silence!” He drug me to my feet and shook me. I was pretty sure I had scrambled eggs for brains by the time he was done. Can an adult get shaken baby syndrome? “You will obey me, woman!”

Oh hell no, he didn’t just use the O word.

“You’re not the boss of me!” I screamed back. I thought I

heard laughter coming from the dining hall but I was too angry to be angry about it, if that makes any sense.

Thor took a few deep breaths, then let go of me and walked away. I rubbed my arms while he stood in front of the fireplace. There were red imprints from his fingers showing up in my flesh already. A fire roared to life suddenly, catching my attention.

"I promised to protect you," he rubbed a hand over his eyes wearily.

"Only to get me to come along and help you in the first place," I walked over to him and wrapped my arms around his waist from behind.

He folded his arms over mine and his body shuddered on a sigh. "I didn't know it could be like this."

"What could?" I asked his back.

"Caring for a human," he said softly as he stared into the flames. "I never felt like this with Sif; all turned upside down and confused. She grounded me and I'd thought that was what I needed. But in the end, my love for her faded away. With you, I've never been happier and I've never been more frustrated. You take me to extremes, each emotion compounding the next until my life is like a ship at sea, constantly rolling beneath my feet. I've lost solid ground but then I was never really at home there to begin with. My heart has always belonged to the ocean."

I went still. Except for my heart, which seemed to have grown wings and was trying to burst free of my chest. Was that a declaration of love? I had no idea. I'd never been good at reading between the lines and all of his ocean metaphors were confusing me. Was I the sea or was the sea the sea? Did his heart belong to me or to a large body of water?

"Oh hell," I let go of him and backed away.

“What’s wrong now?” He turned and faced me like he was afraid I’d bolt.

“This is just too much, too soon,” I ran both of my hands through my hair. “I can’t handle this right now.”

“What’s there to handle?” Thor threw up his hands in exasperation. “Why can’t you just accept what I offer you and stop questioning everything?”

“This is who I am,” I fisted my hands and planted them firmly atop my hips. “I don’t believe in fairy tales or happy endings. I’m not Rapunzel and you’re not Prince Charming. Real life sucks. It’s full of vampire gods who want to use me and ex-wives who want to kill me. I have to be skeptical. I have to be suspicious. If I play it any other way, I’ll wind up dead.”

“Life is not all horror,” he stepped closer slowly, like he was approaching a frightened animal. “Reality can be wonderful and there are even some honorable gods.”

“Maybe,” I smiled sadly, “but a person like me does not go gently into that good night.”

“Who hurt you, that you reference love with a quote about death?” His voice was soft and I couldn’t stand the pity in it.

“Why do you assume I’m hurt?” I felt my jaw clench so hard, I was concerned for my fillings. “I’m not wounded or broken. I’m just smart. I’m wary and cautious but it makes me good at what I do and I won’t stand here and listen to you tell me that I’m somehow less of a woman because I’m too much of a hunter.”

“Vervain,” he reached for me and like I do every time, I retreated. Hell, maybe he was right, maybe I had issues, but I wasn’t ready to admit it.

“No, I should’ve known better than to get involved with a Viking gone soft,” crap, that was unfair and the hurt in his eyes screamed it at me but I couldn't stop; I was on a roll. "You know what your problem is? I'm more of a man than you are."

Oh shit. I knew I'd gone too far as soon as the words came out of my mouth. This was it, the moment it always came to. The moment when I screwed up and they bailed.

"Get out," his voice had gone cold and my gut clenched in response.

Some little part of me had hoped it would be different this time but who was I kidding? I had practically pushed him into dumping me.

I nodded curtly and turned to leave. A vase crashed into the wall beside me, showering me with shards of porcelain, and I spun into a wary crouch. He was slumped in a chair, staring into the fire, clenching and unclenching his hands. I just shook my head. He sure was proving me right; throwing things are a woman's way. No offense ladies, sometimes it's all we can do.

I walked down the hall toward our room. *Our* room, ha, not for much longer. Oh well, it had been good while it lasted. The dining hall was deathly silent as I walked by and I couldn't bring myself to go in and tell everyone goodbye. They'd find out from Thor what a supreme bitch I was soon enough.

What the hell was wrong with me? Why did I say such horrible things? It happened every time a man got too close. Without fail, I'd panic and find a way to screw it up.

I thought of my friends; Jackson and Tristan, as I packed. They had no problem keeping it together. It had taken awhile for them to get together but once they had, it was a done deal. I on the other hand, was the exact opposite. I could get men like crazy. They fell for me hard and fast… exhibit A. Thor. But they also got up and dusted themselves off just as quickly. That was really the root of my men issues. I've heard proclamations of love followed up by awkward silences too many times. Poor Thor had paid the price.

Nick wandered up to me and I gave him a hug. “At least you’ll always love me right?” He purred and I basked in the small comfort before I put him into his cat carrier.

I was packed and ready to go in fifteen minutes flat. I hadn’t actually brought that much with me and I wanted out of Asgard as fast as possible. So I went directly to the tracing room and with my luggage in one hand and the cat carrier in the other, I chanted the spell to take me home. When I finished, I was standing in my living room, breathing a sigh of relief.

“Well, I narrowly dodged that bullet,” I said to Nick as I let him out. “To think I could have ended up falling for that giant pansy.”

I thought about the way it felt to be held by Thor, his electric scent, and the color of his eyes when they filled with lightning. I saw his body over mine, felt the slide of his skin and his hands. The horror of what I had just destroyed washed over me and I sank to the floor next to my suitcase. I don’t know when I started to cry but I know it lasted until I was racked with sobs and gasping for air. Nick rubbed against me and I firmly shook myself out of it. He always knew when I needed him.

“Yes, you’re precisely right,” I scratched his neck. “There’s one more thing I’ve got to do before I can wallow in self-pity.”

I stood in the center of the room and chanted the words to ward my house against Thor again. There’s always that one thing a woman does when she’s decided a relationship is over. Some burn their ex’s picture, some trash his letters, some erase his number from their cell phone. I just learned the closing ritual for leaving a god. You had to reset the wards.

“There,” I stripped as I walked back toward my bedroom, leaving sad little piles of clothing in my wake. “Now it’s over.”

The really messed up part was, I still didn't know what to do about Blue.

Chapter Thirty-Seven

My life was quieter than it had ever been for about two weeks following my departure from Asgard. None of the gods contacted me and I have to admit I was a little disappointed by that. I thought at least Ull would come by to say hi but then again, Thor was his father. Blood before buds.

I sank into a depression deeper than I'd ever experienced before. I never left the house. I couldn't even paint. Thankfully, I'd already finished the commissioned portraits and was able to deliver them on time or I'd have had some very upset customers. My altar was neglected and so was my garden. The herbs I grew for eating and witchcraft were probably overrun with weeds. I didn't really know for sure since I only went outside to get the mail. All phone calls went unanswered until Jackson and Tristan stopped by to check on Nick and found me sleeping. It was two in the afternoon. They held me while I cried, Tristan giving Jackson accusing glances the entire time, like it was all his fault.

But no one can be sad forever. I finally got up one day and decided I'd had enough of pizza and Chinese food. I needed to go grocery shopping. I also needed to clean. I took a good look around my disgusting house and felt the first pangs of renewed vigor. I'd get some food, cook myself a nice meal, and while it was cooking, I'd clean up my life. Or at least my house.

I drove down to Safeway, squinting in the afternoon sunlight like a bear coming out of hibernation. I'd forgotten my sunglasses, dammit. My eyes were a little watery by the time I pulled into the parking lot. I blinked rapidly and walked toward the store with my purse tucked under my arm. There was a dagger in my bag and I'd worn my gloves as well. I was depressed, not suicidal. So I wasn't scared when I spotted Trevor. I was shocked as hell though.

“Hey, Trevor,” I called as he pushed himself off of the wall he'd been leaning against. I glanced around the parking lot warily but didn't see any werewolves.

Trevor gave me a lopsided grin as he stepped up to me, his stride casual but smooth. Animal smooth. He was wearing a black T-shirt that showed off his thick build, a pair of worn blue jeans, and black work boots. His eyes were warm honey peering out from behind the unruly locks of his midnight hair. Too bad Persephone wasn’t there, she would’ve been in werewolf heaven.

“Hey, Vervain,” he leaned in to rub his face along the side of mine. His nose traced my chin and then he withdrew.

“Uh,” I cleared my throat, avoiding the looks I was getting from passerby. “Thanks for that. Now, is there a reason you’re here or is this just a coincidence?”

“It’s no coincidence,” he looked around and sniffed the air before continuing. “I followed some Froekn here and then sent them home. The contract is still valid. I’ll defend you to the death, even against my brothers, but I still can’t betray the confidence of a customer. It’s bad for business.” He smiled and half-shrugged.

I shook my head, “Trevor, I told you; you don't owe me anything. Please don’t endanger yourself anymore for me. I can take care of myself.”

He shuddered and his eyes closed briefly. I frowned at that and was about to ask him if he was alright, when he started speaking again.

“I can’t give you a name but I can give you a hint,” he leaned in closer to whisper. “How do you think we found you?”

“I don’t know,” I shrugged. “That’s one of the things I can’t figure out.”

“Then let me just say that it’s not you we followed,

Vervain."

"Then who?" I looked pointedly around at my lack of companions.

"We only needed to catch your scent," he stared at me like he could will me to understand. "All it took was one time."

"So I guess it's a good thing I haven't left my house in weeks," I huffed.

"Definitely," Trevor looked a little unsteady but his voice sounded strong. "Stay inside. Your home is well warded and I can't watch you twenty-four-seven. I have other obligations."

"To your pack?" I felt a little dizzy for a second and I wavered on my feet. He caught me and steadied me with a hand on each arm. I looked up into his warm eyes. They seemed closer than they should be; bigger and more intense. "What does it mean; Froekn?"

For some reason, it was supremely important that I know.

"It's the name my father gave us," Trevor smiled gently, the honey of his eyes darkening to caramel. "We are the Froekn, his valiant ones, children of the Great Wolf."

"Valiant," I whispered reverently. I felt drugged, blissful. Tingles were spreading along my skin. Did I have low blood sugar?

"Godhunter," he pressed his forehead to mine band then drew his face upward, inhaling and keeping contact with me with the tip of his nose as he went. Then he whispered into my ear, "Call my name into the wind if you ever need me and I'll be there."

"Thanks, I'll remember that," I shivered under his intense wolf stare and tried to shake off the strange way it made me feel.

Maybe I was just overtaxing myself or maybe it was the sun; I hadn't really seen it in awhile.

"You're welcome, Lady Hunter," Trevor smiled in his lopsided way and suddenly the world was back to normal. He loped off before I realized that I still didn't know who was after me.

Chapter Thirty-Eight

The one thing I couldn't avoid was sleep and the one god who wasn't avoiding me was always waiting in my dreams.

"Have you decided yet?" Blue asked as he escorted me through a Victorian garden.

"Why do you always start with that?" I huffed.

I couldn't bring myself to care about anything. I knew I'd have to decide soon but for the first time since I started godhunting, I didn't care. Let the world fall down around me if Thor didn't want me anymore. Thus are lovers selfish bastards.

"It's all that matters to me," Blue said simply. See? Selfish.

"No, I don't want you," it was the first time I'd answered him decisively.

"Not even to save your people?" He stopped and faced me in surprise.

It was mid-day in my dream, the sun glinting off his hair like an obsidian helmet. His eyes were open wounds, his lips pressed into a thin blade. He was battle personified, completely out of place in the garden he'd brought me to. I looked around at the delicate flowers scenting the air with fragile perfume and felt only frustration.

"Why do you want a woman who doesn't want you?" I shot back. "I can't even understand why you'd want me in the first place. No woman is worth this much trouble."

"My life has become one long, blood-drenched nightmare. Even attraction is centered around blood for me. I wake up in the morning and I consume blood. I make my plans of bloodshed and I speak only to people who help me toward these ends. I feel a measure of happiness only when blood fills my mouth or stains my hands." He looked down at his hands as if they were still stained. "Then in the midst of the nightmare, you appeared. You challenged me, you tore at my perceptions and beliefs. You drew from me more than bloodlust. Then you left and I was alone in the nightmare again."

He ran an elegant hand through his thick hair, rubbing at his scalp like it was an annoying barrier to the thoughts he wanted to share. For a moment, I forgot about Thor. I let go of my anger at myself for ruining the best relationship I'd ever had. I let the bitterness over the shackle my life had become fall away and thought about how equally trapped Blue might feel.

"It wasn't the same though. You changed the nightmare with your presence. I began to think of things other than blood and I began to remember things I used to want," he took my hand. "You're my equal, my balance. You're courage and humor, beauty and ferocity. You think me cruel but you know deep down that you kill as easily as I. We do it to protect what we believe in. In that, we are the same."

"No," I pulled my hand out of his. "We're nothing alike."

"The truth can be harsh," he turned and sat down, a stone bench appearing beneath him just in time. "You think you love the Viking because he is so honorable but he only seems honorable to you because he fights on your side. Thor deserted Odin when his father needed him the most. He leaves him to fight for the humans while Odin is ridiculed for Thor's desertion. Where is the honor in betraying your own father? As in all things," Blue spread his hands out, "it is only perspective."

"Thor did not desert his father," I swallowed past the lump that formed in my throat every time I thought about Thor. "Odin deserted him. Don't talk to me about perspective. Either way you look at it, you're trying to kill as many humans as possible for nothing more than power. I kill to prevent that."

"We shall agree to disagree," he patted the bench beside him, his mood shifting like the wind. "Why don't we talk about something else for once? Come, sit. I won't bite," he laughed warmly. "Let me tell you of my childhood."

I couldn't help it, I was intrigued and frankly, I was tired of fighting. I went to the bench and sat down, my full red skirts spreading out around me to drape into his lap. He stroked the fabric, pulling it through his fingers pensively. I continued to watch his hands while he spoke.

"My parents, my baby sister, and I became gods in the valley of Mexico," Blue began. "I happened across a nomadic tribe. They were a strong, resilient people who I sensed would serve my family well. So I decided to become their patron. I led them to an island, telling them to build on the spot where they found an eagle perched on a cactus, devouring a snake."

"Seriously?" I shook my head and huffed a laugh. "Why's it always have to be so complicated? Why couldn't you have just said; *Build over there*?"

"Humans expect it to be complicated," Blue laughed with me. "You don't believe anything great is possible without conditions and we wouldn't want to disappoint you."

"How kind," I grimaced.

"I could have let them wander," Blue shrugged. "Instead, I led them to the perfect place and they built Tenochtitlán which means *near the cactus*."

"Creative," I smirked.

"Another thing humans are good at," he shot back with a twinkle in his eye, "stating the obvious."

"Oh, nice comeback," I nodded approvingly. Was I actually enjoying this? No, of course not.

"To this day, Mexico uses an image of the cactus-perched eagle devouring a snake as its National Emblem," pride oozed from his voice.

"Thanks for the history lesson," I rolled my eyes, completely unimpressed. Or at least trying to be.

The story did more than impress me though. It brought home how large a role the Atlanteans had played in the lives of humans. How much they'd altered our existence, placing their mark on my race like a brand. The gods had twisted us for their amusement and selfish purposes, playing with us without a thought to how their actions may alter our race forever. Of course, these were all things I already knew but the fresh reminder was a bandage torn off a healing wound. I felt the rage rise up like fresh blood but Blue started to speak of his chosen people before I could unleash my fury on him.

He spoke so warmly of their skills, their strength, and their love of beauty, that my anger melted away. There was love in his voice, a deep endless admiration as he told me about the ingenious way they expanded the island. How they made dry land from marsh; with retaining walls and willow trees to prevent erosion. How they loved games and flowers. How they celebrated life with feasts and dancing. He was like a proud parent when he told me how his people had made their little island into one of the greatest cities of their time, home to over fifty-thousand Aztecs.

"Is it true you had four hundred brothers?" I suddenly remembered what the God Squad had told me about Blue's family.

"My father was a very virile man," he smiled wide enough to reveal the tips of his fangs. "There weren't quite that many of them but it was close. They were all my father sons but they had different mothers. We have long lives as you know, and Father wasn't monogamous until he met my mother."

"She had you and your sister?" I asked but his face fell and I instantly regretted prying. "I'm sorry. I heard that she died."

"My father's other sons were angry with him for settling on my mother and naming me as his heir. He acknowledged all of them but it wasn't enough. They wanted to be the greatest of the new gods. They craved the power he passed down to me."

I suddenly remembered why he had killed his brothers and I blanched but I still asked him, "Did they really murder your mother?"

"They attacked my father's temple," Blue's voice had turned into a careful monotone. "This was before gods began to create territories in the God Realm, and we had lived in the pyramid complex of Teotihuacán. My brothers had brought armies with them and although they didn't overtake us, they were able to break through our walls. I… I was too late, too slow to save my family."

I gaped at Blue as tears began to run down his cheeks. His elegant hands lifted to cover his face and I wasn't able to withstand those silent tears. I reached out to him and he flowed into my arms with a sigh. He rested his head on my shoulder, shuddering as he let go. A tide of misery left him as he clung to me, carrying me out to deeper waters with him. My own father's death paled in comparison to Blue's loss but it linked me to him nonetheless, a shared pain reaching through my mind to his.

It was a tenuous touch. At first I hadn't even realized I'd done it. I just felt the need to comfort him and my subconscious responded. Touching Blue in a dream created a closer link to his mind and I felt myself slipping into his thoughts automatically. Blue looked up at me in shock and when our gazes met, the link widened and I fell through. I dove through the blood pools of his eyes and surfaced in his mind. In his memories.

The sound of rushing blood gave way to the blaring confusion of battle. My vision sharpened to reveal a glimpse of Hell. A ferocious war spread out at the base of the pyramid I stood upon. There were hundreds of men in little more than paint and feathers, fighting beside warriors in golden armor, glowing with magic. Men fought beside gods and they were all coming for me. They pressed forward against my own warriors, throwing spears, swinging ancient swords, and shouting battle cries. My fragile humans couldn't hold out against my brothers without my magic supporting them. They needed me behind them.

So I sent my power through them. I strengthened my brave priests, my elite warriors, and led them through the ranks of the traitors. I heard my brothers screaming in fury and in pain but it wasn't enough. There were so many of them spread out through the great city that guarded my home. We would be overrun eventually.

I felt my skin begin to burn and I fought hard to control it. I couldn't lend my strength to my priests if I was under the heat. Commanded by the sun, I would be consumed and focus only on the blood of my enemies. So I controlled it, I pushed it back and used my magic to hold off as much of them as I could, while we fought to hold the front line.

Then I heard it, my father's scream in my mind. His cry for mercy, not for himself but for his wife and daughter. I froze in terror and turned to look at his temple behind me. Somehow they'd made it past me. My brothers were inside my home, killing my family. I roared in rage and traced to them, using our link to find them.

My father was a mass of spears. His head had rolled to a stop against the wall several feet away from his body and his eyes stared at me in flat accusation. Some of my brothers knelt by the pool of blood that flowed from his corpse and lapped at it like dogs. My mother and sister were in the corner, both headless as well, their bodies still holding each other, clinging to one another even in death.

I dropped to my knees and screamed, tears blinding me momentarily. I blinked them away and saw my brothers look up, licking their lips and reaching for their weapons. Several had Atlantean armor, having escaped Atlantis with Father. I had only what the Aztecs could make, being born of this continent. Father was wearing his gold Atlantean armor and his sword was lying next to him but it didn't matter because the heat was coming and this time, I was going to let it consume me.

Hot, I was so hot. I'd burn without blood. Flames ran along the inside of my skin, fighting to get out to the life-granting air. My brothers rushed forward and I flung out a barrier spell to enclose only three of them in with me. They kept coming, confident in their weapons, and I smiled. The smile made them hesitate. They saw my fangs and knew that Father had already passed on his power to me. They'd get nothing from drinking his cooling blood.

Their faces contorted as they howled in rage and ran at me. I batted away their weapons like they were twigs, not steel, and broke their necks, feasting on them one at a time. Discarding the used up corpses, I picked up my father's sword before bringing more of my brothers inside the wards with me.

We fought that way for hours and instead of tiring, I became more energized, more powerful with every body I drained. The bodies piled so deep that I had to take the fight out to the pyramid's steps. My world became an endless series of slash, chop, strike, drink, and move on. All I knew was death. I was death.

My brothers, so arrogant, didn't lose their confidence till the end, when most of their corpses spread out behind me and the power I collected sang out like a freshly rung bell. But by then it was too late for them.

The humans they'd enlisted turned on them, offering my brothers up to me in exchange for their own lives. I accepted, feasting on the blood of my blood. Drinking down so much power, my skin felt near to bursting with it.

When the last of my brothers finally lay dead and drained, I sent away their human armies with a wave of my hand. They left praising my name as their god. Huitzilopochtli, God of War, they shouted with the zeal of the newly converted. My priests took up the chant until I raised my hands for silence. They knelt before me and I went among them, touching each and every head in blessing. I bestowed a little of the power I'd gained upon them. My loyal warrior-priests. Outnumbered, they had stayed strong, even when I left them to battle within the pyramid. They deserved a piece of the power I'd gained, a part of the life I'd live.

They piled the bodies of my brothers at the base of my pyramid and would have burned them but I stopped them. I left the corpses there and went back to my family, to gather them to me and finally give into the agony that I'd pushed aside. I sat covered in their blood and bodies, squeezing them tightly and absorbing their essence into my skin as my tears bathed them. When the last tear fell, I knew they'd never fall again. I'd never feel love that deeply. Never again allow myself to be so weak. The pain was over and through its death, I was reborn.

I carried my sister's body out of the temple and lifted her to the moon with my magic. Below me, my priests sang. They worshiped her and eased her journey with their voices. I felt her body come to rest on the moon she had adored and sank her into it, to become a part of it. There she could remain, forever shining upon me. A soft memory each night, of what I'd lost.

My brothers I sent hurtling, one by one, into the sky. No magic to ease their journey. They burned like meteors as they went. I enjoyed each fiery departure, wanting them as far from me as possible, pleased with the knowledge that their bodies would burn to ash and scatter, to float unmourned in cold, uncaring space.

Around me, I heard the Aztecs gathering. I heard them whispering in awe and saw them kneeling on the blood soaked earth. They spoke of Huitzilopochtli, kin slayer. He who made the stars from the bodies of his brothers and the moon from his sister's head. I didn't want my brothers to be stars, I wanted them to be completely forgotten, but I allowed the legends to grow on the lips of my people. I allowed my priests to go out and counsel them on ways of worship, knowing this was the responsibility of leadership. We would form a covenant; they would sacrifice to me and I would protect them.

Then I went inside my father's temple and buried my parents. It wasn't until I placed the last stone over my father that I realized my vision was tinted red. I picked up my father's sword and held it before me, to stare at my reflection in the shiny metal. My eyes had been jade green, my mother's favorite color, and she'd always said they were the most beautiful eyes in the world. But the eyes that stared back at me from the sword's edge were red, churning pools of freshly spilled blood.

I screamed.

I gasped for air, loudly and deeply, as I returned to my dream body, my own mind, still hearing my screams. No, Huitzilopochtli's screams.

"I'm Vervain Lavine," I whispered over and over, covering my eyes with my hands. "I'm Vervain Lavine."

When my breathing became even, I looked down and rubbed my hands over my body; feeling, remembering myself. I was shaking, traumatized by what I'd experienced, but Blue was horrified. He knelt before me in the grass, his eyes wide and streaming with tears.

"You… I..." he pulled away, wiping frantically at his face.

I reached out for him but he held up a hand and shook his head. He had lost control and wasn't happy about it. I could understand that. I didn't like it when I lost control either.

"You saw it all didn't you?" His voice was hoarse. "You lived my memories and I'm sorry for that. No one should see such horror."

"They made your pain into pretty myths didn't they?" I whispered.

Suddenly, I understood what it meant to be a god. To be worshiped but never comforted. To be prayed to but never spoken with. To be adored but never truly loved. To be feared.

"They knew no better," his eyes held no blame. "They believed the stories and it enriched their lives. It was a small thing to allow. I regret only that you had to see such violence and weakness in me. It won't happen again." He pulled himself onto the seat and brushed off his pants with efficient movements.

"There's no shame in mourning your family," I tried to keep my voice neutral, like I was stating a fact, but it shook with my own unshed tears.

I knew that the worst thing a person could do when you were struggling for control, was speak to you with sympathy. I remembered when my father died. I could only hold it together as long as no one asked if I was alright. I wouldn't do that to Blue. I wouldn't ask him if he was alright. It's a stupid question anyway, he so obviously wasn't.

"I haven't cried since that day. I thought I'd burned the tears out of myself," Blue looked at me then and his face was a mixture of anger, fear, pain, and awe. "You've made me feel love again, Vervain but you've also opened me back up to the pain."

I swallowed hard and did my best to hold his gaze as I spoke, "They often go hand in hand. You can't have one without the other. You can't understand happiness without first knowing loss. I hope someday you'll see the pain as a kind of gift."

I wondered then if maybe he really did love me in his own twisted way. I'd discounted all of his declarations as the ravings of a madman but maybe he wasn't so mad after all, maybe he was just plain angry.

“It always amazes me that humans can gain so much wisdom in such a short time,” one last tear trickled down his cheek.

“Not enough usually,” I wiped the tear away. “I’ve no idea what to do about you.”

“The fact that you’re considering me at all brings me great happiness,” he took my hand and kissed it gently.

“You’re not going to make this easy are you?”

“It's never easy to realize your enemies are not the monsters you'd thought them to be,” he looked down at my hand, still laying within his.

“Or that it changes nothing,” I said sadly as I woke from the dream.

Chapter Thirty-Nine

"So what do you think?" I had done a new series of paintings and my friend Sommer had come over to see them before we did some spellwork together.

"They're the most beautiful things I've ever seen," Kai, Sommer's middle son, stared up at my artwork like he was viewing the Mona Lisa. His mother stood behind him with a slightly different expression.

"They're a little dark," Sommer looked over the first in the series, studying the pile of corpses laid out before the Aztec temple. "What inspired you?"

"I've been doing some research," I smiled at her struggle to come up with something positive to say. "This one is based on the Aztec myth of Huitzilopochtli. The dead men are his brothers. They murdered his parents and his sister, so he killed them all and sent their bodies into the sky to become the stars," I gestured at the next painting which showed the corpses turning into bright points of light.

"That's amazing!" Kai was practically jumping up and down with excitement. "What's this one about?" He pointed at the third painting.

"That's Blue's, um, I mean *Huitzilopochtli's* sister." I looked over the painting critically. I was happy with the resemblance I'd been able to achieve from Blue's memory of Coyolxauhqui. The severed head looked peaceful, beautiful even, as it glowed in place of the moon. "He put her head into the sky and it became the moon."

"Wow," Kai breathed. "And these?" He was already on to the next.

“This is what Huitzilopochtli became,” I took a deep breath as I looked into Blue's blood-colored eyes. It was a close up, his intense gaze matching the blood that dripped over his face. “He's the God of War and the rush of battle inflames him, he can't be stopped until he's drenched in blood.”

“That's the most awesome and wonderful story I've ever heard!” Kai's eyes were focused intently on Blue's. “Can we try some Aztec magic today, Aunty?”

Kai was the only one of Sommer's sons who had any aptitude for magic. She started bringing him with her to our little spell sessions when he was three and he'd been instantly hooked. A gifted natural. Now, at the age of ten, he could hold his own with the grown witches. He also had a knack for stumbling onto brilliant ideas. He probably had some psychic abilities we didn't know about yet.

“Aztec magic,” I whispered. “Kai, you're a genius!”

I should have been researching Aztec magic as soon as I began battling an Aztec. Fight fire with fire and all that. Why the hell hadn't I thought of it?

“Uh huh,” he grinned up at me like I was telling him something he already knew.

“And so modest,” his mother gave him a reproachful look.

“Yep,” he grinned wider.

“I don't know any Aztec spells off hand,” I led them out of my art room and into my magic room. “But I'd love to do some research if you guys are up for it.”

“Sure!” Kai made a beeline for the shelves of books on the far side of my altar room.

“Vervain,” Sommer stopped me with a hand on my arm.

“What's going on?”

“What do you mean?” I blinked innocently up at her.

“The paintings,” she frowned. “They're not your usual style and now an interest in Aztec magic? You're not even interested in shamanic practices and you're part Native American. Now you want to study the Aztecs?”

“Race has nothing to do with it,” I gestured over at Kai, who had found a huge book and already had it open on the floor before him. “Just because Kai's part Filipino doesn't make him better at their magical practices. Is there Filipino magic by the way?”

“I don't know, I'll have to ask Alex,” Sommer said distractedly as she flung a blonde lock out of her face.

“Aunty V look!” Kai shouted as he held the book up to me. “Aztecs could become animals.”

“Let me see that,” I took the book from Kai and examined the passage. “*Nahualli, Aztec sorcerers who could use their animal twin, a Nahual, to collect other Nahuals and use their powers*. This is fantastic, Kai, just what I was looking for.”

“Do you think we could do it?” His little dark eyes were glazed over with intensity. “Could we become animals?”

“I don't think it's literal,” I winked at him, “but I bet with some meditation, we could visualize them. They're supposed to be a twin spirit that everyone has,” I continued to scan the page as my mind raced with possibilities. “Created at the same time as your birth. So just discovering what animal you have may be interesting.”

“Sweet!” He pumped his fist into the air before dropping to the floor. “I'm gonna start right now.”

“Vervain,” Sommer took my arm again. “We've practiced magic together for years. I know when something's up with you, especially when it has to do with witchcraft. What is it you always say? Don't get crafty with a witch.”

“There are things you wouldn't want to know,” I sighed. “Things that, if I were to tell you, you'd think I was crazy for saying. Sometimes ignorance really is bliss.”

“I'm a mother and a witch,” she gave me her mommy face. “I don't have time for bliss. Just give it to me straight.”

“Fine,” I sat down on the carpet and patted the ground next to me. “You may want to get comfortable for this.”

So I told her. As I spoke, I felt a tightness in my chest ease. Confiding in someone human, sharing the struggle I'd been facing alone for so long, was cool water on my parched soul. You don't realize how much you need to speak about your life until you're unable to do so. Years of hiding things from the people I loved the most had taken its toll and I was so relieved to finally let it out. I didn't even care if she thought I was crazy.

As it happens, she didn't try to have me committed. She sat quietly for a bit, staring at Kai, who had been so immersed in his research, he hadn't heard a word I'd said. Then she took a deep breath and let it out slowly.

“Well that explains a lot,” she huffed.

“That's it?” I pushed her shoulder. “I tell you I kill gods and you say it explains a lot.”

“Well religion makes people stupid,” she stated blandly. “It makes sense that it's all a plot created by a bunch of power hungry Atlanteans.”

“Okay then,” I kind of felt let down that I didn't have to defend my sanity. I'd expected a bit more of a fight out of her.

"So," she smiled and cocked her head at me. "You need any help?"

I may have started to cry.

Chapter Forty

After the last dream I had with Blue, I did my best to barricade myself from him. As soon as he entered my dreams, I'd encase myself in a glass bubble and completely ignore him. He'd eventually go away. No one likes to be ignored. But after awhile of that, he started projecting images of us together, all around my barricade. It was a low blow and it was hard to ignore, so I came up with my most cruel and brilliant move yet. I imagined Thor inside the glass with me.

It was cruel not only to Blue but to myself as well. While there, I was so happy. Through these interactions with Blue, my dreamworld had become almost as real as my waking one. So when I brought Thor into it, it was like he was truly there with me. All I had to do was think about him, picture him, and he appeared. But when I woke, I had to face the fact that I had ruined everything between us, all over again. I had to experience the aching loss of him as fresh as the first day.

Anyone who's been through heartache knows it's a pain you'd do almost anything to stop. I was drawing it out by dreaming of Thor, tearing open the wound every morning, and yet I continued to bring him into my dreams every night. Wouldn't you, though? If you could have your lost love back with you every night in your sleep, as real as if he were truly there, wouldn't you do it? Maybe I'm weak, maybe a bit pathetic, or maybe I'm just a masochist.

The first time I imagined Thor with me, Blue went into a rage. All I did was hug Thor, imagine his arms around me, his clean scent enveloping me. It was very PG but Blue reacted like I was performing a sexual act in front of him. He slammed himself into the translucent walls I'd erected, shouting things I couldn't hear but which must've been real doozies. I ignored him and soon he faded out completely in light of the man holding me.

I knew I missed Thor, knew I cared deeply for him, but I had no idea of the extent of my feelings until he held me again. The dream Thor said everything I wanted him to say. Things like how much he missed me too, how he'd been foolish to let me walk out, how much he wanted me to come back. I had simply held him tighter and let all those beautiful words wash over me until I believed them, till I believed the lie.

Like I said, it was cruel to both of us but eventually Blue would leave and I'd be left alone with Thor. So I suffered the worst. I built a whole new relationship with my dream man. I told him things I couldn't tell the real Thor. I bared myself like I'd never done with a man before and my perfect dream Thor listened. He held me and whispered his secrets right back. It was the way I'd always wanted to be with a lover but had never allowed myself. There I could be free. I didn't have to worry about betrayal or the future. Anything was possible in my mind, that's what Teharon had said.

So night after night, I went back to Thor. Even after Blue stopped appearing. It got more and more intense. Long talks and passionate sex that would leave me shaking and wet when I woke up. It was so unhealthy for me. I knew that. I had triumphed over Blue but had created my own hell in the process. I needed to stop dreaming of Thor if I ever wanted a chance to move on. So I finally went to sleep one night, intending to leave Thor out of my dreams.

At least consciously I did. My subconscious must have had other thoughts because he was waiting for me. It was the same room I always envisioned, his bedroom. There he was, sitting on his bed, and when he saw me, he stood and smiled. But the smile disappeared when he saw my face.

"No," he came over and pulled me in tight against his chest. "Don't do this again, darling."

“I can't get over you if I keep dreaming about you,” I jerked away before I gave in to my own fantasy.

How crazy was that? I was basically arguing with myself over an imaginary relationship. I'd officially lost my mind. That's what dwelling on a hopeless situation had done to me. Instead of doing the healthy thing; crying, eating lots of ice cream, and moving on, I'd made a make-believe world where everything had remained the same and it had driven me nutso.

“You don't have to get over me,” his eyes pleaded. “I'm right here.”

“You're not real,” I held up a hand when he started forward.

“Yes, I am,” he'd been telling me for weeks how it was really him, not some figment of my imagination, but that was exactly what I'd wanted him to say. I knew where I was. I wasn't so far gone that I couldn't tell when I was dreaming.

“Stop it,” I forced the room to change. We stood on a stark expanse of cold white marble.

“Vervain,” he ran a hand through his hair in an achingly familiar gesture. “You called me here. We have a link, just like you and Blue. Why can't you believe that it's been me this whole time?”

“Because you say exactly what I want you to say,” I laughed almost hysterically. “Why am I arguing with you? You would never come to me and just immediately forgive me after the horrible things I said to you. Life isn't that easy.”

“We were both very angry that day,” he sighed deeply. “I know you didn't mean what you said. Let's just move on. Let me come to you if you won't come to me. I'll be there in five minutes and you'll have your proof that it's really me in here.”

“You can't,” I shook my head at my own obstinacy. “I've

re-warded the house against you."

"You what?" Oh, there was a look I remembered. It was times like this, when my mind added those little details, that I could almost believe it really was Thor.

"We're over. It was my way of ending the relationship." I wondered if this was my mind's way of ending things. Maybe I should tell him yes and then when he didn't show up, I'd have my closure.

"You think I'd hurt you?" He took my upper arms in hand and turned me to face him. "I'm sworn to protect you. Forever, Vervain. No matter what happens between us, I am *unable* to harm you."

"Physically, yes."

"Ah, here's the truth finally," he let me go. "You're afraid."

"I'm cautious."

"No, you're scared shitless," he ground out. "You're afraid of loving me and of me not loving you back. Or even worse, of me loving you back and then you wrecking it somehow."

"See," I pointed at him. "Only the Thor I imagined would know that."

"Vervain," he let out a frustrated breath. "I've been here in your head with you for weeks. I know you pretty damn well. I even know why you're afraid and I can honestly tell you, you have nothing to fear with me. I love you, Vervain."

"I love you too," I felt a tear drip down my cheek as I sent him away.

I woke with renewed heartache as usual but this time it was accompanied by the hope that it would fade. I had released Thor. Now I could move on. Blue was gone too, so I could actually go back to dreaming like a normal person. The thought got me out of bed with a better outlook. I would go back to my old routine, where I just killed gods instead of falling in love with them. I stopped in front of my bathroom mirror and stared at the pale face reflected there. I loved him. I'd finally admitted it. I loved Thor.

"Too little, too late, you idiot," I hung my head and ran the water as I told myself that all the things he'd said to me in my dreams were just my own imagination. I'd fallen in love with my own ideal man. He wasn't real. "Then why does it feel so real?"

I washed my face and headed out to the kitchen to make some coffee. At least this whole twisted experience had made me realize something important. I couldn't trade myself to Blue for humanity's sake. Yes, I was a selfish bitch. As much as I thought of myself as a soldier for the greater good, I couldn't make the ultimate sacrifice. I wanted to live. I wanted to love.

And I wanted to kill Blue.

As I flipped on the TV and started to make some breakfast, I realized that it was the only solution. I had to kill Blue. After getting to know him, getting to know his motivations, it wasn't something I'd enjoy doing but I knew it was my last hope. There had to be a way. As powerful as he was, removing his head would still kill him. I had to focus on that and on the fact that I had the upper hand. He wanted me. I could use that. I just had to come up with a plan.

"Three bodies were found in an alley off Lewers street last night," the reporter announced dramatically from my TV screen.

Well, that got my attention. I spun around and went into the living room to watch. The petite brunette was standing in front of a taped off alley where a plethora of police people were scrambling about. Hawaii didn't have a lot of crimes like this, so HPD was in a tizzy.

"Honolulu Police are not releasing all the details so far but we've been told that all three victims are Caucasian; two females and one male. The bodies were discovered by this man, Mr. Raymond Delacruz. Mr. Delacruz, can you tell us how you made this gruesome discovery?"

The camera panned over to a young man in an *Ainokea* tank and jeans. His dark eyes were glazed, his entire body randomly twitching. He looked at the camera, at the alley, then back again before answering.

"Yeah, ah," he swallowed hard. "I went out to empty the trash last night after we cleaned the kitchen. I saw what I thought was a stack of mannequins lying by the dumpster," he gestured wildly and then took a deep breath. "But they weren't dummies. When I slammed the lid shut, it hit the pile and one of their arms flopped out and I just knew. I knew they were bodies."

"That must have been a shocking experience for you," the reporter prompted calmly.

"Shocking?" He snorted. "Yeah, shocking. They were so white. I mean, I know they Haoles and all but they were real white. I don't think they had any blood in 'em." He started to shake. "I ran back in and we called 911."

"Thank you, Mr. Delacruz." The reporter droned on but I didn't hear any more of it.

I sat there in a state of shock, my coffee forgotten as I processed it all. Three victims piled neatly in an alley, drained of blood. Who would do that? Who *could* do that? It stank of vampires. Which meant it was probably Blue. Was he so angry at me for the dreams that he'd sent out his minions to kill indiscriminately? The mere fact that I didn't want to believe he'd do such a thing, showed how much Blue had gotten to me.

"I'm the damn frog," I muttered.

You can boil a frog alive by placing it in a pot of water and just slowly turning up the heat. The poor thing would just keep adjusting to the temperature, never realizing it was becoming an accessory to its own murder. All it had to do was jump out to save itself but it wouldn't. Mr. Frog would just sit there enjoying the Jacuzzi.

Blue had done that to me. He'd sweet talked me, showed me parts of himself, opened up about his past and his family, till I thought I knew him. When actually, he was just turning up the heat, little by little. In a way, I was almost thankful to him for showing me his true nature. It would make it so much easier for me to kill him.

"Maybe it's just a human killer," I finally took a sip of my coffee and calmed a bit. "I could be overreacting."

I went back into the kitchen to finish breakfast but after I finally managed to swallow it all, it just sat like a rock in my belly.

Chapter Forty-One

"*A person's day of birth determines which animal twin they are linked to*," I was reading aloud from the book on Aztec magic Kai had brought to my attention. "*Not all are born with the power to become Nahualli, direct English translation;* Transforming witch." Sounded perfect for me. "*Those born under especially strong animal links, such as jaguar or puma, can ascend to the position of Nahualli. These sorcerers, could use their Nahual for good or evil depending on their personalities. They were known to transform into their animal twin, using this form to trick or to help others. Very powerful Nahualli were said to have the ability to enslave another person's Nahual or to take it altogether, leaving an individual bereft without his link to Nature.*"

I peered with fascination at the pictures of men caught in mid-transformation. Were humans actually able to do this? It's hard for me to know what to believe anymore. Five years ago, I would have assumed that the stories were referring to a symbolic change, a magical link to animal energy. Transformations would take place in a metaphysical way only. After meeting werewolves and gods who could shift into anything they wanted though, it was hard to know for sure. Could Atlanteans have given humans such an impressive ability? Or was it possible that we had it all on our own? That this was just another magic that they had stolen from us.

I flipped past the pictures and searched for information on how a Nahualli came into his power. I was hoping there was some kind of ritual described. A hint for me to follow. I could just do some focused meditation but it hadn't worked so well the other day when Kai and I tried it. I had a glimpse of something white and furry but that was it. I needed a little more.

"Here we go," I scanned a page detailing a ritual used to

contact your Nahual. "*Offerings of tobacco and alcohol were common, left on an altar dedicated to the Nahual. Often a bowl of cornmeal, into which the supplicant's blood was dripped, was placed on the altar as a connection.*"

I frowned at the page. Blood was serious business in witchcraft, especially using your own. It linked you to the work in an unbreakable bond. If I did this, there was no going back. There could be serious repercussions to welcoming an animal spirit into my life. I could take on traits of that animal. I could become unpredictable, even to myself. Or I could go insane.

Then I thought of facing Blue again without any kind of edge. I didn't even have the God Squad anymore, I was back to hunting alone. Maybe howling at the moon every now and again wouldn't be such a bad thing. It sounded better than being burnt alive by Blue's heat or becoming his blood ho until he got bored and sucked me dry.

I got up to gather the items I needed. All the mentioned offerings were pretty standard so I had them in stock. The alcohol was in stock for non-magical use as well. I grabbed a bottle of Tequila, which I thought was appropriate. The cornmeal was in the pantry but I poured it into one of my wood ritual bowls and the tobacco leaves went into another little bowl.

I lit a bundle of dried sage, shook it till the flames went out, and took the smoldering herb around the room clockwise, just to make sure there wasn't any bad energy in the room. When that was done, I created a new altar on a hat box I placed in the center of the floor and covered with a white cloth. I lit two white candles and placed the offerings between them, the bowl of cornmeal in the center. Then with my athame, I closed a circle around me and the altar. I needed to be sure I was safe, especially since I'd be working with blood. My house wards were strong but an extra line of defense wouldn't hurt.

I sat in front of the altar and closed my eyes, centering

myself and clearing my thoughts till they were focused on my task. Then I reached up with my energy and felt it connect with the power of the Moon, bright and sparkling, before I went down into the Earth to feel it's stability rush up into me. I took a deep breath, filled with these swirling currents, and opened my eyes.

I picked up the sharp knife I used for bloodletting (I never used my athame for that) and made a small cut in my pointer finger. The blood welled and dripped onto the cornmeal with a little zing of magical intent. I felt the power gathering, like static in a storm, and I knew I was on the right track.

“I come here for knowledge,” I stated firmly as I pulled my hand away from the bowl. “I come here for aid. I am threatened by darkness and need a light to guide me, to protect me. I offer tequila, tobacco, cornmeal, and my own blood. Three delights of the world and one connection to my flesh. Can you hear me, my Nahual? Will you help me? Take these offerings and let me know you, help me to understand you and how I may cultivate our power.”

I sat back and closed my eyes again, trying to be as still as possible. After a few minutes, I began to feel a tingling in my fingertips and a weightlessness, as if the ground had fallen away beneath me. Opening my eyes would ruin the spell, so I kept them closed and concentrated on the sensation. Then came a brush of fur on my arm, like a large animal had nuzzled against me, and it was all I could do to keep my eyes shut.

“Welcome,” I said softly. “Please accept these offerings in peace.”

There was no answering voice or animal sounds but I felt the words inside me, knew that my Nahual was there and was pleased to finally be acknowledged. Then, in my mind, I caught sight of her. She came slowly out of the darkness, just a white glow at first, until the shadows pulled back and revealed her fully.

A white jaguar with golden brown markings and deep brown eyes. She sat there regally, looking at me like she was staring into a mirror. She cocked her head and I cocked mine. She lifted a paw and I felt my hand raise as well. Then I felt an unmistakable wave of humor transfer from her to me. She was playing with me.

It became clear then. She was a part of me. There was nothing here to fear. She had been with me all along; had shared every hurdle, every triumph, and every tear. This was me in my animal form. She knew me like no other because she *was* me.

She opened her mouth in what could have been either a smile or a warning, and I saw her sharp teeth. Yes, she could bring me power to defend myself and she could bring me knowledge of things hidden. This wasn't just my animal form, this was the form of my magic. This was the part of me the gods were drawn to. I giggled a little to think that Thor had actually been attracted to a large jungle cat. The Nahual laughed with me, a wheezing, panting sound, and I laughed harder.

My heartache melted away with our laughter and I suddenly knew that things were happening just as they needed to. That even if they weren't, I could only take responsibility for my own actions and learn from my experiences. I couldn't change the past, so it was best to accept it. The only thing I truly needed in order to live joyously, was this part of me that I had finally found and the knowledge of that was so freeing, a sense of peace drifted over me. I was more calm than I'd ever been but also completely in awe of the wealth of magic I'd just stumbled into. It was like I'd been operating at half-mast for all of my life and someone had finally shouted; *Hey idiot, haul up those sails!*

This hadn't been about calling a new power to me. This wasn't an offering to a strange, unknown spirit. This was an awakening. This was an offering to myself, a way to bring suppressed parts of me into the light. My whole body shuddered as pieces of my soul opened to bring forth undiscovered potential. My eyes shot open as I gasped.

"Time to wake up."

Chapter Forty-Two

"Waikiki cringes in terror while the killing spree continues," the man stared at me accusingly from my TV.

"Son of a bloodsucker!" I scraped my fingers back along my scalp in frustration.

"HPD has now released details on the murders and they are chilling," he continued. "The throats are cut and the victims are drained of blood before being tossed carelessly into dumpsters like garbage. The death toll is now ten and all of the victims have been killed in the same manner. Police have no suspects at this time but believe it to be the work of a group and not just an individual. They advise people to be cautious and avoid going out at night until these murderers are caught. Although all the bodies have been found in Waikiki, the police urge locals to be wary no matter where they live. There has been no blood found at any of the crime scenes and so HPD is assuming the victims are killed elsewhere and then moved."

I took a steadying breath as I went through my options. I couldn't just let the people of Hawaii pay for my sins with their lives. I had a horrible feeling that this was all just an elaborate trap, a way to get me to come out of hiding, but what choice did I have? There was really only one option for me. I had to go hunt me some vampires.

At least I'd kept up with my workouts while I was in my pit of despair. It's funny how good working out feels when you're already miserable. It's like the emotional pain is so overwhelming, the physical feels good by comparison. You also get that great post-workout exhaustion that comes about as close to oblivion as you can manage when your heart is shattered. Plus, it's better for you than ice cream. The main thing was, I felt secure enough to tackle some vampires.

Thanks to the Bloodsucking God himself, I was now even better at killing them. My last run in with his babies had gone a lot smoother, due largely to him. How ironic, that he'd given me the information which made killing his children easier and how convenient that it was the same way I killed gods.

I put on my gloves because they were kind of my security blanket where weapons are concerned but my main weapon was going to be my kodachi, which I strapped to my waist. I'd been studying sword play for five years, ever since the episode with Ku, and I was pretty good but finesse wasn't necessary when you were beheading someone. All that mattered was a good grip, a strong swing, and the ability to follow through with your hips. Oh yeah, and a magically empowered blade helped a bunch.

I took one more look in the mirror before I left. I know; vanity thy name is woman, but can you blame me for wanting to look good on the first night I'd been out in over a month? I'd dressed in Matrix-chic; black leather pants, a black leather zip-front vest (which lifted the girls better than a push-up bra), black leather boots with bladed heels, my kodachi, and my gloves. Basically my normal hunting gear. Black leather might be cliché but it works. It absorbs the light instead of shining, it blends in with the shadows, it's comfortable to move in, and it provides more protection than say, cotton. Kevlar might be even better but it was difficult to move in and really, when it came down to it, Kevlar couldn't protect me from vampires or gods. I had spells for that.

My hair was braided tightly and coiled into a crown around my head. Here's a tip for all you wanna-be hunters; when you fight monsters, don't give them a leash to grab. I hate it when I watch some kick-ass chick-flick and the woman has her long hair in a braid. A real fighter would never give her opponent such an easy handhold. Make it as tight to the head as possible or tuck that braid down the back of your shirt.

I had even put on make-up. My eyes were done smoky and I'd made sure to matte my face with powder but I skipped the lipstick. I wasn't so vain that I was about to paint a bull's-eye on my face (okay, I may have used a little lip balm). Before I left the house, I checked the pins in my hair to make sure they were secure then snatched up my car keys with a smile. I was actually a little excited, isn't that messed up? It just shows you how bored I'd been.

Chapter Forty-Three

I parked at the usual place but Jimmy wasn't on, it was Keoki. He waved excitedly when he saw me, recognizing a big tip when it drove in. I let him take the car and then ran off without my ticket as usual. My purse was already in the hidden compartment but I had a little stash of cash tucked down my vest. I knew this wasn't just a hunting expedition, it was a stakeout and stakeouts required coffee.

Waikiki was always busy. They say New York never sleeps but I think Waikiki really wants second place because at most, it takes power naps. It was ten o'clock and the bars were blaring their music, sending out their siren's calls to lure in tourists and locals alike. The night had just begun.

In all my black I must have looked Goth or is it Emo now? Ridiculous. Back in high school, I wore a lot of black so I guess I was Goth before they had a name for it. They just called us weird. Now everything had labels and whole lifestyles to go along with the looks. Well, my look wasn't Goth or Emo, it was Godhunter and I'm pretty sure my lifestyle was a little too hardcore for the Emotionals. I fit right in with the club crowds though, except for my sword, which was blurred under its protection spell anyway. Then again, with all the Asian influence in Hawaii, people might dig the sword.

I wandered into a Starbucks and grabbed a drink before taking a seat at one of the wrought iron tables outside. I was trying for casual club-hopper; just another lady in leather fueling up with caffeine before the next round of dancing. I needed to blend in while keeping a look out. The kills had all been in this area so I figured it was the best place to start. Blue couldn't have been more obvious if he'd drawn a big red X on the sidewalk. I chose Starbucks in particular since it was raised a little off the sidewalk, giving me a good vantage point of both clubs and alleys. They also had a restroom in case I drunk too much coffee while I waited. It was perfect.

A six-pack of Marines stumbled up the street and I tried desperately not to make eye contact. They didn't seem to need encouragement though. The simple fact that I was sitting alone was enough for them. They wandered over to my low balcony and leaned against the railing to leer at me. I couldn't stop my annoyed groan.

"Hey, cutie," the more loquacious of the bunch started. "We're headed to The Red Lion, wanna come?"

"No, I'm good, thanks," I lifted my cup to show them I was busy enjoying a hot beverage.

"But a woman like you shouldn't be sitting alone," another one puffed out his chest. "Haven't you seen the news?"

"My boyfriend will be here any minute," I looked away, trying to scan the alleys, and thought I saw a flash of violent movement.

"We'll just wait with you then," the first one climbed over the railing and slid into a seat next to mine. Evidently, he knew a lie when he smelled one. Even if the scent of beer rolling off him was strong enough to mask any odor.

I frowned at him for a second bu then I caught the tail end of a scream on the breeze. "Dang it," I stood and jumped over the railing. "Gotta go, boys."

I threw my cup into a trash can as I ran by. The Oorah boys shuffled about in confusion but I didn't give them much thought as I headed across the street and down an alley, unsheathing my kodachi as I went.

Sure enough, a woman was lying on the wet asphalt

beneath a feeding vampire while another waited for his turn. I didn’t didn't even pause, just ran up swinging. The vamp in line heard the thumping of my boots and turned towards me but it was too late. His head bounced off the alley wall and hit the ground with a wet thud. Shocked eyes stared out of the severed head as its body toppled into a heap.

“Holy shit!” Someone exclaimed.

I looked over my shoulder and saw the Marines at my back.

“Get out of here!” I shouted as I spun back around.

It was all the distraction vamp #2 needed. He was on me in a blur of speed, knocking my sword out of my hand to send it clattering across the alley. Fingers dug into my collar and side as he pulled me forward and tried to latch onto my neck with his bared fangs. I struggled to cast a spell as I dodged his bites.

I didn’t struggle for long though. Our country's first line of defense had come to my aid. The vampire was hauled off me and I was freed long enough to release the knives from my gloves. I didn't have time to go after my sword, the claws would have to do.

“Shit, woman, who the fuck are you?” The Marine holding the vampire stared at my gloves with a mixture of jealousy and lust.

“Drop him and back away fast,” I kept my eyes on the strangely docile vampire who was suddenly staring at me like he’d found the prize in a box of Cocoa Pebbles.

“Don’t worry, I’ve got him,” the Marine smirked at me just as the vampire lunged back, dropping him like a bag of bad blood.

His friends rushed forward but the vampire was nearly on me. I did a roundhouse kick and slashed his neck open, splattering the oncoming cavalry and dropping the vampire to his knees. The Marines started shouting but whether it was in horror or appreciation, I’ll never know. Any further conversation was cut off by the arrival of five more vampires.

“Damn, damn, damn,” I swore as I scooped up my sword and chopped the wounded vamp’s head off. Then I ran over to help my rescuers.

They were trying to fight the monsters like humans, trained soldiers but still humans, and they were no match. I couldn’t cover them with a protection spell because they were already hand-to-hand with the vampires and the spell wouldn’t distinguish vamp from human. I had to wade into the mess.

I started a stun spell as I approached, so I was able to lop off the head of one vampire while striking out with the spell towards another. I beheaded the stunned vampire easily, since the spell basically froze him in place. Two down, only three to go.

The remaining three were tangled up with the humans and things were getting bad. Blood was flowing and screams were echoing. I didn't have time to cast another spell and with the way they were fighting, I wasn't sure who I'd hit if I tried. I couldn't get the right angle with my sword either, so I swiped my claws at the back of one of the vampires, separating muscle from spine as I gained his attention in the worst way. He screamed and fell away from the man he'd been trying to maul.

“You may be his *little witch* but for that, you'll die!” The vampire lurched at me.

Okay, so I wasn't being a narcissist; this really was about me.

“Bring it on, gimpy!” I smirked at his left arm, hanging uselessly from his ruined shoulder.

The Marines behind him may not have been faring so well but they were still alive and they were keeping the other two vamps busy for me, so I was grateful for their help. One vampire I could handle, even two, but I hadn't counted on fighting seven. I focused back on the vamp in front of me but before he got close enough to engage, a bolt of lightning hit him and he fell to the ground writhing and screaming.

"Holy fried fangster!" I leaped back.

A haze of magic sealed the entrance to the alley as five forms shimmered into view. Ull, Brahma, Horus, Pan, and Finn came running toward the fight. I was never so happy to see gods in all my life. I started to race in to help them but a large hand grabbed my shoulder and pulled me back.

"You just can't stay out of trouble, can you?" I'd know that rumble anywhere. Hell, the lightning really should've given it away.

"Thor," I whispered his name as I turned and the sounds of battle seemed to fade. I heard a few grunts and the soft tingle of magic crept up my back but my eyes were all for him.

"Come with me," he started pulling me away but I stopped him.

"Thor, wait, I-"

"I don't have time for your protests, Vervain," He bent down and swung me over his shoulder. "Sheath your blades. Now!"

I yanked the latches to pull up the claws as he traced us to Bilskinir. When we stepped out of the Aether, he dropped me rather roughly on his bed.

"What did you think you were doing out there tonight?" He glared at me and I wasn't surprised to see the lightning flashing in his stormy eyes.

"We're still on that?" I snorted. "You don't give up do

you? You're the one who told me I'm the Godhunter. You said it attracted you to me in the first place and yet you don't want me to hunt."

"Damn you, Vervain!" He yelled and the whole place shook.

I laughed with relief. If he was this mad at me, it could only mean one thing, he still cared.

"What the fuck are you laughing about?" He stomped across the room, the floor shivering under his feet, and loomed over me. *The better to glare at you, my dear.*

"Wow, you're really angry," my smile never wavered.

"I asked you what you were laughing about," the vibrations from his voice started to last longer than the actual sound.

"You know, Thor," I kicked off my boots. "There's a lot I find funny about this situation."

He took a step back and frowned, following the arc of my footwear to the floor before returning his narrowed stare to me. "What the hell are you doing now?"

"It's rather funny that the very mess Blue had intended to bring me back to him, has only landed me back here. In your bedroom," I unbuckled my gloves and threw them over by the boots.

Thor's eyes widened and his voice lost its thunder. "Vervain, what are you doing?"

"It's also funny that I got a little overdressed to hunt vampires but I'm glad I did, since you showed up," my smile turned sultry.

"You are?" His voice was just the barest breath of sound.

"And it's really funny that I'm so much of an ass, it took a bunch of vampires to get me to admit how much I've missed you," I undid my hair and shook it out, so that it fell down to my waist in loose waves.

"You are?" His voice came out a little choked. "You do?"

"Even with them out there, killing on my island, I can't stop feeling overjoyed to see you." I stood up and stepped in close to him.

"You can't?" He shuddered as I ran my hands up his chest and around his neck. I stood on my tiptoes and pulled his head down to mine.

"Forgive me, baby?" I whispered against his lips and he groaned.

"Vervain," he pulled me off my feet and kissed me like it was our first kiss.

I yanked his shirt from his jeans and laid my hands on his bare chest. I could feel his heartbeat through his skin, pounding faster and faster. Then my mouth was back to his, a soft sound escaping my lips as I felt the thick muscles of his chest clench beneath my fingers. My hands traveled on a path so well known to them that they needed no direction. It was automatic and effortless; the map of his body memorized in my fingertips.

His hands were at the zipper of my vest and then my breasts were spilling free, the leather thrown on the ever growing pile of clothing. Thor pulled away and looked down at me with those lightning-filled eyes. Pupils dilating, framing the lightning. Nostrils flaring slightly with his rapid breaths. Skin glowing gold beneath my fingertips. I couldn't believe I threw this away because of some stupid fight. Because of my stupid pride.

"Why wouldn't you let me come to you?" His hands slid over both of my breasts as he spoke.

"What?" I grabbed his hands and held them still as I stared up at him in shock.

"I've lived only for my dreams with you," his hands slipped out of my grip and drifted up to my face. "My days were spent in a frustrated haze, anxiously waiting for night. When I could see you, touch you again."

"That really *was* you?" I was horrified, embarrassed, and oddly relieved.

"I tried to tell you, darling," he smiled gently.

"Yeah, you did," I felt my breath catch, constricting my throat as I realized everything that had happened between us had been real. He'd said those things because he wanted to, not because *I* wanted him to. "Then you really...?"

"Love you?" He smiled wider. "Yes, I love you, you stubborn, stupid woman."

"I love you too, you patient, overprotective god."

I glimpsed an expression of fierce joy on his face before he swooped down and kissed me again. Static electricity crackled along my skin and tingled where our mouths met. He tasted of ozone and rain; his tongue hot and his breath cool. A breeze swirled around us, playing in my hair and raising shivers on my back. Then his hands followed, hot and sure, making me lean into his warmth like he was both shelter and storm.

I swallowed past the nervous twitches in my throat and undid his jeans with shaky hands. He pushed them down before kicking them across the room with barely restrained annoyance. I laughed a little until he knelt and covered a breast with his mouth. The laughter turned into a sharp gasp and I arched against him as he lavished attention on me with his tongue. Liquid fire rushed through me, melting my bones, and I went limp. Thor used his free hand to support my weight and I grabbed big handfuls of his hair to hold him against me. By the time he turned his attention to the other breast, I was writhing in need, little snakes of desire twisting in my belly.

"Enough," I groaned as he kissed his way down. He unbuttoned my leather pants and I sighed as they slithered down my legs.

"Never enough," he bit at the front of the red lace g-string that was the only thing remaining between him and I. My heart jumped at his choice of words and the tenderness in them.

I looked down into the ocean-colored eyes and shook my head, "I've been such an idiot."

"At least you've come to your senses," he gave me a big Cheshire cat grin and pulled my panties down.

I stepped out of them and he flung them away like they'd been trying to keep us apart. Thor looked up at me, all lightning flashes and hot desire. Warm, magic-filled hands slid reverently up my calves, over my thighs, and finally came to a stop at my waist.

"You're so beautiful," he whispered.

"Look who's talking," I tugged on his hand to urge him to his feet.

"Men are not beautiful," he chided as he scooped me up and laid me back in his bed.

I struggled with the comforter and finally kicked it onto the floor as he laughed. The silk sheets beneath me slid against my skin with a cool, welcoming caress. Much better. I leaned back on my elbows and enjoyed the show of him crawling over me.

"I don't know about men in general," I licked my lips, "but baby, you are a thing of beauty."

"Call me baby again," he smiled against my mouth.

“Baby,” I whispered and pulled his mass of red-gold hair around me. It smelled of storms on the sea. It smelled like home.

“Mmmmm,” he licked my lips and kissed his way to my ear. “I like the taste of that word on your lips. Try my name now.”

“Thor,” I smiled as his lips returned to press gently to mine.

He breathed in my breath and when he exhaled, he drew it down my body, painting me with sparks of light blue. His lips brushed my skin, sending shivers deeper into me, before he pulled back to continue the fluttering administration of his breath. Then there were his hands. Little sparks tingled from the tips of his fingers to dance across my flesh, jolting my body back to life as if it had been dead without him. By the time he'd covered me completely, I was a shaking shell of my former self. A whimpering halfwit who couldn't remember her own name.

He brought me to the edge of desire over and over again before we even joined together. It all became a blur of pleasure for me after that. Sweat, lightning, shaking legs, clutching hands, and his beautiful face. It became my whole world during the hours I spent wrapped around him. I don't even know how long it was before we finally fell away from each other and laid there catching our breaths. But I will remember forever his first words to me afterward.

“I would remove his mark from you,” Thor had leaned over me, to draw his tongue across the scars Blue had left on my neck. “Will you let me trade his for mine?”

“You can do that?” I twisted my head and met his intense stare.

“Yes, if you’ll let me.”

“Do it,” I bent my head to the side, offering him my neck. Trade Thor's mark for Blue's? Hell yes, any day.

Thor covered the marks with his mouth and I felt his magic gather in great tingling waves. His tongue seemed to spark against me and a sharp jolt of electricity shot into my skin. I screamed from the mix of pleasure and pain as he leaned further over me, one hand going to the bed to hold himself up and the other wrapping around my waist to hold me still.

Thunder rumbled through the sky outside, loud enough to shake all of Asgard, and lightning lit up the room. Shadows spun excitedly on the walls as ancient magic whirled in the air, cooling my flushed skin. Thor lifted his face from my neck, giving me one final lick before he reared up and grabbed my hips. As Bilskinir trembled around us, he filled me with magic and flesh, steering us back into the flow of ecstasy smoothly but fiercely.

Then he began to shake and he shouted my name, a rush of power flowing from him and into me as he came. It filled my blood, my bones, and my very cells with magic before it burst from me in a savage cry of pleasure. We trembled with our completion until we collapsed together in exhaustion. He rolled to the side and pulled me across his chest, where I laid my head so I could hear his heartbeat slowing along with mine. The storm continued to rage outside but in his arms, I felt calm and safe.

"Thank you for this," he brushed my hair away and stroked his fingers over my throat.

"I'm as happy to be rid of those scars as you are to see them go," I snuggled into him and felt his arms settle around me.

"Now all will know you're mine," he kissed the top of my head and my eyes shot open. What was with these guys and their possessiveness? Was it a god thing? I tensed and he must have felt it because he angled his head to look at my face and ask, "You're upset? You gave me permission, Vervain."

"I know," I lifted my head so he could see I had no regrets. "I just need to get used to a possessive god for a boyfriend. The *mine* talk throws me."

He smiled a little but then his eyes went serious. "We have both been fools," he held my face and kissed me gently. "I should never have let you walk out."

"You mean you should never have kicked me out," I smiled to soften my words. "I'm sorry I said such horrible things to you, I didn't mean them."

"I know, darling," he ran a finger over my lips. "It's all better now."

"Better. What a grossly inadequate word," I mumbled as I fell asleep to the sound of thunder and Thor's laughter, unsure of which was which.

Chapter Forty-Four

"Oh God," I groaned as I rubbed my eyes

"Yes?" Thor's voice was low and sultry. He sounded sexier than ever.

"You had to go there?" I swatted him as he pulled me closer under the covers, the early morning chill caressing my face and making his heat all the more sweet. His naked body slid across mine, held up by his forearms so the weight of him was comforting instead of crushing. He was pulsing hard against my thigh. "And good morning," I purred.

"Yes, definitely," he buried his face in my hair and breathed deep, sending tremors skittering through my rib cage. "Do you know what you smell like?"

"I know what you smell like... breakfast."

He chuckled, still buried in my hair, "*You* smell like sex and magic."

"Hmmm, sex and magic," I pushed him over, straddling him and dislodging the blankets as I went. "Yes, please."

He could hardly say no to such a polite request. So we spent most of the morning reinforcing our reunion . Well, at least in my mind it was reinforcement. The previous night had taken on a certain dreamlike quality for me, especially with those sparks of lightning and the way Thor covered Blue's scars. I needed to know it was all real, to have him again in the light of day. I think he knew it as well and made every effort to affirm our new status. Then he carried me to the bathroom and bathed me. Yes, bathed me. Unbelievable. I'd never felt so pampered in all my life. He even washed my hair.

It wasn't till we were done and I was dressed, that I got a good look at myself in the mirror. I had to wear my hunting leathers since I didn't have a change of clothes at Thor's place anymore but I'd left my hair loose and I felt sexier. Funny how actually having sex will do that to you. It wasn't my hair that had caught my attention though, it was the lightning-shaped scar curving down from just below my right ear to the base of my neck. Thor's mark. It was actually kind of attractive but more importantly; it erased that horrible reminder of Blue.

"You *had* to mark me too?" Thor asked as he came up behind me.

"I know," I chuckled when I saw the red bite I'd left on the right side of his neck. "It's very high school, very white trash, but since you got to give me a scar, I thought you could at least suffer through a love bite for awhile."

"You can mark me anytime," he nuzzled my neck as he pulled me back against his chest. He towered over me but it made me feel safe. He lifted his face to ask, "Are you hungry?"

"Oh yeah," I pulled away from him and ran out of the room before he could change his mind. I was happier than I'd been in weeks, especially when I heard his footsteps thudding after me.

Chapter Forty-Five

I'd wasted too much time wallowing in my depression over Thor. Now I had to get back in the game and fast. So as soon as breakfast was done, I headed into the library to spirit-walk into Blue's head. I thought I might be rusty but I guess all those nights of pushing him out of my dreams had kept me in prime mental shape. I slid easily and silently into his mind.

I shouldn't have worried about the quiet part though. Blue was in a mental uproar. His thoughts flew from one angry string to the next. It was so quick, I had a hard time following any particular one through to the end. There were a lot of visions of Thor being hurt and I had to spend some time calming myself before I could continue to sift through the rest of the violent detritus. But the thoughts concerning me were even more disturbing and I passed them by as quickly as possible.

Blue had apparently thought that I'd come to my senses and sacrifice myself on the bloody altar of his desire as soon as I saw all the damage his little vampires could inflict. When his plan failed, he didn't take it kindly. On the bright side, he'd been way too caught up with pursuing me to pursue Maria. In fact, he had decided to explore other options. The latest plot was now centered on the Russian Minister of Defense, Sergei Shoigu.

The last Minister of Defense had been a man named Anatoliy Serdyukov. He had been fired recently due to some real estate scandal. But he also happened to be married to the daughter of the Chairman of the Board of Gazprom, Viktor Zubkov. Zubkov became Chairman when Prime Minister Medvedev had to resign to accept the presidency. Yes, the presidency. Medvedev had been president and Putin had been the Prime Minister but then they traded places. So now Putin is President and Medvedev is Prime Minister. How you like them apples? Confusing, isn't it? What I found especially confusing was the fact that they had both a Prime Minister and a President. Aren't you supposed to have one or the other?

Anyway, when Serdyukov was fired, Putin replaced him with Shoigu. Shoigu didn't seem to have the same connections as Serdyukov but he was a close friend of Putin's. It wasn't surprising that President Putin had put a friend of his in office but it had to have been salt on Serdyukov's wounded pride. He may not be in power anymore but Serdyukov still had powerful connections. This created a volatile situation which Blue was going to take full advantage of. There were several plans he could put into action but they all started the same; with Sergei Shoigu.

Blue had found a way start a war without killing Maria. Great for Maria, bad for Russia and the Minister of Defense. It looked as if Blue's fury over losing me had made him impatient and he'd gotten tired of playing with the middle man. No more games, Blue was going straight to the top. The Minister of Defense is basically Commander in Chief of the Russian military and this Rottweiler was about to become Blue's lapdog. Blue was after the reins of the Russian Federation and he intended to scoop up those reins in Bucharest.

Chapter Forty-Six

There have been many places I've been to that have resonated with me. On some level my body, my very cells, recognized the land. It was like that in both France and Ireland. I'd breathe in and think, *Yes, I know this. This feels right*, and I'd instantly be comfortable.

Bucharest was not one of those places.

I looked around the tired alleys and up at the strings of lank laundry hanging from the lines above me and all I could think was, *I want to go home*. Maybe it was just the knowledge that Blue was conspiring to do horrible things to me and the man I loved. Blue, who for a moment I'd thought might not be past redemption. Then I shut him out of my mind and rejected his love. And he had responded by slaughtering innocent people. It made for an awkward reunion. Especially since I intended to kill him.

I looked around again at the architecture, which must have once been beautiful and should still have had some charm, but all I could see was decay. I sighed.

"Let's get this over with," Horus echoed my feelings precisely.

"There's the cafe," I pointed to the back-alley eatery most people would probably describe as quaint but I just thought was creepy. "And there's Shoigu's men," I indicated the obvious bodyguards standing duty outside the doors.

Blue needed to take Shoigu's blood in order to possess him thoroughly. So the obvious course of action would have been to simply keep Blue away from Shoigu but we couldn't protect him twenty-four-seven and neither could his guards. Blue could snatch Shoigu up in a moment,just like he'd taken me. We needed a more permanent solution.

It was Teharon who came up with the idea and in theory it should work. Unfortunately, we didn't have a lot of time to practice, so a *theory* was kinda all we had. The idea was that if Teharon could drive Blue out of my body and help me keep him out, then he should also be able to shield a mortal's mind who had yet to be invaded. Teharon had tried to shield me from Horus and it had worked but we really didn't know if he'd be able to replicate the process in a normal human with a god as powerful as Blue trying to get past the shields. We also had no idea how long the shielding would last.

It was the first time Teharon had come hunting with us and his eyes were practically glowing with excitement. As a healer, he'd been best utilized behind the scenes and so had never been asked to participate in the field work. He was chomping at the bit to do his part and I couldn't blame him.

"Go get him, tiger," I nudged Teharon and he gave me an eager smile.

"I'll do my best," Teharon disappeared. I assumed he crossed the street and entered the cafe.

"I hate waiting," I bit my lip as I watched for any sign of a disturbance.

All Teharon had to do was go in, lay a hand on Shoigu, and shield him. Then he needed to get his ass out of the creepy/quaint restaurant and we had to watch and make sure that he did. Unfortunately, we wouldn't know if Teharon's shielding worked until Blue tried to take Shoigu's mind. So there would be even more waiting after Teharon returned.

I scanned the empty streets, a knot of fear growing in my belly. Something had me spooked and I couldn't figure out what. There was still no sign of Blue but that didn't mean anything. He could be cloaking like Teharon and standing right next to me, for all I knew. I looked sharply over my shoulder.

"What's wrong with you?" Thor asked me.

"I don't know," I rubbed my bare upper arms. My gloves only reached my elbows. Maybe I should have worn a jacket. I had no idea Romania would be so cold.

"It's done," Teharon appeared before us, startling me. "He's as safe as I can make him."

"Now we wait," Horus leaned against the alley wall, looking even more bored than usual.

"Again," I glanced around.

I shouldn't have worried. Blue was right on schedule. He arrived no more than five minutes after Teharon had returned. Fully visible, Blue strode confidently into the cafe, never bothering to even glance around him. It took half an hour for him to give up and leave. He slammed out of the restaurant and caught sight of immediately. With a nasty glare, he stomped off down the street.

"It worked," Teharon beamed.

"That was way too easy," I stepped back into the alley, frowning.

"Never complain about things being easy," Thor admonished.

"I know but this is Blue," I kept feeling like I was missing something. "He should have learned to expect us by now. This has all been too easy. Why? Why would he go through all of this trouble and just keep walking away? He didn't even come over and confront us."

"Because I was waiting for you to slip up, Godhunter," Blue's voice behind me startled me into a spin. "Only two fighters and a healer to protect you. Then on top of that, you go and hide in an alley. No human witnesses. That's not very smart of you."

He backhanded me and sent me flying further into the alley. I hit a wall hard and then fell onto the cold, uneven stones. The sounds of fierce fighting seemed distant even though I knew I wasn't more than ten feet away. My head spun and I heaved up the contents of my stomach. Acid in my mouth and blood trickling down my neck; I was dizzy but I managed to get to my feet. I squinted down the alley just in time to see a blurry Teharon get struck down.

I screamed, despite the pain it caused in my head, and started forward but a hand caught my arm and yanked me back. I looked down in confusion, still moving a little slow, and saw feminine fingers gripping me tight.

"Huitzilopochtli isn't the only one who's been waiting for you to fuck up."

Before I could focus on my assailant, everything went black.

Chapter Forty-Seven

"Wake up, bitch!" It wasn't the sweetest wake-up call I'd ever had and it was even more startling when I realized who the strident voice belonged to.

I groaned and opened my eyes to see an expanse of gray stone very close to my face. It was dry and cold, sucking the warmth right out of me. It took me a second to realize that I was shackled to a wall, hanging from my wrists. I struggled to my feet, only to find that they were shackled as well. At least they weren't bruised and cut like my wrists were, from supporting my weight. My head was still a little fuzzy, my legs were shaky, and my whole body ached, especially my wrists and shoulders. I guess I should've been thankful that I was still alive but I had a feeling I might be wishing for the alternative soon.

When I turned my head, I could see the rest of an S&M collection; complete with a rack, a wooden X-shaped cross, an iron bed covered in black satin, and a stone altar laid with an assortment of whips and knives. Now when I say whips, I don't mean the soft leather ones you find at Sensually Yours out on Nimitz. I mean the real, pirate on the high seas, strap 'em to the mast, me maties, steel, barb-tipped whips.

Who knew Aphrodite was a sadist?

I guess it made a warped sort of sense. Love hurts and all that. She was the Goddess of Love and wasn't her husband that blacksmith god? The one with the limp. Hephaistos, that was it. I bet I knew where she got all her cool toys.

"Are you awake, you little slut?" She grabbed me by the hair and yanked my head back so she could glare at me.

"Well isn't that the pot calling the kettle black?" I grinned at her and she slapped me, bitch-slapped me actually. I laughed even though my cheek stung bad enough to make my eyes water. “You hit like a girl.”

“You stupid, worthless, human,” she spat and I mean she really spat at me. I had to turn my face to avoid the spittle. “You have no idea what I can do to you.”

“Well, go on then,” I flexed my shoulders and back. “Let’s hear it, Afro.”

“My name is *Aphrodite* and you should be begging by now,” her face was twisted with her hatred and it stole most of her beauty, forcing her features into harsh lines which would have looked more at home on a vulture than a woman. “No matter. You will be soon enough.”

“So what’s this about anyway? Why did you help me escape Blue if you hate me so much?” Keep it casual. Keep her talking. Maybe if I kept her talking, she’d stay away from all the lethal hardware.

“What’s this *about*?!” She screamed and it was like a three-year-old throwing a temper tantrum. “I couldn't kill you after Huitzilopochtli granted you protection. So I helped you escape to get you away from him but you just kept turning up. *I* was supposed to be his Queen. I'm the Goddess of Love and Beauty after all. I deserve to rule beside him. Then you came along and all he could think about was you. Little witch, little witch. You're all he talks about!”

Go figure. Isn’t it always about a man?

“Hey look, I don’t want to be his Queen. I didn’t even know the position was available. I’m in love with Thor for god’s sake... for my sake, whatever. I don’t want Blue.”

“But he wants you.” She sneered at me. “All his plans center around you. Finding you. Luring you out of hiding. Making you chase him. He schemes for hours just to draw you out and see you for mere minutes."

"What?" My mouth fell open, scraping my chin against the wall.

"You said it yourself," she lifted a perfect brow. "Why go through all that trouble just to walk away? He wanted to see you, you idiot! He did it all to make you come to him."

"So he can kill me," I sighed, "I know. He made it pretty clear when he sent me crashing into a wall."

"That's just because you angered him," she waved her hand like she could brush aside my stupidity. "He wasn't going to kill you. He was going to kill your friends and then take you home with him to make you his Queen!"

"Oh, how romantic," I turned my face fully to the wall.

If I was going to feel like I was talking to a brick wall, I might as well be looking at one too. Wait a minute... Queen. Queen of Love. *Aphrodite* was the Queen of Love. I *was* an idiot! How in hell did I not figure that out sooner?

"It *is* romantic, you simpleton," the Queen of Love screeched at my back. "He would have done anything to have you. That's true love. Such devotion shouldn't be wasted on a human."

"You think that's true love?" I was shocked enough to look back at her. "Are you out of your mind?" I looked around the room again and snorted. "Oh, right, sorry. Stating the obvious again."

"You *are* beyond stupid," she planted her hands on her hips, wrinkling the pristine beauty of her white velvet gown. "He's the greatest of the gods. You especially could do no better than him."

"Obviously I'm not worthy. So you just go ahead,

girlfriend." I rolled my eyes. Those two would be perfect for each other.

"I'm not your friend, feeble human," she grabbed a whip from the table and my stomach lurched. "I'm your death."

"Easy now," I eyed her over my shoulder and tried to swallow past the fear that was suddenly choking me. "You don't have to do this. I don't want your man."

"*I'm* her man," a gruff voice made me wrench my head in the other direction and the sudden motion made it spin a little.

Did I have a concussion? It wouldn't be surprising after the blow Blue had dealt me. I blinked and focused on a man of average height who was coming towards me with a distinct limp and a dark glare. He had long brown hair tied at his nape and a rugged handsomeness that spoke of a divine parentage. Oh crap.

"Hephaistos, I presume?" I choked out.

He looked rather pleased for a moment and then started to glare again but this time it was directed at Aphrodite.

"What have you done now?" He motioned to me. "Who's this?"

"She's the Godhunter and I'm going to torture her until she dies, begging for mercy," Afro looked smug. Not exactly the answer I was hoping for.

"So *you* were the one who sent the wolves?" I interrupted and Hephaistos looked me over curiously.

"Of course," Aphrodite sniffed. "I couldn't have it getting back to Huitzilopochtli that I killed you but now I see that the wolves have grown weak and I must do it myself."

"But how were you able to track Thor?" I figured I might as well get some answers.

"Sif is one of my closest friends," Aphrodite's wicked smile belied her words. "All I had to do was comfort her and she told me every move you two made. She's one of those women who torment herself over and over instead of simply getting a new man."

"Hmm," I raised a brow at her, "sounds familiar."

"Shut up, whore," she flung the whip at me and I felt it hit; tearing through the material of my leather vest, my bra, my skin, and then muscle.

There was a blessed second of numb shock before the searing pain hit. Burning, radiating anguish made my back arch as if it could run away from the trauma. I couldn't breathe for a second. It was more excruciating than werewolf claws, which at least had extreme sharpness in their favor. The barbs at the end of Afro's whip weren't nearly as sharp, snagging and tearing as they traveled the length of my back. I'm embarrassed to admit that I screamed like a little schoolgirl.

"Aphrodite!" Hephaistos took the whip as I tried to see past the blinding pain. My vision had gone blotchy and spotty but I could hear just fine and Hephaistos sounded supremely pissed when he demanded, "You will tell me what this is about and you will tell me now!"

"She's trading up, Hephaistos old boy," I choked out. My back was going numb and I was able to think again. "She wants to be Queen of the Gods or some such shit. She's tossing you out on your ass and I'm in her way, so it's the whip for me and the boot for you."

When all else fails, get the bad guys to fight each other.

"Shut up!" Aphrodite swung around and grabbed another whip.

I heard it swish back and I tensed in anticipation of the

blow. But it didn't fall, so I risked another glance over my shoulder. Hephaistos had Aphrodite by the wrist and was staring her down, well up actually, since she had a good four inches on him.

"You want free of me, my love?" He stared hard at her and her eyes softened slightly. "Who will make you such lovely playthings when I'm gone?"

"Hephaistos," she pouted and even to me, it looked practiced.

"No," he released her with a shove that sent her stumbling. "I'm finished. That bloody Aztec is welcome to you."

He turned and walked away as she screamed for him to come back. She demanded that he turn around right this instant. She stomped her feet and cried but still, he kept walking. I was in such deep shit.

I knew the exact moment she remembered me and realized that I'd witnessed her humiliation. The whip swished back and her rage echoed around me as she let it fly. Even prepared, I couldn't stop my scream. Tears ran down my face and I didn't care. I would've begged, I would've done anything she wanted, just to stop that whip from falling again, but she didn't give me a chance. She just kept wailing, kept pulling back the whip until I thought I would pass out. I *hoped* I would pass out.

As I weakened, I instinctively reached for strength from the earth and when the power edged up my toes, I remembered. I saw the circle in my head and the gods falling to their knees around me. Could I do it again? Could I weaken her till she couldn't wield the whip? It was sure worth a try.

I tried to clear my head but it was hard with the pain. My back was burning and I wasn't sure there was any flesh left on it at all. I could feel blood running down my legs in steady streams and my vest was hanging loose at my sides. Since I couldn't escape it, I welcomed the pain. I drew it in and used it. Then I turned it around and pushed it into her as I took power away from her. I saw the circuit in my head and felt the pulsing connection between us. Her magic for my pain. Fair trade, don't ya think?

I heard her gasp as a sweet tingling began to fill me. It was soft and tentative at first but then it started to rush into me with the greatest pleasure I'd ever felt. Wave after wave of liquid sunlight flowed up my legs, licking at me like a lover. It caressed me from the inside out, touching me everywhere, and leaving me feeling more sexually aware of my body than I'd ever been.

I took a deep breath and tried to control the ecstasy but as soon as I did, it started to pull away. I heard Aphrodite choking behind me and knew I couldn't try to control it. I had to let it in completely. I had to welcome the magic and embrace it fully. So I opened my metaphysical arms to it and it flung itself back into my body. Magic rushed through me and I screamed as I came, tremors shaking me from the tips of my fingers to the bottom of my toes. Aphrodite wasn't just a goddess of love, she was also a goddess of lust, and it was pure sex that rode me, filled me, and consumed me. I gasped for air while it settled into my bones and took root. It was mine. I wasn't borrowing this time, I was stealing.

I felt a moment's guilt before a light fluttering started to tickle my toes. I've had butterflies in my stomach before but this was the first time I've had them fly throughout my whole body and roost. It started gentle but then turned wild. A mad heady rush and then back to a steady pace. It was a roller coaster ride. It was the beat of a heart. No, the beat of two hearts together. It was a rhythm of tribal drums mixed with the soft notes of a harp. It was the place where poetry is born. A wide, endless sea of emotion that would never dry up; could in fact, quench the world's thirst and still be full. It was the greatest magic of all. The power that fed all others. It lifted me to happiness so great, I cried violently when it receded, even though it was receding into me.

I saw Thor's face; his soft smile and strong heart. I saw the greatness that love could bring out of him and also the anguish it could cause. I shivered as the magic showed me the other side of love. The ability to destroy completely and leave only despair in its wake. I saw how Aphrodite had twisted her magic and made a mockery of it. She had begun to glory more in the control that love could give her than in the love itself. Ol' Afro had slipped towards the dark side and her power was more than happy to find a new mistress.

I shuddered and began to think it was over but then came an image of Blue. I frowned and tried to push it away but how do you deny something that's inside you, showing you only the truth? It laid him bare before me; his evil nature and his good. To my surprise, there *was* good in him and I saw how it would grow under my care. I saw the man he could become under Love's influence. I shook my head and told myself that I wouldn't be the woman who thinks she can change a man. I didn't want the responsibility and I didn't want his love.

So it showed me the anger inside him, the hatred my rejection would bring, and I cried out in regret. He was pitiful in his withdrawal into rage. I saw him gorge himself on blood and slake himself on countless women in an attempt to burn the feelings away. I moaned and begged the magic to stop. I didn't want this, I didn't ask for him to love me. I refused to take responsibility for his downfall.

You did *ask for this*, something spoke inside me and I knew it was the magic but not just the magic. It was blending with me, becoming me, and forcing me to be honest with myself. *You drew me out and brought me here. Give me your life and I will give you mine but you must accept what I am and what we will be together. You will be held accountable but only to yourself. Aphrodite learned to be cruel to escape the pain of caring but you can choose to be stronger than her. Accept that there will be heartache, that you will feel it and cause it, but that you will also be the cause of soaring happiness; bliss beyond belief. You will be responsible for both but Love, like the butterfly, tends towards lightness and if you're true to me, there will be much more joy than pain.*

"So mote it be," I whispered my weary assent and felt Love settle inside my chest. There *was* lightness to it and I smiled despite my exhaustion. But it wasn't over, a new facet of Aphrodite's magic rushed into me. Now what?

The clash of swords rang in my ears the exhilaration of battle filled me. I suddenly remembered what else Aphrodite ruled; War and Victory. I felt them plow into me together, like brother soldiers. They strengthened my body; tightening muscles, hardening bones, enhancing organs, and sharpening reflexes. I knew I could fight at the head of armies and lead them to victory. I could stand on the field of battle and swing my sword over and over, never tiring. I could make my enemies fall to their knees before me and beg for mercy. I could grant glory and fame to any who would follow me.

The magic was intoxicating. I finally saw why the Atlanteans proclaimed themselves to be gods. It was hard not to believe it when you felt the force of that energy and knew what you were truly capable of. I had to remind myself of who I really was. Vervain Lavine, human witch, *not* a goddess. I may hold god magic now but that didn't make me one of them.

Did it?

War and Victory found their places beside Lust and Love and I felt my body convulse violently, then fall, to hang limp from the shackles. I forced my head around with supreme effort, and saw Aphrodite on the ground behind me. She was beautiful again, peaceful as she laid sprawled across the stone floor. I knew immediately that she was dead. I'd drained her of everything she had, all the magic that was sustaining her, and she had simply laid down and drifted away. I reached deep and tried to feel some horror over her murder but I just couldn't. She was going to whip me to death; flay me open until my heart gave out. I had drained her and she died like Sleeping freakin' Beauty. The bitch was lucky.

However, I was still chained to a wall, filled with a power which couldn't help me with those chains, and bleeding from my shredded back. The magic had taken most of the pain away but it wasn't a healing gift and my back was still bleeding. Just thinking about it brought back the pain. Like it had been sitting there, waiting for me to remember it. Or maybe now that Afro was dead, it had surged back to me from her. Whatever the case, my exhausted mind couldn't take any more. I closed my eyes and let myself fall into the void.

Chapter Forty-Eight

Something cool and liquid was at my lips, and I drank it down greedily. There was soft murmuring around me and warmth everywhere. My body tingled like a foot freshly awakened and I had the urge to stretch everything all at once. I opened my eyes and saw a white feather with a red tip hanging before me. I blinked, refocused, and saw that it was attached to a long, silky, black braid. Teharon. I smiled.

"We have to stop meeting like this," I croaked.

He laughed softly. Everything about him was gentle. He was the perfect healer. "Drink more of this, Vervain."

I heard some movement, it sounded like running. Far away there was a crash, then a slam, and the pound of heavy footfalls. As they neared, I heard angry male voices getting louder with them and I groaned. I was too tired to deal with more anger. Can't we all just get along?

"Tell them if they can't control their hostility, they're not to come in," Teharon looked to his left as he spoke and I saw Mrs. E standing there in a white linen dress, looking like an angel. Or maybe that was just because she was holding a pitcher of water and I was still so very thirsty. She smiled at me, winked, and walked calmly away. I gulped more water from the cup Teharon held as he brushed back the hair from my forehead. His touch was as cool and as reviving as the water. "Easy, Godhunter, you've been through a lot and it's taken many nights to heal you. Don't overtax yourself."

"How many nights?" I frowned as I tried to remember, then tensed as I relived it all at once.

Teharon stroked my face and calmed me with whispered words but soon there were more faces pressing in around him.

Thor's face was pale and anxious. He knelt beside me and took my hand, pressing it to his lips and crying silently as he kissed it. I started to cry too and he dove over me, wrapping his arms around me and burying his face in my neck. My back felt a little tight and achy but there wasn't any pain and I silently worshiped Teharon's healing abilities.

"Are you in pain, darling?" Thor jerked back. "Did I hurt you?"

"No," I smiled as big as I could and looked over to Teharon. "I'm racking up quite a tab with you, Mr. Heaven Hands."

"Remember me when you release your bounty," Teharon winked and I felt my face go slack. He held up his hand, immediately reassuring. "You're still the Godhunter, you're still Vervain Lavine, nothing has changed that. There's just more to you now."

"So now you heal the spirit too, Teharon?" I reached for his hand and he squeezed mine.

"I try my best," he gave me one last squeeze before releasing me to back away, ending up slightly behind the blue silk curtains at the foot of the bed.

"Then so shall I," I smiled with more strength and looked back at Thor. "How did you find me?"

"When you killed Aphrodite, her wards went down and I was able to break through into her territory," Thor winced as he recounted it. "It was bad, darling. I didn't think you were going to live."

"She wouldn't have if she hadn't taken Aphrodite's magic," Teharon admitted.

"The fighting stopped as soon as Aphrodite took you,"

Thor reclaimed my attention, “Huitzilopochtli noticed first, the son of a bitch. He just started screaming and then disappeared. That's when I noticed you were gone too. I thought he'd somehow taken you but Horus pointed out that Huitzilopochtli wouldn't have been upset if that were the case.”

Thor looked over his shoulder at Horus, who shrugged as if it didn't matter to him whether I lived or died. But I caught the glimmer of relief in his eyes and it made me smile.

“I went to Fenrir and asked for Trevor,” Thor continued. “He picked up Aphrodite's scent easily but then he'd known it was her all along.”

“He tried to tell me,” I patted Thor's hand. “I can't blame him for his loyalty to his family.”

“We'll talk of loyalties later,” Thor looked grim and I frowned but before I could ask anything, he continued. “I couldn’t even sense where Aphrodite had taken you. She had you deep in the ground and that, combined with her wards, made you invisible to me. Trevor found the path but we still couldn't get past her wards until she was dead. As soon as they fell, we went in after you. You were horribly abused. If Aphrodite hadn't already been dead, I would have killed her slowly.”

“I love you too,” I whispered and his face lost a little of its ferocity.

“Lady Hunter,” the low roll of Trevor’s voice vibrated in my ears and I looked over to see him at the foot of the bed. I don’t know why but it was strange to see him in Thor's bedroom at Bilskinir. It felt like a misplaced intimacy.

“Trevor,” I started to smile but something in his face made me hesitate. He had something to say but he couldn’t do it in front of the others. I don’t know how I could read him so easily but it suddenly seemed natural, like a childhood friend whose every twitch I could interpret. “Baby,” I looked over to Thor. “I know I just woke up but could you clear everyone out for a minute? I need to talk to Trevor."

Thor looked at me, then the wolf, and back at me again. He gave me a confused nod but before he could get up, I pulled his face down and kissed him thoroughly. When I pulled back, he smiled but his lips trembled and a relieved half laugh/half cry tumbled past them. He got to his feet still holding my gaze.

"Okay, let's give them a minute," Thor turned and I saw for the first time that the room was full.

All of my god peeps were there and each one of them gave me a wink, a smile, or (in the case of Horus) a curt nod as they left. I smiled reassuringly at them, wondering how many more times we'd repeat this bedside scene. It was getting to be tedious, these near death injuries and I'm sure I wasn't the only one who thought so.

When the room was empty of all but Trevor and I, I held a hand out to him and he rushed over with a blur of speed. In a move similar to one he'd done before, he ran his face along mine. This time though, I felt his magic caress me, reach through me questing, seeking to see if I was truly healed. Trevor buried his face deep into the hair at the crook of my neck, then inhaled deep and exhaled with a long shudder.

"I'm alright, Trevor," I felt my body start to tremble and almost groaned.

What was with me? Had I turned into da-da-da-da… Su-u-uper Slut? Able to leap on tall gods with a single bound, fly through feelings faster than a speeding werewolf, and save blood-thirsty Aztecs with love magic. This was ridiculous. I couldn't be feeling anything for Trevor, I loved Thor. I was lying in his bed for fuck's sake. Well maybe not right at the moment but after some rest it would definitely be for fuck's sake. Okay, that was crude. I apologize but cut me some slack, things were getting weird and my mind was having trouble coping.

Trevor didn't pull away like I'd expected. He crawled up onto the bed with me and wrapped all of his muscled, werewolf mass tight against my side. I tried to tamp down the desire his touch ignited but my new magic liked him. It liked him a whole lot. It whispered to me that he was deserving of love. He was worthy of our gift. In fact, he was already ours.

He flung a thickly muscled leg over mine and an arm around my waist.

"Um, Trevor?" My voice was shaky as I looked down at the bulge of his bare arm. He was wearing one of those tight black T-shirts again and for some reason, it made me even more nervous.

"Yes?" He spoke into my neck, his breath hot against my racing pulse.

"Was there something you wanted to talk to me about?" I patted his hand on my belly in what I hoped was a sisterly fashion.

"First, I'd have you know my true name," he whispered, his lips brushing my skin in an irritatingly sensuous way. "It's VèulfR."

Shivers raced down my back. There was magic in the word, at least for me it seemed. I had to catch my breath.

"Why did you change it?" I asked.

"Trevor is easier for people to pronounce," he smiled, a quick movement of lips against my skin, "and I like it."

"Okay," I sighed in delight. "Now I know your name, thank you for sharing. Is there something else you wanna tell me?"

"Have you heard of the Binding?"

"Is this something kinky, Trevor? 'Cause I think I've had

enough kink to last me a year and I really doubt I'll ever be able to do bondage again after that whole scene with Afro," I huffed.

He finally lifted his head to look at me and his face was filled with laughter. He looked so happy, it reminded me of something the love magic had said; *bliss beyond belief.* That was it exactly, Trevor looked blissful. I gaped at him. He was gorgeous when he smiled; heart-stoppingly beautiful. He laughed suddenly; a barking sort of sound that ended on a howl. I gaped some more, this time in curious fascination.

"The binding isn't kinky," he nuzzled my cheek before he went on. "It's an old magic. As ancient as, and bound with, the Law of Three."

"Three times three shall your casting return to thee," I murmured, "Be it for good or evil, three times three it shall be."

"Yes," Trevor nodded, "as old as that and involving the magic of three. A wolf can bind itself only once in his life and nothing can undo the bond."

I was getting a really bad feeling about this but I nodded anyway, "Go on."

"A wolf must vow his life three times to his intended and each time the chosen must offer to release the wolf. He in turn must refuse to be released. Thus there are three times three vows; the offering, the release, and the refusal, each given thrice. On the third refusal, the wolf is bound completely, having been given every opportunity to deny the Binding, he chooses the tether instead."

"So when I saved you?" I whispered the question. The bad feeling was getting stronger and along with it, came a recognition of a connection I had with Trevor; like the glow of honey-colored eyes inside my head.

"I offered you my life," he nodded. "It was your due. You

saved me, so I vowed to try and save you."

"And I told you we were square," I swallowed roughly. It was getting warm and harder to breath. Was this what it felt like to hyperventilate? Nurse! I needed a nurse. Stat!

"Yes," Trevor's hand started to make playful circles on my stomach and I had to take a cleansing breath to try and chase away the butterflies that gathered beneath my skin to investigate the pleasant sensation.

"That was number one. Then later you saved me and Thor," I referenced the night in the alley.

"Yes, again I offered you my life and again you gave it back to me." He stared up at me with glowing adoration and his face was so beautiful to me then. I wanted to kiss the hard angles of his jaw and lick his soft lips. I watched them move as he spoke, "It was almost like you knew just what to say. I accepted then that this must be our destiny."

"And the third time was when you came to give me the hint," I couldn't look away from his eyes. "You chased the Froekn away and offered again to protect me."

"And you released me from my vow," his face was closer but I didn't remember him moving. I could see the double rows of his thick lashes and smell the musky spice of his skin. I inhaled it deep and my head seemed to fill with him, leaving me shivering and panting.

"But you said the wolf must in turn refuse to be released," I was grasping for straws and I knew it but damn it, can't a girl get just one straw please?

"It doesn't have to be a spoken refusal. The desire to refuse is what matters. When he returns to his mate, the wolf's choice is clear." Trevor's lips brushed mine and I shivered more. My chest heaved with my ragged breaths as he whispered, "And I've returned."

"Why would you bind yourself to me?" I asked against his lips. He opened them and inhaled my words like he could taste them. Like they could sustain him.

"My life was yours from the moment you saved it. I had to make the offer but when you refused me, it was you who made the decision. It was you who started the Binding," his body completely covered mine and again I hadn't caught the movement. It was a strange position though; he was centered over me perfectly. His legs hung lower than mine and he had to bend to keep us face to face but we were hips to hips. Our centers were centered.

"But I knew nothing of your culture or I wouldn't have bound you," I trembled from head to toe, my body already knowing something that my mind was trying desperately to deny.

"It was your ignorance that made your release of me so sweet," his breath came faster and I felt him press hard against me. Even through his jeans and the sheet covering me, I could feel his heat. "You give without thought of gain. You're strong, wise, fearless, and beautiful. You're worthy of the Binding and as you have chosen me, I have chosen you."

He lowered his mouth to mine and slipped through my lips. As soon as our tongues met, white light poured between us, around us, and within us. He shuddered against me and I felt waves of pleasure course through me, tightening my body and pushing it into release. Trevor cried out into my mouth and I drank down his rapture as I felt the warmth of his release rush against me. His magic came pouring out with it, past the barrier of fabric and into my flesh.

My body seemed to rebel, tightening and trying to reject the magic. I had no idea what was going on inside me until I saw a flash of white fur in my head and heard a low growl. My Nahual was coming out to defend her territory and she wasn't too pleased to find that the invader was a wolf. My jaguar faced Trevor's wolf inside my chest, both of them ready to tear each other apart over living space.

I slammed down an imaginary wall between the two of them and made my feelings known. They needed to get along or there'd be nothing to fight over because I'd be dead. That seemed to calm them both and I felt my Nahual withdraw reluctantly. She kept her eyes on Trevor's wolf though, even after it backed away and curled up, warm and content. The honey eyes I'd sensed in my mind earlier, closed.

We laid pressed together for a few minutes, breathing hard and staring at each other wide-eyed, until our breath slowed and I began to think clearly again. I closed my eyes and groaned. This wasn't going to make my life any easier. How the hell was I going to explain it to Thor?

"Minn Elska," Trevor whispered into my neck as he slid down into a more relaxed position.

"What?" I brushed the hair back from his eyes. I loved his eyes, such a delicious color, and his hair was silky like fur. Wait; what? No! What the hell was I thinking?

"My love," he smiled up at me with passion-heavy eyes.

"Oh hell no!" I swore and Trevor's eyes shot wide open. "Get off me! I can't do this. There's got to be a way to unbind you."

"It's done, darling," Thor was standing beside the bed, looking down on us with an unreadable expression.

I gaped at him and pushed at Trevor. The werewolf rolled off me and my face flushed when I saw the stain on the front of his jeans. Trevor just curled up at the foot of the bed and continued to stare at me contentedly. It was like he was high. Part of me wished I could stay in that high with him but reality was a downer. I was stone cold sober.

"How much of that did you see?" I asked Thor, completely mortified.

"Enough," Thor's jaw was clenched, so he had to speak through his teeth. That couldn't be a good sign.

"Baby," I sat up and reached for him and he gave me his hand before he sat down beside me. At least he wasn't throwing things at my head. Maybe I stood a chance. I hoped so since I didn't think I could handle losing him again. I cleared my throat and looked over to Trevor, "Trevor, please. I need you to leave."

Trevor stood up and nodded solemnly, finally joining the rest of us on planet Sobriety, but he turned to Thor before he left.

"You know me, Thunderer," Trevor's voice went low and deathly serious. "You know whose scent I carry. I've pledged all to your woman and my legacy is now hers. As long as you treat her well, you are both considered Froekn. I don't ask for her love or her sex but I *will* have my share of her. You know you cannot deny me."

Thor looked toward Trevor but not directly at him. He closed his eyes and nodded curtly before turning back to me. I didn't like that nod and I really didn't like the satisfaction in Trevor's face as he walked out of the room.

"What does that mean, Baby Thunder?" I looked at Thor with my heart in my eyes, begging him not to destroy it.

"He's bound to you," he swallowed hard. "Wolves mate for life. It's like an eternal marriage."

"But I don't want to marry him!" I nearly screamed in frustration. "I barely know the guy."

"This is a complicated situation," Thor took my hands in

his. “Trevor has bound himself to you because you saved him. You haven’t vowed to love him but there will be attraction between you.” He frowned and took a deep breath before continuing. “You’ll desire him, Vervain. It’s part of the magic. It’s meant to keep the species going and the Binding strong.”

“But I still feel attraction for you,” I lifted my hands to his face, stroking the angles I loved. He smiled and kissed both of my palms.

“I’m very happy to hear you say that,” Thor took my hands in his again. “But you’re not the bonded. This wasn't a mutual Binding, as you’ve already figured out. He’s given his life to you but you haven’t offered yours to him.”

“So normally the other wolf would offer their life back?” I frowned and tried to grasp it all. “The process is done by both wolves?”

“Exactly,” he smiled. “You’re not under any restriction regarding him. Only he's bound.”

“That’s unacceptable,” I said firmly. “I can’t have some werewolf bound to me, unable to satisfy his basic needs because I’m already in love with you.”

Thor laughed and it was a surprised sound, like he couldn’t believe I’d made him laugh in such a horrible situation. He hugged me and kissed the top of my head.

“Thank you, darling,” he whispered. “You’ve just made this bearable.”

“Thor,” I gasped. “I can’t breathe.”

He chuckled again and loosened his hold. “We’ll make it work,” he stroked my cheek and kissed me quickly.

“You still haven’t explained what he meant,” I gave him a

reproachful look. "What was all that about scent, legacy, and having his fair share, huh? What the hell was that?"

"Vervain, someday I'm going to introduce you to Hel since you keep invoking her name," Thor rolled his eyes.

"What?" I was baffled.

"The Goddess of the Underworld," he gave my thigh a pat. "The Norse people revered her as the keeper of those who died of old age and illness. Her name is Hel; one L, not two. She also happens to be Trevor's Aunt."

"So that's where the Christians got it," I snorted.

"We all traveled a lot," he shrugged. "Our myths got mixed together and our followers got confused occasionally."

"You're trying to get me off the subject," I pointed at him and thinned my lips. "Wait; Aunty Hel? Oh that's rich. No! You're not distracting me. Tell me the rest."

"Very well," Thor heaved a sigh. "The scent Trevor carries is that of Fenrir himself. All werewolves stem from the Great Wolf but most are generations from the source. Trevor is Fenrir's first cub."

"What?" I felt my face go slack. The bad feeling was getting worse; the butterflies in my belly turning to lead and plummeting. "That means I've bound the Big Bad Wolf's eldest son? His bouncing baby boy? His prime offspring? His-"

"Yes, Vervain," Thor laughed and shook his head.

Then something occurred to me and I asked Thor, "What does VèulfR mean?"

"He spoke his name to you?" Thor didn't sound so much surprised as he did resigned.

"Yes, and I felt something when he said it," I confirmed.

"It's just one more thing that ties him to you now. You of all people should know the power of words when spoken at the right moment," Thor sighed.

"Why do you think I'm asking?" I looked at him expectantly.

"VèulfR means *Sacred Wolf,"* Thor finally explained. "He's Fenrir's holy one; like Jesus to the Christian god."

"Whoa."

"Now you understand why he has a legacy and why it's an honor for you to be a part of it," Thor nodded.

"Yeah but what exactly *is* this legacy?" I tilted my head and narrowed my eyes in suspicion. "I'm not going to need a lot of Nair am I?"

"What?" Thor frowned.

"Am I going to get furry?"

"No, baby," he looked up like there was an explanation for my insanity written on the ceiling. "His legacy is power and now you can tap into it. Trevor has a direct link to Fenrir and you may call on the Great Wolf himself for aid in times of need."

"That's pretty groovy," I lifted my brows.

"Yes, it's all groovy," Thor grumbled, "and now for the bad news."

"No," I groaned. "No more bad news. How's my back by the way? Am I going to scar?"

"What? No," Thor blinked as he tried to follow my train of thought past its derailment. "You're back will heal perfectly,

Teharon's a god."

"Very groovy," I nodded and felt supremely cool.

"Can I tell you the bad part now?"

"If you must," I waved imperiously. I was a powerful girl now; I had connections.

"Too bad I'm not a god of patience," he muttered.

"What was that?" I narrowed my eyes again, with great wolf-empowered menace.

"Nothing, darling," Thor sighed. "Trevor is bound in a one way tie so he'll require you to spend time with him or he'll fall ill."

"He'll get sick if I don't see him?" I blinked in surprise. "Talk about taking rejection hard."

"This isn't funny, Vervain," Thor was losing his tolerance so I gave him my good girl face and nodded. He seemed satisfied enough to continue. "You must have physical contact with him at least once a month. It doesn't have to be big. You don't have to have sex with him or anything like that but it must be skin to skin contact. He's given you a part of his soul and he needs to connect with it or he'll die."

I felt the blood leave my face as I sat back against the pillows with a thud. I had to touch Trevor every month or he died? Well hell, I mean Hel, no pressure or anything. I looked at Thor and noticed the little lines of strain around the corners of his mouth.

"You're not telling me something," I glared at him.

His eyes widened and his head rocked back, "You're getting good at reading me."

"Yeah and what aren't you telling me?" I insisted.

"It's best to touch him as often as possible," Thor looked away and I hit his arm lightly, so he'd turn back. "If you keep the touching to a minimum Trevor could become starved for you and attack."

"Attack, like he'd try to kill me?" I clarified. I *so* did not need a rabid werewolf for a pet. What would Nick think?

"Not kill," Thor looked away again but only briefly. "Rape maybe."

"Oh damn," I gaped at him.

"Yes, very eloquent, Vervain," he swallowed hard. "That about sums it up."

"Okay, so I've got a new doggy who needs to be pet a lot or he may end up humping my leg," I pursed my lips thoughtfully.

"You have such a way with words," Thor's lips were twitching.

"I just wish he didn't have to give up a chance at normal werewolf love for me," I grumbled. "I don't like standing in the way of anyone's happiness."

"You still don't understand," Thor caught my gaze and held it. "You *are* his happiness now. You bring him joy beyond sex. He doesn't need intercourse as much as he needs you. The needs of the body can be managed in other ways, the needs of the soul cannot."

"So he can still masturbate is what you're saying," I chewed my lip as I mulled it over.

Thor rubbed his hand over his face and groaned. "Yes, he can but like you experienced earlier, your touch alone can bring him that pleasure."

"And you'll be okay with this?" I looked at him

apprehensively.

"No, I'm definitely *not okay* with this, but what choice do I have?" He snapped.

"There's always a choice," I whispered and looked down at my hands.

"Not if I want to keep you," Thor pulled me against him so roughly and so suddenly that I couldn't think for a second. His mouth ravaged mine and I tasted the salt of his tears in the kiss. The air sparked around us, our hair starting to lift, and I knew what that meant, so I pulled away breathlessly.

"I don't know if I'm rested enough for mind blowing sex yet, babe," I gave him a saucy smirk, "and that's the only kind of sex I'm willing to have with you anymore."

"I love you," Thor laughed. "You're worth every headache."

"I told you before, be careful you don't speak too soon."

"There's something else," he was smiling, so it couldn't have been that bad but I still went on guard immediately.

"What?" I asked carefully.

"I think you should take a look in the mirror," he suggested.

I looked down at my body quickly to make sure I hadn't turned into a wolfgirl or anything like that. Nope, still me. What the hell? Oh no, my face. My hands flew up to it but everything felt fine to me. Thor laughed and helped me out of bed.

"It's nothing horrible, just go look," he nudged me in the direction of the bathroom.

I was still a little weak and I stumbled but he reached out to steady me. I caught my balance, waved him off with a smile, and made my way over to the bathroom mirror. Then I just stood and stared.

It was still me. Same dark hair, same dark eyes, same curves, but somehow I was different. I leaned in closer. My hair was longer and a little thicker, falling in shining, fat curls past my hips. Normally it grew at a snail's pace and to get those kind of curls I'd have to set it with rollers. My skin was perfect, resplendent with a healthy glow, and when I touched it, my hand glided over its surface like silk. My eyelashes were long and thick, curling up and out over eyes sparkling with vitality. My lips were just a tad fuller and were a soft rose-pink. I felt like a sex kitten and I didn't have a stitch of make-up on. Then I noticed the changes in my body; the way everything felt tighter and stronger, and the way even simple functions like breathing seemed easier.

"Groovy," I whispered.

"Yes, darling it's very nice," Thor's eyes twinkled as he came up behind me.

"Very *nice*?" I turned and lifted a perfectly shaped eyebrow. I wondered if this meant I'd never have to pluck again. "This is about fifty thou in work here. Check me out." I spun around in a circle and felt my hair follow me in a wide arch. "Holy cannolis! Is my ass firmer?"

"Yes," he reached out and pulled me to him. "Like I said, it's very nice but I liked you as you were. This added kick from Aphrodite's magic is just frosting on my Vervain cake," he kissed my neck over the thunderbolt scar.

I laughed and shook my head at him. "I guess I shouldn't be surprised that you're not impressed; it's pretty much what you've been saying all along."

"Ah, so I've proved my love then?" His kisses were heading lower.

“I think I might require just a little more proof,” I sighed.

“Little?” He raised an outraged face to me.

“We’re not back to that again, are we? You’re huge; monstrous. I’m terrified. Eeek, someone help me,” I intoned dryly.

Epilogue

Thor and I settled into couple life fairly quickly. We worked out a system where I spend three nights at his house, he spends three nights at mine, and then he leaves so I can have the seventh day to myself. Hey isn't it like some kinda god rule to rest on the seventh day? I was only being considerate of his culture. Yeah, okay, I admit I just really needed a day to myself every once in awhile. I tell him, “Baby, how can I miss you, if you never leave?” He really hates that line.

The arrangement is perfect though. It gives me time to be home and take care of my housework and plants, as well as a day alone to paint and actually make a living. Thor scoffs at my desire for money, telling me over and over that he'll handle any financial needs I have. I told him to shove it where the lightning don't strike.

Persephone and Hades must be doing well too because nobody’s heard from them in awhile. No news is good news. Last we did hear, they had bought a vacation home in Hawaii Kai, an ultra posh neighborhood across the island from me. So maybe they're just taking their time getting settled in.

Teharon's a source of strength as much as Pan is a source of amusement. I don’t think either will ever change and I wouldn't want them to. Horus and I are growing on each other, like mold, but I catch him smiling at me every once in awhile so I think it's a good mold. The kind you can make into penicillin.

Mr. T and Mrs. E are trying to bring their son over from the dark side but I've yet to even meet Nayenezgani, so I think the chances of that happening are about as good as the chances of Brahma ever being faithful to Sarasvati. Who I still haven't met either, by the way.

Things with Trevor have been going smoothly. He's respectful of Thor and keeps his touching to a minimum. Thor, in turn, respects Trevor's right to keep breathing. The two very different magical beasts inside of me, my jaguar and Trevor's wolf, have seemed to reach an accord as well. I wouldn't say it's exactly harmonious in there but at least they're not fighting like cats and dogs.

Although I still have my concerns over being in a relationship with an immortal, life is pretty great. I'm no longer being stalked by werewolves or hunted by a psycho love goddess. There are no more vampire killings or dream visits from a crazy Aztec god either and when I checked in on him, Blue seemed to have given up on his plan to launch Russia into war. Maybe the thing with Aphrodite gave him a fresh perspective or maybe my new connection to the Froekn was a deterrent. Either way, all was quiet and peaceful. I wallowed in the serenity, knowing it wouldn't last. If there was anything I'd learned from dating a god of lightning, it was that there was only one thing that followed a calm... a storm.

Note from the Author:

If you enjoyed this book and would like to receive a newsletter on important information relating to my books, such as release dates, please sign up here:

http://eepurl.com/buwoMv

You can also follow Vervain on Twitter: @VervainLavine

and check out her life and interests in her blog on Tumblr: http://vervainlavine.tumblr.com/

Or check out the author's Facebook page:

https://www.facebook.com/pages/The-Godhunter-Series/323778160998617?ref=hl

And keep reading for a sneak peak at the next book in the Godhunter Series:

Of Gods and Wolves

Available now on Amazon:
http://astore.amazon.com/amysum-20
or at
http://www.amazon.com/gp/product/B00E9LRYL4/ref=series_rw_dp_sw

Chapter One

Was draining a god's power in self-defense still considered murder?

It's not like the police were going to come knocking on my door. “I swear, Officer, it was a self-defense draining!” I groaned as I looked over my reflection in the mirror. Yes, I killed gods but I did it to protect my race from their manipulations. I did it because gods weren't really gods, they're Atlanteans, yep, from that Atlantis.

After destroying Atlantis with their quest for power and magic, they moved across the world in a diaspora of soon-to-be deities. They found us, humans lacking their skills but full of magical potential, and with their flashy magic, they convinced us they were gods. Then they took the sacrifices we made and used them to make the fiction a reality.

Oh, but we got bored with them. We forgot most of them, moved on, decided to consolidate down to just a handful of gods. Unfortunately, they did not forget about us. They had grown accustomed to our energy, using it to prolong their lives and refresh their magic. So the forgotten ones banded together and found a new way to do things, a new way to steal our power. They manipulated mankind, infiltrated governments, plotted and schemed to bring us to war against each other, and then they took our dead as their sacrifice.

When I first discovered this conspiracy, I thought all gods were bad. I hunted them, tracing through the Aether, a place of thought and magic which binds our world to the God Realm. I didn't know there were gods who viewed relationships with humans as a symbiotic exchange of energy for information. I didn't know there were those among them who still loved us, guarded us, and guided us. But that was before I met Thor.

Now, not only do I know about the division among the gods, I know that as a human witch, I have the ability to take back what they stole. I can drain a god of their magic til there's nothing left to sustain them. Til they die and go wherever the hell it is gods go to when they die. Thus, my current situation.

I killed Aphrodite, the Goddess of Love. Except, you see, she wasn't all that loving. She was in the middle of torturing me to death, when I began to drain her, simply because I had nothing left to defend myself with. Now, I had her magic of Love, Lust, War, and Victory. Also, I had a healthy dose of pretty ladled on me. My hair was longer, shinier. My skin was perfect for like, the first time ever. My lips were fuller, my eyebrows would never need another plucking, and everything felt a little tighter, if you know what I mean.

So there I stood, perusing this new improved Vervain Lavine and wondering why I felt so guilty about it. Maybe it was the way it made me feel less than human somehow. Of course, this new perfection was the least of my current concerns. You'd think hanging with gods would be cool, dating one even better, but so far, all it had meant for me was a lot of drama.

I was dating Thor, God of Thunder, the Sea, yada yada. He was fantastic. Gorgeous. Un-fucking-believable. But somewhere along the way, I'd saved the life of a werewolf. A prince, no less, and had unknowingly bound him to me in some weirdo Froekn(werewolf) ritual. Now Trevor, said werewolf, had to touch me monthly or he'd die. I'm not exaggerating, he'll waste away and die if we don't get skin to skin. Something about being separated from the part of his soul he gave me. So, no pressure.

Thor was handling this surprisingly well. I'd be going apeshit if some hot chick had to touch him once a month or die. But then Thor's a god, he's probably used to all this bullshit. I, however, am only human(I think) and having a sinfully sweet werewolf come onto me all the time, giving me these big freakin' puppy dog eye stares, is driving me insane. Oh, and then there's Blue.

Blue, aka Huitzilopochtli, is the Aztec God of the Sun. His name drives me crazy, so I shortened the English version of it(Blue Hummingbird on the Left) and just call him Blue. It's appropriate in so many ways but let's not digress. He's also the Father of all Vampires. He's beautiful and broken, charming and vicious, evil and brilliant... and out of his fucking mind.

My new magic wants to save him, fix him, but I have no idea how to go about doing that. *He* wants me to be his Blood Bride or some shit. Queen of the Blood? Vampire Empress? I don't know, it's too twisted to think about. At the moment, it's kind of moot, since he hasn't shown his hot Aztec face in over a week. I'm not sure if that's a good or a bad thing. I *am* sure it's one more thing I have to worry about.

Man, I needed a vacation. Or a massage. Or a massage on my vacation. Sighing, I went to lie down and find some peace in my dreams. I had maybe an hour of peace before Trevor came barreling into the room I shared with Thor in Bilskinir, Thor's Hall in the God Realm of Asgard.

"What, you don't knock?" I lost my smirk when I saw the frantic look on his face. "What is it?" I sat up and moved to the edge of the bed.

"We have a problem, Minn Elska," he curled around my feet and laid his head in my lap.

Oh boy, here we go. Trevor was bonded to me but I wasn't bonded to him. That didn't stop the Binding from exerting a little influence on my hormones though. Just being around Trevor made it difficult to be faithful to Thor but when he touched me and called me his love in Old Norse, I turned into silly putty.

"Are we out of ice cream?" I tried to fend off the attraction with humor.

He shook his head a little and stared up at me with wide, honey-colored eyes. “I don’t know. Should I go check?”

“It's a joke, Trevor.” I sighed and stroked his hair. He immediately nuzzled his face into me and hugged my legs with a satisfied grin. “So what’s the problem?”

He looked up, as if suddenly remembering the reason he was there, and blushed, “My father.”

“Fenrir?”

“Yes, him,” he rubbed against me again and sighed, warm breath tickling my bare legs, where my silk slip had rode up.

“What about him?” I was trying to block out the lust spreading in delicious waves from my lap. I wished I wasn't still sitting in bed, a very bad location to be having such a reaction to Trevor.

“He wants to meet you.”

“Well that doesn’t sound so bad,” A sweet feeling of contentment was weakening my limbs, fogging my mind. His hair was so soft in my hands but I couldn’t even remember reaching out. He rubbed his face harder against me and the muscles in my thighs relaxed, falling open so he could shift closer.

“It *is* bad,” Thor’s booming voice snapped my head up and my thighs back together. He fell onto the bed beside us and yanked Trevor from my lap. Trevor started to growl but Thor shoved him away from the bed. “You can’t think straight when you’re touching her, believe me, I have the same problem, and you need to tell her about the trial.”

“Trial?” I looked back and forth between them. “I’m a witch, I don’t like that word.”

Trevor shook his head and frowned. “You’re right, Thunderer, I apologize. The Binding is hitting me hard.”

“Tell her,” Thor gentled his tone a bit.

“Father doesn’t feel that I’ve chosen wisely” he looked down, his jaw clenching and his eyes twitching. “He wants you to be tested for worth.”

“Tested? Does he know I didn’t ask for this?”

“He says you bound me, knowingly or not, and you must prove yourself worthy of the honor or he’ll remove it.” Trevor looked up at me, clearly shaken.

“If your father is so unhappy, Trevor,” I had to handle this delicately but I was ecstatic that there was a way to release him. “Maybe we should just let him remove the Binding.”

“Vervain,” Thor took a deep breath and shook his head at Trevor, who looked so stricken, I thought he’d be in tears at any second. “She doesn’t get it Trevor, relax. Vervain, there’s no way to undo the Binding in the sense you mean. Fenrir is speaking of killing you to free his son, hoping Trevor will live through it. Fenrir thinks the bond is unconsummated and so he believes there’s a chance for Trevor to break free upon your death.”

“Unconsummated?” I frowned and then blushed. “R-i-i-ight, I remember, but since we *are* consummated or whatever, what would happen to Trevor if I died?”

“He’d die too,” Thor watched me carefully as it sank in.

“But you’re immortal,” I searched Trevor’s face for an ounce of hope that I’d misunderstood. “I mean, you can die if someone hurts you bad enough, but otherwise you’d live forever, right?”

“Not anymore,” Trevor didn’t look the least bit disturbed

by his death sentence. In fact, he looked calm, peaceful, happy even.

"You've traded immortality to be bound to me in a one-sided bond?" I was horrified.

"I'd be dead without you anyway." He shrugged casually, his hands deep in the pockets of his jeans. Very flippant, very James Dean. Werewolf without a cause.

"I was the one that nearly killed you in the first place."

"Because I was attacking you," he grinned lopsidedly. "It was the best day of my life."

"This is not our problem right now," Thor stood up and glared at both of us.

"What?" I blinked up at him. "Oh right, so just tell him it's consummated and he needs to get over it."

"I have," Trevor looked away, "he doesn't believe me."

"Why not?" I was so frustrated, I could spit.

"I don't carry your scent," Trevor started to blush a pretty shade of rose.

"What do you mean *carry my scent*?" I stared at him and then Thor. They both had matching looks of embarrassment. "Cheese and rice! No way! He sniffed you to see if he could smell sex?"

Trevor nodded and Thor sighed.

"What it comes down to, Vervain," Thor sat back down and took my hand, "is this. You can either consummate the bond in front of Fenrir or accept the challenge."

"So I'm to either fuck or fight for his entertainment, is that it?" Trevor's shoulders slumped and he looked at the floor in misery.

"That's it," Thor, at least, met my eyes.

"What kind of trial are we talking about?"

"You'll have to face three warriors of my father's choosing," Trevor looked up, smiled, and shrugged. "I know you can win, you're my Lady Huntress. You've fought the wolves before and won. You've even beaten me and I'm the best of our fighters."

"Are you sure it'll be werewolves only?" I looked at Thor and then back at Trevor.

Trevor nodded but Thor was the one who answered. "Fenrir can only use his own power to test you. It's our law."

"Fine, set it up," I slumped back, then shot up again. "Do I have to kill them all or just win?"

"You just need to disable them. They can change and heal if you let them." Trevor smiled and shook his head. "Your compassion is such a treasure to me. It's humbling."

"Yeah, great. Let's just hope it has the same effect on your father," I smiled weakly. "Now when is it going to be?"

"Two days hence," Trevor grimaced and I groaned. "He wanted to test you tonight but I begged him to let you prepare. So he granted us two days."

"He's not too happy with you for giving up your immortality, is he?" *I* wasn't too pleased about it, so I could only imagine what dear old Dad would think.

"He's furious," Trevor nodded.

"Well, let's just hope I can keep us alive till the end of the week and then we'll take it from there."

And here's one more sneak peek into the first book of The Twilight Court Series:
Fairy-Struck

Now available on Amazon:
http://www.amazon.com/gp/product/B011HC6Y1I?*Version*=1&*entries*=0

Fairy-Struck: Several types of conditions such as paralysis, wasting away, pining, and unnatural behavior resulting from an enchantment laid by an offended fairy.

Chapter One

Once upon a time, isn't that how all fairy tales begin? Except this isn't your average fairy tale. There are no charming princes or wicked witches within these pages and the fair maidens are more deadly than any big bad wolf. This is a fairy tale in the truest sense of the words; a story about fairies... the real story.

My name is Seren Sloane and I'm an Extinguisher. That will mean nothing to you, I'm sure, so let me go back a little further. No one knows the true origins of the fey, I don't think even the fey themselves remember, but theories abound. One theory has them evolving alongside us but where we advanced in groups, banding together to become stronger, the fey morphed out of those outcast predators who were too wild for a pack. Those who don't believe in evolution, think instead that the fey stem from divine creations, angels fallen from God's grace. Yet another tale insists they were gods themselves, or demi-gods, led by a mother goddess named Danu.

A final theory suggests they were not gods or angels or outcasts, merely nomads from an advanced civilization. The Scythians or Sidheans, from which the word *sidhe* originates. Myths tell of these talented Sidhe coming to Ireland where they flung about their magic and generally wrecked havoc until the aggrieved locals fought back and forced the fey to retreat into their raths, holy shrines now known as fairy mounds. History has disguised the raths as burial mounds even though originally, they were thought to be royal palaces for portal guardians. Although I cannot validate the rest of the tale, I do know this; the fey don't live under mounds of dirt. The original descriptions strike closer to the truth. The raths shrouded portals not corpses. Hidden paths to the fairy world, a realm laid parallel to ours and not at all underground.

Anyway, we did just fine living side by side with them until humans started destroying the environment around those entrances to Fairy. Fairies don't like it when you mess with nature and when they stroll from their magical abodes to find that mess strewn all over their backyard, they get even more pissy. So they began to fling the mess back. All those old stories about fairies stealing babies and striking people with wasting diseases, stem from this time period. Things got real bad, so bad that those of us who had the gift of clairvoyance and could actually see fairies, joined together to defend the human race.

The first Human-Fey war erupted across Eire, now known as Ireland, and the losses on both sides were staggering. After the third war, a grudging truce was finally attained and councils were created to mediate between the races and support the truce with laws approved by both sides. A good start to be sure but laws flounder and fail if they can't be enforced. Both councils conceded jurisdiction over their people to the other, agreeing upon the penalties to be meted out should someone be found guilty of a crime. Rules for determining guilt and administering justice were set into place and military units were sanctioned to carry out the verdicts of the councils.

The fairies created the Wild Hunt. They gathered the fiercest, most terrifying of their people and trained them to stalk the shadows of our world, watching us like guardian angels until one of us breaks the law. Then the angels become devils who do much more than watch. Trust me when I say you don't want to ever meet a member of the Hunt.

To police the fey, we created the Extinguishers. Formed of the five great psychic families who originally defended humanity, the Extinguishers inspire a fair amount of fear as well. Armed with clairvoyance among other talents which varies by person but can include; telekinesis, pyrokinesis, telepathy, and psychometry, we also have some serious combat skills. Most humans don't have the ability to see a fairy unless that fairy wants to be seen, so both council members and Extinguishers must at least possess clairvoyance. The Council keeps an eye out for humans with exceptional psychic abilities so they can recruit more into their fold but Extinguishers are born into the job. I'm one of those lucky few.

Kavanaugh, Teagan, Sullivan, Murdock, and Sloane. The first five psychic families of Ireland. Over the centuries we've become a secret society so big it spans the globe, gaining strength by breeding only within the five. This has virtually guaranteed powerful psychic gifts in our children. I'm the product of a Sloane and a Kavanaugh. Over thirty generations of contrived breeding(not inbreeding, thank you very much) has given me abilities which rank me as one of the top ten Extinguishers of all time.

I was trained from childhood to become what I am; an Extinguisher, a hunter of fairies, remover of the light of the Shining Ones. Childhood wasn't horrible for me but it was definitely not what most would consider to be normal. Bedtime stories were non-fiction accounts of Extinguisher heroism and instead of receiving platitudes that monsters weren't real, I was told most emphatically that they were and that when checking beneath my bed at night, I should always have an iron blade in hand. My only friends were children from other Extinguisher families and every game or toy had an ulterior motive behind it. Like the dolls my mother made me which showed what each type of fairy looked like... and had their weaknesses written on their backs in red ink.

Still, I was a child and I knew nothing else. Life seemed magical to me, not just in the way that life is magical to all children but in a literally magic way. I was taught to move objects with my mind, create fire in the palm of my hand, and make things materialize anywhere I wanted them to(that's called apportation in case you're curious, not teleportation which is a thing of science fiction). When I got older, I was taught to fight and finally, to kill.

Despite all of that, I wasn't raised to hate fairies. Quite the contrary, I was taught to care for them and protect them if need be.

The job of an Extinguisher exists first and foremost to protect the peace. We kill fairies only when they disrupt that peace and then we do it in the most efficient and merciful way possible... after we receive a warrant of execution approved by the Council. We are, essentially, peace keepers.

That changed for my family when my mother was torn to pieces by a pack of pukas. I know, it sounds funny, doesn't it? A pack of pukas. In reality a bunch of fairy dogs the size of ponies, with teeth sharper than a shark's, shredded the flesh from my mother, gobbled down every last bit of it, and then gnawed on her bones till they could suck out the marrow. That reality killed all the mercy in my father and a lot of the compassion in me as well.

We immersed ourselves in the job, taking every warrant issued for criminal fey we could get our hands on until the Head Extinguisher himself finally noticed and called us to heel. We were sent to a small territory where very little fey crime occurred and where we were supposed to get our shit together. Most humans would love to live where we do now and when I tell you where we were put, I'm sure you'll roll your eyes but let me assure you that this place becomes a slow death for an Extinguisher. Peace keepers need a certain amount of action to keep us sane and Hawaii has very little of that on the fey front.

Yes, I've been exiled to paradise and for someone with my fair Irish skin, Hawaii imitates Hell in so many ways. Sure beauty abounds and the people here embody that tropical temperament of almost Gaelic hospitality but when you're itching for a fight, you don't want to be scratching at your peeling, sunburned skin too. Plus, the only fey to be found, the little local variety called menehune, frolic about causing mischief but never mayhem. Yep, Hawaiian fairies exist. Does that shock you? It shouldn't, I've already mentioned how the Fairy Realm lies parallel to ours. Mounds connect more than merely Ireland to Fairyland, they form bridges between Fairy and places all over the world. The fairies who frequent these paths seem to be influenced by the culture they cross over into.

And the fairies don't just visit. Ever since the creation of the Councils, a lot of fey have moved into our world in an effort to support the peace. There was also the issue of the numerous entrances to Fairy which needed to be guarded. So several fey council members have very human jobs with very powerful positions. I think you'd be pretty damn surprised if I told you which companies secretly belong to the fey.

We don't have any of those powerful companies here in Hawaii because, as I mentioned before, this place isn't all that important in the whole fey-human interrelations department. So my life has become a constant preparation for a battle it doesn't look like I'll ever be allowed to join, in a place whose beauty only feels like salt in my wounded heart. I will admit that my anger has lessened over my time here, as the memory of who my mother was slowly overshadows the memory of how she died, but for my father, this exile has only served to make him even more bitter, more vicious, and more intent on killing the entire fairy race.

About the Author

Amy Sumida lives on an island in the Pacific Ocean where gods can still be found. She sleeps in a fairy bed, high in the air, with two gravity-defying felines and upon waking, enjoys stabbing people with little needles, over and over, under the guise of making pretty pictures on their skin. She, like Vervain, has no filter but has been fortunate enough to find friends who appreciate this... or at least tell her they do. She aspires to someday become a crazy cat lady, sitting on her rocker on her front porch and guarding her precious kitties with a shotgun loaded with rock salt. She bellydances and paints pictures on her walls but is happiest with her nose stuck in a book, her mind in a different world than this one, filled with fantastical men who unfortunately don't exist in our mundane reality. Thank the gods for fantasy.

You can find her on facebook at:

https://www.facebook.com/pages/The-Godhunter-Series/323778160998617?ref=hl

On Twitter under @Ashstarte

On Goodreads:

https://www.goodreads.com/author/show/7200339.Amy_Sumida

On her website:

https://sites.google.com/site/authoramysumida/home?pli=1

And you can find her entire collection of books, along with some personal recommendations, at her Amazon store:

https://sites.google.com/site/authoramysumida/home?pli=1

And you can find Vervain's Blog on Tumblr: Godhunter;

witch, goddess, faerie, & shapeshifter

Or you can write her at: VervainLavine@yahoo.com

Made in the USA
San Bernardino, CA
10 June 2018